Cyberstrike: London

CYBERSTRIKE: LONDON

JAMES BARRINGTON
WITH PROFESSOR RICHARD BENHAM

CANELO

First published in the United Kingdom in 2020 by

Canelo Digital Publishing Limited
Third Floor, 20 Mortimer Street
London W1T 3JW
United Kingdom

Copyright © James Barrington and Richard Benham, 2020

The moral right of James Barrington and Richard Benham to be identified as the author of this work has been asserted in accordance with the Copyright, Designs and Patents Act, 1988.

All rights reserved. No part of this publication may be reproduced or transmitted in any form or by any means, electronic or mechanical, including photocopy, recording, or any information storage and retrieval system, without permission in writing from the publisher.

A CIP catalogue record for this book is available from the British Library.

Hardback ISBN 978 1 78863 824 1
Ebook ISBN 978 1 78863 701 5

This book is a work of fiction. Names, characters, businesses, organizations, places and events are either the product of the author's imagination or are used fictitiously. Any resemblance to actual persons, living or dead, events or locales is entirely coincidental.

Look for more great books at www.canelo.co

Printed and bound in Great Britain by Clays Ltd, Elcograf S.p.A.

To Sally, for putting up with me
James Barrington

To Jenna, Olivia and Henry for much the same
Richard Benham

Factual basis

This book is a novel, but there is a core of fact at its heart. On a minimum of eight occasions that are known about, senior banking officials in London have been placed under covert surveillance by blackmail gangs. These gangs identified and obtained proof of certain activities enjoyed by those officials and then attempted to blackmail them.

Mention is made of the real-world events of 7 July 2005, when for the first time the United Kingdom became the target of dedicated suicide bombers who used home-made devices to cause appalling loss of life and extensive damage on and below the streets of London. A percentage of the sale proceeds of this book will be donated to selected charities working with victims of terrorism and war.

Part 1

Chapter 1

Thursday 7 July 2005
London

Ben Morgan was thirty-four years old, single and at twelve minutes before nine that particular morning he was jammed into one corner of a very full Tube train carriage on the Circle Line and wondering exactly where his life was going.

His short-term future was assured but predictable, and that day was typical. The Home Office project meeting at Queen Anne's Gate scheduled for 09:30 that morning was not something he was looking forward to. It was supposed to last three hours, and from past experience Morgan knew that it would take at least that long, maybe even longer. It would be dull and dry and probably largely unproductive, and punctuated by the kind of refreshments that no normal person would ever wish to consume: the cheapest possible teabag tea or instant coffee, both typically topped up with UHT milk which tasted disgusting in coffee and worse in tea, accompanied by the most appalling stale biscuits that appeared to have been purchased as emergency survival rations early in the decade following the last World War. His personal belief was that the cellars underneath Queen Anne's Gate contained storerooms full of the blasted things, probably enough to last for the next half-century.

He glanced at his watch. It was exactly 08:49, which meant he had plenty of time to reach his destination without hurrying. In fact, he thought he might even get off at Victoria, the station before his usual stop at St James's Park, and walk the rest of the way. The fresh air would do him good.

He was thinking about the points he needed to make at the meeting, his input into the project, when the lights went out and the Underground train instantly slammed to a halt. Commuters lurched into one another as they lost their grips on the hanging straps and bars. A couple of people squealed in alarm, and Morgan heard muttered curses and apologies as people regained their feet.

Almost immediately, the emergency lights came on, imbuing the crowded carriage with enough light for people to see what was around them, but not enough to see it clearly. It was, he thought somewhat irreverently, almost exactly the kind of illumination that the directors of horror movies worked so hard to achieve just before the mummy or the zombies or the monster from the cellar made their inevitable appearance. In some ways, the darkness might have been better.

The loudspeaker crackled and the driver made a broadcast, stating the obvious.

'Ladies and gentlemen, as you can see we've come to a stop, but we should be moving again within a few minutes.'

Morgan didn't think it was his imagination, but it sounded as if the driver's voice had faded away at the end of his announcement, as if the power to the loudspeaker system, as well as to the electric motor driving the train, had failed. That wasn't good news. But surely that would be battery-powered, so maybe the driver just had nothing else to say.

Unexpected stoppages on the Underground system were not exactly rare, and Morgan could see some of his fellow passengers shrugging, murmuring to their companions and checking their watches to try to estimate exactly how late they would be getting to work or wherever they were going that day.

But he knew instantly that it was more than just a signal failure or a train stuck at a station. If it had been that kind of problem, then the lights in the carriages would still be on and the driver would have told the passengers the reason for the delay. He guessed that the driver, very probably sitting in almost complete darkness at the front of the train, had not the slightest idea why his train had suddenly come to a dead stop, without power. And he wouldn't find out unless whatever communication system was in use on the Underground was still functioning and somebody in the control room told him.

The fact that the lights were out and the emergency lanterns had been activated meant that at the very least there had been a massive power failure somewhere in the system. Underground trains run on electricity. If the power stops, the trains stop. Simple as that.

And it was quiet. Tube trains are never silent. There's always the background noise of the ventilation system running, but in that carriage on that day there were no mechanical noises whatsoever, and Morgan found the absence of sound particularly disturbing. There was also a smell. Something like burning rubber, only much worse, something he had never smelled before anywhere on the Tube, but which was unpleasantly familiar to him, reminding him of another chapter in his life.

In the faint illumination of the emergency lights, he could see what he thought was smoke outside the carriage. Smoke meant a fire or perhaps an explosion, although he had heard nothing to suggest that. But Tube trains on the move were noisy, and if a power transformer had blown up it could have been inaudible inside the carriage. After 9/11 the knowledge that terrorists could strike almost anywhere, and at any time, influenced everybody's thinking and Morgan was a little paranoid, partly because of where he now worked.

He remembered reading an article in some management journal about how people reacted in a crisis: roughly eighty per cent would do nothing, fifteen per cent would panic, and the remaining five per cent would stay calm, think things through and take whatever action they could. Being stuck dozens of feet underground in a non-functioning Tube train stopped between stations was not exactly conducive to calm and measured thought. And even less so because of the real possibility that a fire was raging somewhere in the nearby tunnel system. But what he did know was that he wasn't going to panic.

The unpleasant smell grew stronger and Morgan could almost feel the tension rise in the carriage as people stopped being annoyed at the disruption to their journey and realised that the situation was serious. That the train was not going to start up and simply resume travelling to the next station on the line. Tendrils of smoke were now clearly visible outside.

And then a new sound intruded: a kind of high-pitched keening noise that Morgan couldn't immediately identify. At least, until its pitch changed. Then he recognised it. At the forward end of the carriage, close to the connecting door, a middle-aged woman was standing with her fists clenched and her eyes tightly shut, and her scream was just starting to build. There was nothing he could do, because she was just too far away, and forcing his way through the packed crowd of commuters probably wouldn't be a good idea.

A man standing near her, possibly her husband or partner, stepped in front of her. He wrapped his arms around her and began murmuring in her ear. Almost as soon as the embryo scream had started it stopped, but the man continued to hold the woman close and kept up his presumably soothing and reassuring monologue.

Smoke started seeping into the carriage and it was obvious to Morgan that they needed to keep it out. Nobody else seemed inclined to take charge or react to the situation, so he shouted out in his best parade ground voice: 'Close the windows and the vents. That'll keep the smoke out until this gets sorted.'

He was rewarded by the sound and sight of the passengers at either end of the carriage closing the glass windows on the connecting doors, and those at the sides of the carriage sliding shut the ventilation controls. He knew the ventilation system wasn't working but closing the vents should help.

But Morgan knew they were all potentially in a *Titanic* and deckchairs situation. If there was a fire outside the train, the smoke and flames would eventually get inside, and the carriage doors were firmly shut. There was no way to escape except up or down the train through the internal doors between carriages. He believed – and he certainly hoped – that Underground trains weren't particularly flammable, but that really wasn't the point. In fires, more people die from smoke inhalation than from the flames, and a serious fire fed by fuel or oil could easily produce enough smoke to choke them all.

Morgan was a user of the London Underground system, not an expert on how it worked, but as far as he was aware most of the tunnels weren't ventilated. It was the passage of the trains that moved the air. If the trains stopped moving, so did the air. And, more importantly in the present situation, the smoke from a fire wouldn't dissipate because there would be nowhere for it to go. If it got really thick and choking, their only possible means of escape would be to get to the very last carriage, open the rear door and take their chances walking along the unlit railway track. And that was not a prospect he relished.

The sound of voices continued to rise as the passengers looked about them. Strangers uncharacteristically began talking to other strangers. There was nothing visible outside the windows of the carriage apart from the thickening clouds of smoke. Some of it was finding its way in, neither the vents nor the windows providing a proper seal. Morgan guessed that the situation was probably going to get a lot worse before it got any better, and the most important thing was to avoid panic. The woman beside the door still worried him, and he had no doubt that some other people in the carriage would be suffering from claustrophobia, exacerbated by the potentially very dangerous situation they had been thrust into.

Panic is contagious. The moment one person loses it, it's almost certain that others will temporarily also lose their reason. That's why the death toll in nightclubs and football grounds and other places with restricted exits is so high when a fire or other emergency occurs: if one or two people run, others will follow in an escalating stampede and inevitably people will be trampled in the crush to get out.

If that happened in the crowded carriage, a location that had the narrowest possible exit points at each end, just wide enough for one person at a time to use, the result could be catastrophic. Morgan knew he had to try to prevent that at all costs.

'The controllers of the Tube system will know exactly where we are,' he said in a voice that he hoped would carry to every corner of the carriage. 'I think what's happened is a complete power failure. Maybe a generator or transformer has blown and affected this part of the network, but they'll either restore power or they'll send out a rescue crew. In the meantime, we need to stay calm, keep the windows closed and wait for rescue.'

Nobody responded in any way, as far as Morgan could tell, which didn't surprise him. If he'd been wearing a uniform and a peaked cap, no doubt what he'd said would have carried more weight, but there was nothing else he could do.

For perhaps a couple of minutes nothing happened. Then they all heard raised voices, shouts and yells. Behind the woman who'd screamed the connecting door to the next carriage opened, and Morgan saw a press of bodies behind it. But it was already standing-room only, and the absolute last thing they wanted was a bunch of panicking passengers crowding into the carriage.

'Don't let them in,' Morgan called out urgently. 'There's no room in here.'

A couple of heavily built men at the end of the carriage apparently saw the sense of what he was saying and stepped forward to lean their weight against the door to stop it from being opened. There, at least, the narrow opening helped them: only one person in the adjoining carriage could push on the door in the narrow gap between the carriages, but two people could use their weight to keep it closed.

When the door didn't budge, whoever was trying to gain access from the other carriage began banging on the glass window of the door and shouting. It looked as if the smoke outside the train could be the least of their worries.

Then there was a sudden flash of light outside the carriage windows and for a brief moment Morgan wondered if the power had been switched on again and he'd seen an arc as a circuit was made. But the emergency lights were still burning, and if the power had been restored the carriage lights would have come on and the ventilation restarted. It had looked to him a bit like a flame, but more like an electric light. Or a torch.

Then they all heard a voice outside the carriage, and moments later a dim face topped by a yellow safety helmet appeared at one of the side windows, the man gesturing back towards the rear of the train.

'Go back to the last carriage,' he shouted, his voice muffled. Then he walked further up the track towards the engine.

'Slowly, walk slowly,' Morgan cautioned, fearing a stampede if everybody moved at the same time.

He went the other way, towards the front of the carriage, where the two men standing beside the door were looking around them somewhat uncertainly. What he hoped was that the sight of the worker outside the train would calm down the possibly panicking passengers in the neighbouring carriage.

'You reckon it's okay now?' one of the men asked him.

'I bloody well hope so,' Morgan replied. 'You go. I'll wait here.'

He leaned his back firmly against the door and watched until about half of the passengers in his carriage had made their way out of the connecting door at the other end. Then he turned and opened the door.

Whether it was because the commuters in that carriage had seen a railway worker or simply because they knew they were now able to leave the train, Morgan didn't know, but the people who filed past him appeared calm, albeit still apprehensive. They simply walked out of their carriage and moved steadily towards the rear of the train.

Morgan waited a couple of minutes just to make sure that the evacuation was proceeding in an orderly fashion, and then joined the line himself.

They moved through one carriage after another, everybody seeming calm. At the end of the last carriage, the open doorway showed a crowd of people walking along the tunnel, all keeping to one side and away from the live rail, although the current had clearly been switched off. A short ladder had been placed against the rear door to allow passengers to climb down it and onto the track.

It was something of a vision from hell. A handful of torches provided fitful and erratic illumination in the hands of the Underground staff as the mass of people shuffled slowly along, fearful of losing their footing in the darkness, and with the ever present threat of electrocution should the current to the live rail suddenly be restored. The drifting clouds of smoke reduced visibility and caused some commuters to cough harshly. Others were clinging onto other people as they made their way towards what they hoped was safety.

There was almost no talking from the passengers as they stumbled along the track, but the workmen and officials kept up a constant stream of encouragement and instruction, telling them to keep moving, that the live rail had been turned off, and that the platform, and the way out of the Underground system, was only a matter of yards away.

Morgan thought that might have been slightly optimistic, but then he remembered that the train had left the previous station only a matter of seconds, certainly no more than half a minute, before the power was cut, and it couldn't have got very far before it stopped. He joined the queue of people walking along, and in about a minute he saw that they had reached the nearer end of the previous station, Paddington. Underground staff in yellow high-vis jackets were standing on the platform and on the track to help people climb up to safety. Morgan stepped on the rail, easily boosted himself up onto the platform and then looked around.

The thing he noticed immediately was that the station itself was also using emergency lighting, which meant the escalators would not be working. That suggested the cause had probably been a failure of a part of the National Grid rather than something local to the Tube system. No doubt he'd read all about it in the *Standard* that evening.

There's something about climbing up a non-working escalator that feels completely wrong, but it was the obvious way out, so he followed the people who were steadily making their way up to the street. Almost everybody was silent, the commuters saving their breath for the effort involved in the climb.

When he got to street level he knew he needed to get cleaned up. In daylight he discovered that his hands were smudged with soot from the walk along the track and the climb up onto the platform. Both his jacket and trousers were badly stained and he suspected his face and hair were covered in soot. There was nothing he could do about his clothes, but at least he could wash his hands and face in the station lavatory.

Or rather he couldn't, because Paddington Station was in utter chaos, with hundreds of commuters milling about. But he should have time to get cleaned up at Queen Anne's Gate before the meeting started.

His next surprise was what he saw when he walked outside onto Praed Street. The junction outside the station was filled with a galaxy of flashing blue lights mounted on the roofs of ambulances and police vehicles. That seemed something of an overreaction, but it was presumably a precautionary measure: far better to send too many vehicles and personnel to the scene of an incident rather than too few.

The dust- and soot-covered commuters were being funnelled over to the right as they stepped outside the station, to a point where half a dozen police officers and a couple of paramedics were standing. But although some people were probably suffering from shock nobody was hurt and so the line was moving quickly. When Morgan reached the head of the queue he said he was uninjured, just dirty, and asked one of the police officers what had happened.

'We don't know yet, sir,' the constable responded. 'Some bloke I talked to from the Tube reckoned it was an overload that tripped the power, but nobody's told me anything official.'

Taxis and buses were presumably still running, but with the number of passengers spilling out of the station, finding an empty cab or a bus that wasn't jammed to capacity would be difficult or impossible. And with the state of his clothes a lot of cabbies might not want him in their vehicle. His best option was probably just to walk it.

Morgan strode away briskly, heading north-east towards Hyde Park. He pulled a handkerchief from his pocket and did his best to clean the soot off his face and hands, then took out his mobile to ring his contact at Queen Anne's Gate and advise him that he might be a few minutes late. But his phone simply beeped at him, and when he looked at the screen he realised he had no signal.

Whenever you add two and two together, you almost invariably get four. The Underground system power cut and the failure of the mobile phone system meant that the incident was much more serious and widespread than just an electrical overload somewhere. No doubt he'd find out more when he reached the Home Office.

He covered the two miles in about three quarters of an hour, and by the time he reached his destination he knew beyond doubt that something was very wrong. London is always busy with traffic and pedestrians, but the air was full of the wail of sirens and it looked as if every emergency vehicle in the city was on the streets, trying to get somewhere as quickly as possible. Most of the vehicles were heading north as far as he could tell. Something had obviously happened. Something major.

At Queen Anne's Gate he showed his pass to the security guard, who looked somewhat disapprovingly at his grubby attire and told Morgan that teams of suicide bombers were on the loose in London.

'Teams?' Morgan echoed. 'I didn't know they operated as teams.'

'That's what I've been told, sir,' the guard replied. 'Right, you're expected, so I can let you in, but we've been ordered to keep the doors of the Home Office locked and to refuse entry to all non-official visitors.'

Morgan spent about five minutes in the gents' loo trying to tidy himself up. He doubted if London really was under attack by groups of suicide bombers. There was probably a core of truth in what the guard had said but it had been magnified and exaggerated in the retelling. What irritated him was the possibility of being locked in the Home Office for an indeterminate period of time, if it turned into some kind of a siege because the bombers – assuming they existed at all – were targeting government buildings. And potentially worse than that was the prospect of having to exist on Home Office biscuits as the only available food source.

'What happened to you, Mr Morgan?' Stephen Willoughby, the career civil servant who headed the group asked, looking at him closely.

'My Tube train was stopped just outside Paddington with a total power failure. I had to walk along the track from the carriage and then all the way here. You're lucky I made it at all.'

'And you're luckier than you know,' Willoughby replied, 'because you're alive. We don't have the full details yet, but at least three terrorist bombs were detonated this morning on the London Underground network, two of them on the Circle Line. That's the line you take, it is not?'

Morgan actually felt himself going pale as he realised that the statement by the security guard at the main door had not been much of an exaggeration after all.

As the morning wore on, and details of what became known as the 7/7 attacks were clarified and confirmed, he knew that Willoughby had been right: he had been very lucky. Quite often, when attending meetings of this type, Morgan would come in earlier than the start time to take a look round a part of London that he didn't know well, and that usually meant catching an earlier train. He hadn't bothered that morning because he was familiar with the area around Queen Anne's Gate, and he'd timed his journey so that he would only have about twenty minutes in hand to allow for any delays. If it had been the first time he'd visited that part of the city, he could well have been on one of the Circle Line trains targeted by the bombers.

Morgan felt shocked but also angry: a kind of cold, deep and unyielding fury enveloped him as the first casualty figures were released and the full scope and extent of the terrorist attack became clear. It had hit close to home for him because he could easily have been one of the victims. Dozens of innocent lives had been taken at random in a terrorist attack of a sort that had never been seen in the United Kingdom before.

As more information became available over the next few hours, it became clear to Morgan that the forces of law and order in Britain were facing a brand-new enemy. An enemy that held all the cards, that operated below the radar and could strike at any target they selected at a time and in a manner of their own choosing. An enemy that only needed to be lucky once, while the counterterrorism people needed to be lucky every single time.

The scale of the problem was almost incomprehensible. How could any counter-intelligence or counterterrorism organisation hope to detect an attack planned by a group of disaffected and angry men who were prepared to sacrifice their lives to cause massive death and destruction? Britain was facing an enemy that played by its own rules, and at that moment he had no idea what anyone could do to counter that kind of attack.

Fate always plays its cards close to its chest, and often the hands that people are dealt seem hopelessly random. Sometimes, though, things work out in ways that almost appear to be planned as the number of coincidences grows.

As it happened, Ben Morgan turned out to be exactly the right person in precisely the right place at absolutely the right time.

Chapter 2

Sunday 10 July 2005
Vauxhall Cross, London

'I've got two questions I'd like answered. First, why the hell didn't we see this coming – or something like it? And, second, who exactly is that man and what's he doing here?'

'To be pedantic about it,' Simon Greaves said smoothly, 'that's three questions, possibly four, and realistically I should be asking you to answer the first two. But right now we need to wait, because he's not the only stranger you're going to be meeting today. I'll do the introductions once everyone else is here.'

'What is this? Some kind of party?'

'Not the kind you'd normally expect to be invited to on a Sunday, James, but of a sort, yes.'

Greaves, the Assistant Chief and Director of Operations and Intelligence of the Secret Intelligence Service, leaned back in the chair at the head of the conference table, picked an almost invisible piece of fluff from the sleeve of his immaculate dark jacket and steepled his fingers. He was slim and clean-shaven, with dark hair and the kind of face and bearing that screamed 'officer class' and 'home counties' in equal measure.

James Welby, more or less his opposite number at Thames House, the Millbank headquarters of the Security Service, known to intelligence professionals as 'The Box', also leaned back, but with his bulky frame and far less expensive tailoring the action looked clumsy and forced. He plastered a neutral expression on his ruddy face and looked again at the man who was sitting at the far end of the long table.

The stranger returned his glance with a slight smile. He was wearing a prominent red badge on a lanyard around his neck displaying the unambiguous legend 'VISITOR – TO BE ACCOMPANIED AT ALL TIMES', so all Welby knew for certain was that he wasn't employed by the SIS.

'I take it this person has the requisite security clearances?' he asked.

'Relax, James. He's here in the building, so it should be quite obvious that he's been checked.'

'On a Sunday, I note,' Welby commented neutrally, 'so I also assume that this is a classified meeting?'

'Everything in this building is classified to some extent. Some matters more so than others.'

'And it's easier to do this at a weekend, when the place is pretty much deserted?'

Greaves smiled and made a gesture intended to encompass the entirety of the very distinctive avant-garde building located on the south bank of the Thames at Vauxhall Cross.

'There are some advantages in doing things when the clerks and administrators are sitting at home with a beer watching the box or mowing the lawn, but because of what happened last week most of the desks are working.'

Before Welby could reply there was a brisk double tap and the door of the conference room opened. A well-built man peered inside and scanned the room and its occupants keenly, as if looking for some evidence of impropriety, then stepped back to usher three men inside.

'Your guests, sir,' the security man stated briefly, and withdrew.

Each of the new arrivals was wearing a badge identifying him as a visitor who needed escorting everywhere. Two of them paused by the door, while the third stepped forward and looked somewhat pointedly at the table.

'I've been on the sodding road for half a day,' he said, addressing the room at large, 'and I've only just managed to avoid that hefty bastard outside giving me a full body cavity search. The least you could have done was organise some bloody coffee.'

'It's on its way, Dave,' Greaves said, depressing a button on a small control panel on the table directly in front of him, 'so take a pew and we'll get started.'

A couple of minutes after the three of them had taken their seats a smartly-dressed woman pushed a trolley inside the room, dispensed refreshments and then left. When the door had closed behind her Greaves made the introductions.

'My name,' he began, 'is Simon Greaves, and my post here at Vauxhall Cross is Assistant Chief and Director of Operations and Intelligence. On my left is James Welby. He works for the Security Service – what the media insist on calling MI5, because they don't know any better – at Millbank, where he's the Director in charge of G Branch, International Counter-Terrorism. He's the man who should have known about last week's attack here in London and nipped it in the bud, but we'll get to that.'

Welby gave him a hard stare but didn't respond.

Greaves picked up a pencil and sighted along its length, aiming the point at a balding, slightly overweight man wearing a dark, dusty suit, who looked back at him through black-framed spectacles. He looked like he might have been a secondary-school science teacher, but he clearly wasn't.

'This is Michael Hollings, who's a part of NARO, the government's Nuclear Accident Response Organisation. They're the people who respond to any kind of nuclear accident or incident. Before anyone gets too twitchy, let me tell you that he's here as a precaution, just in case we need specialist advice about nukes or dirty bombs.'

Greaves moved the end of the pencil to point towards the man who had complained about the lack of coffee.

'Most of us here at Vauxhall Cross are thinkers and planners, or that's what we believe,' he said, 'but we need doers as well, and Dave North is definitely one of them. He's fondly known as a 'Rupert'. He's a major in the Special Air Service, based up at Hereford. If we need muscle and firepower, he's the man who's authorised to supply as much as we want. In fact,' Greaves added, 'he's actually a Rupert-plus, because a few weeks ago he slid sideways into the SRR.'

Hollings looked baffled. 'The what?' he said.

'Dave?' Greaves prompted.

North, a stocky and solid figure dressed casually in jeans, an open-necked shirt and leather jacket, inclined his head and reached out for another biscuit.

'The SRR is the Special Reconnaissance Regiment,' he said.

'Never heard of it,' Hollings said.

'I'm not entirely surprised,' North replied, taking a bite. 'I've barely heard of it, and I'm actually in it. It's a new and highly specialised Special Forces outfit set up a few months ago that concentrates on surveillance. It's highly classified and that's really all you need to know.'

Hollings nodded and Greaves altered the aim of his pencil to point at the last new arrival, a tall, thin smartly dressed man with thick black hair and a fussy small trimmed moustache.

'And this is Nigel Fanning,' he said. 'He's a technical consultant in the telecommunications industry. We didn't invite anyone from the phone companies to this little get-together, because we needed someone here who actually knows what he's talking about.'

Hollings chuckled and the others smiled. Fanning inclined his head and gave his moustache a discreet stroke.

'And that,' Greaves concluded, looking at the man sitting at the opposite end of the conference table, 'brings us to the last of our visitors. His name is Ben Morgan.'

The other four men followed his gaze.

Morgan was visibly the youngest person in the room and right then he both looked and felt slightly out of place. Not because he was unfamiliar with the world in which he found himself – he had previously been involved in covert operations and intelligence gathering, two of the core activities of both the Secret Intelligence Service and the Security Service – but because he was wondering if the action he had taken in the last few hours had been a mistake.

'His expertise,' Greaves continued, 'lies in IT security, which I know is rather a broad-brush statement. Until last Friday he was working at Hendon on the PNC. We decided he has the skill set we needed and that's why he's here. Don't ask him too many questions because a lot of what he's been involved in is still covered by the Official Secrets Act. In short, he's probably the most important person in this room, at least in the context of what we're involved in.'

'And what context is that?' Welby asked.

'I'd have thought that was quite obvious,' Greaves replied. 'We all know what happened last Thursday. Our job – or, to be exact, *your* new job as instructed by the Prime Minister, because I'm only really here as a coordinator, to provide oversight – is to make sure that nothing like that can ever happen again.'

There was a moment of silence, finally broken by Dave North.

'Oh, shit,' he said.

Chapter 3

Sunday 10 July 2005
Vauxhall Cross, London

'That shouldn't have been too much of a surprise, surely?' Greaves asked, looking at the SAS officer. 'Why else did you think you'd been asked to turn up here?'

North shook his head.

'That was the obvious bit, and you're right. That was no surprise to me. But I had hoped that whatever we were going to be tasked with doing would be funded and acknowledged. The moment a senior SIS officer tells you he's only providing oversight, it means we're in the shit whatever happens. If it works, nobody will even bother to thank us, and if it all turns into a clusterfuck, officially nobody will ever have heard of us and we could all end up in the slammer. That's the short version, isn't it, Simon?'

Greaves had the grace to look slightly embarrassed.

'This will be off the books and totally deniable, yes,' he said. 'It has to be, because of what I expect you'll be doing and how you'll be doing it.'

Michael Hollings stirred uncomfortably in his seat.

'Are you implying that we may be required to carry out illegal actions?' he asked. 'If you are, then I will be forced to decline. I actually work for the government, so I cannot be involved in any form of impropriety.'

'Relax, Michael. Your role in this is strictly advisory.'

Greaves looked down the table at Fanning and Morgan.

'Technically,' he went on, 'you're all here as advisers, but some of the areas that we wish to investigate could be considered sensitive under current UK law.'

'You mean you want me to act as your secret hacker?' Ben Morgan asked, speaking for the first time.

'In a manner of speaking, yes.'

Like North, Morgan had an immediate sinking feeling. He had the skills, but years ago he'd had a major brush with the law and he'd been lucky to walk away. The case file had been sealed because of what the investigating officer called an 'ambiguity'.

While Morgan had been flattered when the MI5 officer had phoned him at Hendon on Friday, saying the Home Secretary needed his technical expertise at a meeting, he now wondered if he had been selected for some other reason entirely. Sealing a police file was one thing, but he was in no doubt that both the SIS and MI5 could probably bring enough pressure to bear to get it reopened. His fear was that he had been chosen as a fall guy because of that incident. He would have to tread carefully and make sure that the deck was stacked in his favour.

'I presume that's the reason there's nobody here from the Metropolitan Police?' he asked.

'The police, Mr Morgan,' Welby said, 'will do exactly what we tell them to do. As usual.'

Simon Greaves glanced at his watch and then rubbed his hands together briskly.

'Right,' he said. 'Let's crack on. James, why don't you tell us what you know.'

'You saw the news last week,' Welby began. 'At 08:49 last Thursday morning, 7 July, what the newspapers are calling the 7/7 attacks took place. You know how they like their shorthand stuff. Three bombs exploded almost simultaneously on different Tube trains after they left King's Cross St Pancras station. That's the first anomaly, because we've now established that all three detonations occurred within fifty seconds, which could mean pre-set timers attached to the explosive charges, remote triggers using a radio link or calls to mobile phones wired in as detonators. Or, most likely, did these people synchronise their watches and press their buttons at 08:49?'

'They wouldn't have used timers,' North said, 'because there'd be too much chance of a delay. It was right in the middle of the morning rush hour. They couldn't have set the timers beforehand because they wouldn't have known how crowded it was going to be, and they definitely wanted things to go bang after the trains had left the station so they'd blow up in the tunnel system, not on a platform. Radio signals and mobile phones don't really work on the Tube, so they probably did it the easy way. They synchronised their watches and picked a time. Simple as that.'

'We concur at Millbank,' Welby agreed. 'The first bomb was in the third carriage of an eastbound Circle Line train between Liverpool Street and Aldgate, which had just left Liverpool Street station. The second device was in the second carriage of a westbound Circle Line train out of Edgware Road station. Both trains had left King's Cross roughly eight minutes earlier, and that's why we think the bombers had picked a specific time to trigger them. For the maximum blast effect, maximum casualties, and to make the rescue work as difficult as possible, they should have waited until the trains were midway between stations. Presumably they'd decided that they wanted simultaneous blasts to make it clear that it was a coordinated attack.

'The third bomb was in the first carriage of a Piccadilly Line train heading south from King's Cross to Russell Square, and was detonated when the train was about five hundred yards from the station. If the bombers had decided to wait until their trains were midway between stations, that could have doubled the number of casualties and made the recovery operation a lot more difficult than it is right now.

'There were also clear differences between the explosions in terms of their effects. The Circle Line runs in what's called a "cut and cover" tunnel, only about twenty feet below ground, which has two parallel tracks, making it fairly wide. This allowed the force of the explosion to dissipate within the tunnel and significantly reduced the number of casualties. Not including people with life-threatening injuries, the bomb at Aldgate killed seven people and the Edgware Road device killed six, plus the two bombers.

'The Piccadilly Line is different. It's a deep-level tunnel, running about one hundred feet below the surface, with a single-track and only about six inches of clearance around the trains. When the device was detonated at Russell Square the explosion was magnified and concentrated by the solid walls of the tunnel, increasing the effects of the blast, and that's reflected in the number of deaths. Twenty-six innocent people died at Russell Square.'

That bald statement hung heavily in the air.

'We were lucky. If these bombers had done their homework a bit more thoroughly, if they'd only picked single-track tunnels to hit and timed their detonations so that the trains were between stations, we might have been looking at over thirty deaths from each explosion, and a total death toll of well over one hundred, twice what we have now.'

'What about the bus?' Greaves asked.

'I'm coming to that. There was initial confusion in the Underground control rooms because they thought they were dealing with a series of power surges that had explosively tripped various breakers. In fact, it was the explosions that had caused the power to fail. And there were confusing reports, like one incident being described as a body under a train and another as a derailment. Both statements were true, but these had been caused by the explosions and weren't standalone events. Then there was the timing. The police first thought the bombings had taken place over about half an hour, not the fifty seconds that was the case. At 09:19 London Underground declared a Code Amber alert and shut down the entire network. Train drivers were told to stop at the next station and all services were suspended.

'The fourth bomb was detonated on the top deck of a number 30 double-decker travelling from Marble Arch to Hackney Wick. It left Marble Arch at 09:00 and got to Euston bus station at 09:35. There were crowds of people there because the Underground network was shutting down and passengers were taking buses to continue their journeys. At 09:47 the fourth bomber detonated the device he was carrying in Tavistock Square, near the headquarters of the British Medical Association, a building full of doctors. They hadn't got much in the way of medical supplies there, but they did what they could and their actions undoubtedly saved lives. The explosion tore the roof off the bus and virtually destroyed the rear of the vehicle. Most of the passengers in the front of the bus, on both the upper and lower decks, survived. If it had been under a bridge when the explosion took place the results would have been worse.

'We think another thirteen people died in the explosion, the same number of casualties as was caused by both of the bombings on the Circle Line. That's our best estimate, but the damage caused by the bomb was so great that the forensic people are having to patch together what's left of them to get an accurate figure. Identifying all the victims will be a nightmare. We'll have to wait for families to register missing person reports and start from there, using DNA analysis to provide an indication of which bits belong to which victim.'

'Are you sure that this attack was linked to the other three?' Greaves asked. 'That we're not looking at two bombing campaigns that coincidentally decided to launch their attacks almost simultaneously?'

'I'm not a fan of coincidence,' Welby stated flatly, 'and logically we can discount it. Despite the different target and the delay in detonating the last weapon, we're certain that all four attacks were part of a single operation. King's Cross is a major transport hub and we think the four bombers had intended to attack only the Underground network. Two of them went in different directions on the Circle Line, the third took the Piccadilly Line, and it makes sense that the last bomber's target was the Northern Line. But he couldn't do that because the service was temporarily suspended. Or maybe something spooked him at King's Cross. But whatever happened he obviously decided that a crowded bus was his next best option.

'You might think that an explosion on a bus would be much less effective than detonating a device in an underground train in a tunnel, and you'd be right, but actually he managed to achieve the second highest death toll. This was probably, ironically, due to the earlier bombings. Because the Underground network was shutting down there were more passengers than normal on all bus routes in the city.

'The media still haven't got accurate figures, but we're looking at fifty-two dead, excluding the bombers, and about seven hundred injured, making this the worst terrorist attack in the history of Britain.'

Chapter 4

Sunday 10 July 2005
Vauxhall Cross, London

'You're discounting Lockerbie,' Greaves said.

'Yes,' Welby agreed. 'When the bomb tore Pan Am flight 103 to pieces over Lockerbie in 1988 it wasn't an attack on Britain per se. It was a terrorist attack that killed 270 people but the location was almost incidental. The trans-Atlantic air routes are altered daily because of the jet stream and oceanic weather systems. If they had been different that day, the explosion could have occurred over Ireland or over the Atlantic itself. This was different. This was an attack aimed deliberately and directly at the people of Britain.'

'Do we know what type of IED they used?' North asked into the silence that followed. 'One report claimed they'd had access to commercial-grade plastic, C4 or Semtex. And what about their identities? Have we any idea who they were or what group they represented?'

Welby nodded.

'It's early days yet, but they didn't use plastic explosive, despite what the papers may be saying. The bombs were home-made devices using organic peroxide compounds, most probably TATP, triacetone triperoxide. And we know who three of them were already. The bus bomber was an eighteen-year-old named Hasib Hussain from Leeds – we found the remains of his driving licence and credit cards in the wreckage. The bomber on the westbound Circle Line train was Mohammad Sidique Khan, again based on the remains of his documentation, and the Aldgate bomber was a man named Shehzad Tanweer. We're still waiting for confirmation of the Russell Square bomber, but we think he might be Germaine

Morris Lindsay. These names won't be released to the press until later.'

'Anything known about them?' Morgan asked.

Welby shook his head.

'Nothing yet. We think they were cleanskins, which means they hadn't previously come to the attention of the security forces.'

'I think we could all have worked out what that word meant,' Morgan said. He was still mildly irritated at the possibility he was there under false pretences. 'And if you're trying to stop a repeat performance, that's your biggest problem. If future terror attacks are planned by people who have never surfaced before, how are you going to identify them and find out what they're doing before there's another bloody great bang somewhere?'

There was a short silence, and then Greaves spoke again.

'Actually, that was where we thought you might be able to lend a hand.'

'Ah.' Morgan's heart sank a second time.

'The other aspect of last week's attack is the failure of the mobile phone network in the part of London where the explosions took place,' Greaves said. 'Which is why Nigel Fanning was asked to be here for this meeting.'

Fanning picked up the ball and ran with it.

'I've read the preliminary analysis,' he said. 'The assumption was that the network had been shut down to avoid other bombs being detonated by mobile phones – that's a technique used by terrorist groups to remotely trigger IEDs – but in reality it just got completely overloaded. The Vodafone network crashed at about ten that morning. Other providers had outages as well and it affected some landlines. There's a workaround for this kind of problem called the ACCOLC, Access Overload Control, which gives priority to emergency calls. Vodafone activated this inside about a half-mile radius around Aldgate Underground station that morning. This was because many of the victims of the bombings were being treated there, and it ensured the emergency responders had reliable communications, at least if they had ACCOLC-enabled phones.'

'We know the identities of three, maybe four, of the bombers,' North said, 'so I assume the police will be mounting raids on their houses, seizing their vehicles, and hauling in their relatives for a bit of one-on-one interrogation? That sort of thing.'

'That's in hand, obviously,' Welby replied. 'We already know that two of the bombers lived in Leeds, and possibly the other two did as well. It looks as if King's Cross was the starting point, so we've already impounded the CCTV footage from the station to be analysed. We'll be looking at footage from other stations, street cameras, stations at Leeds, car hire firms and the other usual avenues. Not for public dissemination, obviously, but raids will be mounted on the two addresses we already know in Leeds on Tuesday, and on the homes of the other two bombers if we've identified them by then, and on the addresses of any other persons of interest.'

'The expression "stable door" springs to mind,' Morgan said. 'I've no doubt that you'll identify all the people involved in this attack, the bombers and their helpers and their enablers, but all you're actually doing is clearing up a mess that's already happened. Unless you're wrong about these people being cleanskins, that'll be the end of it. You won't find any links to any other potential suicide bombers, because these people won't have known any, so you'll have no idea where or when the next attack will happen. And my guess is that you're expecting another attack.'

'We are,' Greaves said. 'Because of what's going on in Afghanistan and Iraq, and the perception by at least a part of the Muslim community that their countrymen are being targeted deliberately, we think more attacks are a virtual certainty.'

'And you're expecting me to somehow track down any future suicide bombers so that you can stop them in their tracks. Like a kind of home-grown, one-man version of Echelon.'

'Technically,' James Welby stated, 'details of the Echelon system are still classified.'

Morgan laughed.

'If you really believe that, then MI5 is even more hopelessly optimistic and deluded than I thought. Just go onto the Internet and you'll find chapter and verse about Echelon in Wikipedia and a bunch of other sites. And while you're there you can check out Fairview and Carnivore and Pinwale and Turbulence and Topsail and a raft of other covert surveillance systems and data analysis tools that the general public are not supposed to know about. That particular genie is already out of the bottle and has been for some time.'

'I do know that. I was just clarifying the official position. And we're not expecting you to replicate the monitoring facilities used by Echelon. In fact, quite the reverse. We'll be very happy to provide you with access to all of the surveillance systems over which we have any degree of control, because you're going to need that capability to have any hope of doing what we want, of identifying the next attack before it happens.'

Morgan shook his head.

'GCHQ out at Cheltenham is already doing that, unless its remit has changed, and I don't think it has. If the analysts at the Doughnut, with their access to pretty much every form of electronic communication known to man, can't find these nutters, how the hell do you expect me to do it? I mean, every time some Talib farts in the Hindu Kush GCHQ is listening in.'

'I think that's a slight exaggeration, Ben,' Greaves said smoothly, 'and even if it was true that the wind emissions from some Afghan's bowels could be detected at that range it wouldn't actually help us. The threat we're dealing with here is almost certainly home-grown. As far as we know at this stage, there's no evidence that this attack was planned by anyone other than the perpetrators themselves. They were probably influenced by events in Afghanistan but nobody over there, not the Taliban or al-Qaeda or anybody else, was involved.'

'That's a broad-brush statement,' Welby said, 'and I don't know what your basis is for making it. We don't know exactly what motivated these four people to turn themselves into walking bombs. Until we check their family backgrounds for international links, look at airline records and credit card expenditure and all the rest of it, we'll have no idea how or why or when they were radicalised. And that's the key. Find out what triggered them to do it and maybe we can find a way to stop the next attack.'

'Let me clarify that,' Greaves replied. 'We don't *know* that these bombers were home-grown but that is the most likely scenario. As far as GCHQ is aware there's been no traffic or any other indications that these people were acting on behalf of any group. If it had been a sponsored attack, there would probably have been an immediate claim of responsibility after the event, and possibly two-way traffic in the immediate run-up to it. We saw nothing like that, and what we know so far about Hussain and Khan has revealed no links to radical Islamic groups. That's why we think this was domestic in origin.'

'Let me get back to the main issue,' North said. 'There almost certainly were other people involved. Learning how to cobble together a bomb by looking at a couple of websites doesn't always work out that well. It doesn't often make the press because we try and keep a lid on it, but assorted Muslims pitch up at their local A&E fairly frequently, missing a few digits or a hand or two from when things have gone wrong. That's wrong for them but right for us, obviously.

'According to a couple of sites on the Web, the improvised explosive TATP – triacetone triperoxide – has been nicknamed the "Mother of Satan" by the radical element among the followers of Allah, because it can explode so easily and unpredictably. Pretty much anything can make it go bang – friction, heat, static electricity, UV radiation, or shock. A decent fart could probably trigger it if the bomber's arse was close enough to it. About forty Palestinian bomb-makers working for Hamas have made the acquaintance of Allah way sooner than they ever expected to because the stuff is so unstable.'

'And you know this because…?' Morgan asked.

'Because we're in the loop,' North replied, 'along with all the other special forces' outfits. There are Executive Liaison Groups that act as a kind of link between The Box and the police and enable the two-way sharing of raw intelligence. The local police get told by hospital administrators when somebody walks in off the street and presents an injury that raises a flag, like a stabbing, a gunshot wound or damage caused by an explosion. So they tell Millbank and Millbank tells us, but none of us usually gets involved in stuff like that. And we keep it quiet. The media tend to do what MI5 tells them. They just quote the usual national security bollocks and most editors will play ball.'

'I think there's probably an argument that keeping it quiet is counterproductive,' Morgan suggested. 'Maybe if the papers showed a few moderately gruesome pictures of failed would-be suicide bombers who would then be known to their friends as "Stumpy", we might get a lot fewer repeat offenders.'

'That's true, but we don't want to give the impression that there are dozens of these guys out there building bombs and getting ready to light the blue touch-paper on the evening commute.' James Welby glanced round the table at the other men as he spoke. 'That tends to freak out the voters and our political lords and masters don't want that to happen in case they don't get re-elected and have to go out and find a real job. Questions in the House, all that kind of thing. We prefer to keep some things off the public radar if we can.'

'These amateur bombers who blow their hands off,' Nigel Fanning said. 'What do they say happened to them when they pitch up at the hospital?'

'Fireworks,' Welby said. 'They normally say they were lighting fireworks or carrying them when the whole lot went off. Or they were working on a car or motorbike engine and the carburettor exploded. Nobody believes them because the injuries caused by an explosive are distinctive, and a handful of fireworks going off and a petrol explosion produce quite different results.'

'I think we're getting side-tracked here,' Simon Greaves said. 'What excuse a failed suicide bomber uses really doesn't matter. We'll be picking apart the lives of the perpetrators of these attacks. We'll be looking at their local imam up in Leeds, or wherever they prayed, in case he radicalised them, and scrutinising their families and friends. Who else would they have needed? What equipment would they have used?'

'One of the most vital components of the bombs,' North replied, 'would have been the detonation mechanism they used, the fuse. Mixing up a home-made peroxide explosive is not that difficult but persuading it to go bang isn't easy unless the concentration of hydrogen peroxide is high enough. They'd certainly need a decent-quality detonator to make sure. I'll want to know what the techies pull out of the rubble that might give us a clue. If they knew somebody competent enough to make blasting caps that would be another trail to follow.

'We also need to look at safe houses and the bomb factory where they manufactured and stored the weapons. We'll find whatever vehicle or vehicles they used to travel down to the Smoke and pull those apart. And these idiots might well have done video interviews to justify what they were going to do. If any surface, we need first-generation copies of them and we'll do a full analysis of the room or wherever they were filmed. It's amazing what you can get from a video or even a soundtrack.'

'There's a good chance Al Jazeera will get them first, if there are any,' Morgan said. 'That seems to be the pattern these days. But if you can get copies, I know people who can extract whatever data they contain.'

'No doubt the police will identify the four bombers and roll up whatever network they had in place around them,' Greaves pointed out, 'but that's nothing to do with us. What we're actually supposed to be doing is working out a way of detecting and stopping the next attack.'

Chapter 5

Sunday 10 July 2005
Vauxhall Cross, London

There was a brief double tap on the door. A youngish man wearing a light grey suit and looking slightly harassed stepped into the room and walked across to Greaves. He bent down and muttered something in the SIS man's ear, then left.

'Some progress,' Greaves said, turning back to the table. 'As you know, the Met have pulled in CCTV and one of the cameras at King's Cross shows four young men carrying backpacks arriving at the station at 08:23 on Thursday. Comparison with driving licence pictures of Hussain and Khan held at the DVLA suggest they are two of the figures.'

'Did they walk into the station from outside,' James Welby asked, 'or did they use the rail network?'

'It looks like they travelled by mainline rail, but that's being checked. The Met are backtracking to find out where they travelled from, which was probably Leeds. I think we can assume they were travelling together rather than arriving from four different places and meeting at King's Cross.'

Greaves looked down the table towards Ben Morgan.

'You'll need time to formulate a plan,' he said, 'but now you know why you're here and what we need, what steps can we take? We have to detect and stop the next attack before it's too late. How can we do that?'

Morgan nodded slowly, then leaned back in his chair, looking almost exactly unlike a man who has just been told that the safety of an entire nation – in a manner of speaking – now rested on his shoulders. He had assumed he would merely be advising or undertaking a bit of covert hacking, but it was now clear that they wanted him to own and solve the problem. And from their point of view he was a good choice. He had no political career to protect, no family to worry about, and was totally expendable if it all went wrong.

His career hadn't started particularly auspiciously. After leaving university he had moved almost seamlessly into banking, a logical start for someone with his IT skills. It hadn't worked out, for several reasons, and so he'd left, swapping his City business suit for the slightly more relaxed dress code and lower salary at the Police Training Centre in Hendon.

The British police force had needed IT specialists to service the needs of the Police National Computer, which was vital to combat not just domestic crimes but international terrorism after the US 9/11 attacks. Instead of attending meetings in the City to discuss somewhat nebulous and frankly dull concepts like margins, remittances and reserves, Morgan found himself very close to the sharp end of policing, receiving briefings about firearms, long frauds, heists, identity theft, kidnapping and – most alarmingly – national security. His time there helped shape and hone his skills, and his access to some of the finest brains in the world on computer hacking and cyber defence was invaluable.

He'd moved from coalface computing to IT management. Unlike many IT specialists, who genuinely did act like the kind of geeks portrayed on television, Morgan found he worked well with people, and was particularly good at making IT work in the real world, outside the computer room. It was a comfortable niche and his work was valued – something of a novelty after his years in the City.

But the present challenge was very different to anything he had faced before.

'I'm a simple soul,' he said, after a few seconds. 'I look at problems as things that can be solved with small steps, working towards the desired solution.'

'We don't have time for small steps, Ben,' Greaves said. 'The next gang of radicalised Islamic nutters might already be packing their rucksacks with TATP bombs and nails and screws to use as shrapnel.

We're in a race here, and right now we're not really winning it. In fact, we're still hanging about somewhere behind the start line.'

'I know that. You've just dumped this problem on my head without any warning. You're asking me to invade the privacy of tens of thousands, maybe hundreds of thousands of assorted citizens of this great nation who might be entirely innocent but who just happen to be Muslims – or at least I assume that's what you want me to do – which is against the law as far as I'm aware. You probably won't be surprised to learn that I don't have some magic program that will automatically identify groups of putative bombers building explosive devices in their back bedrooms and send carloads of heavily armed rozzers screaming up to their doors.'

'You mean you can't help us, or you won't help us?' Welby asked, his tone frosty.

Bloody hell, Morgan thought. These guys are desperate. I bet all the civil servants and senior police officers are running away from this one in case it dents their chances of a knighthood.

'I hadn't finished,' he replied shortly. 'I was just stating the reality of the situation. Snooping on private citizens in the UK is illegal unless you can come up with some kind of credible probable cause. Believe me, I've been on the receiving end of the law and it's not pleasant. To the best of my knowledge, neither having Middle Eastern genes nor worshipping Allah would constitute anything like a good enough reason for initiating surveillance of any of them. So before I do anything, that situation needs to be clarified. And in this case the word "clarified" means an absolute and enduring written and signed immunity from prosecution for me and any of my colleagues that work on this problem.'

'I don't think that will be necessary, or achievable,' Greaves said.

'I do. I will not permit the British legal system to bite me in the arse a second time for helping my country. I heard what Dave North said. I have no doubt whatsoever that if what we're trying to do goes tits-up, you lot at MI5 and MI6 would be perfectly happy to hang me out to dry just to save your own skins and pensions. So this is non-negotiable. If I don't get this, in a form that my personal legal eagle is certain will protect me, then I'm out of here right now.' Morgan glanced across at North. 'I'm not familiar with the way your outfit operates, Dave, but maybe you should think about doing the same.'

North smiled and shook his head.

'We're covered on that score,' he said, 'just in a slightly different way.' He lifted both his arms and pointed his index fingers at Greaves and Welby, his thumbs vertical so that his hands looked like pistols. 'I have a lot of friends, and I know where both of these gentlemen live, and if they try and fuck me about they'll bloody soon learn the real meaning of meeting a stranger in the night, Hereford-style.'

The expression on his face made it clear this was no idle threat.

Welby's complexion paled slightly and he opened his mouth to reply. But then he apparently thought better of it and shut it with a snap.

'Very well,' Greaves said, sounding resigned, 'we can probably organise something like that. Who are you expecting to sign the document?'

'The word you're looking for,' Morgan replied, 'is "definitely" not "probably" and I'll want it signed by your bosses. That's the Foreign Secretary for Six and the Home Secretary for Five. Not some faceless bureaucrat or invisible administrator at Vauxhall Cross or Millbank. Two recognisable signatures and two printed names over two ministerial seals at the bottom of the page. That's the deal. Nothing more, nothing less.'

Greaves didn't reply for a few seconds, then nodded slowly.

'Very well,' he said, 'I'll make sure I get the wheels turning, but it may take a week or two.'

'I'll give you three working days,' Morgan said. 'That should be long enough. After that, it'll be good night from me because I'll be gone.'

'I had hoped you were more patriotic than this,' Welby said, his tone contemptuous.

'This has nothing to do with patriotism,' Morgan replied, not trusting the man from Five an inch. 'I've dealt with the British government often enough to know that they'll trample over the rights of any individual without so much as a second thought if it suits their purposes. You're asking me to do something illegal, and I'm happy to do it because I know how important it is, not just for the intelligence services but for the country. But what I'm not prepared to do is risk getting arrested again and prosecuted for helping you if the whole thing turns into a bugger's muddle. That's the deal, and it's my way or the highway. Your choice.'

'Enough,' Greaves said, sounding exasperated. 'You'll get your immunity, Ben. I'll make sure of that personally. Now, as I asked before, what can we do about this? I presume that before the letter of immunity arrives you can at least discuss this?'

Morgan nodded.

'Of course. Talking about doing something illegal isn't a crime in this country, at least not yet. And there are things we can do right now.'

He had the undivided attention of everyone in the room.

'But first there's one thing I want to emphasise, though you probably know it already. I doubt if these cleanskins spontaneously decided to bomb themselves into immortality just because they saw TV reports about the fighting in Iraq or Afghanistan. I do know something about Islam, and for a devout Muslim his religion dominates his life. The constant requirement to pray and read the Koran to a large extent negates any Muslim's free will. For these four men to do what they did means they must have had spiritual guidance, for want of a better expression. So somewhere, maybe at their mosque in Leeds or perhaps on the Web, there will be an imam who pointed them in the right – or rather the wrong – direction. I presume Five and the police will be investigating this?'

James Welby nodded.

'That's pretty much standard procedure, obviously. We will be picking over every aspect of their lives from conception onwards, believe me. Do you have another angle on this you want us to explore?'

'Not exactly. I'm hoping that the imam up in Leeds proves to be entirely blameless in this matter, because if they were radicalised by visiting a website run by one of the hate preachers that would give us a starting point to look for possible new attacks. We can set tripwires around the site and grab the location and other details of anyone who visits it.'

'Even if they use a VPN?' Greaves asked.

'Even if they use a virtual private network,' Morgan confirmed, 'though that does add an extra layer of complication. That's why I'd like to know the results of this part of the 7/7 investigation as soon as possible.'

'I'll make sure you get them,' Welby said, jotting down a reminder in his notebook.

'So for the future,' Morgan said, 'the first thing we do is go backwards. I'm slightly surprised you didn't have a GCHQ rep here this morning, but if you had I'm sure he'd have made the same suggestion. We have the probable identities of the 7/7 bombers, so the first step has to be to identify every communication system and method they had access to. Everything from the landline phones in their homes to their mobiles and email accounts. They couldn't have done this in isolation. They had to have been communicating with each other by some method. We might find nothing useful, but they might have been stupid and careless and left traces all over the place. We won't know until we look.

'Then we need to kick all that information out to Cheltenham so GCHQ can scan the Echelon take for any available recordings. We need to know every website they looked at. We need transcripts of every telephone call these people made, and every email or text message they sent.'

'GCHQ are already on that,' Greaves said. 'I was speaking to one of the section managers this morning. We would have done this anyway, because tracing communications between the bombers is an obvious first step to help us identify anyone else involved. So this isn't exactly ground-breaking stuff, Ben.'

Morgan smiled.

'I know, but this is just the first step. More relevant for our purposes, we need to tell the people at GCHQ that they're probably looking for the wrong things.'

Chapter 6

Sunday 10 July 2005
Vauxhall Cross, London

'You need to explain that,' Greaves said.

'Gladly,' Morgan said. 'Checking phone calls and stuff might give us the names of the people who supported them and GCHQ will be establishing links, maybe using a program like Promis, to identify anybody these guys talked to. But I'm not really interested in that. That's just a police matter, to identify the players. What I want to see are the transcripts of any conversations the various systems managed to record.'

'You don't think these people would have rung each other up and said "We'll do the bombing tomorrow morning at eight thirty, starting from King's Cross", or something like that?' Welby asked mockingly.

'If they *are* cleanskins, they might have done that if they didn't know about Echelon and that their emails and phone calls might be recorded. Most people in this great nation are completely unaware that numerous government organisations can snoop on what they say and do virtually at will, and for the flimsiest possible reasons. They could easily have communicated using plain text emails or phone calls, because they wouldn't have known any better. That would help establish their guilt but wouldn't help us. I'm hoping that somebody told them about Echelon or they looked at a website about it and they took precautions.'

'I wish somebody would tell *me* about this bloody Echelon thing,' Michael Hollings said, the tone of his voice revealing how out of his depth he felt. 'I've never even heard of it.'

Before Morgan could reply Nigel Fanning responded.

'Echelon's been around for a long time,' he said. 'It's run by what are often called the "Five Eyes" – the United States, Canada, the United Kingdom, Australia and New Zealand. Echelon monitors and records all telephone calls, faxes, texts and emails that originate in, terminate in, or pass through any of the participating nations. Bearing in mind that most of the major network hubs are located in those countries, and that the worldwide web is optimised to send traffic by the fastest possible route, those servers handle the vast majority of all Internet traffic. Phone systems work in a similar way.'

'So these Echelon people listen in to everything?' Hollings said. 'Who are they?'

'It's not "who", not a person,' Morgan replied, 'but "what". The monitoring is done by computers, but there's an alert system based on a thing called the Echelon dictionary. Any intelligence organisation in any of the participating countries and in other nations that are on friendly terms with one of them, like Germany or Israel for example, can ask to add words or names or phrases to the dictionary. Any message that contains one of those words will be flagged and copied, and sometimes analysed by a human being. The results of any analysis and the original text will be sent to the organisation that initiated the request.'

'You seem to know a lot about a subject that's supposed to be classified,' Greaves said.

Morgan looked over at him.

'It's a part of my world,' he said simply. 'Cybersecurity doesn't just mean identifying a virus some script kiddie has bolted together and pulling it off an infected computer. It's literally a whole and very real new world out there, and Echelon and Carnivore and all the other systems are an important part of it. It's what I did at Hendon and before.'

'Echelon can be a big help in counterterrorism,' Welby said, 'but how effective it will be in any particular circumstance depends on a lot of different factors, and on how much the targets know about the way it works.'

'Exactly.' Morgan picked up the thread again. 'They must have been communicating with each other. I want to see what those conversations involved and what words they used. You all know about al-Qaeda weddings, I suppose?'

Michael Hollings looked even more confused than he had a few moments earlier, but the other four men nodded immediately.

'Okay,' Morgan said to Hollings. 'Terrorist groups around the world know about Echelon and the other monitoring systems, so what they never do is describe their plans in plain language. They always use innocent-sounding words. So instead of saying "We will place the bomb in the station at nine thirty on Saturday", they'll say something like "We will sell the car at the garage at nine thirty on Saturday". They'll always use substitute words.'

'And al-Qaeda weddings?' Michael Hollings prompted.

'American intelligence officers have discovered that al-Qaeda terrorists refer to forthcoming attacks as "weddings" and there's an obvious cynicism in that. A wedding is a celebration, and as far as radical Islam is concerned a bombing attack is also a cause for celebration. It's just that it involves blowing people apart rather than bringing them together. Trying to identify an al-Qaeda wedding out of the hundreds of thousands of weddings being discussed on any one day on the Internet is virtually impossible unless there's some known factor, like the name or IP address of one of the people involved.

'So what I need from GCHQ is an analysis of the expressions and words that the bombers used. I'm hoping that they would have decided their code word for a bomb, for example, might be "bicycle" or something equally innocuous, and a fuse might be a "fish", say. If they did use code words, they might well have taken the first letter of the word they meant and picked another beginning with the same letter. I want an analysis performed on every text or verbal communication they exchanged, so we can see which nouns and verbs were most commonly used. Then we can analyse the context and see if the sentences are clumsy or clunky or don't really make sense, which might confirm we're looking at code words.'

'That's a good idea,' Welby conceded.

'That's just the start, of course,' Morgan went on, 'and it might be no help whatsoever. If these people were cleanskins they may have devised their own code, but I'm hoping they may have been in touch with other people with the same mindset, maybe when they were trying to work out how to mix the explosive or something, and there may be a kind of common underground code used to describe different aspects of this kind of attack. GCHQ may have detected something like this already, and if they haven't they should definitely be working on it. The worst-case scenario from our point of view would be if the bombers did everything face to face and never put anything in writing, but they would still need to communicate to a limited extent, if only to arrange meetings.

'Cleanskins would have needed expert help in building a bomb, to be told what chemicals to buy and shown how to mix them, how to pack the explosive and the shrapnel to create the maximum damage and so on. Unless they had a friendly neighbourhood explosives expert up in Leeds who could give them a crash course in bomb-making, they might have had to travel to get instruction. That might show up on credit card statements as bus or train tickets or petrol receipts, and I presume the police and Five will be checking to see if they took any holidays in Pakistan or Afghanistan where they might have done al-Qaeda training courses or the like.'

'That's all really useful stuff and good suggestions, Ben,' Greaves pointed out, 'but we're still looking backwards at what's already happened, not towards the future.'

'In the initial stages,' Morgan said, 'that will be inevitable. Nothing like this has ever happened here before, so we have no past experience or data to guide us. One thing you might think about is sending somebody over to Israel to talk to Mossad and Shin Bet, because they've got more experience in dealing with suicide bombers than any other nation.'

'That's already in hand,' Greaves confirmed. 'We're sending a two-man team out to Tel Aviv tomorrow to liaise with both organisations and exchange data. The Israelis have produced a kind of checklist telling people employed in law enforcement how to recognise a suicide bomber by what they look like and how they behave. We'll be distributing copies of that list to every British police force, the transport police and even traffic wardens, with instructions that their personnel memorise it as a matter of urgency. And hope they never need to use it.'

'I'd heard about that list somewhere,' Morgan said. 'Anyway, we need to know how this attack was constructed and where and how the bombers were educated in their craft. Once we have that, we'll be in a much better position to predict the future. But I do have some other ideas that would be worth trying.'

'Go on.'

'It's really a matter of the signal-to-noise ratio, and we need to do two things. We need to establish a kind of baseline, to analyse the level and type of communications of the Muslim communities or anyone else that might spawn this kind of atrocity. That means identifying the most likely target areas, the places where radical Islamic preachers are operating or where racial tensions have been reported. Places where a handful of young men might be so brainwashed at what's happening in Iraq or Syria or Jerusalem or wherever that they decide to protest by blowing themselves up along with anyone standing near them.

'Today we have mobile phones, text messages and emails, and there are services like Skype becoming popular as well. Even if we concentrate our efforts on analysing the two types that we can most easily intercept – texts and emails – there'll still be a huge volume of traffic that we'll need to look at, and almost all of it will be entirely innocent. That's the noise and what we need to find is the signal, the tiny percentage of messages that people planning terror attacks will be sending. The signal-to-noise ratio will be extremely low, and the signal very difficult to detect. That's why I want the message analysis from GCHQ as soon as possible, to tell us what we should be looking for. Once we've identified any suspicious terms used by the 7/7 bombers we can program the Echelon dictionary to flag those words and pull out any matching messages to be analysed.'

'There is one obvious problem with what you're suggesting,' Simon Greaves pointed out.

'I know,' Morgan replied. 'If the 7/7 bombers were cleanskins and never used electronic media to discuss what they were going to do, apart from setting up meetings, then we're not going to find any code words that we'll be able to use to detect another bombing in the planning stages. We'll be blind, and that's why I think as well as taking mainly passive actions we also need to be proactive, to try to attack the bombers, or at least try to fuck them up before they attack us.'

'What exactly do you mean by that?' Welby asked, leaning forward.

So Morgan told them.

When he'd finished, there was a moment of silence and then Welby shook his head.

'I'm not sure if that's a good idea, and it's probably not legal. It's certainly not ethical.'

'I don't know if you've noticed, James,' said Greaves, 'but this whole thing is off the books, so the legality of it doesn't matter. And as I presume it won't be attributable, even if it was illegal it wouldn't matter because it would be untraceable. And in this situation I don't give a toss about the ethics or otherwise, so go for it. How long before you could go live with this, Ben? Next week? The week after?'

Morgan shook his head.

'Longer than that?' Greaves asked.

'No,' Morgan replied. 'It's already running. It went live this morning, and I just need to do an update on the data as soon as I leave here and get back on the Web, now that we know who these bombers were. It would have been live sooner than that, but I had to find a chemist on Saturday afternoon before I could complete it.'

'And not a man in a Boots Pharmacy, I assume?' Dave North said.

Morgan shook his head.

'A rather different kind of chemist,' he agreed.

'And that was before we met and I told you what we were hoping you could do,' Greaves said.

Morgan nodded, knowing he would need to justify himself to win the trust of those in the room who already – and quite correctly – suspected he might be something of a loose cannon.

'I'm not an idiot, Simon. On Thursday morning four bombs exploded in the middle of the morning rush hour in London and over fifty citizens ended up in body bags. The media were all over it like a rash and most of what they said turned out to be correct, which is rather more unusual. Within hours of the attack, the fact that the perpetrators had been Islamic fundamentalists was pretty well established.

'First thing on Friday morning I got a call from somebody who declined to give me his name but who claimed to work at Millbank. He invited me to this meeting on Sunday morning. Knowing what I do from my day job and my past indiscretions and putting it all together into a single picture wasn't that difficult. You didn't invite me here for coffee and biscuits and a gentle chat about the state of the nation. The only reason for letting me walk through the hallowed portals of James Bond land was because you wanted me to do something. I'm a white-hat hacker and a counter-espionage IT specialist, so it wasn't rocket science to work out that you'd be asking me to try to do something in response to the 7/7 attacks. So I figured I'd get that something running sooner rather than later.'

Morgan switched his glance from Greaves to Welby and back again.

'It's already out there,' he said defensively, 'but I can stop it if that's what you want.'

Greaves shook his head decisively.

'No chance,' he said. 'Let it run and let's see what it can do. It can't do any harm, or not to anyone who matters. If a handful of terrorists blow themselves up trying to make their bombs, I won't lose a second's sleep over it.'

Chapter 7

Friday 22 July 2005
Vauxhall Cross, London

'This time we dodged the bullet,' James Welby said.

'That's perfectly true,' Simon Greaves replied, 'but it really isn't the point. We never saw 7/7 coming and now, exactly two weeks later, we didn't see this attack coming either. I'm getting pressure from above, from inside and outside the Service, and I'm at the point where I have no idea what to say. But countering threats and attacks like these is not a task for which Six was established or is responsible for, and it's one that we're certainly not equipped to handle. This, James, is definitely down to Five and the British police, and that means the buck stops with you and Millbank and the Met.'

At 12:26 the previous day, the first of a series of four explosions had occurred on an Underground train on the Hammersmith and City Line at Shepherd's Bush Station, West London. Four minutes later there was a similar detonation on a Northern Line train at Oval Station. At 12:45 a third explosion occurred at Warren Street Station on a Victoria Line train, and at 13:30 an explosive charge was detonated on a number 26 bus en route from Waterloo to Hackney Wick.

In almost every respect bar one, these terrorist attacks mirrored the 7/7 explosions that had occurred exactly two weeks earlier. But the vital difference between the two sets of attacks was that all four of the improvised explosive devices triggered around lunchtime on 21 July had failed to detonate. In each case only the blasting cap exploded, producing a detonation no louder than a firework. Apart from a single individual who suffered an asthma attack, there were no casualties caused.

However, once it became apparent that London was again under attack by a gang of terrorists, even if those terrorists were manifestly incompetent, action was initiated to evacuate the principal target, the Underground system. All the stations where the failed detonations had taken place were cleared of commuters, as well as other stations, shutting down Archway, Moorgate, St Paul's and Green Park. Trains were suspended on the Victoria, Northern, Hammersmith and City, Bakerloo and Piccadilly lines.

'The situation is still very confused,' Welby said, not responding to Greaves's blunt criticism of both himself and the Security Service. 'I don't think anybody could have anticipated a second attack so soon after the first, or that it would be so similar to what happened on 7/7, virtually a mirror image. Except that this attack was a failure.'

The group was meeting again at the headquarters of the Secret Intelligence Service at Vauxhall Cross. They'd all been summoned as soon as the full extent of the attack had been established.

'We've obviously been very lucky,' Nigel Fanning said. 'If these bombs had detonated, London would now be in a state of siege.'

'Actually,' Dave North said, the leather of his jacket creaking slightly as he leant forward across the table and looked towards Ben Morgan, 'I'm not entirely sure that it was only luck. I have a feeling that our colleague at the end of the table might have something that he needs to tell us. Or something that we need to know, which isn't exactly the same thing.'

The other four men followed North's gaze.

'I'm not certain what I did made too much difference,' Morgan said. 'What do the forensic people say about the devices? Why did none of them explode?'

The information was fresh in James Welby's mind and he had no need to refer to the notes on the table in front of him.

'This information is based on a preliminary forensic examination,' he said, 'but it looks as if the devices only contained a low concentration of hydrogen peroxide. Not enough for it to explode, anyway.'

Ben Morgan nodded.

'That makes sense. This isn't my field, but you need about a seventy per cent concentration of hydrogen peroxide to guarantee an explosion, and at least thirty per cent for the mixture to become explosive at all. The good news is that nobody can buy thirty per cent concentrations without the proper paperwork, and the stuff that's readily available is only about three percent, or double that if it's used in the hairdressing industry. So the terrorists have to boil the hydrogen peroxide to concentrate it, to evaporate some of the water. If they can't get at least a thirty per cent concentration, the device won't detonate.'

'And?' Simon Greaves prompted. 'The first bunch of terrorists managed to do that so how come this second group made such a Horlicks of it? Did you do something that influenced them? In the wrong direction, I mean?'

Morgan smiled slightly.

'Maybe,' he admitted, almost shyly.

'So what did you do?' Dave North asked. 'You told us you'd put something on the Deep Web, but you didn't give us details.'

'I figured that any terrorist group wanting to emulate the 7/7 bombings would probably get their information from the Deep Web, so after I got the call to attend our first meeting I built a site really quickly that contained most of what we already knew about the first attack, and structured it so that it looked like the information had come from the terrorists themselves, or from people who were involved. If you remember,' he added, looking at James Welby, 'I gave you the website address to pass on to the Met so that they wouldn't waste their time trying to track down the author. As soon as the identities of the bombers were confirmed, I included their names on the site as martyrs for the cause. That was intended to give the site credibility, to make anyone who visited believe it was a genuine jihadist site. And that was important.'

'Why?' Michael Hollings asked, an angry undertone to his voice. 'It sounds to me as if that would fan the flames and make it more likely other groups would try to emulate the first attack. What you did might even have prompted this second terrorist group to act.'

'Definitely not,' Morgan said firmly, shaking his head. 'You can't put this kind of operation together in a couple of weeks. Just buying enough hydrogen peroxide to build the devices would take time, unless they could persuade a friendly hair salon to give them their entire stock. But even then, physically boiling the hydrogen peroxide to concentrate it would take days at least. And they would need to buy the acetone to mix with it, find containers to hold the mixture, buy the shrapnel to put around the explosive charge, buy or make blasting caps to detonate it, and most importantly find half a dozen people who were so utterly committed that they were prepared to blow themselves to pieces to make a political point. I don't believe an operation like this could be mounted in less than two or three months at the very least. It certainly couldn't be done in a fortnight.'

Hollings looked slightly mollified but didn't reply.

'That makes sense to me,' Dave North said, 'but you still haven't explained why you created the site. From what you've said, the contents could have inspired potential terrorists, and I'm not happy about that.'

'That,' Morgan replied, 'was the whole point. I had to build a totally credible, inspirational site that would be accessed by potential terrorists so that the information I provided would be accepted without question and hopefully used by them.'

'What information?' Greaves asked.

'Do any of you know anything about hydrogen peroxide?' Morgan stared at shaking heads. 'Well, I don't know much about it either, but I did a bit of research and I discovered something I thought was interesting. Hydrogen peroxide breaks down into water and oxygen. In fact, you could almost consider it to be an unstable isotope of water, and in its pure form it's a clear and pale blue liquid. If it's exposed to light it slowly decomposes. It's used as a bleaching agent, as an oxidiser and an antiseptic. In high concentrations it can be used as a propellant or an explosive.

'Terrorists must obtain the highest concentration of hydrogen peroxide that they can and then combine it with acetone and sulphuric acid, which makes acetone peroxide, also known as APEX, and that produces triacetone triperoxide or TATP. That's the explosive, and it's got a similar yield to trinitrotoluene or TNT, so it's a serious weapon. It's one of the few types of high explosive that doesn't contain nitrogen, which means it can't be detected by traditional scanners. That's why it's become the weapon of choice for terrorist groups, despite its extreme sensitivity. All that information is available on the Web, and if you search deeper in the Deep Web you can find step-by-step instructions on how to make TATP.

'What I was counting on was that the people wanting to manufacture TATP would read enough about it to produce it, but not study its chemistry. There are three inorganic catalysts that increase the decomposition of hydrogen peroxide. In decreasing order of effectiveness these are manganese oxide, lead oxide and zinc oxide. The first two of these catalysts are often named on the web, but few sites seem to mention zinc oxide.

'On my website I explained the problems the 7/7 bombers had had in making the explosive and said the solution to increasing the effectiveness of hydrogen peroxide was to mix zinc oxide with it before combining it with acetone. I said the amount of acetone could be significantly reduced because of the presence of zinc oxide, especially if it was mixed with flour as a binding agent. I said this would increase the yield of the mixture, but what the zinc oxide would actually be doing was speeding up the decomposition of the major component of the explosive.'

'That's bloody sneaky,' Dave North said. 'Did you know if it would work?'

'I talked to a chemist who wasn't sure but reckoned it was worth a try. I have no idea if the group responsible for yesterday's attack saw my website and seeded the hydrogen peroxide with zinc oxide. But the fact that the devices didn't explode suggests they might have done. When we see the final analysis of the chemical compounds we'll have a better idea why they failed to detonate.'

For a few seconds nobody spoke, then Simon Greaves made a suggestion.

'Whether they did or not, it was a good idea, and that could be an indication of the route we should take to try to combat these groups. Get enough disinformation out there and we might confuse them to the degree that any devices they make will be less effective than they could be.'

Morgan looked unconvinced.

'Maybe, or maybe not. There are enough authoritative sites on the Deep Web to tell them exactly how to fabricate a bomb. I think at best we might be able to muddy the waters.'

'Every little helps.'

Simon Greaves stopped talking as they heard a brisk knock on the conference room door. A smartly dressed man walked briskly over to Greaves, murmured a few words and handed him a sheet of paper. Then he left.

Greaves read the brief paragraphs printed on the page.

'Now the shit is really going to hit the fan,' he said. 'Just after ten o'clock this morning, the Met police shot and killed a man at Stockwell Underground Station because they thought he looked like one of the suspects from the failed attacks yesterday. They were wrong. They managed to execute a Brazilian named Jean Charles de Menezes who had nothing to do with what happened. The Met is going to have to do a lot of backpedalling and arse-covering to sort this out. Heads should, and probably will, roll.'

Greaves looked again at the paper he was holding, then glanced at Ben Morgan.

'Going back to what you were saying, Ben, we've now got a very quick analysis of the devices used yesterday. According to this, the failed weapons contained a mixture of chapati flour and hydrogen peroxide, which is pretty much the suggestion you made on your website, so maybe what you did helped. But we still have work to do. My masters have agreed that we will continue with this arrangement for the foreseeable future to try to forestall any further terrorist attacks on the United Kingdom, and this group has been blessed in the last three days with three things. First, it will now be known as C-TAC.'

'Sea what?' Michael Hollings asked.

'C-TAC, which stands for the Counter-Terrorism Advisory Committee. A nicely innocuous name suggesting that it's a committee, which means that it just talks but doesn't do anything, and advisory because that implies we just give advice and nothing more. The intention is that it will be regarded as just another quango, a toothless talking shop.'

'You've told us what it won't be,' Morgan said, 'but what will it be?'

'These two attacks,' Greaves replied, 'the one that failed and particularly the one that succeeded, have got our lords and masters in something of a tizzy.'

Morgan had never before heard an adult male use that word in normal conversation.

'A tizzy?' he repeated.

'A state,' Greaves clarified. 'They're desperate to make sure that nothing like this will ever happen again. So although we started out just looking for ways to detect another terrorist attack before it could be launched, our – or rather your – remit is now much wider. C-TAC is intended to be Britain's first line of defence against disruptions and attacks of all sorts. Anything that the police or Millbank detect that has potential as a terrorist attack or that could cause any serious form of disruption will be advised to you for information and if necessary for action.'

Dave North laughed shortly.

'There are precisely six of us in this room,' he said. 'We have a man who knows about telecoms, another who can tell us all about nuclear weapons, a third who can hack his way into most computer systems, and I'm basically a licensed killer for the government. I presume that you and Mr Welby here have no intention of getting your hands dirty, so that leaves the four of us. What the hell are you expecting us to do? Exactly?'

'That's the third factor. C-TAC has been given an effectively unlimited budget and access to whatever resources and information you think you need, subject to the usual caveats. You can second anybody you like for assistance so the manpower question is irrelevant. You, gentlemen, are the new front line in an undeclared war.'

—

The name C-TAC, Ben Morgan thought, as he walked away from Vauxhall Cross a couple of hours later, had a good ring to it. He paused for a moment on the pavement and looked back towards the building, cynically referred to by most intelligence officers as 'Legoland'.

Then he shrugged, turned and walked on to find a Starbucks.

Part 2

Chapter 8

Three months ago
Hong Kong

Condemned prisoners in American jails can spend decades on Death Row as their lawyers submit appeal after appeal in attempts to get the verdict overturned or commuted. Some people believe that this long period of uncertainty and legal manoeuvring after a guilty verdict constitutes a cruel and unusual punishment in addition to the death sentence itself.

The man who called himself either Wang — which was his real name — or Mr King if dealing with somebody who didn't speak Cantonese, was a big fan of the death penalty. He was also, when time permitted, a big fan of cruel and unusual, because he believed it sent an unequivocal message to people in his criminal organisation and to anyone else who got to hear about it. But what he did not like was delay, which possibly served as a small degree of comfort to those people who seriously displeased him, because although they might well end up dying in screaming agony, at least they knew in advance that they would die relatively quickly in screaming agony. As far as degrees of comfort went, it wasn't much, but that was the point. The people who worked for him invariably did their best because they knew what would happen to them if they didn't.

Which was why he had been surprised when one of his most trusted underlings — a Macau-born enforcer named Zhao — had turned out to be working for himself by siphoning off some of the profits generated by a particularly successful stable of prostitutes in Wan Chai. The girls were based near the notorious Hop Yee building on Lockhart Road in the Causeway Bay district of Hong Kong Island, but in a more upmarket establishment. That was bad enough, but Zhao had also been feeding details of some other operations being run by Mr King to the Hong Kong Police Force.

In the eyes of Mr King, either offence was quite sufficient to merit the man's execution, and his biggest regret was that he could only have him killed once.

So he departed from his usual routine and decided that Zhao would die painfully and slowly and in an unusual manner. He spent some days pondering exactly how this would happen, and then came to a decision. The man was taken to a deserted area in the New Territories, gagged and stripped naked. Mr King's underlings had procured a large board of thick MDF, which they laid flat on the ground. Zhao was then tied to the board, arms and legs outstretched, and the ropes secured to nails driven into the MDF.

Mr King never normally concerned himself with the details of such activities and was driven to the site only when the execution was about to commence. He inspected the preparations and declared himself satisfied, and then explained to the terrified man that because he had tried to break up Mr King's criminal empire, Zhao himself would now be broken up.

The man selected to carry out the execution approached the condemned man and tied rubber bands loosely around his ankles and wrists and above his elbows and knees. Those would act as tourniquets when the dismemberment began, to ensure that Zhao did not die too quickly.

'I will be back here at the same time tomorrow,' Mr King told them. 'I expect him to still be alive when I come back. Make sure you give him water. Do not attack him during the night and cover him with a blanket. I don't want him to freeze to death. You may begin now with his left hand.'

The executioner nodded, bowed to his master, then took a simple claw hammer, walked back to the prisoner, and with three swift and brutally hard blows smashed the man's left hand to a bloody pulp. Not only was Zhao to be dismembered, but virtually every bone in his body was to be broken first.

Mr King nodded his satisfaction as he watched Zhao writhe and twist in agony, straining against his bonds and almost choking on the gag.

'Wait two hours and then continue as ordered,' he said. 'His hands and arms first, then his feet and legs, with two hours between each assault. Keep reminding him of the time and which part of his body will be destroyed next. I want him to fully appreciate the depth of his treachery and my displeasure with him.'

It took Zhao almost three days to die from pain and shock and, inevitably, blood loss despite the tourniquets, and he was mercifully already deceased when he was disembowelled and then beheaded, as the final parts of the punishment Mr King had selected for him. What was left of the man was chopped up into even smaller pieces and placed in two wooden barrels which the executioner and his assistant then drove to a farm a couple of miles away that was owned by an associate of Mr King. There, the body parts were fed to about a dozen large pigs over a period of two days, pigs being generally accepted as capable of eating almost anything.

As a fairly obvious precaution, Mr King never ate pork dishes anywhere in Hong Kong. Or seafood dishes either, as Mirs Bay and Tung Wan had also been used as convenient disposal areas for people who had fatally incurred Mr King's displeasure.

But that was not the end of the matter.

Zhao had passed on enough information to the police about Mr King's operations in and around Hong Kong that his sudden and unexplained disappearance raised immediate red flags. A handful of raids and the interrogation of men known to be a part of Mr King's criminal empire unsurprisingly produced no leads, none of his underlings wishing to end their days as Zhao had done. Mr King himself was arrested by the police, something that had only rarely happened to him in the past, and it began to look as if that particular enquiry was not one that he would be able to walk away from, and that his future would include decades in Stanley Prison or one of the other six maximum-security penal facilities in Hong Kong.

But before he could be formally charged with any offence, he received two unexpected visitors in the holding cell at the Mong Kok police station in Kowloon.

Neither man introduced himself, but the deference with which the police officers treated them told Mr King that they were important and powerful men, and probably important and powerful men from mainland China rather than from Hong Kong itself. They spoke only in Cantonese and offered Mr King a fairly stark choice. They had, they said, compelling evidence that a Macau citizen named Zhao had met his untimely and protracted demise in the New Territories at the hands of members of Mr King's criminal organisation, and they had produced high-quality aerial photographs, presumably taken by a drone, showing his broken body still nailed to the MDF board, as well as two photographs of the pig farm.

'The Hong Kong police know that this man has vanished,' one of them said, 'and with the photographic and other evidence we possess we can ensure that you will be successfully prosecuted for his murder.'

'We can also,' the other man chimed in, 'take you to mainland China for prosecution there. You are no doubt aware that the death penalty was abolished in Hong Kong in April 1993, but capital punishment is still carried out in mainland China. In fact, every year about half of the total number of people executed worldwide end their days in China. We have no doubt that your crimes would merit this ultimate sanction.'

Like an amateurish double act, the first man then spoke again.

'You may also be aware that our government has a policy of charging the families of executed drug dealers, for example, with the cost of the bullet used to kill them. And we also see no good reason why executed murderers should not contribute to the well-being of others after their deaths, so we routinely harvest their organs. China now performs more organ transplants than any other country in the world, and condemned prisoners executed by lethal injection form an important part of the supply chain. In your case, bearing in mind what happened to the man from Macau, it would seem only reasonable that you also should be dismembered, not by losing your limbs but by losing those parts of your body which have a cash value. We might also decide that the removal of those organs could be performed before your death, and not necessarily involve the use of anaesthetics.'

'Unless,' Mr King said, speaking for the first time since the two men had entered his cell.

He didn't doubt for a moment that his two visitors had the power to do exactly what they were claiming, but he also knew that they would not have travelled all the way to Hong Kong from Beijing or wherever unless they were looking for some kind of a deal. And he had been making deals – sometimes perhaps with the devil – for almost all his life.

'Unless?' the first man said questioningly.

'You didn't fly down here to Hong Kong just to visit Mong Kok and try to frighten me. I already know what could happen to me, so nothing you've said is new. You're here because I have something you want or because I can do something for you. As far as I know, I have no possessions that would interest the Chinese government, so presumably you want me to do something. So why don't you tell me what it is, and then I can either agree to do it or refuse and accept my fate.'

The two visitors glanced at each other, perhaps not expecting such a forthright response from the man they had come to see. Then the first man shrugged and nodded.

'Very well,' he said. 'I'm glad that you appreciate the reality of your situation. We do have a proposal for you. If you accept it, then the evidence we have assembled will not be given to the Hong Kong police, though we will retain it in Beijing in case you decide to change your mind, and you will be able to walk out of this police station no later than tomorrow afternoon. If you do not accept what we propose, then the evidence will be used to formulate charges for you to face. We will not make a formal extradition request for obvious reasons, but we will simply take you into our custody and deliver you across the border to the mainland. That would be much easier.'

'So what's the deal?' Mr King asked.

The two men leaned closer and told him exactly what they wanted him to do, which was nothing like he had expected. Basically, it was the kind of thing he had been thinking about for a couple of years.

Times change and the methods he had employed with great success in Hong Kong had become less and less appropriate and effective in recent years. Like any business, crime and criminals had to change, had to react to altered circumstances, and what the men suggested was a simple but major change. A switch, in effect, from blue-collar to white-collar crime that would mean not only changing the way he did business but would also necessitate moving to a different country.

Mr King didn't hesitate.

'I'll do it,' he said.

Chapter 9

Present day – Wednesday
London and Essex

It's a truism that the only reason anyone in the world is alive is because nobody wants them dead badly enough. Everybody, irrespective of their personal or professional security precautions and awareness of their immediate surroundings, is vulnerable at some time and in some location to some people.

Nicholas Michaelson became aware of his personal vulnerability precisely twenty-six minutes and thirty-seven seconds after he sat down in the rear seat of his chauffeur-driven Mercedes saloon outside his office building just north of Canary Wharf. His driver, Frederick Daley, fifty-something, slim and grey-haired, had been sitting in the car with the engine running, ready to leave, and his bodyguard had been standing beside the vehicle waiting for him. Michaelson didn't like that word but he couldn't think of a better way to describe the bulky man with the shaven head whose suits always seemed just that little bit too small. As Michaelson had approached, Ivan – and that name did seem appropriate because there was more than a hint of Russian hard man in his appearance – checked the road in both directions and then opened the rear door for Michaelson.

Ivan wasn't employed by Michaelson, but by the company he worked for. At the last meeting of the main board the decision had been taken to insist that all their most senior executives would be accompanied by a minder or bodyguard on their journeys to and from work, and enhanced security measures had been installed in their homes as well. Michaelson thought the whole thing was overkill.

'I know bankers aren't the most popular people in this country right now,' he had said, though he wasn't actually a banker and certainly didn't work for a bank, 'but I hardly think anyone is likely to attack us in the street.'

But the decision had been made and Ivan had dutifully made his appearance and for the last two months had been sitting in the front passenger seat of Michaelson's Mercedes every time he travelled from his home to the office or vice versa.

The other thing that Michaelson found slightly irritating was that Ivan had insisted from the start on varying the route they took in and out of London so as not to establish too obvious a pattern, making any attack more difficult. The slight problem was that there were some roads they really couldn't avoid using without making the journey ridiculously lengthy, simply because of where Michaelson lived.

With the three men inside and the doors locked, the car pulled away from the kerb on the roughly one-hour journey to the large country house that Michaelson called home, situated on the edge of a pleasant village just over the border in Essex.

The accident, though of course the impact was anything but accidental, occurred after they'd driven under the M25 orbital motorway and were heading north-east along the A113 London Road – one of the roads that was difficult for them to avoid – about two miles beyond the village of Stapleford Tawney. That stretch of road was two-lane and straight and could get busy during the morning and evening rush hours as drivers did their best to avoid the inevitable jams and chaos on the M25 and to a lesser extent on the M11, but at just after lunchtime on a Wednesday it was fairly quiet.

Sutton's Manor Hospital was on the east side of the road about a quarter of a mile beyond the M25 underpass, and about another quarter of a mile beyond that was a minor road that led to Mitchell's Farm. As the Mercedes passed the end of the road, the car passed a Range Rover there, waiting to join the main road. That wasn't unusual. Four-wheel-drive vehicles were a common sight in the area because the farmers needed their off-road ability, unlike the yummy mummies of Kensington and Chelsea for whom a big four-by-four was merely a pointless status symbol. What was slightly unusual was the substantial bull bar bolted to the front of the vehicle.

When he had begun his close protection duties, Ivan had installed a second interior mirror in the Mercedes alongside the standard fitment, angled so that a person sitting in the front passenger seat could see the road behind. He automatically glanced at it as they continued their journey and saw the Range Rover pull out behind them once they'd passed the turning.

About a hundred yards beyond on the left-hand side of the road was a farm track and public footpath that headed north-west, and as the Mercedes approached, a long-wheelbase white Transit van pulled out directly in front of them. But the van driver didn't continue the turn, just drove his vehicle straight across the road so that it blocked both carriageways, effectively closing the road.

Daley muttered a curse under his breath and stamped hard on the brake pedal.

In the back seat, Michaelson was thrown forward against his seat belt by the force of the deceleration and looked up from the document he had been studying to see the windscreen filled with the side of a white van. The rebuke that he had been intending to deliver to Daley died on his lips.

Ivan's attention had also been captured by what had just happened in front of them, apparently a thoughtless and dangerous action by a careless or incompetent van driver. But the moment he glanced at the mirror he realised that it was nothing of the sort. It was entirely deliberate.

'Brace!' he shouted, and instinctively pulled his seat belt tight across his chest.

Less than half a second later, the heavy-duty bull bar on the front of the Range Rover smashed into the right rear quarter of the Mercedes, spinning it sideways across the road. The driver of the four-by-four kept his foot on the accelerator pedal, forcing the Mercedes across to the opposite carriageway, over the grass verge and into the hedge that bordered the road, turning the car through a half-circle so that it faced the way it had come.

The moment the Range Rover came to a halt, the front passenger door and one rear door opened and two heavily built men, both wearing balaclavas so their faces were hidden, ran over to the wrecked Mercedes. One of the men was carrying a whippet, a double-barrelled twelve-bore shotgun with a cut-down stock and the barrels sawn off just beyond the wooden fore-end. Bigger than most pistols, utterly devastating at short range, it was an ideal close-quarter handgun, but hopelessly inaccurate at more than about thirty feet.

Inside the car, both the driver and the bodyguard were fighting a battle against the cluster of deflating airbags that had deployed at the moment of impact.

The man stopped about ten feet away from the driver's door of the Mercedes. He lifted the whippet to shoulder height and grabbed the fore-end of the weapon with his left hand to steady it. He took careful aim, making sure the angle was right, and then pulled the left-hand trigger.

That barrel of the whippet was loaded with a three-inch magnum shell filled with a single sabot round, basically a single solid slug inside a plastic sleeve. Illegal for use in Britain, except in very specific circumstances, the round had been hand-loaded. Bearing in mind that simple possession of the whippet would guarantee him a long term in prison, the gunman wasn't bothered at all about the legality or otherwise of the round it was firing.

The solid slug hit the car precisely where he was aiming, the right-hand side of the driver's door window.

The sound of the glass shattering was lost in the massive explosion as the weapon fired. The slug drove through the side window and into the laminated windscreen of the Mercedes with such force that the entire glass panel was ripped from the frame of the car and driven across the bonnet to slide off into the undergrowth.

Inside the wrecked car, glittering blue-green jewels of safety glass exploded from the side window all over Daley and Ivan, the tiny missiles opening up shallow cuts on their hands and faces. Deafened by the sound of the shot and the crashing impact of the solid slug with the window and windscreen, neither man had even had time to react before the gunman covered the remaining few feet and aimed the whippet directly at them through the opening where the windscreen had been.

'Don't move,' he snapped. 'That was solid shot, but the other barrel's loaded with buckshot. If either of you do anything other than breathe, I'll pull the trigger and they'll still be picking the last bits of you out of the car in a week's time.'

The two men registered the sight of the gaping side-by-side barrels of the whippet pointing straight at them and instantly froze.

'Lace your fingers together and put your hands on top of your heads,' he ordered.

It wasn't a difficult decision. Faced with either doing what the gunman told them or having their heads blown off, the two men in the car instantly complied. Ivan, of course, was unarmed, civil close protection staff in Britain not being permitted to carry weapons, unlike the people they expected to have to confront.

The second man from the Range Rover had acted almost as quickly, but his job was very different. He was carrying a tactical baton, identical to those issued to the British police. The moment the whippet fired, he stepped up to the battered and twisted Mercedes, snapped open his baton and swung it to shatter the rear side window.

He reached inside and popped the lock, then wrenched the door open. The driver of the Range Rover knew his stuff, and the bull bar had only hit the rear wing and boot lid. If the impact had been on the rear door as well, there was a good chance that it would have been jammed shut.

On the leather bench seat, Nicholas Michaelson was struggling with a collapsing airbag and his seat belt, an expression of total panic on his face.

The attacker slid onto the rear seat beside him, deftly released the seat belt, grabbed Michaelson by his right arm and hauled him bodily out of the car. As they emerged from the vehicle, the man who'd been driving the Transit van grabbed his other arm.

'Hold him.'

The Transit driver forced Michaelson to bend forward, then leaned back as his accomplice swung the baton again, this time aiming it at the back of Michaelson's head. It wasn't a hard blow, because they wanted him alive, but it was hard enough to render the man instantly unconscious.

The man slipped the baton into a pocket, ducked back into the Mercedes and grabbed Michaelson's computer case, checked that his laptop was in it, and picked up his mobile from the floor where it had fallen in the crash.

The two men dragged Michaelson across the road to the Range Rover, opened the back door and unceremoniously tossed him into the luggage area. Working quickly, they immobilised his unconscious body with plastic cable ties, lashing together his wrists and ankles, and then tied a makeshift gag across his mouth.

Then they climbed into the rear seats of the four-by-four.

Behind them, Michaelson was already starting to come round. He'd only been unconscious for a matter of a minute or so.

The moment the Mercedes had come to rest, the driver had backed the Range Rover away from it and turned it round so that it was now facing south-west, the way it had come.

When the doors slammed shut on the Range Rover, the gunman backed away from the wrecked car, still aiming his whippet at the two men in the front seats. When he reached the vehicle, he opened the front passenger door and turned back to face them.

'Duck, you suckers,' he shouted.

He waited a couple of seconds as the driver and bodyguard guessed what he was about to do and desperately ducked down below the dashboard of the Mercedes.

He laughed as he watched them trying to get down as low as possible in the front seats. And then he fired the second barrel of his weapon. The spreading cloud of buckshot tore through the thin metal of the bonnet, punching holes and driving deep gouges into the steel. He was still laughing as he climbed into the Range Rover.

Just under ninety seconds after the Transit van had blocked the road, the four-by-four, now carrying five passengers – four willing and one very unwilling – drove away from the scene.

On the other side of the abandoned van, traffic was beginning to build up and the first angry horn blasts sounded as the Range Rover moved off. Two other cars, both family saloons, were now approaching the improvised roadblock from the south-west, their occupants gazing curiously at the vehicle as it passed them going in the opposite direction.

'There's no traffic in front of us,' the driver said, 'so you can lose the balaclavas now.' His own face was obscured by sunglasses with particularly large lenses and he had a baseball cap pulled down low on his forehead.

His senses heightened by his predicament, Michaelson had heard every word spoken and every sound made. And even as he was fighting a rising tide of panic, that single statement by the driver frightened Michaelson so much he almost lost control of his bladder.

He had attended security briefings on what could be expected in a kidnapping, and one of the things he remembered very clearly was that the kidnappers would always hide their identities. The fact that the men in the car with him were prepared to let him see their faces meant only one thing in his mind: they didn't care if he could identify them because he wasn't going to live through the experience.

'That went smooth as silk,' the driver said. 'Good job, all of you. Now we'll get off this road and change the plates. How's our guest?' he added, glancing in the rear-view mirror.

'Pissed off and frightened fart-less, probably,' the man in the front passenger seat said, unloading the fired cartridge cases from his whippet, 'or he will be when he comes round. Make sure he keeps quiet, Jack, if he's awake. Here,' he added, handing over the unloaded whippet.

The man in the back seat took the shotgun and leaned over into the luggage area at the back of the Range Rover.

'He's awake and looks terrified,' he said. 'Just the way we want him.'

He leaned further over and rested the sawn-off barrels of the shotgun against Michaelson's chest.

'Just lie still, don't say a word and you'll live a little bit longer,' he said. 'You going to do that? That's a nod for yes or shake your head if you've got a death wish.'

Michaelson nodded.

'I figured you'd see sense.' He reached down and roughly pulled the gag away from Michaelson's mouth. 'But let me just give you a reminder.'

He pressed the muzzle of the whippet more firmly against Michaelson's chest, then pulled the two triggers one after the other. The clicks as the hammers dry fired were clearly audible even over the engine and road noise as the Range Rover headed towards London. Michaelson flinched each time, his whole body shuddering.

The man laughed, then tucked the whippet out of sight in the footwell in front of him.

Michaelson knew he had to do what he could before it was too late. What most kidnappers wanted, obviously, was money, and he was a seriously wealthy man.

'I can pay a ransom,' he said, a quiver of emotion in his voice. 'I'm a rich man. Just name your price.'

The driver laughed shortly.

'We know who you are,' he said, 'and we know you've got money. But that's not why you're sitting in the back of this car.'

'Then why?'

'We picked you because you've got something that we need.'

'What?' Michaelson asked. 'What have I got?'

'You'll find out soon enough. Now shut up, lie down and enjoy the ride.'

Chapter 10

Wednesday
Chelsea and Fulham, London

Everybody has secrets and everybody tells lies. It is almost a requirement of civilised society that people are consistently deceitful. There's the husband who cannot respond truthfully to his wife when she seeks his opinion about some item of apparel, or the dinner party where the meal is a disaster but which polite convention requires the guests to apparently enjoy. In a polite society lies and evasions and half-truths are a part of everyday living. Without them, marriages would break up, friendships shatter and daily life would be much, much more unpleasant.

These are the little lies, the lies told in the interests of domestic harmony or kindness or simple courtesy, but there are also big lies. And in a class of their own are the kind of lies that have a habit of making the front pages of the tabloid press should they ever be revealed.

George Kenton was very familiar with that kind of lie, because he'd been living one for most of the last decade. That was why he took extreme care to keep one particular part of his life completely hidden, because he knew that if his 'hobby' ever became public knowledge – or to some people, even private knowledge – then his career and the comfortable lifestyle that it funded would end very abruptly and he would probably be required to spend some years contemplating the error of his ways at Her Majesty's pleasure.

So when he left his large terraced house in Chelsea on one or two evenings each week, apologising to his wife about the 'little problem' that one of his subordinates had identified and that Kenton, as the man who ran the place, needed to fix as a matter of urgency, he always took care to make sure that he wasn't followed. And to complete the illusion for his wife's benefit there was always a telephone call to his work mobile a few minutes before he left the property.

But none of these calls originated from any member of the bank's staff. They were made by Kenton himself using an unregistered mobile phone set up to hide the outgoing number and fitted with a pre-paid SIM card. He had about a dozen of these cards locked away in the safe in his study and he swapped them regularly, never using any card more than half a dozen times before destroying it. That way, in the event of him ever being questioned, he could claim that they were unwanted cold calls, the kind of irritating and pointless conversations that everyone with a mobile phone has from time to time.

And before he made that call to his work mobile he made another call on the unregistered phone to a number that he had memorised. That call was invariably answered quickly, and all Kenton had to do was confirm his likely time of arrival and that the facilities, as it were, would be ready for him when he got there.

When he left the house, Kenton always knew he had time in hand, because his office was on the outskirts of the City, not a huge distance from Chelsea, but with London traffic the journey could take quite some time in either direction. On these call-outs, his wife would never expect him back in less than about three hours. But his actual destination was in Fulham, near Parsons Green Underground station, a distance of about a mile. In his experience it was no more than a ten-minute drive on any evening, even in unusually heavy traffic. That always gave him at least two and a half hours of complete privacy.

Black cabs cruised the area on a regular basis and provided anonymous transport for Kenton, who always paid the driver in cash and never asked for a receipt. He wouldn't hail a cab near his home but always walked a few streets away, and he would get out two or three hundred yards from his destination. He then walked to the building, even in inclement weather. The entire journey had never taken him more than twenty-five minutes each way.

That gave him a chance to make sure that he was as unobserved as it was possible to be in London, with its countless thousands of CCTV cameras monitoring the streets. He also took precautions to avoid presenting a recognisable image to those cameras, so even on summer evenings he wore either a raincoat or an overcoat, a hat with a wide brim and a pair of spectacles – his eyesight was near perfect – with slightly tinted plain lenses. To the cameras, and to anyone else who might have been watching, Kenton believed he looked like just one more Londoner heading home.

He was, of course, untrained in the art of counter-surveillance, and a halfway decent team of watchers could very easily have followed him from his home and through the streets to his ultimate destination. If this had happened, then he would never have known about it unless the members of the surveillance team were particularly clumsy or obvious in their activity.

–

And they weren't. He had been followed, but the men in the team knew what they were doing and had been behind him on three evenings during the previous ten days. That was all they'd needed to do, because George Kenton only ever travelled through the streets of London to one destination on his nocturnal ramblings. Once they'd identified the building, the surveillance team didn't need to follow him again, though they maintained a watch on his home each evening.

Instead, they turned their collective attention in a different direction.

Kenton only visited the building in the evening so they timed their arrival for mid-afternoon on Wednesday, two days after his last visit.

Getting inside most apartment buildings in London, or anywhere else for that matter, is not normally particularly difficult. Simply pressing one of the doorbells at random and telling the person who answers that the caller is there to read a meter or service the lift or fix a problem with the hallway lights or some other more or less plausible suggestion usually results in one of the residents pressing the button to open the main door. And if the first occupant refuses to comply, there are other doorbells, and eventually somebody will open the door, if only to stop the incessant buzzing.

Once inside, the two-man team, both wearing anonymous workman's overalls, quickly inspected the layout of the building. It was on three floors with four apartments on each, making twelve in total. One of the men was carrying a folding stepladder and the other a toolbox that contained little in the way of tools, but a dozen small motion-sensitive surveillance cameras, each with a battery life of at least a month. With three floors to cover, they decided to fit two on each, one at either end of each hallway.

The cameras were already prepped and SD cards formatted and inserted, so they only needed positioning and switching on. The man carrying the stepladder snapped it open beside one of the end walls, then held it securely while his companion climbed up carrying one of the cameras and a dry rag. He used the piece of cloth to clean the appropriate area on the wall, then pulled a circle of clear plastic film off the camera's suction mount to reveal a layer of contact adhesive for additional security on a less than ideal surface. He took a brief glance over his shoulder and down the hall, then pressed the mount firmly into position and closed the over-centre catch. He checked the alignment to ensure the apartment doors would be visible to the lens and pressed the on/off switch on the top of the camera body. A telltale red LED flashed twice to show that the camera was on and working.

The whole operation took less than fifteen seconds, and to fit all six cameras on the three floors a little over twelve minutes.

Once outside, they walked around the corner and down a side street to where they had parked a white Ford Transit van, opened the rear doors to tuck the stepladder and toolbox away, and then climbed into the front of the vehicle.

'Piece of piss,' the driver said, turning the key to start the engine.

The man in the passenger seat nodded. Both of them knew that the chances of the cameras being spotted by any of the residents were virtually nil. Most people viewed the world at eye level and below and rarely looked up. But if one of them did, the cameras were just small white cubes – the colour chosen deliberately – that were barely visible against the white paint of the hallway ceilings. They knew the building was tenanted and even if the cameras were spotted the assumption would be that the owners had installed them as a security measure to cover the public areas of the building, potentially a good idea. And the cameras would only be in place for about a week if all went as planned.

'We've got one more to do,' the passenger said, looking at a printed sheet of paper.

'Where? Which way do I go?'

'I'll program the satnav, but for the moment just head north. It's up in Holland Park.'

The driver indicated, waited for a gap in the traffic and then pulled out, driving with noticeably more care and attention than was usually exhibited by members of the White Van Man species. They didn't want to get stopped by a Met traffic car, because although the van was legal in every sense, and both men were insured for the vehicle and had full driving licences, some of the equipment in the rear of the Transit was forbidden to the citizens of the United Kingdom. Both men knew that if the vehicle was stopped and searched they would be looking at potential custodial sentences for what was called 'going equipped'. So the driver took extra care and was supremely conscious of the other vehicles on the road.

Chapter 11

Wednesday
Undisclosed location

Nicholas Michaelson hadn't known what to expect when he was pulled out of the back seat of the Vauxhall saloon – the kidnappers had changed cars in a small car park just off a country road about ten minutes after they'd grabbed him – and was half carried and half dragged by two of the men through the back door of an obviously run-down farmhouse at the end of a short driveway.

His waking nightmare on the journey had conjured up images of a cold, damp cellar populated by rats and other vermin, where he would be chained naked to the wall and provided with stale bread, stagnant water and a bucket in lieu of a bathroom. Or perhaps he'd be shoved into a kind of modern *oubliette*, the pre-medieval dungeons where unwanted prisoners were thrown and literally forgotten about – hence the name – to die of thirst and hunger over days or weeks. The logical part of his brain kept telling him that these possibilities really didn't make sense in view of what had happened, but that didn't stop the images from crowding his imagination.

What he hadn't anticipated was what actually happened to him.

His ankles still bound, he was dragged down a short passage and pushed face-first against the wall.

'Hold him still,' one of the men ordered, and Michaelson felt strong hands grabbing his shoulders.

He heard a metallic click from behind him that might have been a knife snapping open: he'd seen people using switchblades in films and that was what it sounded like. Then he felt a tugging on his bound arms and seconds later the sharp and unyielding grip of the plastic ties around his wrists vanished. The man with the knife then bent down and freed his ankles as well.

'In you go,' he said, opening the door beside Michaelson and giving him a shove.

He took a couple of tentative steps forward, rubbing his wrists where the plastic ties had cut into his skin, then glanced behind him. One of the men had already walked away and was out of sight, while the other stood looking at him, closing a large black-handled switchblade.

All of his captors appeared to have come from the same basic mould, broad-shouldered and well-muscled, some sporting tattoos and all with short-cropped hair. They looked like the kind of people Michaelson would expect to find propping up the bar in a cheap East End pub, not that he had ever ventured into that part of London. What they were was physically intimidating, which he assumed was the point.

'Make yourself at home,' the man said, then pulled the door closed.

Michaelson heard the sound of a key turning in the lock but stepped back to the door anyway. He turned the handle and pulled on it but the door didn't budge. Then he looked around him.

It wasn't a large room, and a single metal-framed bed bearing a thin mattress and bedding was the biggest thing in it. There was a somewhat battered armchair, and beside that a small wooden table. On the wall opposite the door was a window with steel bars on the outside, which was not unexpected. His captors would hardly be likely to shut him in a room with an available exit of any sort.

The other feature was a door in the left-hand wall, facing the foot of the single bed. Michaelson walked across the room and opened it. Inside was a small square space that contained a compact shower, a sink with a mirror above it, and a toilet bowl, but no window. On a shelf were two towels, a stick deodorant, a bar of soap, toothbrush and toothpaste, a bottle of shampoo, a can of shaving foam and a packet of disposable plastic razors.

It absolutely wasn't what he had been expecting. He felt more like a house guest – granted, a house guest in a seriously down-market establishment – than a prisoner. For the first time since the Range Rover had slammed into the rear of his Mercedes, Michaelson started to hope that maybe he would be able to walk away from this. Whatever 'this' was.

He stepped back into the bedroom. The room was warm, the heat coming from a radiator bolted to the wall below the window, and it was even carpeted. The room was scruffy, faded and in need of some TLC, but as prisons went it really wasn't bad. Whoever the men who'd taken him were, and whatever their motives, they seemed to want to keep him fit and well.

He heard the key turn in the lock and the door opened again. One of his captors entered – Michaelson still didn't know their names, but it was the man who'd fired the cut-down shotgun during the attack and who'd used the switchblade on his bonds – carrying a tray bearing a mug from which steam was rising and a packet of sandwiches. The man was probably the shortest of the four men with almost white hair cut very short, his face heavily marked by old acne scars on both cheeks. He put the tray down on the table beside the easy chair and then looked at Michaelson.

'You can call me Karl,' he said, though Michaelson doubted very much if that was any part of his real name. 'This is maybe not what you're used to but it's all we've got. The coffee's instant and we don't run to a chef, so it'll be sandwiches and maybe the occasional takeaway. Don't even think about trying to get out of here. There are four of us and one of you, and you're miles from anywhere. Do what we want, and this'll all be over quickly. Bugger us about and it won't only be you that suffers, if you take my meaning. Now eat your dinner. Somebody will be along to have a word with you later.'

In fact, he was being slightly economical with the truth. Four people had been directly involved in the kidnapping and they would provide the muscle should Michaelson suddenly develop the nerve to try to escape, but in fact there were five people in the building in addition to the captive. The fifth man had not taken part in the assault that had led to Michaelson's capture, but he had been deeply involved in the operation from the start. He was also by far the most dangerous man in the farmhouse.

As 'Karl' locked the door behind him, Michaelson looked at the tray. The coffee was black, with a couple of sachets of UHT milk and sugar beside the mug, and the packet contained a chicken salad sandwich, maybe bought from a garage or convenience store because he didn't recognise the brand name.

His laptop and mobile had been taken away from him and there were no books or magazines or anything else in the room to distract him. And it was then late afternoon and he was getting hungry, so he sat down. He smelled the coffee and took a cautious sip before ripping open the packet of sandwiches.

Michaelson had finished eating before he really noticed the picture on the opposite wall. It looked like a watercolour because of the simple and narrow black frame, but the colours were particularly vibrant, so maybe it was a small oil painting. For some reason it looked familiar to him and after a minute of staring at it, he walked across for a closer look.

When he got within a few feet of it, he realised two things. First, it was neither a watercolour nor an oil but a colour photograph. And, second, the reason it looked familiar was because it was a picture of his own house. It had been taken from more or less the centre of his front lawn on a sunny afternoon, judging by the shadows cast by the trees lining his driveway, and that meant whoever had taken the picture had climbed the wall or the gate. The other thing he knew was that the picture had been taken within the last month, because the ivy on the left of the house had been cut back by his gardener about four weeks earlier, and in the photograph it was definitely cut.

He turned away and scanned the small room, looking for any other images, but all the walls were bare.

Michaelson was still standing there when the door was unlocked and one of his captors walked in. He recognised him as the driver of the Range Rover, the youngest of the four by about ten years, he guessed, and the man who had also seemed to be in charge. Both his forearms were marked by a plethora of small tattoos that left virtually none of the skin untouched.

'Call me John,' the man said, picking up the tray with one hand. With the other, he reached into the back pocket of his jeans, pulled out an envelope and tossed it onto the chair. 'That's for you,' he added. 'Just something you can think about before we start talking.'

Michaelson stood where he was until 'John' had left, then walked over and picked up the envelope.

It wasn't very heavy, and he guessed it just contained a sheet of paper, but when he peered inside he saw he was mistaken. In it were three colour photographs, and when he looked at them he knew he was right out of options.

Chapter 12

Thursday
Vauxhall Cross, London

Ben Morgan handed a twenty-pound note to the driver of the black cab that had stopped to let him out in the stream of traffic turning off Vauxhall Bridge and onto the Albert Embankment.

'That's close enough,' he said, looking through the drizzle at the double line of unmoving brake lights in front of him. 'Keep the change. I don't need a receipt.'

He climbed out of the cab, flipped open a folding umbrella and walked briskly towards the SIS headquarters building.

It had been an unusually long and irritating journey from Cheltenham. Normally the train took about two hours to reach Paddington but for some unspecified reason it had taken over half an hour more. Morgan had almost been expecting the driver to complain about leaves on the line or the wrong kind of rain, but there had been no announcements during the journey. Traffic in London had been heavier than he had hoped, the ride from Paddington taking much longer than usual, with a major jam near Hyde Park Corner, apparently caused by a minor fender-bender.

Morgan used his C-TAC pass to get through the security checks and was directed to one of the smaller briefing rooms.

The core members of C-TAC sitting around the long oblong conference table that dominated the room looked at him as he entered. He nodded to the formidable grey-haired woman at the head of the table and murmured 'Ma'am' almost under his breath, then pulled out a vacant chair, slumped into it and glanced around.

'Sorry I'm late, people. Blame it on Britain's steam age public transport system. Okay, tell me what the hell's happened to get us all excited. And is there any coffee left?'

Angela Evans, the other female in the room and the youngest person there, nodded and pointed at an insulated pot on the table. Then she slid a mug across in front of Morgan and left him to do the honours himself.

'Thanks,' Morgan said, poured the coffee, put in a dash of milk and took a sip. 'I needed that,' he added, glancing round the table. 'It's been a dry day for me so far.'

In the more than a decade since the events of 7/7, C-TAC had inevitably moved on and to some extent sideways. For about five years it had been virtually mothballed, though not disbanded, due to a couple of not particularly well-known factors.

As well as alarming the British people and especially the residents of London, the 2005 attacks had sent tremors through the international community, tremors that resonated particularly with Russia and the Arab states. The capital was the recipient of substantial financial investments originating in Moscow and the area around the Gulf, and the investors had purchased extensive property in the Greater London area. The last thing they wanted was any kind of prolonged terrorist campaign that might reduce the value of their investments.

The result was a kind of self-policing operation that saw Arab intelligence officers recruiting informers around the country to attempt to spot the earliest signs of any hint of dissent or rebellion. When anything was detected, anonymous messages were sent to the British police along with documentary proof and, if possible, surveillance footage to support the accusation. The perpetrators were then identified and dealt with, usually without any public fuss or acknowledgement.

The Russian technique was very different but equally effective. They let it be known in all the major Arabic enclaves in the United Kingdom that if anyone from those communities were to become involved in terrorism, then their entire extended families would suffer. Every female in the family between the ages of five and fifteen would be sold as a sex slave, probably to somewhere like Algeria, and every male over fifteen would suffer a painful death.

Morgan was aware of two occasions when surveillance by MI5 had identified an extended Arab family that had suddenly been denuded of both adult males and female children, all unexplained disappearances. In neither case did the remaining family members make any report, but the implications were fairly clear.

These unofficial tactics worked and after the events of 2005 there was an extended period when the nation was free from any major terrorist incidents.

In the same period, C-TAC had nothing useful to do and although the unit still technically existed the members rarely met. Ben Morgan had returned to IT postings in various police forces around the country, freelancing after handing in his notice at Hendon, and taking on different jobs and challenges as the mood took him, including a couple of spells working for the Ministry of Defence on classified projects.

Things changed after the first decade of the new century when cybersecurity became a recognised science in its own right because of the increased reliance on computers systems in all aspects of the modern world and the need to combat hackers and malicious individuals intent on identity theft and other types of cybercrime. And, once again, Morgan found himself the right man, this time possibly in the wrong place but certainly at the right time. He had even become a part-time academic, a professor of cybersecurity.

The new discipline had expanded to cope with an increase in state-funded attacks, particularly from Russia, China, North Korea and Iran, which used cyberattacks for economic and, more alarmingly, warfare purposes. The rise of artificial intelligence techniques meant that the United Kingdom started falling behind the threat. The normal rules and laws simply didn't apply in this world without borders, a world almost impossible to police.

It had been decided at the very highest level, and after the US President demanded action from the United Kingdom, that C-TAC was to be resurrected. No longer regarded as a detached group of civilian visitors, perhaps even as interlopers, within the hallowed portals of Vauxhall Cross, the members of the unit now had passes that granted them access to the building without the necessity to sign in and be accompanied everywhere they went. And the unit had changed and grown, expanding to include additional personnel essential for it to function effectively and efficiently.

NARO, the Nuclear Accident Response Organisation, was no longer involved because there had been no signs that any terrorist group had either the means or the intention of using nuclear materials in their improvised devices. The spectre of a dirty bomb, a weapon seeded with radioactive material, was, thankfully, a nightmare for another day. And Morgan's knowledge was sufficient that a separate telecoms expert was no longer needed either.

'So what's happened? Why are we here?' he asked.

Communicating by mobile phone is reasonably secure with the new generation of handsets and communication systems, but there's always a potential risk. So the only information that Morgan had received when he took the call at his home outside Cheltenham at eight that morning was that there'd been an incident and his presence was needed. Soonest.

'Glad you *finally* made it, Professor,' Dame Janet Marcham-Coutts said, her tone somewhat icy.

She'd taken over the direction of C-TAC from Simon Greaves a few years earlier. Her background was allegedly pure civil service, although Morgan thought there was more to it than that, and she was a senior mandarin on first-name terms with the PM. She had gained a reputation for extreme competence and for never taking any crap, at any time, for any reason, from anyone. Of more immediate concern to Morgan was that she had also specified maximum response times for all members of the team and had never entirely approved of Morgan's insistence on living so 'close to the frontier' as she termed Cheltenham and its proximity to the Welsh border. On a good day Morgan could reach Vauxhall Cross within Dame Janet's time limit, but that morning he was about thirty minutes late.

'Circumstances completely beyond my control,' Morgan replied. 'I can apologise, but that's all I can do.'

'Quite. Right, the short answer is that there's been a snatch,' she said. 'It may be something significant or it might be nothing to do with us. That's what we have to decide.'

'A kidnapping?' The doubt in Morgan's voice was obvious. 'I think I've probably had a wasted journey. We leave that sort of thing to the old Bill.'

'There's a bit more to it than that,' Dame Janet said. 'I'll let Cam explain.'

'You're right,' Cameron Riley said. 'Normally the only time we'd know about a kidnapping would be if we read it in the paper or saw it on the news. Even a kidnapping by a bunch of Johnny Foreigners in far-flung bits of the world wouldn't bother us. We'd just tell the FCO to get off their arses and sort it out. But this one is a bit different. Yesterday afternoon a man named Nicholas Michaelson was kidnapped near the Essex border. It was a violent and professional attack, involving a Range Rover, a Ford Transit van and four men, one of whom was armed with a sawn-off shotgun.'

'Was anybody hurt?' Morgan asked.

'Nobody was killed, but it was a close-run thing because of the man with the whippet.'

'They had a dog with them?' Dame Janet queried.

'No, ma'am,' Riley explained, a slight smile on his face. 'A whippet is the slang term for a sawn-off shotgun. We don't know what condition Michaelson is in. But we do know that one of the attackers hit him with a baton, because his bodyguard watched it happen.'

'He didn't intervene?'

'No. Right then, he was too busy picking bits of glass out of his face.'

He recounted exactly what had happened to Michaelson's Mercedes the previous afternoon.

Riley — almost a clone of Dave North, a whisker under six feet tall, stocky build, clean-shaven with brown hair and a face that was craggy rather than handsome, and known during his military career as 'Cam the Man' for reasons lost in time — had crammed more into his fifty-odd years than most people could manage in a couple of lifetimes. He'd joined the Royal Navy after leaving university, developed a strange attraction to the electronic rock band *Depeche Mode*, and then moved sideways into the SBS, the Special Boat Squadron, the Navy's equivalent of the Army's SAS. After officially leaving the SBS, he'd joined HSBC and then moved through the various incarnations of what was now the Financial Service Authority. His military background meant he concentrated on the security aspects of the industry. Cameron was not only the keeper of secrets, but also knew where the bodies were buried, in both a metaphorical and allegedly a literal sense. The position he occupied also meant he was a frequent attendee at Cabinet Office and COBRA meetings.

Morgan had known Cameron Riley for a long time. Soon after C-TAC had been formed, the question of its chain of command had arisen and it had been decided that it should be affiliated to the Special Reconnaissance Regiment. This was probably because at the time of its creation its members were primarily civilians drawn from several different sectors and the only serving military officer was Major Dave North, who had been seconded to the SRR from the SAS. And, besides, C-TAC was in its own way a kind of surveillance and reconnaissance unit.

Morgan and the rest of the group had attended training courses run by the SRR, which actually meant they were being run by the Special Air Service. SAS recruits go through what is known as Selection, a physically tortuous and mentally gruelling process that only the very fittest and most determined soldiers can complete successfully.

The SRR officer who had put Morgan through a cut-down and rather gentler training, on the grounds that he was too old and unfit to even think about doing the full Selection, was Riley in yet another of his various incarnations and wearing a different hat. The purely physical stuff didn't happen, but Morgan was taken through escape and evasion training at Hereford, and he was given crash courses covering firearms, offensive and defensive driving techniques, and covert intelligence gathering.

'The driver and the bodyguard survived,' Riley finished, 'but it'll be a while before they win any beauty contests. Safety glass is supposed to fragment on impact and not cause any physical damage, but when it's hit by a twelve-bore solid slug fired at a range of about ten feet, it's a really good idea not to be sitting right behind it. Their faces were pretty torn up. And they both had minor injuries from the buckshot the guy fired at the car just before the kidnappers drove away.

'It wasn't a random attack. The timing was impeccable. They completely blocked the road using the van, and according to Michaelson's driver and bodyguard the whole thing took less than two minutes, start to finish. The attackers were wearing balaclavas, even the man driving the Transit. They obviously knew exactly who Michaelson was, where he lived and the various routes his driver took. And Michaelson had left work early yesterday to attend an afternoon meeting in Norwich, so they had to have been watching his office to set it in motion.'

'They know a lot more than I do,' Morgan said, 'because I've never heard of him.'

'That's because you spend your life sitting in front of a computer screen and don't get out enough,' Andrew Nuffield said before Riley could answer.

Another recent addition to C-TAC, he'd worked in the City for over twenty years but had been seconded to the group because he really was one of those people who knew almost everyone. Morgan sometimes joked that Nuffield was the only man he knew who genuinely had the private telephone numbers and email addresses of just about every senior current and retired politician in the world in his address book. And if he didn't know somebody, he knew someone who did.

'I'm always telling you that you need to circulate and network and meet people. And you drink far too much coffee. I don't trust any drink you can't read a newspaper through. A decent Calvados is far better for you than that brown muck you keep pouring down your throat.'

'Thank you for that diagnosis. Just let me remind you that if we followed your medical recommendation to its logical conclusion, the only thing we'd ever drink would be water.'

'Nothing wrong with water,' Nuffield replied, his smile half hidden by his beard. 'Or nothing that a dash of alcohol wouldn't fix, anyway.'

'So who, exactly, is Nicholas Michaelson, and why is he important?'

'Michaelson was – and I hope still is, because if these people had wanted to kill him they could have done so on the road – the head of corporate relations for one of the biggest venture capital groups in the City,' Nuffield said. 'He's a bit like me. He knows everybody. Or at least he knows everybody of importance in the financial world because he operates at the highest level with banks the whole time, putting deals together.'

Morgan didn't look impressed.

'So he's a banker, or at least he works with bankers,' he said. 'So what? Why are we interested? Presumably he's been grabbed because he's a wealthy man and these four thugs will be expecting a hefty payout when they finally let him go.'

Dame Janet shook her head.

'That's one way of looking at it,' she said, 'but because of how the kidnapping happened, I have my doubts. We all have doubts.'

'Think it through, Ben,' Angela Evans said. 'All men have pressure points, and in most cases their most important vulnerabilities are their wives and children. Threaten a man's kids and it's almost certain that he'll do whatever you want. Michaelson has two children, a son and a daughter. They go to a local school in Essex and his wife is a stay-at-home mum and lady who lunches. If they were actually after a ransom, they could have grabbed his wife or his children and just left a note on his front door saying pay us five million pounds or we'll start mailing your wife and kids back to you in small individual cardboard boxes. That would have been easy, obvious, and they would probably have got away with it.

'But they didn't do that. Instead, they prepared and then executed a complicated and time-critical kidnapping using a Transit van that they stole about a week earlier from a company in Suffolk and presumably had to store somewhere away from ANPR and traffic cameras until they were ready to use it. They parked the van on a farm track, the driver waiting for confirmation by two-way radio or mobile phone that Michaelson's car had passed the other vehicle involved in the ambush, and at precisely the right moment the man in the Transit drove it out to completely block the road.

'At almost the same moment, the three men in the Range Rover had to be right behind the Mercedes to drive it off the road and disable it. Snatching Michaelson's wife or children would have taken minimal planning, ten minutes, two men and a closed van. But what these guys did involve stealing a van and fitting an illegal bull bar on a probably stolen Range Rover. We can't be certain about the four-by-four because it was running on false plates, assuming the two people who claimed to have made a note of its number are right. According to the DVLA the number they gave belongs to a scrapped Ford Orion. We're talking about at least four men and roughly a month of preparation work.

'They'd have had to check the route his car took driving him home, decided on a suitable location for the attack and found the vehicles they would need. And at the site they picked there were plenty of things that could have gone wrong. It's fairly busy so there could have been heavy traffic that would have prevented them blocking the road, or the Mercedes could have taken a different route or Michaelson's driver might have been able to drive around the van before it completely blocked the road, or something else could have cocked it up. What happened just doesn't make sense as a kidnapping for ransom. It's far too difficult and uncertain.'

'So if we're ruling out ransom, he must have been kidnapped for a different reason, most likely because of something he knows,' Morgan said.

'Or because of *someone* he knows,' Nuffield suggested.

'Or that, yes,' Angela agreed.

'That does make sense,' Morgan said, 'but it still seems a bit unlikely. Granted, he obviously knows most of the people in the banking industry but their identities are not exactly a secret. If you grab a copy of the annual report of every big bank in London you'll find the names of all the directors and senior staff listed. So what was the point?'

'You're right about that,' Nuffield said, 'and if all you want is a list of names and positions, that's fine. Once you'd collected half a ton of annual reports and spent a week or so extracting the data, that's what you'd have. The real point is what exactly you mean by the word "know". Someone like Nicholas Michaelson actually *knows* the senior men in the banking business, and on more than a casual everyday basis. He doesn't just know their names. He probably knows where they live, the names of their immediate family members and, far more importantly, he might even know if they have any weaknesses. If they drink, if they gamble or have a penchant for expensive call girls. The kind of information that might make negotiating a financial package for a takeover a little bit easier.'

'You really think he'd know that much about their private lives?' Morgan sounded doubtful.

'He wouldn't know chapter and verse, obviously,' Nuffield said, 'but the City really is an old boys' club and almost everyone there knows something about somebody else. When they get in their cups they start to talk and often they're a lot less discreet than they should be. You'll hear a man with a wife at home talking about some girl he's wined and dined and probably bedded. Or some young City boy will mention his new source for cocaine or heroin. Nothing concrete, necessarily, but certainly enough for someone like Michaelson who's been in that environment for over a decade to have acquired plenty of scurrilous information that he can use to his advantage. I've met him, several times, and he's a very good listener with an extremely retentive memory. All it would take during the negotiations would be for Michaelson to drop something into the conversation like "Still enjoying your Thursday evening meetings, Clive?" to show that he knows what's going on.'

'A few years ago,' Dame Janet said, 'a friend of mine wrote a book called *Snakes in Suits* which concluded that most successful bankers are either sociopaths or psychopaths, and I do know that in interviews for the highest positions in the banking industry psychopathic tendencies are seen as a positive advantage, because people of that type are prepared to take risks and worry about the consequences later. In fact, most of them don't ever worry about the consequences because it's not in their nature to do so. And when it comes to the seamier side of life, they usually just go ahead and do whatever they want, drugs or sex or anything else, because they really don't think that the law should apply to them. They know they're special – and they're right, just not in the way that most of them think they are. I know these are broad-brush statements and generalisations, but they're basically accurate.'

'The slightly less polite way of putting it,' Cameron Riley said, 'is that most senior bankers have about the same moral compass as a shithouse rat.'

Dame Janet looked at Riley and smiled.

'Anyway,' she finished, 'assuming that Michaelson fits into the same mould, which he probably does because of the position he's achieved, I've got no doubt that he'd be prepared to use a little professional level blackmail to secure a higher level of funding from a particular bank, or maybe a slightly more favourable interest rate. And I think it's that kind of information that the people who grabbed him might be after.'

Something didn't make sense to Morgan.

'You might well be right,' he said, 'but whatever their motives, it's still a kidnapping, and so nothing to do with us. Our job is fighting terrorism.'

'You worked in banking, Ben,' Dame Janet replied, 'though I know that was a long time ago, but I'm slightly surprised you don't see the connection. There's something here that you're missing.'

Chapter 13

Thursday
City of London

'I don't see people who wander in off the street,' James McEwan said, sounding irritated. Comfortably built and in his late forties, his square well-scrubbed face was reddish and plump, a probable testament to too many expense-account lunches, an impression accentuated by his large black moustache which acted as a horizontal divider between his very black and neatly combed hair and his expanding triple chin.

'I know, and I've already told him that.' Jeremy Somerville, essentially McEwan's right-hand man in the merchant bank located just off Poultry in the City of London, looked and sounded equally irritated. 'But he keeps on stressing that he has to see you about a strictly personal and private matter, and he won't tell me anything other than that.'

'What's his name again?'

Somerville glanced down at the business card in his hand, a card that displayed frustratingly little information about the man who had handed it over. It contained only his name, a logo, a position and a telephone number.

'John Harrison,' Somerville replied, 'and according to this he's a director of a company called PSP4. I've never heard of it.'

'Nor have I,' McEwan said. 'Use suitably polite language but tell him to fuck off. And you can explain to him that if he wants to see me or anyone else in the bank he should make an appointment in the usual way.'

Somerville pulled McEwan's office door closed on his way out, but returned less than two minutes later, this time holding a sealed white envelope in his hand.

'As soon as I told him you wouldn't see him, he gave me this and said he would wait for another three minutes, and after that he would leave.'

'Bloody hell,' McEwan muttered. He took the envelope that Somerville proffered and picked up a stainless-steel letter opener. He slid the point under the flap of the envelope and cut it open. Inside were three colour photographs. McEwan looked at the first one and the colour seemed to drain from his face.

He looked up at Somerville and nodded.

'I will see him. Bring him in right now.'

'But I thought—'

'Which part of that last sentence didn't you understand? Bring him in now.'

Somerville left the office and almost immediately stepped back into view, leading another man.

'This is Mr Harrison,' he said. He pushed the door to but didn't completely close it.

McEwan didn't get up from his seat or offer the man his hand. Instead, he leaned back in his chair and regarded him with obvious distaste.

Harrison looked every inch the successful businessman, from his short and neatly combed light brown hair and his clearly expensive suit to his highly polished black shoes, and he seemed completely unperturbed by the coolness of his reception.

'I'm pleased to meet you,' Harrison said.

'The feeling isn't mutual,' McEwan snapped.

'It rarely is in my business, but like most long-term relationships it's quite common to get off to a somewhat frosty start.'

McEwan jabbed his finger angrily at the three pictures lying face-down on his desk.

'You call this a frosty start? And this is never going to be a long-term relationship.'

Harrison's good humour seemed unaffected, and he smiled again.

'I think you'll find our relationship will last for longer than you expect, unless of course you decide that you have no wish to avail yourself of our services. The pictures are quite good, aren't they?

Especially, I think, the one showing you snorting a line of the best quality snow through what looks to me like a fifty-pound note. That does show a bit of style. Most junkies have to make do with a fiver, if they're lucky. I appreciate that you and your friends are in something of a different league to the jakeys on the streets, but basically you're all doing the same thing.'

McEwan turned over the three photographs and stared down at them. His face on the middle picture was clear and completely unmistakeable, as was what he was doing. He remembered the occasion well – a private party a couple of weeks earlier – and Harrison was certainly correct about the quality of the blow: he had rarely experienced such immediate euphoria after snorting cocaine.

But what McEwan didn't know was how the hell this man Harrison had obtained the picture. In fact, he didn't even know how the picture had been taken, because one of the rules that they always applied at their private get-togethers was that all mobile phones were both switched off and left outside the room where the party was being held. Somehow, obviously, either somebody had smuggled a tiny camera into the room or it had been professionally bugged. As far as he could see, those were the only two possibilities.

Harrison pointed at the other two pictures that flanked the one showing the drug-taking.

'These perhaps aren't quite as pin-sharp,' he continued, 'just because of the constraints in that lady's bedroom, but it's certainly clear enough to identify both you and her, and we can see exactly what you're doing. Did you know, by the way, that until November 1994 that particular act was illegal between a man and a woman? Interestingly, if your partner had been an adult male over the age of consent it would have been legal to do that as long ago as 1967. One of the odd quirks of English law. Quite funny, really.'

'I don't find any of this amusing,' McEwan said. 'I suppose you want money. You're just a filthy little blackmailer, aren't you?'

'Oddly enough, the answer to that is both yes and no. Yes, I do want money, but I have no intention of blackmailing you. Instead, I'm here to offer you a service.'

That wasn't the answer that McEwan had been expecting and despite himself he was intrigued.

'What service?' he asked.

Harrison leaned across the desk and passed McEwan another business card.

'As that says, I'm a director of a company called PSP4. The initials stand for Professional Security Providers 4, and what we specialise in is offering security services to high net worth individuals, people like yourself, in fact. We have no interest in your – what should we call them? – hobbies, perhaps? We appreciate that all people have needs that might not always be satisfied by conventional domestic bliss or polite society, and we fully understand why some people may feel the need to engage in certain types of recreational activities. Really, we're on your side.'

McEwan didn't believe that for a moment, but he gestured for Harrison to explain.

'My company will ensure that you can continue to pursue whatever hobbies you're interested in, and we will maintain a watching brief over the locations you use. If we find any hint that the police are taking an interest in what you're doing, then we'll tell you so that you can take whatever steps are necessary to avoid arrest or prosecution. What we're offering is almost a public service.'

'And I presume there's a charge for this?'

Harrison smiled encouragingly.

'Nothing truly worthwhile is ever free,' he replied. 'We offer a single grade of service, and the cost to you will be a comparatively modest ten thousand pounds per month, which you can charge to one of your company accounts as a legitimate expense because PSP4 is a private security company providing an important service to our client base. We only accept payment by credit transfer and we will send to your personal email account all the details you need to make the transfers, the IBAN number and so on. The first payment is due within seven days of today's date, and then on the same date every succeeding month.'

Harrison pointed at the card he had placed in front of McEwan.

'If you encounter any difficulties with your hobbies, call that number and we'll render whatever assistance we can. Please understand that there's no period of grace with the monthly payments. If the money is not in our account within twenty-four hours of the due date, then we will sever our connection with you immediately and permanently. We will then have no further use for the images and videos and other information that we've obtained because you will have ceased to be a client, so we will send it anonymously to a police station of our choice. We will also send a DVD just like this one—' Harrison leaned forward slightly and placed on McEwan's desk a jewel case containing a disk with the printed label JAMES McEWAN '—containing edited highlights, to your wife, to your superior if you have one, and to all the senior executives of this bank or whichever bank you happen to be working for when payments cease. Is that clearly understood?'

McEwan nodded, reluctantly. He had absolutely no option and he knew it. And Harrison was quite right: a payment of ten thousand per month was not unrealistic. McEwan knew personally of three or four people who worked in the City who paid far more than that every month for security services, and it wouldn't even be his money he was spending. As the CEO he could simply tell the finance people that he was concerned for his personal safety and had engaged the services of this PSP4 company and instruct them to pay the monthly charge forthwith. Even if he paid it himself, it would barely dent his annual seven-figure salary and anticipated bonus payments.

The alternative did not even bear thinking about. If knowledge of some of the things he did in his spare time ever reached the ears of his wife, he could virtually guarantee that the divorce papers would be submitted within a matter of days, and if the main board of the bank received the same information, he would be out of a job. And not just temporarily. He'd never be employed again in the City in any meaningful post. And banking was all he knew.

He would be permanently ruined, personally, professionally and financially. He had no choice at all.

Chapter 14

Thursday
Fulham and Brent Park, London

In the apartment building at Parsons Green, tenants and visitors came and went, the cameras faithfully recording all movement in the halls.

The lone watcher outside George Kenton's Chelsea home had recorded him leaving four times over the previous seven days. On the first occasion he was accompanied by his wife and they hailed a cab outside the front door. The obvious deduction was that they were going out for dinner or some other evening entertainment. The second time Kenton was wearing a tuxedo and black tie and was collected by a Jaguar saloon as soon as he stepped onto the pavement, so presumably he was attending a function. But the other two occasions saw him wearing his usual basic disguise and walking some distance away before looking for a cab.

Each time he appeared, the watcher on duty recorded the date and time, what he was wearing, and anything else that appeared relevant, though in fact he was only interested in Kenton's appointments down in Parsons Green.

On Thursday, the day after Kenton's last visit to the apartment building, the two 'electrical contractors' parked their van on an adjacent street and gained entry. They knew the cameras would have done their job, but they left them in situ and simply changed the SD cards, carefully placing each card they removed in an envelope already marked with the location of the relevant camera. This took a little longer than installing the cameras in the first place, but it was still less than twenty minutes later that the two men walked out of the building. They would make another visit in a few days to finally remove the cameras.

And at the same time they would have another operation to perform there.

–

In some ways the art of camouflage can be described as showing people what they expect to see, but not what is actually there.

The group – Professional Security Providers 4, or PSP4 – had needed a base, somewhere they could come and go without attracting attention, and the obvious choice was a commercial property where they would appear to be the employees of a small company.

Mr King had taken out a one-year lease on a somewhat run-down but still functional combined office and warehouse premises on an industrial estate near Brent Park. It wasn't very big, because it didn't need to be, but the warehouse was spacious enough to accommodate half a dozen cars behind the roller shutter door, as well as concealing their various weapons and other specialised equipment they needed to ply their trade. The office beside it had two rooms, one of which they'd set up as a single bedroom, plus a combined shower and lavatory. It was pretty much ideal for their purposes.

The only unusual aspect of the operation, from the point of view of an outsider, was that there was someone in the building at all times, day and night. Nobody had ever asked why, but if the question were to be posed the men had been told to say that it was a requirement of their business insurance policy because of the value of some of the equipment there. Which was, in one way, absolutely true, though anyone inspecting the interior of the building would be hard pressed to find anything there of significant value.

They had had expensive business cards printed, which looked good but were notably short on detail, like where the company was based or the real names of any of the people involved in it. Companies House, predictably enough, had never heard of Professional Security Providers 4. Funds received by the company were paid into the British branch of a foreign bank and then funnelled out to a compliant bank in the Cayman Islands as soon as the payment had cleared. But this British Overseas Territory in the Caribbean was not the final destination of any of the money.

When the two-man team returned to the warehouse from Parsons Green, they used a remote control to lift the roller shutter door and then drove the white van into the large open space behind it.

Mr King, as usual, was not in the building. In fact, he hadn't been there for a couple of days, being deeply involved in a separate facet of the operation they were running. He'd driven away from London three days earlier in a Jaguar saloon car. The vehicle was legal in all respects, although the identity of the owner of the car and the type of insurance policy that had been taken out on it were a trifle unusual. Not illegal, but definitely unusual.

The two men checked in with the guard in the building, then took the envelopes containing the SD cards into the office. On one side was a comparatively wide wooden desk on which sat a Dell desktop computer and large monitor. Unusually, the machine's internal hard drive contained no data that would be of the slightest use to an examiner looking for incriminating evidence. Particularly to the kind of person who might be, say, a police forensic IT specialist. That was because everything of value was stored on a six-terabyte external hard drive that was securely hidden in the property and was only linked to the system unit when it was needed to transfer something sensitive. Something like, for example, the video sequences gathered from a cluster of hidden surveillance cameras.

USB peripheries need to be located fairly close to the host computer, meaning less than 3 metres for a USB 3.0 device unless the cable includes an active repeater. But when the computer system had been installed in the building, Mr King had been adamant that no cables were to be used. Instead, he had purchased the highest-capacity wireless hard drive on the market. That in turn had permitted him to secure the hard drive in a location where he doubted it would be found even in a quite thorough search of the building.

'We'll do the ground floor first,' said Vince, the driver of the van, switching on the computer as he spoke.

His companion, Mike, nodded agreement and selected the SD card that they'd taken from one of the two cameras on the ground floor of the target building.

Analysing video footage, whether from security cameras installed by a householder or by police officers or other specialists scanning CCTV footage looking for a person or vehicle or event, is excruciatingly and mind-numbingly boring.

But Mike and Vince had two important and very significant advantages over people carrying out that kind of surveillance. First, they knew exactly who they were looking for – George Kenton – and they also knew what he looked like. And second, thanks to their ongoing surveillance of Kenton's building, they knew to within about ten or fifteen minutes when he was likely to appear.

Vince slid the SD card into the slot on the system unit and opened File Explorer. He navigated to the card and waited while Mike checked a handwritten list of dates and times.

'Okay, he left home yesterday evening at eight seventeen. That means he couldn't have reached the target building any earlier than eight thirty, so start looking then.'

Vince nodded and started the search.

All the cameras were motion-sensitive, so until a moving object appeared within each camera's field of view no recordings were made. That, too, cut down enormously on the total amount of video. The start and stop times of each sequence of filming were recorded on the SD card, so it was just a matter of picking the right one.

'We have movement at 20:31,' he said after a few moments, and both men looked at the computer screen as the video began to play.

One of the apartment doors on the ground floor opened. A middle-aged woman appeared in the doorway clutching a set of keys in one hand and a dog lead in the other. At the far end of the lead a small terrier-like animal tugged and lunged as she paused to lock the door. Its panting and squeaking were clearly audible on the recording. Obviously the dog was desperate to get outside. Both woman and dog moved out of shot and a few moments later the footage ended.

'I hope she remembered her poop bags,' Mike said. 'I bloody hate people who leave dog crap on pavements.'

The next timed recording began at 20:43, and they saw no movement in the first few seconds. But then a figure wearing an overcoat and hat came into view, having obviously entered the hall from outside the building.

'I didn't hear the sound of a buzzer,' Vince said, 'so Kenton must have a key to the building. If that is him, I mean. Or maybe the recording started after he'd opened the door.'

'That guy's wearing the same outfit Kenton usually does, but if we swap to the camera at the other end of the hall we'll see his face.'

They changed SD cards and viewed the same scene from the opposite end of the hallway. This time the man was facing the camera as he walked down the hall and started to climb the staircase.

'That's confirmation,' Vince said. 'It's definitely Kenton. Give me the card from one of the first-floor cameras.'

The two men watched as a few seconds later the figure wearing the overcoat appeared at the top of the stairs and walked to the door at the far end of the landing. What was slightly unexpected was that he knocked on the door and waited perhaps two seconds. Then it opened, though nobody appeared in the doorway, and he stepped inside the flat, disappearing from view as the door closed behind him.

'I would have expected him to have a key,' Vince said, leaning back in his chair. 'Or maybe he has, but the routine is that he always knocks to give whoever's inside time to get ready. I mean, to put out a cigarette or empty their drink down the sink before he walks in, that kind of thing, just the final touches before they open the door to him. I wonder who's in the apartment.'

Mike nodded.

'Now we know the flat number, we'll find out soon enough,' he replied. 'It's a decent building and the apartments are quite big, so my money's on an expensive mistress. I'll get the names of the tenants and then we can go back and finish this.'

Chapter 15

Thursday

Vauxhall Cross, London

'What have I missed?' Ben Morgan asked.

'It's not definite,' Cameron Riley replied, 'but it's possible that we're not looking at a local problem. Michaelson could have been snatched by a London blackmail gang who'd found out who he was and what he was likely to know and saw him as a shortcut to help them identify people in the City with something to hide. If that is the case, then it's nothing to do with C-TAC, and the police can sort it out.

'A kidnapping for ransom would net a single big payout but it would be a high-risk strategy. If the gang started blackmailing a bunch of bankers, on the other hand, they could create an income stream that would run for years. The guys at the top of the major banks are pulling in six-figure salaries as a minimum along with massive annual bonuses. Persuading a man like that to fork over five or ten grand a month to avoid the details of, say, his underage boyfriend being given to the police wouldn't be a difficult sell. If they could find a dozen victims in total and charge them ten each, they could be hauling in over a hundred grand every month, over a million a year, and it would be pretty much risk-free because the only person who could tell the police would be the banker himself, and he obviously couldn't, just for self-preservation.'

'I think I'm in the wrong job,' Morgan said slowly. 'Okay, that does make sense. So where are we on the kidnapping? Or rather, how far have the police got with it?'

'No arrest is imminent,' Nuffield said. 'I had a word with the local chief constable this morning and he said that their examination of the car had turned up nothing useful, which isn't surprising as the witnesses – Michaelson's driver and bodyguard – said both the men who attacked the car and the driver of the Transit had been wearing gloves. Everything they arrived with they took away with them, apart from the van. They've checked the business premises in Suffolk where the Transit was stolen but the only CCTV camera covering the parking area was fixed and didn't show the part of it where the van had been left. And they've got nowhere so far with trying to trace the Range Rover. There's nothing on the CCTV or ANPR cameras in the area that looks relevant.'

'But none of this is really our concern,' Angela Evans said. 'Eventually the kidnappers will release Michaelson or they'll kill him and dump his body and maybe the police will be able to backtrack from that point and find out what happened to him. But all of that is down to local law enforcement. What we need to look at are the wider implications, and that's the possibility that worries us.'

'You mean this could be the start of a trend?' Morgan suggested.

Angela nodded, but it was Dame Janet who answered.

'Not only are we possibly seeing the beginnings of a campaign,' she said, 'but my concern is that these kidnappers aren't blackmailers in the usual sense of the word. Suppose they're not just blackmailing senior bankers for money, but also trying to get them to fix interest rates or the FOREX market? Or maybe persuade some bankers to facilitate money laundering or account manipulation? This isn't my field, but I would have thought something like that could net them a far bigger return than some grubby little blackmail scheme. And there's a far bigger concern too.

'Just suppose their ultimate aim is to crash the markets. Because of Brexit, the UK economy is fragile and it probably wouldn't take much to start a downturn. Remember that in October 1987 well over a quarter of the value of the British stock market was wiped out in less than two weeks in the Black Monday crash, and economists still don't really know what caused it, though programmed trading was certainly a contributor. That was a worldwide crash that started in Hong Kong and hit every other market within hours. If these people have a stable of influential bankers under their control, they could crash one or more of the City's markets and that could be just the excuse some people want to kick everything east to the Euronext group and Frankfurt. London might never recover.

'This isn't some hacker stealing customer account or credit card details and flogging them on the Dark Web. This is economic warfare and that's a whole lot more dangerous. The PM and Chancellor know anything that produces economic instability could seriously damage the United Kingdom, though personally I suspect they're far more worried about being re-elected. So if we find that these people just want to make a quick killing using insider trading information, then we can walk away and leave it to the police. But until we can do that, we're involved.'

'Got it,' Morgan said.

There was silence in the conference room as the assembled members of C-TAC considered what had happened and what they should be doing about it.

'What we can't do,' Morgan said eventually, 'is provide guards for the senior executives of every leading bank in the City. Quite apart from anything else, what happened to Michaelson, who had a chauffeur and a bodyguard in the car, proves that if the bad guys want to get you, they will. I suppose we could produce some kind of a security awareness round robin that Millbank could send out to all the major financial institutions.'

'But if Angela and our esteemed leader are right,' Cameron Riley pointed out, 'the people who orchestrated Michaelson's kidnapping could get all the information they need from him, so there may not be another direct attack on somebody working in the City. If so, then what we should be doing is monitoring the markets and the exchanges looking for spikes or troughs that aren't predictable. Or are less predictable than the spikes or troughs that we normally get. I can set that up through the systems in my virtual office at the Old Lady.'

Morgan nodded.

'That would be helpful, Cam, but with the volume of trading in the City I don't think it would be easy to spot any kind of manipulation. It's worth doing, though. What other options do we have?'

Nobody responded, but Dame Janet looked down the table at Morgan somewhat expectantly.

'You've got an idea, Ben,' she said. 'I can tell from that slightly smug look on your face.'

Morgan shrugged, then nodded.

'As I see it, there are three components in the present situation. The first was the actual kidnapping of Nicholas Michaelson and we can do nothing about that. The second is the fact that Michaelson is being held somewhere by this gang while they pump him for information. I know that's an assumption, but it does seem to make sense. And the third factor, again assuming that our analysis is correct, will be the blackmailing of senior banking officials to force them to perform various illegal actions. Is that a fair summary?'

The others all nodded, and Nuffield gestured for Morgan to carry on.

'We'll have to rely on Cam's monitoring through the Bank of England to detect any signs of manipulation, but that does leave the matter of Michaelson's imprisonment, and there is something we can do about that. We have systems and contacts that the police don't. They'll be relying on physical surveillance of East Anglia and hoping that a camera somewhere captured an image of the Range Rover after it left the scene of the attack. And I suppose they'll be questioning people who use that road in case any of them spotted members of the gang surveying it in the days before the attack was carried out. Given the observational skills, memory for numbers and descriptive abilities of the average member of the British public, in a hurry and heading to or from work along a fairly busy road, I don't think they're going to get very far with that.'

'Agreed,' Cam said, 'so what can we do that's different?'

'Off the top of my head,' Morgan said, 'there are at least two things we can do just because of who we are. First, it's at least possible that the four men involved in the kidnap weren't acting alone but were part of a larger gang. In that case, they may not all be in the same place and might be communicating by phone, so we can use Echelon.'

Cameron Riley laughed shortly.

'Echelon? Isn't that using a very large sledgehammer to crack an extremely small nut?'

Morgan nodded.

'It is, but clearly both SIS and MI5 are worried about this incident, not because of Michaelson himself but because of what he knows, which is why we've been summoned here. They're expecting us to do something about it, and using Echelon is one of our options. We can program the Echelon dictionary with maybe forty or fifty words, including the obvious like Michaelson, kidnap or kidnapping, blackmail and so on, and just see if the servers come up with anything. Based on how professionally they carried out the attack on the car, I think if they do communicate by phone they'll use code words and won't ever speak the name Michaelson. Instead they'll call him Fred or something. And it's quite possible they won't make any phone calls about him. But if they do and mention his name in clear and they're stupid enough to use a mobile phone, then obviously we can triangulate it and send in the heavies. I don't think this will work but I think we would be derelict not to put it in place.'

'Agreed,' Angela said. 'It's simple enough to do and we can implement it virtually immediately. If you want, I can draft a suggested list of words for the dictionary and we can finalise it while we're here. Strike while the iron's hot and all that. So what's the other option?'

Morgan smiled slightly before he replied.

'It's a bit sneaky. In fact, it's very sneaky and there's no guarantee that it'll actually work. I'll need to make a phone call and then have a meeting really soon, like today, to put it in place. Oh, and it's also highly illegal.'

'Sounds like it ticks all the usual boxes, then,' Dame Janet said. 'Well, don't keep it to yourself. Let's hear what it is.'

Morgan told them.

'That's not just sneaky and illegal,' Angela said when he'd finished, 'it's also problematic for a whole bunch of reasons. But it might just work. If the company does play ball, have you any clue how much data you'll have to analyse?'

'Terabytes at least, possibly petabytes,' Morgan replied.

'Shit,' Cameron Riley murmured. 'I guess you won't be running the analysis software on the kind of computer you can pick up in PC World. Where will you do it? Here in Legoland?'

'GCHQ out at Cheltenham, probably. I do have a sort of relationship with a couple of the wheels there, and if a formal request comes from here at Vauxhall Cross there shouldn't be any problems. The biggest difficulty will be getting the company to agree, so I'll need to go there and make my case in person. Can I leave the rest of you to sort out the stuff for the Echelon dictionary and get that implemented and running?'

'No problem,' Dame Janet said. 'Take Cam with you. And good luck out there.'

Chapter 16

Thursday
Undisclosed location

He felt he'd hardly slept at all. After the man who called himself John had left the room with the tray, Michaelson had sat for several minutes just staring at the three photographs he had been given, feeling the familiar world around him begin to collapse.

After about twenty minutes he had taken off his clothes, walked into the tiny bathroom, showered and cleaned his teeth, because that was what he did every night. Then he'd put on his underpants because he had no pyjamas and didn't like the idea of sleeping completely naked, turned off the light and climbed into the single bed.

And then he'd lain flat on his back staring up at the ceiling, dimly visible in the darkness. Sleep had finally come, but not for what seemed like hours.

There were no curtains on the single window, which he thought faced east, and the early morning light and a somewhat deafening dawn chorus woke him just after six. Again, he followed his normal routine, taking a shower, shaving and cleaning his teeth before getting dressed in the only clothes that he had.

The driver – John – unlocked the door and walked into the room just after nine, carrying a tray on which was a mug of instant coffee and a couple of what were euphemistically referred to as breakfast bars, presumably on the grounds that they were about as unlike an actual breakfast as it was possible to get.

Michaelson was sitting in the armchair when John arrived, again looking at the three photographs.

Each picture displayed a familiar image: his wife, his son and his daughter. They weren't portraits but showed each member of his family outside the house in Essex and were in almost every way completely innocuous. They had obviously been taken at different times and from some distance away and weren't even very good pictures, but that wasn't the point. What had stopped Michaelson in his tracks was the reticule on each one.

Like a faint overlay, each image included a sharp and clear set of cross-hairs in a circle, the centre positioned directly on the upper torso of each of the subjects. In fact, it wasn't just a simple set of cross-hairs. The reticule included other marks and faint numbers that Michaelson didn't understand, never having handled any kind of gun in his life. But he was certain he was looking at photographs taken through the telescopic sight of a sniper rifle.

'You've seen the pictures,' John said – a statement rather than a question – as he set down the tray. 'If you're interested, it's a Leupold scope and the rifle's a Savage 110 in .308 Winchester. All we need to do is get within about half a mile of the target, get a clear shot and it's Goodnight, Vienna.'

John was gilding the lily slightly. The US Army works on the basis that the .308 round has an effective range of 800 metres, while the US Marine Corps extends that to 915 metres, so a target half a mile away would be at the extreme limit of the rifle's – and the shooter's – capability.

'Of course, we'd be able to get a lot closer than that.' John smiled at Michaelson but without any humour in his eyes, the tone of his voice conversational. 'I reckon we'd probably be able to shoot from less than a hundred yards. Wouldn't even need the optical sight at that range. And we'd probably go for a gut shot for each of them. Takes a long time to die from that, and it hurts like hell.'

Michaelson thought he was going to vomit.

'Please,' he said, swallowing hard, 'please don't hurt my family. I'll do whatever you want.'

'I know you will,' John said. 'That's the point, obviously. We just thought you ought to know what would happen if you didn't.'

'So what *do* you people want?' Michaelson asked.

'Eat your breakfast. I'll be back in twenty minutes and then I'll show you.'

John returned half an hour later and led Michaelson out of the bedroom and into a sitting room. On one side of the room was a small table with a laptop, and a chair on either side.

'Sit there,' John instructed, 'and I'll lay out the ground rules. That's your laptop in front of you. We used a utility program to get around your password, and we've copied the contents of your hard drive onto an external disk. We have a Wi-Fi network here but you're not getting the password for that. If there's something you need from the Web, we'll get it for you using a different laptop. You've probably got a lot of data stored in the Cloud, so we'll need your log-in credentials to download it. And we'll need the PIN for your mobile so we can access the data on that.'

Michaelson suddenly thought he had an inkling of who these men were and why they'd kidnapped him. Venture capitalists sometimes swam in murky waters, with hostile takeovers and the like, and occasionally faced attempted financial sabotage from companies that had no wish to be bought primarily so their assets could be stripped and sold for the benefit of the new owners. Perhaps these people had been hired by such a company to combat a takeover, though driving his car off the road, kidnapping him and threatening to kill his wife and children seemed an extreme overreaction. The counter-argument was that his company wasn't involved in any contentious actions at that moment.

But if that deduction was correct, then he guessed – or rather hoped – there was something he could do about it, because ultimately it all came down to one thing: money.

Whatever these men had been paid for kidnapping him, Michaelson was certain he could outbid whoever they were working for, because he was sure they were employees rather than principals. If they were working for somebody else, that meant they were doing it for money. Offer them more, and he could shift their allegiance. It was a basic premise when doing deals in the City that the highest bidder almost always won.

Michaelson stopped beside the chair and looked at John.

'Look,' he said, 'whatever you're being paid for this, I'll double it.'

John just looked at him.

'You have no clue what's going on,' he said, 'so I'll make this as simple as I can. Listen, and inwardly digest. You can't buy your way out of this because you don't have anything like enough money. Now sit down and shut up.'

Michaelson sat.

'Right,' John said, 'we have your data, so that's the skeleton of what we want. Now you're going to put flesh on the bones.'

'I have no idea what you're talking about.'

'Don't worry. I'll make everything very clear to you.'

Chapter 17

Thursday
Beijing, People's Republic of China (PRC)

Plausible deniability is only necessary in a country that enjoys a free press, where reporters can and do ask awkward questions and expect sensible answers. Then the ability of senior government officers and executives to truthfully deny their involvement in any particular matter is essential. In the totalitarian regime operated in the PRC, the words 'free' and 'press' are very rarely found in the same sentence, with monitoring and censorship of all kinds of media, including the Internet, the norm. In 2018, the Press Freedom Index ranked China at number 176 out of 180 countries in terms of media repression and control.

But despite this freedom from unwanted oversight, the team directing what they had named the *Lúndūn yùnyíng* or 'London Operation' comprised only four men, two of whom had travelled to Kowloon to recruit the criminal Wang, and they always met in a private house in the Guanzhuang Residential District in the eastern outskirts of Beijing, never in a government building. Their meetings were invariably short and factual, essentially just weekly reports of the progress being made.

Communication with Wang – 'Mr King' in the UK – was done only by mobile phone, both the Chinese handset and the one in Britain using pre-paid and unregistered SIM cards. Hoeng, the more senior of the two men who'd recruited Wang, was principally responsible for communicating with him, and for providing the information the other members of the group needed. On this occasion, his report was typically brief and upbeat.

'Recruitment—' the other three men smiled slightly, as they always did, at his use of this word '—is proceeding satisfactorily, and

Wang is following another avenue to speed up the identification of suitable subjects. He has kidnapped an influential businessman from the City of London who will be able to supply not only the names of targets but also their probable weaknesses. This information will greatly assist Wang in his task.'

The man sitting on the opposite side of the table opened his mouth as if to speak, but Hoeng had a very good idea of the question he was about to ask.

'Needless to say,' he went on, 'once Wang has obtained what he needs from this businessman, he will be disposed of permanently.'

The other man closed his mouth and nodded.

'So we are on schedule,' Hoeng concluded, 'and we will be able to initiate the third phase of the operation at a time and in a manner of our choosing. And once that has been concluded, the City of London will be nothing more than an archaic memory.'

Chapter 18

Thursday

London

'You do know what you're asking, Ben?' Adam Cross said. 'And that it's illegal under British and European Union law? And that it goes against everything this company stands for? And that if we did it, and that information was ever made public, we would at the very least end up facing massive lawsuits?'

'Yes, obviously, Adam. If I didn't know what I was asking I would hardly be sitting here talking to you.'

In the context of their conversation, 'here' was a comfortable and spacious office on the top floor of a modern steel and glass building that was the United Kingdom headquarters of a global technology giant and Adam Cross was the man who ran it.

Like many really successful people in the IT industry, he looked too young to be in charge, an effect enhanced by the casual clothes – designer jeans and an open-necked white shirt – that he was wearing. He looked about thirty, though Morgan knew he was nudging forty, with blond hair worn long at the back of his head and the kind of chiselled looks and blue eyes that advertisers tended to associate with surfers.

'And you're obviously expecting me to say yes,' Cross added.

'I don't think "expecting" is exactly the right word,' Ben Morgan said. 'I think "hoping" is closer to the mark. If you say no, which you have a perfect right to do and which is almost certainly the correct answer from your perspective, then Cam and I will get up, thank you for the coffee and leave the building. And your decision will have no effect whatsoever upon our relationship.'

'But?'

Morgan looked at him and smiled.

'You're right, of course. There should have been a "but" tagged onto the end of that sentence. But we really do need your help. If we can use your resources then the only people who will ever know about your involvement will be Cameron, me, the other members of my team who know that I'm approaching you, and no more than four people at GCHQ in Cheltenham, who'll manage the supercomputer that'll be used to run the analysis. And you already know, but I'll tell you again anyway, that all of those people are bound by the Official Secrets Act so none of them can ever say a word about it. And because in this matter I'm speaking for the British government through the Secret Intelligence Service, I can guarantee that even if word did leak out, there would be no possibility of a prosecution. We could give you a signed letter of immunity, but it's better for everyone if no evidence exists.'

Adam Cross still didn't look convinced.

'You know me, Adam,' Cameron Riley said. 'You know my position in the City and you know I wouldn't be here unless this really mattered.'

Cross nodded.

'You think what Michaelson knows could lead to a financial crash or meltdown or whatever you want to call it? I mean, really?'

'In the wrong hands, definitely, but indirectly, if you see what I mean,' Morgan replied. 'It's not what he knows himself, it's the dirt we believe he can supply about senior men in the City. We think they're the real targets of these kidnappers, because that's the only scenario that makes sense. Snatching Michaelson is a way of identifying people they can pressurise to make that meltdown a reality. If it had been a straight kidnapping there'd have been a ransom demand by now, and if they'd only wanted money they wouldn't have taken Michaelson but grabbed his wife or kids.'

'And if you know when a crash is going to happen, you can make hundreds of millions from options trading,' Riley said. 'In the City, knowledge is power. This wouldn't be insider trading because these people would be timing the crash to suit their own agenda. In effect, they would be controlling the FTSE, not market forces, and that's incredibly dangerous. The City might take years to recover.'

Cross looked from Morgan to Riley and back again.

'I see your problem,' he said, 'and I know you can see mine. This isn't the kind of thing the company would ever do. Or even consider doing. And there's another problem that you might not have thought about, and that's simple practicality. After you called me I did a tiny bit of research. The population of East Anglia, which is basically the area you're talking about, is well over six million people. The population of Greater London is around nine million, so let's say that north-east London is home to about two million people. Add that to East Anglia and you're looking at around eight million people in all. I don't know, and I wouldn't tell you if I did know, how many of them own mobile devices or apps supplied by us, but I would be quite surprised if it was much less than two or three million people. If we went ahead with this, the amount of data that would need analysing would be colossal. Petabytes for sure. Could GCHQ cope with that extra load?'

Morgan nodded.

'You've heard of Tempora?' he asked.

'Yes, of course.'

'Well, compared to the volume of data routinely handled by Tempora, what this monitoring program would collect is comparatively insignificant.'

Ben Morgan's plan had been simple in concept and execution. He wanted the company to silently activate one of its apps in every device located in the area where the police thought the kidnap gang had gone to ground. With the microphone enabled he wanted to stream the recorded data back to the company headquarters and then pipe it to GCHQ so that one of the supercomputers there could monitor it, listening for specific words in the same way that the Echelon system used its dictionary to analyse telephone calls and other media. If they could pick up a conversation about the missing venture capitalist, they could identify the device involved and triangulate its location or get its IP address. And if possible they could enable its camera so they could witness what was happening at the scene.

Technically, there was no particular problem in carrying out what Morgan was suggesting. That particular app was programmed to listen out for a specific word followed by a question, which the device would then attempt to answer for the user using the resources of the Internet. So the microphone was effectively live the whole time anyway, the difference being that in this scenario all the sounds the microphone picked up would be recorded and streamed to GCHQ for analysis.

Remotely switching on the camera in a computer, a mobile phone or other device was also possible. This had been demonstrated by the Americans during what became known as Titan Rain, a series of organised and persistent attacks carried out against American and British computer systems beginning in about 2003. The attacks were Chinese in origin and launched from Red Army buildings in Guangdong province. American counter-espionage cyber experts identified the buildings used and sent a small program, hidden in a data packet, back to the originating computers. This remotely switched on the cameras built into the PCs being operated by Chinese technicians. The images they obtained allowed them to positively identify several senior Red Army officers wearing military uniform in one of the rooms from which the cyber-espionage attacks had originated.

But Morgan's plan was very much a shot in the dark and astonishingly speculative. And it would remain nothing more than speculation unless they could persuade Adam Cross that it was crucially important.

'Let me explain why we need this,' Morgan said. 'The police have no idea of the identity of the kidnappers because they left no clues at the scene of the attack and the getaway vehicle was using false plates. The police believe the location where Michaelson is being held is fairly close to where he was snatched. They think it would have been too risky for the gang to drive very far with him in the vehicle because there'd be too much chance of the Range Rover being involved in a traffic accident or the plates getting pinged by an ANPR camera or a cop in a patrol car. They think he's being held at a remote location, probably a farm, within about ten miles of the location where his Mercedes was attacked. That cuts down the population density a hell of a lot, because it's mainly rural, not urban.'

Morgan opened the black leather briefcase he had brought with him and pulled out a sheet of paper with a map printed on it. He put it on the coffee table in front of him and used a slim gold pen to point at it.

'The small red dot in the centre is where the attack happened,' he said, 'and the blue line I've drawn around it is about ten miles away, but I've altered it to include some villages and isolated houses.'

The rough circle included Chelmsford and smaller towns like Epping and Cheshunt to the west, Brentwood and Billericay to the south-east, and Romford and Enfield within the M25; but as Morgan had said, most of the area enclosed within the line was rural, dotted with farms and small villages.

Cross leaned forward and pointed out a single feature.

'You've got the M25 running right through the middle of it and the M11 just to the west. These bad guys could have snatched Michaelson, driven back towards the orbital motorway – that's the direction the witnesses said the Range Rover was heading – and in half an hour they could have been thirty miles away in either direction.'

'The police looked at that but they don't think it's very likely. For one thing, getting onto either of the motorways wouldn't have been easy. There's a network of small roads there that cross or pass close to the motorways, but they don't link up with the junctions. To get onto either would have meant driving north to Hastingwood to join the M11, or south to Brentwood to pick up the M25 at the A12 junction. Either route would have taken some time. The only other place is down at Chigwell, but that's a limited access junction. You can leave the M11 there, or join it to head south, towards London, but not to go north.

'Michaelson was snatched during the early afternoon but traffic on the M25 was running slowly in both directions and the M11 was busy. The kidnappers wouldn't have wanted to stop on the motorway in case Michaelson attracted the attention of people in other cars, and the traffic cameras didn't detect any similar Range

Rovers. That vehicle had a probably illegal bull bar bolted to the front, and that would have made it very distinctive.'

'Okay,' Cross replied, 'that makes sense. And you don't think they drove under the M25 into north-east London, because it's too built-up and crowded.'

'Exactly. The police have included some parts of Greater London like Enfield and Romford, but I think they're unlikely. Dragging a man out of a car and bundling him into a house would be a lot more difficult to do unseen in a built-up area, so a rural location is more probable. There's also the camera problem. There are a lot of them in urban areas but they're comparatively rare out in the countryside.'

Morgan paused and Riley took up the story.

'We think the area that the Essex police are concentrating on is too limited. We don't believe the kidnappers would have taken him inside the M25, but they'd have wanted to get more than ten miles from the kidnap site. So we think it's more likely that they'd have headed north, up into East Anglia.'

Morgan pointed to another shape he'd drawn on the map, a rough oblong with its base along the M25 from the A1(M) interchange south-east to the A12 junction, north-east to Stowmarket, west to Bury St Edmunds, Cambridge and Bedford, and south back to the M25.

'There are lots of towns in this area,' he said, 'but most of it is rural and all of it can be accessed without going on a motorway or passing traffic cameras. That's where I think we should be looking.'

Cross nodded but didn't respond immediately, just sat staring at the map. Morgan was too canny a negotiator to say anything. He knew that Cross would think through the risks and potential rewards – that was the reason the company employed him, because of his ability to quickly assess a situation – and then say yes or no.

He said neither. He stood up, walked over to his desk and depressed a button on his intercom system.

'Oliver, my office, please, in ten minutes.'

Then he walked back to where he'd been sitting, resumed his seat and looked at Morgan and Riley.

'I'm not hands-on about the way the systems work,' he said. 'I know the basics, and I make the overall business decisions, make sure everything is functioning the way it should, that kind of thing. But I'm heavily involved in the marketing of the products we sell, because if that goes tits-up, so does the company.

'We're constantly checking our strategies,' he went on. 'We assess our market share, target demographic take-up, area penetration, all that kind of corporate gobbledegook, to make sure we're on track. That's mainly done on a national basis, looking at responses to advertising campaigns and promotions, but what we've not done is select an area and work out the percentage of residents there with our app and devices and how many actually use them. Maybe it's time we did.'

Morgan immediately understood what Cross was really saying, the sub-text.

'It would need to be a largish area,' he suggested, 'and probably a mix of rural and urban environments to widen the spectrum. Say a part of East Anglia, which is urban, rural and commuter belt.'

Cross nodded and pointed at the map.

'I think we should be looking at an area like that,' he said.

'Do you want me to brief whoever you'll be tasking with the job?'

Cross shook his head.

'Definitely not. This is my own idea as CEO. It's purely a marketing decision. The last thing I want is some semi-spook like you sticking his nose in.'

'Semi-spook?' Morgan asked. 'What the hell's a semi-spook?'

Cross grinned at him.

'Well, what else would you call yourself? I've known you for years as a computer expert and from what you've told me this afternoon you're now spending most of your time in that bloody awful building at Vauxhall Cross, mixing it with a bunch of James Bond-wannabes. I think semi-spook covers it neatly. Now get out of here, both of you, while I tell my tech expert what I want him to do without telling him what I actually want him to do. Give me a call later with details of how you want us to funnel the stuff to Cheltenham.'

Chapter 19

Thursday
Fulham, London

The two men got the main door of the building open the same way they'd done it before, by claiming to be workmen who needed access to carry out a minor repair. Vince was carrying a collapsible stepladder and Mike a small toolbox.

They first visited each floor to remove the cameras they'd previously installed. Then they went to the first floor and walked towards the door of the apartment George Kenton had visited, stopping a few feet away. There was something they needed to do before they went inside.

For every technological problem there's usually a technological solution. Legitimate problems generate legitimate solutions, but from almost the first moment when a handful of early computers were connected into a rudimentary network, there have been people who have seen computers as challenges rather than tools.

The most destructive early attack took place in November 1988 when a graduate student at Cornell University named Ben Tappan Morris released what became known as the Morris Worm. Since then, viruses, worms and malware have become ubiquitous.

With the advent of Wi-Fi networks hackers could obtain direct access to a particular computer if they could log on to the network and bypass some of the firewalls and other controls. In response, the use of log-in passwords became almost universal. Many people believe their networks are completely protected from hacking because their Wi-Fi router requires a password before the system can be accessed. In fact, hacking into a Wi-Fi network is comparatively straightforward.

In the apartment building, Mike took out a smartphone. It wasn't one of the Samsung or Apple mobiles that everybody over the age of eight appeared to own. It had a six-inch display and the name on the back was Nexus. Inside, it had a 2.7 GHz quad-core CPU and 3GB of RAM, not exactly a leading-edge specification, but what made it different to a regular mobile was its software.

Kali Linux NetHunter was the first commercially produced open source penetration testing program. As it loaded Mike saw the familiar Kali logo appear: the head and neck of a stylised dragon surrounded by white smoke against a black background.

He went back to the home screen, accessed Settings and selected Wi-Fi. Still staring at the screen, he walked over to the door of the target apartment, then turned to look back at Vince and nodded.

'I'm detecting a network,' he said.

'No surprise there,' Vince replied. 'Can you crack it?'

'Is the Pope Catholic?'

Mike switched back to the Kali app, selected the 'Wi-Fite' utility and let it run. The screen display changed to show two fields requesting data input: the name of the Wi-Fi network and the type of encryption in use. The name of the network that Mike had detected in the target apartment was 'MarisoL2' and he input that and selected WPA2 from the drop-down menu.

Then he pressed 'Connect'. A sequence of screen messages appeared, culminating in the message 'Wi-Fi network hacked successfully' and 'Wi-Fi network name MarisoL2. Password is FortNum88'.

'Got it,' he said.

Mike had over thirty miniature cameras in his toolbox, all with fully charged batteries and all both motion-sensitive and Wi-Fi-enabled, meaning that the images the cameras recorded could be transmitted anywhere in the world, as long as they were connected to the wireless network in the apartment. These were smaller and more discreet than the ones containing micro-SD cards. They would be easier to hide and, more importantly, wouldn't need to be accessed. Talking their way into the target apartment on a single occasion was one thing but getting regular access to it would be an entirely different matter.

Both men squatted down and Vince opened the toolbox. He took out ten cameras. Each had the highest capacity battery available, which should last for at least a month – more than sufficient time to record what they needed.

As Vince switched on each camera, Mike identified it using a utility program on his Nexus mobile and logged it into the Wi-Fi network in the target apartment. They probably wouldn't use all of them – three would most likely be enough – but it never hurt to have redundancy. Each man took five of the cameras because they didn't know which of them would have the best opportunity to plant them.

'We good to go?' Mike asked, and Vince nodded.

Both men stood up, walked across to the apartment door and Vince rang the bell.

For about twenty seconds there was no response from inside, and then they saw the viewing peephole darken as a figure moved to the door.

'Hullo. What do you want?' a female voice demanded from inside.

'Building maintenance, Miss Hart,' Vince replied, holding up a worksheet to the peephole, a worksheet he had prepared before they left for Parsons Green. 'We need to check your wiring and circuit breakers.'

They'd got her name – Amanda Hart – from the list of tenants and confirmed it on the bell-push panel outside the entrance door.

There was another short delay before the door was opened by a young woman wearing a velour tracksuit, the kind of comfortable garment designed for lounging about. Her long coal-black hair hung loose and her face wasn't made up, but there was no denying her natural beauty.

'How long will this take?' she asked. 'I have to go out in about an hour.'

'Well,' Mike said, 'that really depends on you.'

'What do you mean?'

Mike gave her his best cheeky boy smile.

'Well, we work better and faster with the right kind of lubrication, see. If you were to make us both a cuppa, I can guarantee we'll be out of here in twenty minutes maximum.'

The woman looked at him for a few seconds, apparently deciding how to reply, then nodded and smiled.

'I'll see what I can do,' she said, and walked away. 'The fuse box thing is in that cupboard on the right-hand side of the door,' she added over her shoulder.

The moment she left the hall, the two men started work. Vince opened the cupboard the woman had indicated, but they weren't going to do anything with the breaker panel.

The apartment was clearly expensive, or at least expensively and tastefully furnished, with thick carpets, cream leather sofas and easy chairs, a very large flat-screen television mounted on the wall, and several oil paintings. Which was what they'd been hoping to see.

The worst possible kind of home to rig for sound and vision was one decorated in a minimalist Scandinavian style, all clean lines, white walls, modern furniture and a complete absence of stuff. The more cluttered the property, the easier it was to conceal the cameras.

Of the two men, Mike was the more personable, Vince's general demeanour and appearance – he had a line of scar tissue on his forehead and a nose that had clearly encountered at least one hard and unyielding object in the past – suggesting that he was more of a fighter than a lover. Which in his case was absolutely true.

While Vince, who despite his heavy build was actually light on his feet, headed towards a short corridor that had to lead to the bedrooms and bathroom, Mike took a voltage meter and current detector from his toolbox and followed Amanda Hart into the kitchen.

She was standing beside the worktop where an electric kettle was just getting into its stride and dropping individual teabags into three china mugs. She turned as Mike entered.

'It looks as if your fuse box might be okay,' he said, 'but we're still getting some odd readings from the wiring system, so there may be something else that we need to look at.'

Mike always lived in fear of the day when the person he was talking to and providing a line of ill-informed bullshit would turn out to be a fully qualified electrician or plumber or whatever, but he doubted if the woman in front of him had ever done any work of that kind with her hands. He strongly suspected that her talents lay in a very different direction.

'So we might have to start looking in other rooms to see where the wires and conduits have been run,' he added.

The woman looked startled.

'I haven't had any problems in here,' she said.

'Ah, well, you wouldn't, necessarily. But there might be some kind of short-circuit or leakage of current in here that's affecting other parts of the building.'

He had no idea if electric current could leak anywhere, and frankly doubted it, but Amanda Hart didn't even blink.

'You won't have to start taking down walls, will you?'

'No, nothing like that,' he said reassuringly. 'Look, I can show you.'

He lifted the voltmeter and switched it on, then held it close to the wall above the mains power point to which the electric kettle was connected. The red telltale light on the meter remained dark and the needle in the gauge below it didn't move at all. He waved the meter from side to side along the wall with exactly the same lack of result.

'Now, if there was a power cable running behind the tiles here,' he said, 'then this little gadget would detect it. But what you have here is what we in the trade call a ring main, and to supply your electric sockets—' Mike gestured with his other hand at the numerous power points located above the work surface '—there's a set of wires that run all the way round the room but lower down.'

He lowered the meter until it was just below the socket where the kettle was plugged in. Immediately the red light came on and the needle jumped on the dial below it.

'By using this, we can trace the wiring all the way around the apartment, and that'll help us pinpoint whatever the problem is. And it might not be in this apartment at all. Until we've had a good check round, we won't know.'

Amanda Hart still looked concerned and shook her head as she poured water into three mugs.

'The sugar's over there,' she said, pointing at a metal storage container bearing the word 'sugar' in italic script, 'if you or the other man take it. Where is he, by the way?'

'He's probably checking the circuit breakers,' Mike replied. 'Don't bother taking a mug out to him. I'll bring him in here.'

'It's no trouble,' she said, picking up two of the mugs and making for the door.

Mike had no option but to follow. He just hoped he'd bought Vince enough time to get the cameras into position.

He was crouching by the wall near the television holding a meter identical to the one Mike had in his hand, apparently checking for the location of embedded conduits.

'Tea?' Vince asked, and Mike nodded.

'Have you got anywhere?'

Vince took a sip from the mug before he replied.

'I have. I don't know where the fault is in this building, but I can tell you that it's not in this flat. Everything in here, the wiring, the breakers, everything, it all checks out.'

Mike looked over at the woman and gave her a broad smile.

'See, I told you so.' He glanced at his watch. 'Reckon my estimate of twenty minutes might have been a bit pessimistic. We'll be gone as soon as we've had this tea, and thanks for that, by the way.'

Just over fifteen minutes after they had stepped through the door of the apartment, the two men left the building and returned to their van. Vince got behind the wheel while Mike put the stepladder and toolbox in the back of the vehicle. Then he sat in the passenger seat and stared at the screen of his mobile phone.

'Where did you put the cameras?' he asked.

'One in the lounge in an artificial potted plant,' Vince replied, 'and three others in the bedroom, because that's where all the action is going to be.'

Something about the way he spoke caused Mike to glance at him.

'You sure about that?'

Vince started the engine and put the van into gear.

'Definitely. Can you see her? Is the lounge camera working?'

'Yes,' Mike replied. 'She's just sat down on the sofa, still drinking her tea. The bedroom?'

Vince grinned at him.

'I think our Mister Kenton only goes to see Miss Hart when he's been a very, very naughty boy. It's a big bedroom and it's been set up like a dungeon, heavy curtains, low lighting and a St Andrew's cross bolted to the wall at the foot of the bed, complete with chains and straps to hold somebody on it. Plus what I think is a flogging rack on the other side of the room. And there are handcuffs and ropes and canes and whips and paddles and all sorts. This isn't my scene, but it looks to me like Miss Hart turns into something a bit different to what we saw once the sun goes down and some poor sod like Kenton turns up at her door. More Miss Whiplash than anything else.'

Mike nodded.

'I was expecting something a bit different to that, to be honest,' he said, 'because that woman is really built. You could tell even through that shapeless bloody jogging suit thing she was wearing, and I had her pegged as an expensive call girl, not some sadomasochistic dominatrix, all whips and chains and leather and latex. But it'll make exciting viewing for George Kenton when John shows him a few still pictures of his next session and gives him the DVD.'

Chapter 20

Thursday
City of London

'I know you don't know. That's the point. If you had known, I'd probably have fired you on the spot. What I'm telling you to do is find out. Just make absolutely sure that nobody knows what you're doing. Or why.'

James McEwan was the kind of Chief Executive Officer who was almost always the first to arrive at his place of business and the last to leave. He was also the kind of Chief Executive Officer who made sure that as many people as possible on his staff knew that. More pertinently, his 'full days' in the office tended to be interrupted by long business lunches, meetings and conferences that were not necessarily anything to do with the bank for which he worked. And it was the consequence of one of those extracurricular activities that had prompted him to summon his personal assistant to his office minutes after his arrival at work that morning.

Jeremy Somerville had worked for him for just over two years, and this was not the first time he had found himself facing his boss and being given instructions that either made no sense to him or which were possibly or definitely illegal.

Somerville was even more confused than usual at what he had been told this time. McEwan's orders seemed straightforward, just a peculiar way to obtain what appeared to be a fairly simple, uncomplicated and not particularly sensitive piece of information. Which meant there must be more to it, something that McEwan was not telling him. But Somerville thought he could do the whole thing at arm's length and avoid being directly involved. He could get other people to do the dirty work so they would take whatever risks were involved and he would be insulated.

Somerville had learnt a lot while working for McEwan, not least the fact that they really were two of a kind, just occupying different positions in the hierarchy of the merchant bank.

But over the last day or so McEwan seemed to have changed, beginning immediately after the unexpected visit of the man calling himself Harrison. Ever since then, McEwan had seemed on edge, and Somerville had a very good idea why.

'Is there a timescale?' he asked.

McEwan nodded.

'As soon as possible, obviously, and ideally by yesterday. But in this case quick results are less important than staying under the radar. Nobody must know about this.' He glanced up and held Somerville's gaze for a moment, then nodded. 'Why are you still here? Get on with it.'

Somerville returned to his own office, pressed the space bar to wake up his computer and began scanning the list of contacts, picking out those who were in positions to provide the information that he had been told to obtain.

But he didn't call them directly, because what he was trying to do definitely merited a circuitous approach, and that would take him a couple of hours at least to work out.

Chapter 21

Thursday
London

'I still think this is probably a waste of time,' Adam Cross said, using his private mobile phone, 'but we're ready at this end if you can specify the destination. The IP address or wherever you want this stuff sent.'

'Thanks, Adam,' Ben Morgan replied. 'I really owe you for this. You'll get a text within the next two minutes with all the information you need.'

Ever the optimist, Morgan had prepared the text some time earlier, and the delay was not in the preparation of the message but purely to give him enough time to call his contact at GCHQ and warn her that the data transfer was about to start.

Less than five minutes after Adam Cross's call to Morgan, the analysis of the data stream began. Of necessity, Morgan had had to specify a severely reduced list of trigger words, which was comparatively straightforward because he was only looking for references to Nicholas Michaelson and the gang of people holding him. So his list contained the name of the target and his wife and children, the company he worked for in the City, a list of some fifty words including references to the kidnapping, and the names of the banks and bankers that Michaelson was known to be involved with professionally.

Then all Morgan could do was wait and hope. He wasn't particularly optimistic in this case, but he still believed that either Echelon or the app offered the best chance of finding the man.

The police investigation appeared to have stalled completely. As far as the Essex police were concerned, Nicholas Michaelson and the four men who'd kidnapped him appeared to have vanished without trace. No new witnesses had come forward with sightings of the vehicles involved, and the traffic and ANPR cameras had recorded no hits. The Essex police helicopter had scoured the area looking for the Range Rover but this had also drawn a blank. Their assumption was that Michaelson was being held somewhere near the kidnap location, but without any idea where to look there was nothing further that could be done.

Chapter 22

Friday
Brent Park, London

'We've got movement,' Mike said as his mobile emitted a warning chime.

'I'm on it,' Vince replied, opening a window on the desktop PC and staring at the feed from the remote camera. 'Okay. Miss Whiplash is back.'

The cameras in the lounge and bedroom of the apartment in Parsons Green had been triggered several times that day as Amanda Hart moved around the property, but about three hours earlier she'd left the flat. Now she'd returned but she wasn't alone.

'Is that her son?' Mike asked. 'Has she got a son?'

Her companion was clearly young – accurately estimating his age was difficult but he looked about fifteen – and he was very scruffily dressed, but no more so than most school-age children. He was carrying a battered rucksack over one shoulder.

He wasn't in view for more than a few seconds, as he followed Amanda Hart into the kitchen and out of sight. The targets were too far away from the camera for their voices to be clearly heard, and then the camera shut down as the motion sensor stopped detecting movement.

'I can override it and switch to live view if you want,' Mike said.

Vince shook his head.

'There's no point. It'll switch on again when they come out, and we can't hear what they're saying anyway. We can wait.'

'And whoever the boy is, he isn't George Kenton,' Mike pointed out, 'so we're not really interested in him.'

Nothing happened for about ten minutes, and then the camera was triggered again as Amanda Hart came back into view, the boy a couple of paces behind her. Both of them turned down the short internal passageway that led to the bedrooms and moments later the lounge camera shut down.

'Maybe her personal tastes run to really young men,' Mike suggested, 'not old farts like George Kenton who just want to get a good spanking. Anyway, we'll soon see.'

But they didn't.

The hidden cameras in the bedroom remained dormant, meaning that wherever they had gone it wasn't there. Then the lounge camera came on again when Amanda Hart reappeared with a glass in her hand. She poured herself a drink from a selection of bottles on a sideboard, sat down on the sofa, picked up a magazine and began flicking through its pages. The boy remained conspicuous by his absence.

Mike asked the obvious question.

'You went down that corridor when we bugged the place,' he said. 'How many bedrooms are there?'

'Two,' Vince replied, 'but the second one is a regular guest room. Just a double bed and en-suite bathroom. There's nowhere else he can go down the corridor, so he must be in that bedroom. Maybe he's her son or nephew or something and he's staying the night.'

'Maybe. Or maybe something else is going on here, and George Kenton doesn't visit to enjoy a good flogging. Maybe Amanda Hart provides more than one kind of evening entertainment. That boy doesn't look like her – he's fair-haired for starters, and she's dark – and he doesn't look like a schoolboy. I know these days schoolkids seem to think it's cool to dress like tramps or druggies, but that lad looked more like a runaway to me, and he just looked unwashed.'

'You think she's got a sideline in pimping underage kids?' Vince asked. 'And this guy's a bit of rough she found at King's Cross or somewhere?'

'Maybe. If she really does like them that young, why didn't she take him into the main bedroom? I think she's probably stuck him in the spare room and told him to take a bath, and that could mean we've bugged the wrong bedroom. We need to get back inside that flat again, and we can't pose as electricians this time. We'll have to wait for her to go out and then pick the lock.'

'Shit. Okay, nothing we can do right now except keep an eye on what's going on. This might all be innocent and we've got the wrong end of the stick, but I don't think we have.'

About half an hour later Amanda Hart stood up. She glanced down the internal corridor, then picked up her mobile phone and walked into the kitchen, presumably intending to make a call. A call that perhaps she didn't want the boy to overhear.

She sat down again in the lounge and ten minutes later the boy reappeared, this time apparently wearing nothing but a large white dressing gown. He stepped forward tentatively, as if unsure of his reception, but Amanda Hart immediately smiled at him and stood up. The audio from the lounge camera was perfectly clear.

'Excellent, Robert,' she said. 'Does that feel better?'

The young blond boy nodded.

'Yeah. And thanks, Miss Nicholson.'

'So she's got at least two names,' Vince said, watching the screen. 'And I bet her real name isn't Hart or Nicholson.'

'Please call me Amanda. Are you hungry? Would you like a sandwich?'

'Yeah. Please. That'd be good.'

'Right. Just sit down and I'll make something for you.'

The boy took a seat on the sofa. He appeared nervous and fidgety, and made no attempt to lean back or relax.

A few minutes later Amanda Hart returned carrying a tray that she handed to the boy. The camera angle allowed them to see what was on it: a plate of sandwiches made with white bread and cut into quarters, a packet of crisps and a can of Coke.

'They're ham and cheese. I hope that's okay with you.'

The boy simply nodded, grabbed the first sandwich and stuffed it into his mouth.

'He's hungry,' Vince said. 'I think you might be right. He's probably a runaway and he's likely been sleeping rough.'

The sandwiches disappeared with impressive speed followed by the crisps, and then the boy finally leaned back on the sofa, put the tray on a side table, popped open the can of Coke and took a long swallow.

'Better?' Amanda Hart asked.

'Shedloads, ta,' he replied.

He finished the drink and placed the empty can on the tray.

'When's he due, this bloke?' he asked.

'About an hour, I expect. Why don't you go back to your bedroom and get ready? I've shown you the clothes I want you to wear, and what you need to do in the bathroom before you get dressed.'

The boy nodded slowly, then stood up. Now he was washed and clean, he didn't look to Vince or Mike as if he was older than thirteen or fourteen.

'I ain't much into this kinda thing,' the boy said, looking across at the woman, 'and I ain't had much experience. I mean, I've done it twice or maybe three times before when I needed a bed and couldn't pay for it. I ain't much good at it.'

'I'm sure you'll be fine,' Amanda Hart said. 'My friend is very experienced and he'll take good care of you. He likes people who are new to this.' Her voice changed slightly, a hint of menace creeping into it. 'Just remember that we have a deal, and that you won't get paid until afterwards. And if you do well you might get the bonus I mentioned.'

The boy nodded again, then stepped out of the lounge.

'As soon as you're completely ready, Robert,' Amanda Hart called after him, 'come out here so that I can check how you look.'

'I think you nailed it, Mike,' Vince said. 'I think she multi-talented. She's a dominatrix, possibly a hooker and probably a pimp. I know most pimps are men but when you think about it a female pimp makes good sense if she's targeting kids. They're probably more likely to talk to a sympathetic woman than some hairy-arsed man who's trying to get them into the back seat of his car.'

'Okay. What's your money on? How's this lad Robert going to look when he comes out for his final inspection?'

Vince thought for a few moments.

'Probably a schoolboy,' he suggested. 'Or a schoolgirl with a wig on, in case Miss Whiplash's client likes the idea of a girl with a hidden surprise. You?'

'Schoolboy,' Mike said. 'Nothing else makes sense, as far as I can see.'

They were both right.

Chapter 23

Friday
Undisclosed location

'I don't understand,' Nicholas Michaelson said desperately. 'I don't know why you need—'

'You don't need to know the reason,' John said. 'All you have to do is answer the fucking question.'

'But I don't—'

'You need some encouragement, do you? We can give you that right now.'

Michaelson had been providing answers to the best of his ability, though he still had no idea who these people were or why they needed the information. But over the last few hours the probing had got much more personal, and despite the situation he was in and the overt threat to his family, Michaelson was reluctant to give the answers his interrogator wanted.

John stood up, opened the door and gestured to someone outside the room.

A few seconds later Karl walked in and crossed to where Michaelson sat in the wooden armchair on one side of the table.

'Wrists and ankles,' John instructed.

Karl took some cable ties out of his pocket, clamped Michaelson's right wrist to the arm of the chair, slid one of the cable ties over his wrist and pulled it tight. He repeated the treatment on his left arm and then on each ankle. Michaelson didn't react in anyway, recognising the futility of any resistance. Outnumbered by men who were both bigger and stronger than he was, he knew that trying to struggle would only make things worse.

'Watch him,' John said and left the room.

He knocked on the door of the adjacent room and stepped inside. It was set up something like a home office, with a desk, a leather swivel chair and a large wall-mounted television that was acting as a monitor, the screen displaying four different views of the table and chairs where Nicholas Michaelson sat immobile, the feeds simultaneously being stored on a high-capacity external hard drive.

The man behind the desk was different in almost every way from the other four men. He had a different ethnic background, and where John and the other three were heavily built, his frame was light, almost delicate. But there was no mistaking the aura of ruthless power that he appeared to exude. John appeared cowed in his presence.

'You heard?' he asked. The unidentified man nodded. 'What do you want me to do?'

'You shouldn't even have to ask. Go back in there and hurt him. Break one of his bones. Nothing incapacitating, just a finger or perhaps two of them.'

John nodded and almost backed out of the room. He stood for a moment looking down at Michaelson, who stared defiantly up at him.

'Are you right-handed?' John asked.

'What? I don't know why—'

'You're beginning to sound like a cracked record. Most people are right-handed, so we'll go with that.'

He walked around behind Michaelson, then reached down, placed his thumb on the knuckle of the captive's left little finger to use as a fulcrum, hooked his index finger around the end of Michaelson's finger and pulled. He screamed as John increased the pressure and the delicate joints started to pop, and then howled in absolute agony as one of the bones snapped. John pressed down on the break to emphasise the point.

Karl looked down at the traumatised man and laughed. Then he turned and walked out.

'In the trade,' John said, 'that's what we call an attention-getter. You've got another three fingers on that hand we can play with, four on your right hand, plus your thumbs. And then we can start on your toes. We don't bother breaking those, just snip them off with bolt-croppers and use a soldering iron to cauterise the wound. Stings like a bitch, but I've always found that it really concentrates the mind.'

He sat down again on the opposite side of the desk and stared at Michaelson, whose entire attention was fixed on his broken little finger, the digit already visibly swelling and discoloured.

'So, I'm assuming that I now have your full attention,' he said, his tone conversational and almost friendly. 'That was one small bone in a part of your body that's really easy to fix. If we start on your toes, it's a whole different game.'

John pulled a knife out of his pocket. Not a switchblade, just a lock-knife with a four-inch curved blade. He snapped it open and cut through the two cable ties that had been holding Nicholas Michaelson's arms rigidly in position on the chair.

As soon as his hands were free, Michaelson grabbed his left hand with his right and let loose a howl of anguish as a solid bolt of pain pulsed up his arm from his broken finger.

Then the questioning started again and this time Michaelson showed no hesitation. Whatever John asked him, he gave the fullest possible reply. A few times he had to refer to either his phone or his laptop to pull up detailed information, usually dates, mobile numbers and the like.

An hour into the new session, John cut Michaelson's ankles free from the chair when it became obvious he was going to throw up, the shock and pain working in combination. About half an hour after that he took Michaelson back to his room and locked him in.

The man's attention had started to wander and he was making mistakes, but probably not deliberately. John decided to start again in the morning.

Chapter 24

Friday

London

An hour after the analysis of the data had started running at GCHQ, Morgan took a call from Angela Evans that changed the focus of the search.

'They've found the Range Rover,' she said. 'The police are all over it like a rash.'

'I presume it was dumped somewhere?' Morgan said.

'Yes. And it's caused some embarrassment because it was abandoned only about three miles from where the kidnapping took place.'

'I suppose nobody reported it?'

'That's where the embarrassment comes in,' Evans replied. 'It was reported three times to the police by the owner of the land where it was left, and they did nothing about it. The kidnappers were quite clever. They used a completely false registration number on the Range Rover when they did the kidnapping, but they'd had another set of plates made for the vehicle, and the number on those was for a properly taxed and insured Range Rover of the same colour, so when the police ran a check, as far as they could tell it was all legitimate. But actually it was running on cloned plates, what the police call a ringer, and they can only detect that by looking at the VIN, the Vehicle Identification Number.'

'So where was it?' Morgan asked.

'In the car park of a cafe on the Ongar Road south of the M25. The car park has gates, and when the owner locked up at the end of the day he saw a Range Rover parked there. He checked it, found it was locked, noted the registration number and then went home. But he didn't lock the car park because he didn't want to trap the vehicle inside. There's a garden centre behind the cafe and he thought the driver had probably left the vehicle in his car park because there wasn't room at the garden centre. When he opened up the next day he expected it to have gone, but it was still there. So he made a non-emergency call to the police so they could arrange to move it, which they declined to do.

'He called them twice more with the same request because his car park isn't that big and the Range Rover was taking up a parking space one of his customers could have used. It was only during his third call that somebody in the control room realised the vehicle he was reporting and the vehicle they were looking for were the same make, model and colour, and had the same type of bull bar bolted to the front. A squad car turned up within fifteen minutes, and a transporter vehicle half an hour after that, and the Range Rover is now being taken to pieces forensically at some cop shop in Essex.'

'They'll probably find nothing useful,' Morgan commented, 'but of course this does change the situation.'

'Quite. The kidnappers swapped vehicles probably within fifteen minutes of grabbing Michaelson, so checking the ANPR and traffic cameras was a complete waste of time because they were looking for the wrong vehicle. Before you ask the question, no, the cafe had no CCTV cameras covering the car park, and neither the owner nor any of his staff have any idea what cars might have been parked there. It's a very popular cafe and there are always vehicles entering and leaving the car park. The kidnappers made a good choice, and I don't think it was by accident. In fact, I don't think they did anything by accident.'

Morgan was silent for a few seconds, then replied.

'So now it really does all depend on what we can pull out of Echelon or from the surveillance using the app. I'll call Adam and see if he can expand the search, because Michaelson could be almost anywhere by now.'

Chapter 25

Friday

Brent Park, London

There was almost no movement from the flat at Parsons Green but Mike and Vince kept watching the screen anyway as Amanda Hart slowly finished her drink.

About twenty minutes later the boy returned. He was wearing black shoes with knee-length socks, short trousers, a white shirt with a tie, and a dark blue blazer with some kind of badge on the breast pocket.

'That's excellent,' Amanda Hart exclaimed as he reappeared, then stood up and walked over to examine the clothes more carefully. 'They're a better fit than I expected,' she said. 'They could almost have been made for you.'

She walked around him, pausing only to straighten his collar and slightly tighten the knot of his tie.

'You did what I told you to do in the bathroom?' she asked.

Robert nodded.

'Right, you should go and wait in the bedroom now. My friend will be along in a little while.'

She took a brief call on her mobile about five minutes later, and the knock on the door came twenty-five minutes after that. Amanda Hart, or Amanda Nicholson, or whatever her real name was, immediately went to answer it.

'Now why am I not surprised he's here?' Vince muttered, as George Kenton stepped into the lounge and embraced Amanda. It was a professional greeting, the kind exchanged between a man and a woman in a business environment, rather than two lovers.

'Good to see you again, George,' she said.

'And you, Amanda. You've got me somebody new, I think.'

Kenton seemed keen to proceed to the main event.

'I found him near Paddington Station,' she said, nodding. 'He claims to be eighteen, but if he's a day over fifteen I'd be surprised.'

'Dark or fair?'

'Blond, just the way you like them. I told him one hundred. I know that's more than usual, but I think you'll find he's worth it. And if you feel like a return bout, I can keep him here for another four or five days.'

The surprise on Kenton's face was quite obvious.

'Have you asked him?'

'No, but I think he'd agree. It's not the first time he's done this, by his own admission, and if I dangled another hundred in front of him and promised him board and lodging here for a few days I think he'd be happy to stay. My next appointment isn't until Wednesday, so that would be the deadline.'

Kenton nodded.

'That might work for me too,' he said. 'I might be able to manage another evening and perhaps an afternoon session as well.'

'Good. He's in the spare bedroom.'

Amanda Hart walked across to the internal corridor, George Kenton eagerly trotting along behind her.

The two watchers heard the sound of a double knock on a door and then the camera shut down as usual because it was detecting no movement. A few seconds later, the image reappeared as Amanda Hart returned to the lounge and her seat on the sofa.

'I think we both know what's about to happen in that bedroom,' Mike said, 'but knowing something and proving it are very different animals. We definitely need to get cameras into that room.'

'If the boy does stay on with her, getting inside might be difficult.'

Mike shook his head.

'I doubt it. He's a runaway off the streets and that flat is full of attractive and saleable items. She won't be going out to the shops to buy milk or something and leaving him alone there, because if she did he could just grab a couple of bags full of stuff and leg it. If she goes out, she'll take him with her – a mother and son out shopping

– or she'll lock him in the flat and make sure there's no way he can get out.'

The rest of the evening was something of an anti-climax, at least in Brent Park. About ninety minutes later, George Kenton reappeared in the lounge, fully dressed and looking pleased with himself. He took out his wallet and handed over what looked like four fifty-pound notes to Amanda Hart, presumably her fee and the money for the boy, then simply said he'd call her and left the apartment.

The boy didn't reappear in the lounge and about three hours after Kenton had left Amanda Hart switched off the lights. In the master bedroom the camera recorded her climbing into bed wearing a T-shirt and shorts.

Chapter 26

Saturday
Marble Arch, London

Ben Morgan's mobile rang as he was approaching the hotel where he'd booked a room for the next four nights.

Because the kidnapping situation was still fluid – or still fucked up, as Cameron Riley had described it – Morgan had decided to stay in London rather than return home. He wanted to be on the spot should Echelon or the app-based surveillance detect anything. He still reckoned they offered more hope than routine police enquiries.

Essex police had started visiting isolated buildings within their theoretical ten-mile radius of the kidnap location, but he frankly doubted if that would get them anywhere, especially since the kidnappers had dumped the distinctive Range Rover. About all the patrols could do was knock at the door of a target property, spout whatever cover story they'd been told, and take a look around while they were on the premises. That was it, and to describe it as anything more than hit and miss was optimistic.

In the final analysis, the ten-mile radius had been nothing more than a guess. Because the kidnappers had changed to another car, they could have driven as far as they wanted outside that distance, and the police would have no idea where they should be looking. Michaelson and his captors could realistically be anywhere in Britain.

The phone announced that it was a private number, suggesting it was probably a cold caller, but he answered it anyway.

'Yes?'

'Ben? It's Natasha.'

'Oh, hi. How are you?'

Natasha Black had been recruited by GCHQ years earlier because of her undeniable mathematical and other abilities, but she'd raised eyebrows there from the first day she'd turned up for work, not least because of the broad pink streak in her hair. Morgan had known her for about five years, and in conversation with her always felt slightly inadequate.

'I'd have been better if somebody else had been told to process this stream of crap that you've decided to send us,' she replied. 'Is this a good time to talk?'

'This is a very good time to talk,' Morgan replied, 'as long as you've got something useful to tell me. You're calling about the analysis?'

'Yes,' Natasha said, 'but this is an open line so I can't provide any details.'

'Just a broad hint would do,' Morgan replied, ducking into a side street and away from the traffic noise.

'Okey dokey. You gave us a list of names and words, but it's so bloody general and non-specific that we're picking up hits from all over.'

'The list was non-specific,' Morgan replied, 'because of the situation. And we've had to widen the search area so the amount of data you'll be getting will be increasing.'

'It already has,' Natasha responded. 'I've had to put two additional analysts on it. You'll get listings by email on an hourly basis from now on, but that's not why I called.'

'It isn't?'

'Of course not. You know as well as I do that assumptions are always dangerous, but sometimes they're inevitable. You won't be surprised to learn that this is one of those times.'

'It is?'

'Do try and keep up, Ben. Of course it is. We're going to have to use a form of MVR on the data or it's going to swamp us. Tempora takes priority, and I can't keep pulling analysts off that.'

Morgan was familiar with the concept of Massive Volume Reduction, a way of reducing the amount of data to be analysed based on certain criteria. Or more accurately certain assumptions.

'What filters do you want to use?' he asked.

'I'd have thought that was quite obvious. You're looking for a gang of male kidnappers holding a male victim. How likely is it that they would have their wives and children in the property?'

'Not very.'

'Exactly. So we can eliminate any location where we detect children's or women's voices.'

'Yes, that makes sense,' Morgan said. 'Please implement it.'

'Already done,' Natasha replied. 'And you owe me dinner for this. At least.'

Chapter 27

Monday
City of London

'I'm not sure if this is what you want,' Jeremy Somerville said, placing a single sheet of paper, laser printed on both sides, on James McEwan's desk. It was a list of names, their positions in the City, their home and business addresses, their contact telephone numbers and email addresses.

The CEO picked it up and read every piece of information printed on it. Then he looked up and stared at his subordinate.

'Nobody knows about this apart from the two of us, I hope.'

'Nobody. Your instructions were very specific.'

'So how did you get the information?'

Somerville shrugged.

'I did a combination of things,' he replied, 'but mainly I used staff in the target banks. I persuaded them to complete a survey of security companies used by the City, based on the rates charged and the services provided. I told them it was strictly confidential but that we needed the names of the clients and the companies, and the fees that they were paying.'

'And they believed you?' McEwan sounded incredulous.

Somerville nodded.

'I did take a slight liberty. I told them that the survey was being conducted under the auspices of the Bank of England and I made sure that there were no links to me or to this bank.'

'That was good thinking. And did you carry out the final step, as I instructed?'

'I did.' Somerville produced another sheet of paper. On this page was the name of a single company and below it the contact details and other information that he had been able to discover, which was remarkably sparse. 'This is all I could find out about this PSP4 outfit. It looks like their financial base is in the Cayman Islands, though they do have at least one bank account here in the UK. There's not much in it, and I reckon they use it as a funnel. People pay them here in London and as soon as the transfer's cleared they bung it straight out to the Caribbean,' he said. 'All of the people listed on the other sheet are clients of PSP4. Some of them have contracts with other security firms, but there's no particular pattern in the other companies that they selected. It does look as if this PSP4 outfit is offering something special.'

James McEwan not only knew that was true, but he also knew precisely what PSP4's unique selling point was. And he wished he didn't. Since he'd seen Harrison in his office for that brief and unpleasant meeting, he didn't think he'd slept for more than about an hour at a time.

'Good. That's what I needed to know. Is this the only copy?'

'I have a backup on my work laptop and one hard copy.'

'Right. Shred the hard copy backup, delete the file or files from your laptop and anywhere else you've put copies, including the Cloud. In fact, don't just delete them because that's not secure enough. If you haven't got one already, download a military-spec wipe utility and run that over the files to shred them completely. If I find you've retained any of the information about this, including your mocked-up survey form, you'll be looking for a new job within twenty-four hours. Is that clearly understood?'

Somerville nodded because there wasn't much else he could do. Dismissed by McEwan, he sat behind his own desk for a few minutes wondering about the exact depth of the hole that his superior had fallen into.

And working out the best way that he could protect himself from the fallout and the shrapnel when the whole thing blew up in his face, as it was almost certain to do.

Chapter 28

Monday

Fulham, London

The focus of the two men was still on Amanda Hart and her so far unidentified young house guest who called himself Robert, and both Vince and Mike knew that they needed to get back into her apartment so that they could set up two or three cameras in the guest bedroom ready for George Kenton's next visit. It had already taken them far longer than they had expected to get to this point. What they dared not do was annoy the man they knew as Mr King. He gave them their instructions and paid them, and they knew exactly the kind of trouble they'd be in if they failed, so they needed to finish this. They parked the van near the building in Fulham and waited for her to leave so they could get inside and complete the job.

Checking her movements was the easy bit, because the camera in the lounge was recording her whenever she came within range, and they monitored this on their smartphones.

When they'd already been parked for nearly two hours, Vince suddenly nudged Mike, who was sitting in the driving seat and starting to doze off.

'She's on the move,' he said. 'She's putting on a coat and the young lad looks as if he's going with her.'

Vince adjusted the volume on his smartphone – he'd had the sound muted to help preserve the phone's battery life – so they could hear the conversation.

'—can watch television when we come back,' Amanda Hart said, 'but we just need to pick up a few things for lunch, and it will do you good to get out of this flat for a little while. Just don't do anything stupid while we're shopping. I've told you what my friend will be paying you, but you'll only get the money when you leave, not before.'

Robert – whether his real name or just one he'd picked when he dropped off society's radar and into the usually unseen undercurrent, the sub-surface society of the drunks and druggies and runaways – nodded at the woman who was looking after him on a strictly temporary basis. An arrangement that, perhaps strangely, seemed to suit them both.

'I know that,' he said. 'You told me before. It ain't my ideal world, this, but it's keepin' me warm and fed and I don't reckon I need to do that much to keep your dodgy friend comin' back for more. I've 'ad a lot worse on the street.'

Amanda Hart smiled at him encouragingly.

'He was very pleased with you and he'll be coming to see you again, perhaps even tonight.'

The boy actually looked happy at that prospect, though he was probably thinking about the fee he would collect – assuming that Amanda Hart and George Kenton adhered to the arrangement, which they probably would, because that would suit everybody and not lead to messy complications – rather than the encounter itself.

'Okay. They've left the flat,' Vince said. 'We need to move.'

The two men, Mike carrying a canvas tool bag, walked briskly to the end of the street and then peered cautiously down the road towards the entrance of the building. They saw the unmistakeable figure of Amanda Hart, her right hand holding Robert's left, heading towards a local parade of shops.

'She might not be gone for all that long,' Mike said. 'If she's just nipping out for bread and cheese or something, she might be back in ten minutes.'

At the main door of the apartment building Vince took a device from his pocket. It looked a little like the frame of a small handgun, complete with a trigger and a thin needle-like prong where the barrel would be. They already knew that the main door lock was a standard old-type Yale, and that meant the Brockhage manual lock pick gun, also known as a snap gun, should work on it.

Vince inserted a slim torsion wrench, an L-shaped length of steel, into the lower part of the keyhole to apply turning pressure to the lock, then slid the needle of the gun into the keyhole and squeezed the trigger three or four times to allow the gun to move the pins inside the lock.

Vince felt the torsion wrench begin to rotate and applied a little more pressure. The lock turned smoothly, the door opened and he removed both tools from it. It hadn't taken him much longer to open the door than if he'd used a key.

Thirty seconds later they were standing outside the door of the target apartment.

The Yale on that door succumbed to the action of the snap gun in less than ten seconds. With a final look around the deserted landing, the two men slipped inside.

They had half a dozen small cameras fitted with fully charged long-life batteries and already programmed for the apartment's Wi-Fi network. The guest bedroom was just as Vince had described it: plain and simple with a minimum of clutter, although now some of Robert's few possessions were sitting on a chair and his rucksack was on the floor in one corner, making the place look a little untidy.

'We need to cover the bed,' Mike said, and pointed out three locations their tiny cameras could be secreted where they would be difficult, though not impossible, to spot. It was a much smaller room than the lounge, but both men were certain that when George Kenton entered the room again his mind would be on other things.

And it wouldn't matter if the cameras were detected later, as long as they had already recorded what happened in or on the double bed.

'Happy with that?' Vince asked, as Mike stood at the foot of the bed and looked around the room.

'I'd have preferred more hidden locations, but I reckon these will do. I can't see the cameras from here, and I know where they are.'

'Let's go.'

'Two minutes,' Mike said. 'I need to check I'm getting a feed from each of them.'

'We might not have two minutes,' Vince said forcefully. 'We go now.'

Both men glanced around the bedroom to make sure they had left nothing out of place. In the lounge Vince looked through the spyhole, saw nothing outside and pulled open the flat door.

The good thing with a conventional Yale is that closing the door also locks it. As he closed it, Vince heard another door open and close. From the sudden increase in traffic noise, followed almost immediately by its cessation, it was probably the main door of the building.

He didn't speak, just pointed at the staircase that led to the floor above.

Both men climbed the stairs as quickly and quietly as they could manage and stopped out of sight on the next floor. Realistically, the door could have opened and closed as somebody left the building, and if somebody had entered it wasn't necessarily Amanda Hart and the boy. But Sod's Law meant that the worst possible scenario would be the one that took place, so they stood and waited in complete silence.

They heard footsteps on the floor below, a jangle of keys and then another door opening and closing.

Mike took out his mobile and opened one of the apps.

He looked at the screen, smiled slightly and held the phone so that Vince could see it as well. They saw Amanda Hart walking into her kitchen carrying a bag of shopping, Robert a couple of paces behind her.

'Good call,' he said. 'That was a really short shopping trip. Let's get out of here.'

An hour later Vince and Mike were placing four covert surveillance cameras in the master bedroom of a spacious and comfortable apartment on the northern outskirts of Ealing. The flat was empty while they were inside it, the tenant having left by taxi about fifteen minutes before they used the Brockhage snap gun on the lock, and they expected they'd have plenty of time to complete the job.

The resident looked like a remarkably beautiful woman, at least until he took his trousers off, and was visited on a regular basis by a senior banking executive whose photograph appeared fairly frequently in the British financial press.

Chapter 29

Monday

Vauxhall Cross, London

'Ben? It's Angela. We have some more possible hits but you need to listen to them. Where are you now?'

'In a taxi near Piccadilly Circus,' Morgan replied. 'I'll be with you in a few minutes.'

The recording, the sound of two male voices, was short, not particularly informative and frustratingly incomplete. It sounded as if they had walked past the recording device mid-conversation, so perhaps it was in a hallway or something of that sort.

One man could be heard saying '—move him if he lives—' while the other speaker responded 'We've got no choice. That Michael—'

Morgan listened to the recording half a dozen times, the last two through a pair of extremely high-quality headphones, and at the end of it he just shook his head.

'That could be the kidnappers deciding to move Michaelson somewhere different if he survived whatever tortures they've been subjecting him to,' Evans said, studying the look on Morgan's face. 'And I know Michael's not the same as Michaelson, but that's where the recording stops, and he could have moved out of range of the microphone before he finished the word.'

Morgan looked unconvinced.

'You could be reading too much into this,' he said, 'or you could be right on the money. But there are other possibilities. It could be a couple of men talking about an aged relative and deciding that if he survives whatever problem he's suffering from now they're going to put him in a home or hospice. The second man could be referring to a doctor. That's a fairly obvious alternative scenario.

And I don't think that the kidnappers would refer to Michaelson by name because that would humanise their victim. I doubt if they would refer to him except in the most general terms: "Take him a glass of water" or something like that.'

'So you don't reckon this is worth following up?' Evans asked.

'I didn't say that,' Morgan replied, 'because I could be wrong and you could be right. Let's face it, that would not be a situation with which I am entirely unfamiliar.'

She smiled at him.

'I'm glad you recognise the inherent superiority of the female brain over whatever you've got stuffed inside your head,' she said.

'And I didn't say that either. I think we should identify the IP address and give it to the Essex police. We can just call it a rumour we've heard or an anonymous tip-off or something like that. Let them check the place out and decide if it's worth going in mob-handed and kicking down the door. As far as I know they've got no other leads.'

'Good decision,' Evans said, 'because that's exactly what Dame Janet – in your absence – told me to do. The Essex police already have that recording plus the IP address, along with another four snippets that also sounded interesting. And,' she added, 'GCHQ pulled out another eight fragments of conversation from the petabytes of data that might be worth further investigation. Dame Janet's leaving the decision up to you. And me, actually. These thirteen recordings – these eight plus the five I've already sent to the Essex Constabulary – are all that have risen to the top of the heap to date, but there are hundreds of other snippets they've sent because they contain one or more hits from our list of trigger words.'

'Okay. Let's play them and see what we've got.'

Just over an hour later Morgan pulled off the Bose headphones he had been using and looked across the table at Angela Evans.

'In my opinion, none of these really stand out apart from the last one, and that's only because of that one sentence, the only one we can hear clearly. And I can think of at least a couple of explanations that don't involve kidnapping a venture capitalist.'

'It is pretty unambiguous, though,' Evans responded. 'That man clearly says "we're going to kill him". Not much room for misunderstanding there, I'd have thought.'

Morgan nodded.

'None at all,' he agreed, 'but unless you know exactly who the "him" is, you're not much further forward. So the meaning is clear but we don't know what they're talking about. It's another one worth passing on, just in case we have stumbled on their lair. The other seven recordings are less interesting, and we don't want to overload the corporate brain of the Essex police force. Hopefully they'll check it, so that when the squad car goes screaming up to the door, they'll know it's the right one.'

'I don't think squad cars are likely to be involved at this stage,' Evans pointed out. 'I was talking to Andrew Nuffield this morning, and he'd just been having a tête-à-tête with the Essex chief constable through the magic of mobile telephony, and it looks like the police chopper crews will be earning a fair bit of overtime in the next few days. The eye in the sky and all that. They've got thermal imaging cameras and all sorts of other stuff, and they can do their surveillance at a distance.'

'I thought they'd already had a helicopter in the air.'

'They did, beginning on the afternoon that the kidnap took place. The problem was they had nothing definitive to look for apart from a Range Rover, and there are plenty of those in that part of the country. We now know that was a complete waste of time unless the kidnappers had for some reason decided that their second getaway car was also going to be a Range Rover, and that seems to be spectacularly unlikely. We don't know what they drove away from the cafe, but my guess would be an anonymous saloon car, a Ford or Vauxhall, something like that. But what they can do with this information is check out the buildings where these conversations have been recorded.'

She reached for her mobile as it rang.

'Evans,' she said, then listened for about half a minute.

'All copied,' she said briskly. 'With any luck we'll be there to watch.'

'And that was?'

'Dame Janet.'

'And she wants us where? And why?'

'Essex. About half a mile south of a place called Toot Hill. The Essex police have apparently taken one of our leads and run with it, and in just over an hour they'll be kicking in the door of some farmhouse where they think Michaelson could be. I don't know what else they've managed to find out, but I presume it's fairly conclusive otherwise they wouldn't be sending in whatever passes for a SWAT team out there.'

'As it's Essex, they'll probably all have fake suntans and teeth so white that they glow in the dark.'

'Not everyone in Essex looks as if they work on the set of *TOWIE*,' Evans pointed out. 'There must be some normal people there. Now we need to move. There'll be a car waiting for us on the Albert Embankment within the next five minutes.'

A sudden thought struck Morgan as he stood up.

'If they're kicking down the door in an hour,' he said, 'there's no way we're going to be able to get there in time. Not through London traffic, and certainly not at this time of day.'

'I know,' Angela replied, 'but we won't be going all the way by car.'

Chapter 30

Monday
Undisclosed location

Unsurprisingly, when John had led Michaelson out of his room that morning for another day of interrogation the executive was looking the worse for wear. The reason was obvious: denied medical treatment, the broken and grotesquely swollen little finger on his left hand would have ensured he'd have got little sleep over the previous three nights. That, combined with the uncertainty of his situation, would have been enough to turn most people into gibbering wrecks. Michaelson wasn't gibbering, but he did look a wreck.

John sat him down at the table, then left the room and came back with a mug of coffee that he put down in front of the captive.

'Drink that,' he said. 'You look as if you need it.'

Michaelson nodded and took a sip, but it was still too hot to drink.

'You know what I want,' John said, then pointed at Michaelson's damaged hand. 'If you don't play ball I won't snap another finger, not yet, but you'd be amazed how much it'll hurt if I hit the break with a hammer or just squeeze it with a pair of pliers. You got that?'

'I'll tell you whatever I can,' Michaelson said, his voice breaking. 'Just don't hurt me again.'

John consulted a printed list of questions and then started at the top, Michaelson dredging up facts from his memory and occasionally checking a specific piece of information on his laptop computer which John had placed on the table in front of him.

It didn't occur to Michaelson to wonder where the questions had come from, or why somebody had thought it necessary to print them. Or, for that matter, why John had a pile of about a dozen sheets in front of him.

Chapter 31

Monday

London

The car – a black Jaguar XJ saloon with tinted rear windows – was already waiting for them outside the building, and the moment Morgan and Evans pulled their doors closed the driver moved out into the traffic. It was immediately clear to Morgan that they were going the wrong way.

'You do know where you're going?' he asked the driver.

'Yes,' the man replied, never taking his eyes off the road as he carved through the traffic, 'and I know where you're going as well. Darkest Essex, and good luck with that, by the way. I'll be letting you out at Battersea in about ten minutes and then I've got another job to do.'

That statement made their route clear.

'So we're taking a chopper from the heliport,' Morgan said to Evans. 'I presume this has been laid on by Dame Janet and we won't be presented with a substantial bill when we land in some field in rural Essex?'

'You presume correctly. That woman seems to have a huge number of strings she can pull whenever she wants, and nobody ever bothers to ask her how she does it.'

If you fly over some cities, New York being a good example, it seems as if almost every other building has a helicopter landing pad on its roof, marked by the distinctive 'H' inside a circle, but London isn't like that. There are very few landing sites within the city and overflying by helicopters is very strictly controlled. There are exceptions, of course, such as police helicopters, air ambulances and other types of emergency aircraft.

There's only one licensed heliport in London, situated on the south bank of the Thames between Wandsworth Bridge and the Battersea Railway Bridge, on the H4 helicopter route, which starts at Barnes and then follows the river east to the Isle of Dogs. This route is mandatory and any shortcuts are prohibited. The idea is that helicopters follow the route of the River Thames, on the reasonable grounds that if they fall out of the sky – something that helicopters are far more prone to do than fixed-wing aircraft – the main casualties will be whatever enterprising fish have ventured into the dark and muddy waters of the river, rather than assorted citizens of London.

A black Bell 206B JetRanger with no markings apart from its British registration was already on the T-shaped jetty that juts out into the Thames. The helicopter was parked precisely on the 'H' symbol, which itself is more or less the midpoint of what is almost certainly the shortest runway in the world: runway 02/20 at the Heliport is a mere 125 feet in length.

'You the people from the Home Office?' a staff member asked as they walked into the NetJets London Heliport building, bolted like an afterthought onto the end of the Crowne Plaza London Battersea hotel.

From the start of her tenure as Director of C-TAC, Dame Janet Marcham-Coutts had insisted that in any dealings with the general public and non-governmental organisations the unit would be attached nominally to the Home Office, which most people perceived as rather dull, rather than the Secret Intelligence Service at Vauxhall Cross, which she thought might generate unnecessary speculation about C-TAC's function and remit.

Morgan simply nodded in response, and the man ushered them through the building and straight out onto the tarmac helicopter parking area.

'That's your pilot,' he said, pointing.

The man standing at the edge of the runway looked to be no more than eighteen in Morgan's eyes, an impression that he was experiencing increasingly frequently, especially when he looked at police officers. He had four gold bars on the epaulettes of his short-sleeved white shirt, black trousers and a black tie.

As Morgan and Evans approached, the man briskly closed the distance between them, his right hand extended.

'Mr Morgan and Miss Evans, is it? I'm taking you to Essex, I gather. My name's Roger Wilson. Just Roger is fine.'

They shook hands and Wilson led them to the aircraft and opened both the front and rear doors on the left-hand side.

'One of you can ride in the front if you want,' he said.

'In you get, Angela,' Morgan said. 'I'll be fine in the back.'

She glanced at him as if suspicious of his motive, then smiled.

'If we come back the same way, we'll swap,' she suggested.

A couple of ground crew from the heliport walked over to assist them with climbing aboard and getting strapped in.

Wilson himself made sure their seat belts were done up and their headphones on, then climbed into the right-hand side of the helicopter.

'Can you hear me?' he asked and Morgan and Evans both confirmed they could. 'As you can see this is a full dual-control aircraft, so please, Miss Evans, don't touch anything while we're in the air. Now, I'll be off intercom while I get clearance to start.' About twenty seconds later he came back online. 'Okay, we're good to go.'

Morgan had never flown in a JetRanger before and watched with interest as Wilson began the start sequence.

'Can you talk me through it, Roger?' he asked. 'I've flown a Gazelle before with an instructor but never one of these.'

Wilson glanced round at Morgan and smiled.

'No problem. Nice aircraft, the Gazelle. One of the fastest choppers ever built, too. It does nearly two hundred miles an hour. Okay, Bell 206 JetRanger start-up.'

He reached down to the bottom right of the instrument panel and pointed at a switch protected by a red plastic gate.

'That's the master fuel switch, and it's always a good idea to make sure that's switched on, otherwise things have a tendency to go very, very quiet at a very, very awkward moment.' He pointed below the collective. 'That's the hydraulics and that switch needs to be up as well. Then we go to the roof console to make sure that all the fuses are in and no circuits have been tripped.' He moved his left hand to the front of the console and pressed the second switch on the right-hand side. 'That's the battery on.'

He pointed at the gauges on the control panel in front of him.

'All these should be reading zero before engine start and we're now ready to do that. Finally what we have to do is adjust the throttle on the collective.' He grasped the throttle with his left hand, rotated it fully clockwise, then fully anticlockwise, and pressed the red détente button and turned it the final few degrees. 'The détente is the idle position, but you never start the engine in that position because it will allow fuel to enter the combustion chamber too early and that could start a fire. Now we're ready to go.'

Still holding the throttle on the collective with his left hand, Wilson pointed at a black button next to the détente. 'That's the start button,' he said, pressed it and held it down.

Immediately they could hear the turbine beginning to spool up, the whine getting louder with every passing second.

'We watch the gauges to make sure that the engine oil pressure is starting to climb, and at the same time check the N1 gas pressure gauge. When it reaches fifteen per cent we can add fuel to the engine.' As he said that, Wilson turned the throttle slightly so that it moved past the shutdown position and to the idle stop, the détente button clicking into place. 'Now it's just a matter of monitoring the gauges to make sure the temperatures and pressures are within limits. Once the N1 gauge reaches fifty-eight per cent we can release the starter button and the engine start will become self-sustaining.'

The rotor blades – only two on the JetRanger – were already turning, and as the turbine noise grew to a wail the rotor disk became a blur.

'Not quite like starting a Ford Fiesta, is it?' Evans commented to no one in particular.

'It seems complicated but you very quickly get used to it. I'll just set up our squawk – that's the secondary surveillance radar response that identifies us to ATC, the air traffic controllers – and get take-off clearance, and then we're good to go.'

A few moments later, Wilson opened the throttle, eased up on the collective and the JetRanger lifted smoothly into the air. He turned the aircraft through ninety degrees so it was pointing directly away from the heliport and aiming at the opposite side of the river, held it there for a couple of seconds, glanced both ways, and then turned back to follow the Thames downstream, climbing quickly.

'A bit like the Green Cross code?' Morgan asked.

Wilson laughed.

'I know we've had clearance from ATC, but there's absolutely no substitute for using the mark one human eyeball to take a look both ways before we commit ourselves. The airspace around London is about the busiest in the world, and although air traffic down here on the river is both limited and controlled, I always make sure that the only aircraft that's heading for the particular bit of sky right in front of me is the one I'm sitting in.'

'Check once, check twice, check thrice,' Evans said. 'That mantra works for me.'

The JetRanger climbed to its cruising altitude – Wilson explained that he had been allocated 1,000 feet by ATC – and followed the river to the north-east.

'We're on route H4,' Wilson explained, 'and we have to follow the Thames unless ATC gives us different instructions for traffic separation or something of that sort. I have to report passing Chelsea Bridge and then Vauxhall Bridge, and finally at the Isle of Dogs, but after that we clear the route and then we can go more or less straight up to Toot Hill.'

'How far is it?' Evans asked. 'Twenty miles or so?'

'The straight-line distance is about sixteen or seventeen miles,' Roger replied. 'This bird cruises at a little over a hundred, so once we leave the route it should only take me about ten or twelve minutes to get you on the ground, unless finding a landing spot ends up being a bit trickier than I expect.'

Chapter 32

Monday
City of London

James McEwan did nothing immediately with the list that Jeremy Somerville had produced for him. He'd been surprised at some of the names on it, though a couple of them were there for reasons that he already knew about, or at least he suspected he knew about. The question really was what action he should take now he had the information.

What he couldn't do was ring them up to talk about it, because he knew without the slightest shadow of a doubt that they would simply clam up and deny all knowledge. And that would be that.

He needed to get them all to a secure location, to a place where they could relax and where hopefully their tongues might be loosened.

In the end, he decided there was only one thing he could do. It needed to be short notice, it needed to be for a very brief period, and he needed to get as many of them as possible to that location without them knowing that other people were also attending. Until it was too late and they were all in the same room.

It wasn't ideal, but his final solution was to call each of the men personally and tell them that he had a private and sensitive professional problem and he needed their help and advice. An appeal for help, in his experience, normally generated a positive response, because it made the person feel superior. They were being asked by one of their peers for the benefit of their wisdom and experience, which very clearly meant that they were more knowledgeable and reinforced their egos. Not that the egos of most people involved in any capacity in the City of London needed much reinforcing.

So, McEwan would finish, could they possibly amend their diaries so that they were able to meet him at his country home the very next evening for a very short private meeting? And if they wanted to stay for dinner, they would be more than welcome. There were a few decent restaurants in Chislehurst a short taxi ride away from his house, and they would be his guests.

By the middle of the afternoon, McEwan was feeling somewhat drained from the seemingly endless talking he had been doing on his mobile, but he had achieved what he had set out to do. The following evening, all the men on his list bar three who would be out of London would be arriving at his home just outside Chislehurst between seven and seven thirty, and all of them believed they would be speaking privately with him.

Once they were through his front door, he would explain his subterfuge to each of them in turn, and reveal that other bankers would also be attending because he had some financially critical information to share with them as a group.

Which was, if you looked at the situation from a particular point of view, a reasonably accurate description.

Chapter 33

Monday
Essex

The JetRanger touched down with the gentlest of bumps just eleven minutes after Wilson had turned the aircraft north-east about a mile beyond the Isle of Dogs. He hadn't even had to search for a landing ground, because as the helicopter approached the coordinates south of Toot Hill, he saw an almost level field right in front of him, at one end of which was a collection of police vehicles.

'A bunch of bad news and breathalysers right there,' Wilson said as he started the engine shutdown procedure. 'Hopefully they're on your side, but if it all turns to rat-shit and you need to make a quick getaway, I'll be right here.'

'I hope they're on our side too,' Angela Evans said, 'but thanks for the offer.'

She and Morgan unclipped their seat belts and climbed down from the aircraft as soon as the rotors had stopped turning and the engine had shut down.

The closest police vehicles – cars and vans – were about two hundred yards away, parked in a straggly line along the edge of the lane that bordered the field where the JetRanger had landed, and a couple of men, both clad in normal uniform and peaked caps rather than the tactical clothing most of the other officers were wearing, approached them.

'And who are you two, exactly?' the leading police officer asked. He was a tall and excessively thin man, with sharp features and dark, almost black, eyes. He was a superintendent and he looked irritated, perhaps with life in general, but certainly with them in particular.

'My name is Ben Morgan and this is Angela Evans. We've come from the Home Office and we're here as observers. You should have been told to expect us. And who are you, exactly?' he finished, turning the man's question around.

'Superintendent Crenshaw. I'm the ground commander for this operation. That means you do what I tell you, and what I'm telling you to do is keep well out of my way and out of the way of my men as they do their jobs.' He punctuated his remarks with a jabbing forefinger.

'And good afternoon to you too, Superintendent,' Evans snapped. 'We haven't come here to get shot at, so you needn't worry about us getting too close. And you can lose the attitude unless you want me to have a quick chat with your chief constable.'

Crenshaw seemed a little taken aback by the response and looked slightly uncertainly at Morgan, who grinned at him.

'Miss Evans sometimes functions as my personal attack dog,' he said, 'and if you annoy her you'll very quickly discover that her bite is very much worse than her bark. So what's the situation here? What's your evidence and what do you know about the occupants and the target property?'

Superintendent Crenshaw switched his gaze back to Angela, who responded with a dazzling smile.

'Well,' he said, almost hesitantly, 'we had a tip-off, an anonymous call, from somebody who'd seen the news about the kidnapping of this man Michaelson, and claimed he'd seen two men dragging a third person into the farmhouse that's the other side of those trees. He said he saw it as he drove down the lane over there.' He gestured to the nearer side of the field they were standing in. 'We had the chopper up to do a recce but told the pilot to keep his distance and use the on-board sensors to check the place out. We got images of two men who broadly fitted the descriptions given by the people at the scene of the kidnapping. And the building is just a small farmhouse, typical of this part of Essex. Is there anything else you need to know?'

Morgan glanced at Angela, who shook her head.

'Right. I'll go and get things started,' Crenshaw stated, then turned away towards the waiting police officers, his unidentified companion – a chief inspector – a couple of paces behind him.

'So it wasn't one of our intercepts that kicked this into gear,' Evans said, 'and it doesn't sound that likely to me. I mean, if this anonymous witness genuinely did see some bloke being dragged into a farmhouse, why didn't he report it straight away, instead of waiting until the TV news was carrying the story? And we know there were at least four people involved in the kidnapping, so how come the cameras on the chopper have only managed to detect two men?'

'So you think this is a mistake?' Morgan asked. 'It's not where Michaelson is being held?'

'Yes, I do think it's a mistake, and Michaelson could well be hundreds of miles away from here. Mind you, it's not our job to stop the Essex police making complete idiots of themselves, so what happens next might prove to be quite entertaining. Or not.'

For the next few minutes they watched the activity as the police officers got kitted up and checked their equipment, ready to make a forced entry into the target premises. There were about forty officers in all, and about half of them were clad entirely in black, wearing heavy utility belts and armed with handguns in leg holsters.

'I presume the guys in the black tactical outfits and bristling with weapons loaded for bear, as the Americans say, are members of the Essex police SWAT team,' Angela said, watching them.

'Oddly enough,' Morgan replied, 'they're not. Obviously somebody in Essex decided that calling them a SWAT team was far too simple or perhaps far too American. So what you're actually looking at are members of the Essex police FSU, the Force Support Unit, a name that conveys absolutely nothing about what they do. They could be the people who make the tea or service the cars.'

Evans's mobile phone began ringing and she immediately answered the call.

But before she could speak, Morgan's mobile also sounded. He moved a few paces away from her so as not to disturb her while she was talking.

'Morgan,' he said.

And then he just listened for about two minutes to what Dave North, then manning the C-TAC cell at Vauxhall Cross, had to tell him.

'Are you sure?' he asked when North finished speaking.

'In this business, Ben,' the former SAS officer replied, 'there's almost never such a thing as certainty, but GCHQ flagged it up, I've listened to it and so have a couple of the desk officers here, and we reckon it's about ninety per cent certain that the app has picked up a conversation between two of the kidnappers, one of them – from the sound of it – being the man in charge. And if it isn't the kidnappers, there's still some pretty nasty stuff going on in that house that needs to be stopped. We've already pinpointed the location from the IP address.'

'Somewhere in Essex, like Toot Hill, for example,' Morgan suggested.

'Where? Never mind, it's not in Essex. The site is about halfway between Bedford and Cambridge, not too far from a place called Gamlingay. The whole area is rural with lots of scattered farms and cottages. Where are you now? And can you get to the location quickly? We've already scrambled the Cambridge plods and they should be en route.'

'We came by chopper and it's still here, so we can get there just as quickly as a convoy of police cars from Cambridge.'

'Don't just stand there talking to me, then,' North said. 'Get your arse into gear and get a move on. I'll text you the coordinates.'

Morgan ended the call and opened his mouth to speak to Evans, but she was already jogging across the field towards the assembled police officers.

'Crenshaw!' she called out. And again: 'Crenshaw!'

The superintendent turned round, apparently reluctantly, as she drew near, clearly wondering what on earth was going on.

Morgan ran after her and arrived as she was telling Crenshaw what had happened.

'This is the wrong location, Superintendent,' she said crisply. 'We've just had confirmation that the kidnappers have been located near Cambridge, so whatever your anonymous witness has told you about this farm is almost certainly either a lie or he's misinterpreted what he saw.'

Crenshaw looked neither pleased nor convinced.

'How certain are you about this?' he asked.

'Better than ninety per cent,' Evans replied. 'We're going up there right now in the helicopter. My advice is to tell your men to pack up their toys and go back to where you came from. If you still think that the farmhouse is worth a visit, then just send a couple of uniformed bobbies to knock on the door.'

'You have your orders, Miss – er – Evans,' Crenshaw said, 'just as I have mine. My superiors gave me the most explicit orders to follow, and I cannot abandon my tasking just on the say-so of some third party.'

'That's up to you. But if I was in your shoes, at the very least I'd give my direct superior a bell and tell him what I've just told you and get him to confirm that he still wants the raid to go ahead. But it's your choice and nothing to do with us. We're gone.'

And with that Evans turned round, and she and Morgan began walking quickly across the rutted ground of the field towards the JetRanger.

'Do you think he'll make the call?' Morgan asked.

'I have no idea. It's not my problem, and frankly I don't care one way or the other, but I would feel a bit pissed off if his shock troops crashed their way inside that farmhouse and gave some innocent old biddy sitting by the fire a heart attack. That really would irritate me, and if that happens I will certainly do something about it.'

'I assume the natives were hostile,' Roger Wilson said, climbing out of his seat as they approached the helicopter. 'Back to London?'

'No,' Angela said. 'What's your fuel state? How much petrol have you got?'

Wilson gave a half-smile and nodded.

'I'm assuming you know that jet engines don't actually run on petrol,' he replied, 'but I was tanks-full at the heliport when you arrived, and that gives me a total range of roughly 370 nautical miles or 430 statute miles, so from here I could probably get you as far north as Edinburgh, if that's where you want to go.'

'No, thanks. We want to go to a place near Cambridge – I'll give you the coordinates and the name of the nearest village on the way. When we get there it'll be the same deal. A field full of police and a bunch of people in a nearby house who don't know that their front door is about to be kicked in by cops toting pistols and assault rifles.'

'On the other hand,' Morgan pointed out, 'at least this time we're reasonably sure that the people inside the house are definitely not on the side of the angels, and they probably need their door kicking in just for that reason.'

Chapter 34

Monday
Undisclosed location

'I think we've got as much out of him as we're going to,' John said, closing the door and turning to face the man sitting behind the desk. 'In fact, I reckon he was starting to make stuff up, just to keep us thinking that he had more to give. I had to provide another bit of persuasion to make him stop doing that and just give us the facts. To only give me the information you need.'

Mr King nodded slowly. He'd been watching the progress of Michaelson's questioning through the camera system on the TV in front of him. He was far more used to watching interrogations than the man who called himself John, though he had never taken part in one personally. He was fastidious in most things and never enjoyed witnessing another person's pain and suffering, though he accepted the need for it – it was just a part of the business he was involved in. He preferred to remain in the background, watching what happened and directing operations from a distance, exactly as he was doing at that moment. Throughout his career, he had always been able to find and employ people who had a talent for interrogation and torture, and there had never been a shortage of that kind of individual among the Chinese community in Hong Kong.

He hadn't necessarily expected to find people with the same mindset in Great Britain. John had proved to be the most capable, ready and prepared to carry out his instructions, but he always needed specific direction. He had no natural talent or ability for harsh interrogation, probably because he was just a career criminal, readily able to draw blood and break bones but only in the course of a violent robbery or something similar. The idea of torturing somebody for information had very probably never crossed his mind until he had accepted his present employment with Mr King.

'Lock Michaelson in his room,' Mr King ordered, his English fluent and colloquial, his native Chinese accent detectable only on certain words. English being one of Hong Kong's official languages, he had been speaking it since he was a teenager. 'Tell him that you will question him again later this afternoon. Also tell him that our patience has been exhausted. For every wrong or incomplete answer that he gives you, you will break another one of his bones. But if he supplies the information, we will provide medical treatment for his broken fingers and release him otherwise unharmed.'

John looked uncertain at this suggestion.

'But we can't really just let him go, can we?' he asked. 'I mean, I know he hasn't seen you, but he has seen the four of us and he could probably pick us out in a line-up.'

Mr King looked at him as if he was mad.

'Of course we're not going to let him go,' he snapped. 'Today is the last day of Nicholas Michaelson's life. Once you've finished with him this afternoon, you are to take him out into the field behind the farmhouse and kill him. I don't care how you do it, or which one of you carries out the killing, but it is to be videoed so that I can inspect it later. I will be leaving here later this afternoon, after the questioning has been completed.'

John looked almost shocked at what he had just heard.

'I didn't sign up for killing him,' he said.

Mr King smiled, but there was not a trace of humour in his expression.

'I don't care what you signed up for,' he replied. 'You may be the leader of this group but that doesn't mean you can't be replaced. Jack or Karl, I'm sure, would be more than happy to take your place, and in my experience getting rid of two bodies is not that much more difficult than getting rid of one.'

John didn't immediately respond to the obvious threat, just stood in front of the desk and clenched his fists. As he stared at Mr King, he noticed for the first time that the man's right hand was holding a small black automatic pistol, and that he was staring straight down the muzzle. And he knew the man well enough to realise that the gun would be loaded and that he would have no hesitation whatsoever in pulling the trigger.

'Nobody messes with me, John,' Mr King said, his tone cold and bleak. 'This venture will turn you into a millionaire in eighteen months, virtually risk-free, if you do exactly what I tell you. If you want out, the only retirement package I can offer you measures nine millimetres in diameter and comes courtesy of this Walther pistol. And don't think that the other three men outside this room will help you. If you're dead, their share of the take goes up, and for them that's more important than anything else.'

'Okay, okay,' John said. 'I'll make sure it gets done.'

'I don't want the body left in the field,' Mr King said. 'There are plenty of woods around here where you can bury him. If you want to do a bit less work, there are lakes in the area too, according to Google Maps, but if you dump him in the water you must ensure that the body is weighted down, so you'll need to wrap it in chains and use concrete blocks or something as well.'

He paused for a few seconds before continuing.

'Neither of those are my preferred method because some dogs are very good at smelling out buried bodies, and even the most heavily weighted corpse does sometimes work its way free of the chains and bob up to the surface. I do not want Michaelson's body to be found, ideally for ever, but certainly for at least a year.'

'How would you prefer us to dispose of him?'

Mr King smiled again.

'This is a predominantly agricultural area,' he said, 'so I'm sure there must be a pig farm somewhere nearby.'

Chapter 35

Monday
Near Gamlingay, Cambridgeshire

Ben Morgan, again sitting in the rear seat of the Bell JetRanger, experienced a distinct sense of déjà vu as they flew over the agricultural patchwork, heading towards Gamlingay.

The landscape of southern Cambridgeshire looked virtually identical to the area around Toot Hill: oddly shaped small fields, different colours indicating different crops being grown, tracks suitable only for tractors to negotiate, narrow tarmac lanes, and a scattering of cottages, farmhouses and agricultural buildings of various sizes.

He had used the mapping app on his mobile to identify the location of the target house, then switched to Google Earth and zoomed using the street view option to give him a photographic image of what they were looking for. Helicopters were noisy and the racket they made unmistakeable, and it was important that they avoid flying over the target farmhouse or landing so close that people inside would hear the aircraft. In that they were helped by the Bell's performance.

Wilson confirmed that the JetRanger had a service ceiling of 13,500 feet, and if they were flying above 8,000 feet the noise would be much less audible on the ground. And although they were flying VFR or Visual Flight Rules – meaning that the pilot was responsible for his own navigation and avoidance from any other aircraft – Wilson decided that he would tell somebody where they were and where they were going.

'I'll be off intercom for a few seconds,' he said, 'because if we're going up to nine or ten thousand feet we should be in solid radar cover most of the way. Farnborough is the controlling authority for the LARS – the Lower Airspace Radar Service – in this area, so I'll give them a bell.'

Wilson selected 132.800 on the VHF radio, passed the Farnborough LARS controller their flight details, confirmed the Bell was squawking the conspicuity code – 7000 – on its SSR transponder, and asked for information on any known traffic in their vicinity.

It wasn't a long flight and a few minutes later they started to descend. Wilson pointed the nose of the helicopter below the horizon and eased off the power. They were still about five miles from the target and Morgan had identified a couple of possible landing sites to the east of the farm that were far enough away for the aircraft noise to be inaudible to anybody in the building.

Just as at Toot Hill, as Wilson dropped the Bell to about two thousand feet, they saw a collection of police vehicles parked inside one of the fields beside a lane, figures wearing dark, combat-type clothing milling around them.

As soon as they'd landed Morgan and Angela Evans walked the hundred yards or so across the field to the police officers, looking for the man in charge, and this time their reception was rather different.

The senior police officer was another superintendent, a broad and solid man about six feet tall with short grey hair.

'You must be the people from the Home Office,' he said, shaking their hands. 'My name's Waterson, John Waterson, and I'm in charge of this tea party.'

'This is Angela Evans,' Morgan said, 'and I'm Ben Morgan.'

'Good. I gather from the people at Cambridge who claim to know about these things that the intercept came from you. I don't need to know how the Home Office managed to listen to a conversation taking place in a farmhouse in Cambridgeshire, but I would like to know how sure you are that Michaelson is being held prisoner in that particular building.'

'We can't be completely certain without actually seeing him but we are ninety per cent sure that he's in there,' Morgan said, and took out his mobile phone to access the data he had been sent. 'The data collection method is classified but we have a recording of two men talking, one of whom seems to be in charge. One man apparently enters a room and says, "You heard?" and then "What do you want me to do?" The boss, for want of a better term, replies, "You shouldn't even have to ask. Go back in there and hurt him. Break one of his bones. Nothing incapacitating, just a finger or perhaps two of them." About a minute later, the recording picks up a scream from elsewhere on the property.'

'As Ben said,' Evans added, 'we can't be certain that they were discussing Nicholas Michaelson, but we believe he was kidnapped to be interrogated, to obtain financially critical information. And if he was reluctant to talk, then applying physical persuasion – torturing him – is what we would expect to happen. But whoever is in that house,' she finished, 'definitely needs rescuing, and quickly.'

'The other thing that's relevant,' Morgan added, 'is that the intercept I've just described was recorded on Friday, but because of the volume of data it was only identified this afternoon. We hope that Michaelson is still alive, but it's critical that we get inside that building as soon as possible. What orders were you given?'

Waterson nodded.

'I appreciate the urgency. I was told the kidnap victim was in that farmhouse and we were to extract him. Exactly how we do that will depend upon what we see when we reach the building, but in broad terms I'll be ordering a stealthy approach so that we remain out of sight of the occupants, and then a simultaneous forced entry using our big red keys – the hand-held rams – if the doors are locked.'

'I presume that these men are a part of your SWAT team?' Angela asked.

'Yes, and at the same time no. What we have here are twenty members of our APU, the Armed Policing Unit, which is our equivalent of a SWAT team, plus another ten unarmed officers. I understand the suspects are likely to be armed.'

Morgan nodded.

'During the kidnapping, one of them was carrying a whippet and he fired both buckshot and solid shot. We have to assume that the other members of the gang – we believe there are four of them – will be armed as well. Ideally, we'd like them alive at the end of this, so we would rather you used your tasers than your Glocks or whatever pistols you carry, but the safety of your men's lives, and of course Michaelson's safety, is paramount.'

'Understood,' Waterson said. 'Right, we'll get going. I presume you'll both want to come along as observers, but please don't get too close because you have no body armour and I don't want you to be a distraction to my men. Or casualties,' he added.

The lanes in this part of Cambridgeshire were bordered by hedges and fences and there were copses of trees that provided cover as they advanced towards the building. They stopped in one of the wooded areas that provided an uninterrupted view of the farmhouse. The street view facility on Google Earth had offered a clear picture of the farmhouse from the lane that ran beside it, and from their vantage point they could see the rear of the building. Waterson checked it through a pair of compact binoculars, then briefed his men.

'The windows are quite small,' he said, 'so unless one of the kidnappers is standing up and looking out they probably won't see us. It looks like there are only two doors, the one we can see from here, which leads into the yard at the rear, and the front door shown on the Google Earth picture, so we'll need two big red keys and two groups for the assault.

'It's quite a small house and an undetected approach is vital. I don't want you falling over each other when you get inside, so the breaching attack will be carried out by two teams of five APU officers each, one on each door. The moment the doors are open I want the remainder of the APU to get to the building as quickly as possible, but to wait outside unless the first team need assistance. At the same time, the remaining officers will close up and form a cordon around the farmhouse to make sure nobody gets out. Any questions?'

There were a couple of minor queries which Waterson dealt with quickly and competently.

'Right,' he said. 'Go.'

The two teams of heavily armed APU officers moved slowly out of the copse of trees. One group followed a thick hedge that completely concealed them from view and would take them to within about thirty yards of the farmhouse, while the other approached from the opposite direction, moving along the lane towards the front of the building.

Both teams faced the same problem, in that there was no cover at all available for the final ten yards or so of the approach from either direction. They would just have to sprint to the farmhouse doors and hope that nobody inside saw them.

Behind them, the remaining APU officers began following the same route and the unarmed officers also prepared to move out.

Morgan was reasonably familiar with police operations from his time working at Hendon, and it looked to him as if Waterson and his men were doing everything right.

The front-door team was invisible from where he was standing, but he could see the second group of five officers preparing to rush towards the back door of the farmhouse.

But as they stood up from cover and started to run towards the building, Morgan heard a sudden yell of alarm from inside the house, followed almost immediately by the noise of breaking glass and three rapid shots from a semi-automatic weapon.

The stealthy approach they had been hoping to achieve had suddenly turned very noisy indeed.

Chapter 36

Monday
Near Gamlingay, Cambridgeshire

They'd rented the farmhouse for a week, paying cash up front to avoid the owner having to bother the taxman. No references and no questions. Because it was so isolated, they hadn't seen much point in mounting watches, but Mr King had insisted that they should be aware of anything happening outside the building. So whenever one of them passed a window, they always looked outside.

The man who called himself Jack Bellow was walking into the kitchen as the first of the APU officers ran towards the door. As usual, he looked to his left, glancing through the window to the yard outside.

He did a double take that would have been comical under different circumstances, dropped the coffee mug he was carrying and yelled an alarm. He snatched his Browning Hi-Power pistol from the waistband of his jeans.

Bellow took two quick strides to his left so that his body was protected by the wall of the farmhouse and pulled back the slide of the pistol to chamber a round.

He slammed the muzzle of the weapon through the glass and took aim through the opening at the group of running men. Then he cracked off three rapid shots.

Chapter 37

Monday

Near Gamlingay, Cambridgeshire

Mr King had spent most of his life in and around Hong Kong and he'd committed his first serious crime – using a cosh to knock down and rob a European businessman – at the age of eleven. By the time he was fourteen he was a member of a gang working the waterfront in Kowloon. Six years later he was that same gang's planner and coordinator, the man who made the decisions about how, when and why they should select a particular target. Five years after that he was the de facto head of the organisation. He was used to thinking on his feet, to changing his focus in a fluid situation, and he never panicked.

When he heard the first shout of alarm, followed by breaking glass and shots – deafeningly loud shots – being fired from inside the farmhouse, he reacted immediately. He yanked the lead out of the external hard drive, picked up the unit and put that and his pistol in a pocket. He put on sunglasses to hide the shape of his eyes and ran out of the room and straight to the side door, the third exit from the farmhouse, visible neither on Google Earth nor from the direction he guessed the police had approached the building.

Outside, he was confronted by an encircling line of heavily armed police officers who instantly bellowed at him to stop and aimed their assault rifles directly at him.

But Mr King knew a lot about the British police force, because it was always prudent to learn as much about your enemy as possible, and he was certain that although they were pointing their weapons at him, the one thing they wouldn't do was open fire. That was why he appeared to be unarmed, with his Walther in his pocket instead of in his hand. Carrying the pistol, there was probably an even chance that they would shoot him.

Although the police officers had virtually surrounded the farmhouse, the Jaguar was between him and them. The car was pointing towards the road outside the property, it had keyless ignition, and the fob was in his pocket. As he ran the few feet to the vehicle the doors automatically unlocked. He wrenched open the driver's door, jumped into the seat, put his feet on the brake and accelerator and simultaneously pressed the start button.

The engine roared into life. Mr King engaged drive and floored the accelerator. The Jaguar fishtailed out of the farmhouse yard, police officers dodging to both sides as he accelerated away. He swung the wheel as he reached the lane outside and simply carried on accelerating, clipping his seat belt into place as he did so.

The Jaguar's central locking engaged and Mr King took his hand off the steering wheel and selected the navigation option on the dashboard screen. He wasn't familiar with the area except in the most general terms, but he knew that one of the country's fastest roads lay only a few miles to the west.

So that was where he headed.

If he could make it to the A1 before the police intercepted him, he could blend in with the London-bound traffic. He even had a set of cloned plates in the boot of the Jaguar that he could use to cover the car's genuine registration number, in case one of the police at the house had made a note of it.

And the Jaguar XF was such a popular car that there was no possible way the police could stop every such vehicle on the busy A1.

Mr King had no doubt that one way or the other he would manage to slip away.

Chapter 38

Monday
Near Gamlingay, Cambridgeshire

As the shots sounded across the quiet countryside, one of the police officers in the team that was running for the back door stopped abruptly and then fell backwards to the ground.

But the other four continued, racing across the remaining part of the yard and crashing to a stop beside the door. One of them had a steel battering ram in his hands and drove it into the wooden door just above the lock. The door shuddered but didn't give. He repeated the action with even greater force a second and a third time, and the door burst open, slamming back against the inside wall of the farmhouse.

Immediately, his three companions ran past him and into the house, yelling orders to anybody inside. The officer dropped the ram, grabbed his assault rifle on its tactical sling and followed them through the open doorway, less than a second behind.

The farmhouse echoed to the sound of bellowing voices as both teams got inside at almost the same moment. In the confusion of noise, Morgan could hear the officers shouting the standard phrases: 'Armed police', 'Stand still' and 'Stay where you are'.

—

As the steel ram slammed into the kitchen door for the second time, Bellow strode across the room. He stopped by the heavy oblong oak table, stuck the Browning back in his waistband and used both hands to tilt the table over onto its side for cover.

John appeared in the doorway, a CZ-75 pistol in his hand.

'Armed fucking police,' Bellow shouted, his comment superfluous as the door was smashed open by the third blow from the ram and four black-clad police officers, each aiming a Heckler & Koch G36 assault rifle, burst in through the open doorway in a kind of starburst pattern, each heading in a different direction, spreading out.

John swung his pistol to point at one of the police officers and squeezed the trigger. The CZ-75 bucked in his hand.

Two of the officers fired two shots each – the classic double tap – from their assault rifles and John fell backwards onto the floor, the pistol falling from his lifeless hand.

Bellow was slower to react, which saved his life. As he turned to face the open door he reached for his pistol but then stopped, his hand still six inches away from the weapon. He was facing four armed police officers and looking straight down the barrels of their assault rifles. He realised in that instant that if he drew his weapon he would be committing suicide – at that range none of them could possibly miss him. John's dead body was a mute testament to that fact.

The police officers were yelling at him to lie down on the floor. Bellow froze. Cautiously and slowly he raised both hands above his head. Then he turned round, equally slowly, so that the pistol in his waistband was clearly visible. Moments later, his pistol had been taken and he was flat on his face on the flagstone floor of the kitchen, his wrists handcuffed behind his back while one of the officers read him the standard caution.

—

At almost the same moment, on the other side of the farmhouse, Karl snapped his whippet closed as the front door crashed open and immediately pulled the trigger for the left-hand barrel. A spreading cloud of buckshot tore across the confined space and ripped into the group of police officers.

Two of them opened up with their assault rifles and Karl felt twin punches to his chest as the bullets hit home. But he still pulled the second trigger of the shotgun. If he was going down, he was determined to take them with him. But he was already falling backwards and the massive recoil from the whippet had forced his right arm upwards, so the contents of the weapon's second chamber ploughed harmlessly into the wooden ceiling.

Ten feet away, the fourth member of the kidnap gang let loose a fusillade of shots from his pistol, two of which knocked a pair of officers off their feet as three of them returned fire.

One of the bullets tore through his right shoulder, and that was the end of his resistance as his pistol clattered to the floor.

—

Locked in his bedroom, Michaelson had been nursing his injured hand when he heard the racket, the shouting and the shots. He dropped down to the floor and crawled into the shower room. Seconds after he reached it, two stray bullets slammed through the thin internal walls of the room at about chest height.

He squealed in terror and lay flat with his arms cradling his head. The rational part of his brain knew this wouldn't help if any of the bullets reached him, but there was nothing else he could do.

—

Evans, Morgan and Waterson heard the shouts and yells and the fusillade of shots from the farmhouse, and moments later other shouts from the same direction, followed almost immediately by the sound of a car engine running at high revolutions. Then a dark saloon powered away from the house and up the lane.

'Oh fuck,' Waterson said.

The problem was obvious. The police had surrounded and entered an isolated building to rescue a kidnap victim. They hadn't been anticipating a car chase and they had no pursuit vehicles immediately available. There were police cars parked in the field, but all the drivers were in or near the target property.

Morgan sized up the situation in an instant.

'Angela,' he instructed, 'stay here and talk to Michaelson when they get him out. I'll take the chopper and try and follow that car from the air.'

Angela Evans was used to reacting quickly and effectively to a changing situation.

'No problem,' she replied briskly. 'Be careful.'

Morgan was already jogging away as she spoke.

By that time, the second half of the APU group had reached the farmhouse. Two of them crouched beside the fallen officer and quickly dragged him away from the building and behind the stout stone wall that formed the perimeter of the yard. It was impossible to tell whether the man was alive or dead, but the mere fact they had moved him suggested he was probably still breathing. Angela certainly hoped so.

Waterson used his mobile to summon the two ambulances and the medevac chopper he had placed on standby. Then he used his radio to tell the leader of the unarmed officers to get one of his medics – an officer with medical training – to check the downed man and if possible get him away from the scene.

'He's still alive,' he said to Angela. 'That much I do know from the radio chatter, but I have no idea what state he's in.'

They watched from the safety of the trees as two of the men crouched beside the fallen policeman. Moments later, they picked him up by his shoulders and feet and began carrying him away from the farmhouse.

'That means he's basically OK,' Waterson said. 'If he was badly injured they'd have left him where he was.'

'Let's hope his body armour did the job,' Angela murmured.

Chapter 39

Monday
South-west Cambridgeshire

The other person who was clearly used to reacting quickly was Roger Wilson, because before Morgan had covered even half the distance back to the JetRanger he could already hear the escalating whine of the Allison 250 turboshaft engine spooling up. The rotors were turning when he reached the helicopter. He wrenched open the left-hand front passenger door and clambered inside, secured the seat belt and put on the headphones.

Instantly, the noise level dropped by what seemed like a hundred decibels and he could clearly hear Wilson when he spoke.

'From the racket I've just heard,' the pilot said, 'I assume that the faeces have impacted the air conditioning with some force.'

'You could say that,' Morgan agreed. 'Quite a lot of shit, a very large fan and a very high-speed impact. What we never expected was that somebody from the farmhouse would simply get in their car and drive away. Sod's Law says it was one of the kidnappers and maybe this man Michaelson we were supposed to rescue.'

Wilson increased the throttle opening, simultaneously lifted the collective lever and the JetRanger rose smoothly into the air.

'So, in the absence of a police helicopter, we become their eye in the sky?'

'Exactly,' Morgan replied. 'The target vehicle is I think a Jaguar saloon, but maybe a beamer or a Mercedes, dark in colour.'

The JetRanger accelerated towards and then over the farmhouse, both men looking down through the Perspex nose panels to try and spot the fleeing car.

'All those cars are quick,' Wilson said. 'In fact, in terms of straight-line speed they're probably faster than this helicopter because our top speed is just under 140 miles an hour and they can probably do at least 150. But that makes no difference, because up here there are no bends in the road, or roundabouts, or traffic lights or anything else, and we can fly in a straight line, so we will catch them. What I'm not sure about is what we do then.'

'I'm on it already,' Morgan said.

He took out his mobile phone, dialled 999, then slid the mobile under the headphone covering his right ear. It wasn't ideal, because the noise of the helicopter was still extremely intrusive, but it was the best he could do, and at least he could hear what the female operator on the ground was saying to him.

'Emergency. Which service do you require?'

'Police.'

'Stand by, caller.'

There was a brief silence and then Morgan heard a male voice.

'Police.'

'Please listen carefully,' Morgan said. 'Cambridge police are carrying out a hostage rescue operation near Gamlingay. The officer in charge is Superintendent John Waterson. One of the suspects has escaped from the property in a dark coloured saloon car and I'm following him in a helicopter. We need ground units to stop the car and apprehend the suspect. I can provide the car's location from the air.'

There was a short pause before the man replied.

'Can I assume this is not some kind of joke?' he asked.

'You can. Check with Cambridge and they'll confirm what's happening but do it now. We need to get this car stopped ASAP.'

'Very well, caller, stay on the line. And who are you?'

'My name is Ben Morgan, and I'm an observer from the Home Office.'

The line appeared to go dead, which Morgan guessed was the operator switching to another circuit to contact the Cambridge police.

'There he is,' Wilson said, 'right in front of us.'

Still holding the mobile phone to his ear, Morgan looked down and ahead. About two hundred yards in front of them, a distance that was rapidly lessening, he could see a black saloon car, obviously travelling at speed.

The driver had already got clear of the tangle of narrow lanes around the farmhouse and was now driving south-west on a virtually straight road towards a small village. Wilson slowed the JetRanger so as not to overtake the car.

'Can you drop us down low enough so I can see his registration number?' Morgan asked.

Wilson nodded and the helicopter descended towards the rear of what Morgan could now tell was a Jaguar XF. He memorised the registration number.

'What's that?' Wilson asked, looking at the right-hand side of the Jaguar, where the driver had obviously just lowered the window.

There was a sudden flash from the man's hand, and then another.

Morgan had spent enough time on various firing ranges, including a couple of sessions in the Killing House at Hereford where the SAS train in Close Quarter Battle tactics, to tell what it was.

'That's a pistol,' he said urgently. 'He's shooting at us.'

Wilson instantly threw the helicopter into a tight left-hand banked turn to get them away from the threat as quickly as possible.

'Better safe than sorry,' he said, 'although I reckon his chance of hitting us from a car travelling at that speed on that kind of road are pretty much nil. And it isn't like you see on the films, where some bloke with a twenty-two rifle shoots down a Chinook a quarter of a mile away. Helicopters are quite tough, and it takes a lot to bring one down.'

'I do know that,' Morgan said, 'and he isn't even aiming. He's just trying to frighten us, which from my point of view is working extremely well. I'm not keen on bullets unless I'm the one firing them.'

'And he only needs to be lucky once,' Wilson said. 'We need every bullet he fires to miss us.'

He took up station behind and over to the left of the car, keeping about a hundred yards clear of it to provide a decent safety margin.

Morgan slipped his mobile back under his headphone and was immediately aware that the emergency controller was talking to him, repeatedly asking the same question.

'Mr Morgan. Are you there?'

'Yes, sorry,' he replied. 'Things got a bit hectic just then.'

'We checked, and what you said is correct, so where is the car now?'

'Hang on.' Morgan pointed ahead at the village the car had almost reached. 'Where's that?' he asked.

'According to the map,' Wilson replied, 'that's a place called Everton.'

'It's just approaching a village named Everton which is probably almost due west of Gamlingay. The vehicle is a black Jaguar XF.'

Morgan passed the registration number he'd memorised.

'We're just bringing the map up on one of our displays here,' the controller said. 'Okay, he could go left or right or straight on when he gets there. Let me know as soon as you can which road he takes.'

Morgan didn't have long to wait. Barely slackening speed, the Jaguar swept past a kind of elongated crossroads in the centre of the village and continued straight ahead.

'He's gone straight on,' Morgan said. 'He's still heading—' he glanced at the compass in the JetRanger's instrument panel '—more or less south-west.'

'Right, that means he's on Sandy Road, which turns into Everton Road a bit further on. He has to be heading for Sandy itself because there are no other junctions he could take before he gets to the town. Or none that make sense if he's trying to get away. Our guess is he'll probably go through Sandy to pick up the A1 on the other side and then tank it straight down to London. We've got units north and south of Sandy heading there to try to box him in, and now a couple of cars from the Gamlingay operation following him.'

The controller paused for a few seconds, then continued speaking.

'He'll reach a fork in a few minutes, and he'll have to take the left-hand road because the other is a dead end. That'll take him to the centre of Sandy. From there, he'll probably head west to the A1 roundabout near the Co-op garage, and we do definitely need to know whether he goes north or south from there so we can organise a TPAC or roadblock to stop him. That's if none of our units get there before he reaches the roundabout.'

'Understood,' Morgan replied. 'The other thing you need to know is that he took a few shots at us in the helicopter, so he's obviously armed with a pistol. Your men need to be aware of that before they get too close.'

That seemed to stump the controller for a moment.

Morgan knew that all police forces practised TPAC – Tactical Pursuit and Containment – on a regular basis, but these presupposed that they were trying to stop a fleeing driver and not, significantly and very differently, a fleeing *armed* driver who was clearly quite prepared to use his weapon.

'Thanks for that, Mr Morgan. We'll probably have to go a bit more carefully then. We have got a couple of ARVs – Armed Response Vehicles – in the area, but we'll have to work out how to deploy them to end this.'

Morgan resumed his commentary as Jaguar reached the fork.

'Okay, as you said he would, he stayed on the main road at the fork and is now coming up to the T-junction with the main road. Traffic is fairly light. Now he's turned right and is just merging in with the other vehicles on the road. In other words, he's no longer tanking it and probably hoping not to attract attention.'

Wilson moved the helicopter to the south of the road the Jaguar was following, so that they could both keep it in sight.

'There's a big roundabout in front of him now,' Morgan continued, 'and his fastest route to the A1 is to turn left there. Where are your closest units?'

'The nearest one is just turning off the A1 right now at the main roundabout. If you look west you should see its light bar flashing. They'll kill the blues any minute now so as not to spook the driver. Their orders are to get behind the Jaguar and tail it until we can get it stopped somewhere that nobody's likely to get hurt. There's a second car about two minutes behind them.'

It was, Morgan supposed, quite a decent plan, and if the Jaguar's driver had done what they expected him to do, then it would probably have worked. But as he watched the scene below from the Bell JetRanger in a near hover over the southern part of the town of Sandy, he saw it all turn to worms.

Whoever the driver was, he had clearly been aware of the presence of the helicopter because he'd shot at it, and it wouldn't have been a particularly big leap of logic for him to assume that the crew of the chopper were vectoring ground units onto his location.

And that was obviously why, about a hundred yards before he reached the large Sandy roundabout, more or less in the centre of the town, the driver did something entirely unexpected.

Chapter 40

Monday
Sandy, Bedfordshire

The sudden appearance of the helicopter had been an extremely unwelcome surprise as far as Mr King was concerned. The only thing he could take any comfort in was that the aircraft wasn't a police chopper with its tracking and surveillance equipment. He thought it looked like a JetRanger, but aircraft of any sort, and especially helicopters, were not his strong point. He was certain it was a civilian aircraft, which begged the question why it was following him.

He took his Walther, stuck his hand out of the window and fired three or four wild and largely un-aimed shots towards the helicopter to see if that would make it go away. It didn't, though the pilot did significantly increase his height and horizontal separation. But it was still following him.

Despite not being a police helicopter, Mr King knew that it would be fitted with a radio, because all aircraft were, and so he knew that his plan for turning onto the A1 and heading for London wasn't going to work. Evading police cars on the ground was difficult enough, and only really worked if the driver of the fleeing vehicle took so many chances that the lives of members of the general public were placed at risk. But evading police cars on the ground when they were being assisted by a helicopter in the sky was another matter. That wasn't just very difficult, it was actually impossible as long as the helicopter had fuel.

What Mr King needed was an entirely different way of escape, and as he swung the Jaguar right to head into the centre of the town of Sandy, still aiming for the A1 junction, he realised he might have found one.

A little under two minutes later he switched off the Jaguar's engine, reached behind him to pick up a hat from the rear passenger seat and pulled a plastic carrier bag from a door pocket. He put the hat on his head and the bag in his pocket and stepped out of the car. Limping heavily, he made his way the few yards across the car park to a supermarket on the High Street and walked inside.

The moment he was inside and out of view of the people in the hovering helicopter, he lost the limp, walked briskly over to a rubbish bin and dumped his hat in it. Then, making sure that he was unobserved, he emptied the contents of his jacket pockets, including the hard drive and his pistol, into the carrier bag and put the folded jacket on top. He walked out of the building and turned right down the High Street, moving at exactly the same speed as all the other pedestrians.

His destination was about eight hundred yards away and he knew he needed to get there as quickly as possible. But he dared not run because he could still see the helicopter maintaining a hover just to the south of the town centre. He knew the crew of the aircraft would be scouring the streets below them, searching for anyone who seemed to be in a hurry, so he walked steadily down the almost perfectly straight road that led to the railway station.

Once there, he would buy a ticket for the first train to arrive, irrespective of its destination, and get off it more or less anywhere.

As soon as he knew he was safe from pursuit, he would be able to work his way back to London in his own time.

Chapter 41

Monday
Above Sandy, Bedfordshire

'Where's he going now?' Roger Wilson asked, slowing the JetRanger still further so as to keep the Jaguar both in sight and in front of them.

'He's turning off,' Morgan replied, stating the obvious.

Down below them, the black Jaguar, which had been moving at the same speed as the rest of the traffic on the High Street, slowed down and turned into a car park on the left-hand side of the road.

'Maybe he's turning round to go back the way he came,' Wilson suggested, then immediately corrected himself. 'No, if he wanted to do that he could just carry on to the roundabout and do a U-turn there. It's only about a hundred yards away.'

'I think it's a decamp,' Morgan suggested. 'He might have heard the siren of that police car—' he pointed further ahead along Bedford Road to where the patrol car was clearly visible, its flashing blue lights now extinguished '—and decided to take his chances on foot. We'll have to watch what he does and relay it to the guy in the control room I've been talking to.'

Wilson brought the helicopter to a virtually stationary hover over a small playing field adjacent to a school due south of the car park and they watched.

The voice in Morgan's ear told him that the police controller had heard what he'd just said.

'Can you confirm a decamp?' he asked.

'Stand by,' Morgan said, his attention focused on the now stationary Jaguar. As he watched, the driver's door opened and a figure emerged.

'Yes, it's a decamp,' he confirmed. 'One person only, wearing dark trousers, a dark jacket and a hat. He's heading for the shop – I think it's a Co-op supermarket – but he's walking at normal speed. In fact, he's limping. Maybe he was injured when he got away from the farmhouse.'

Morgan shifted his attention to the approaching police car, which was then under a quarter of a mile away by his estimation.

'Your first car is right here. It's near the main roundabout. Tell the driver to turn right down the High Street and then take the first on the right. They'll see the Jaguar straight away. The driver's gone into the Co-op. If they're quick, they can grab him. Just remember that he's armed.'

Wilson turned the JetRanger in a very tight circle, maintaining more or less the same position over the playing field.

'Just checking there's nothing else in the air anywhere near us,' he said.

On the ground below, Morgan watched as the police car, a white Volvo estate, braked sharply to a stop in the Co-op car park. Two officers got out and ran into the shop.

'I haven't seen him leave the building,' Wilson said. 'Have you?'

'No, and it's not that big a store. But there are a lot of people around.'

About five minutes later, with the JetRanger still hovering to the south of the shop, the two police officers emerged from the building, obviously empty-handed, and almost immediately the police controller spoke to him.

'There was no sign of him,' he said. 'They found a hat in a waste bin, so he must have walked in, dumped the one item of clothing that could identify him, and then walked out of the other door. The limp was probably deliberate. We've got officers on the scene right now, so there's probably not much more help you can give us.'

'Right,' Morgan replied. 'I'll get off the air.'

'So where to now?' asked Wilson.

'Back to the farmhouse, I suppose, but do a quick circuit over the town on the way, just in case we happen to spot him.'

'Tricky when we don't actually know what he looks like,' Wilson replied, but turned the helicopter in a slow gentle circle, both men looking downwards the whole time.

'It's quite a big place,' Morgan remarked, as Wilson straightened up the helicopter and headed north-east, 'and he could have gone in any direction. We've lost him.'

Chapter 42

Monday

Near Gamlingay, Cambridgeshire

Despite the fact that the inhabitants of the farmhouse had had a warning – albeit an extremely brief warning – that the police were at their door, the outcome was never really in doubt. Nineteen highly trained police officers, each carrying a semi-automatic handgun and an assault rifle, were always going to prevail against four armed men taken by surprise.

The farmhouse echoed with the sounds of the shots, a confusion of noise, interspersed by the shouts of the officers as they fought their way in. But less than ninety seconds after the first bullets had been fired it was all over.

Angela Evans was standing right next to Superintendent Waterson when the leader of the APU team reported in by radio.

'Building is secure, occupants disarmed. We need medics in here right now.'

Waterson glanced behind him at the lane alongside the field where all the police vehicles were parked. An ambulance had drawn to a stop there a few seconds earlier, and Waterson stepped out of the copse and into plain view to wave it on towards the farmhouse. Then he pressed the transmit button on his radio.

'The first ambulance will be with you in ten seconds, and there's a second one on the way plus the medevac chopper. How many casualties?'

'I'm still counting, but one of the Tangos didn't make it, two of them are wounded and the last one is in handcuffs, unhurt. I've got four officers down with pellet wounds from that fucking sawn-off shotgun and another one took a bullet in his thigh from a pistol.

He's the one I'm worried about. Two of the officers took chest shots from pistols which their vests stopped, so they're just hurting but not wounded. How's Mason?'

He was the first man to go down before the police had even reached the farmhouse.

'He took two pistol bullets to the chest,' Waterson said. 'His vest worked but the double impact knocked him out, so he's okay. What about the kidnap victim?'

'We found him in a locked room, which was probably the best place for him when we came in through the doors because he was out of the way of the bullets flying about the place. He's alive and well, just a bit damaged, but nothing to do with us. To persuade him to cooperate, these guys broke two fingers on his left hand, so he'll need attention as well.'

Waterson looked at Evans.

'Not the nicest specimens of humanity on the planet, obviously,' he said.

'I'd have been surprised if they were.'

'Right, we'll need to get Michaelson sorted out with splints or painkillers or whatever and I assume you'll want to ask him some questions?'

Evans nodded.

'I do need time with him before he leaves this place,' she replied, 'but I don't need that long, probably only about ten or fifteen minutes.'

The first thing that struck her as she walked into the farmhouse a couple of paces behind Waterson was the distinctive smell of what she assumed was cordite from the shots that had been fired. The building was full of police officers, almost all of them armed, and it was predictably something of a mess, with chairs and tables overturned and a few brass cartridge cases littering the floor.

'This is turning into a disaster,' Waterson said, looking around.

'I don't know,' Evans replied. 'You achieved the objective and Michaelson is safe. And you took three of the kidnappers alive.'

'I know, but that's the least of my worries. The amount of paperwork that this is going to generate will probably bury me until Christmas. Most years in the UK, police firearms officers might fire a dozen rounds on duty. I reckon we fired about three times that number in under two minutes. There'll have to be a full investigation here. So don't touch anything, because we're standing in the middle of a crime scene.'

A heavily built man was lying on his back at one side of the room, his expression almost peaceful and his eyes wide open as if he had found something fascinating to look at on the ceiling. The almost circular pool of blood surrounding the upper part of his torso and the bullet wounds in the centre of his chest confirmed that he was the kidnapper who'd been killed during the assault.

Another man with a similar build was sitting on the floor a few feet away from the corpse, his wrists handcuffed behind him and leaning against the wall, an armed police officer a couple of feet away, presumably to make sure he stayed where they'd put him.

'The other kidnappers?' Angela asked. 'I assume you've got them separated for the moment?'

Waterson nodded.

'Yes, these gentlemen,' he said, somehow making the word sound faintly obscene, 'will be spending a number of years in one of Her Majesty's less salubrious guesthouses once we've finished with them, and exactly how many years will depend to a very large extent on what story each of them tells us. We keep them separate so that we get three different stories, one of which might actually have a tenuous connection to the truth, rather than a single story that they've worked out together.'

'That's what I expected,' Evans said. 'So where's Michaelson?'

The APU officer who had led the raid pointed to an open door, the lock splintered and part of the frame missing.

'That was locked when we arrived and got the situation calmed down,' he said. 'We had no idea where the key was, or if there were more Tangos inside the room, so we kicked it down to check. Michaelson was hiding in the shower room, which was probably a good move on his part. We left him there while we cleared the rest of the house.'

As well as the armed and unarmed police officers, the ambulance crews and paramedics were working there, finding plenty to do in the bullet-riddled farmhouse.

'You might as well go and see Michaelson now,' Waterson suggested. 'It'll be a while before any of these people are free to treat him, by the looks of it.'

'Good idea,' Evans replied.

The venture capitalist was sitting in a chair, a half empty bottle of water beside him, and looking intensely relieved.

'Nicholas?' Evans said. 'My name's Angela Evans and I'm from a small unit attached to the Home Office. We managed to locate this building as part of a surveillance operation,' she explained, managing to be both factually accurate and suitably vague at the same time, 'and we pointed the police in the right direction to rescue you. How are you feeling?'

'I'm so glad to see you, and the officers outside, that I doubt if I can find the words. I was absolutely sure these bastards were going to kill me.'

'That would be very unusual. Kidnappers normally keep their victims alive and in good health.' She glanced at Michaelson's left hand, resting on the arm of the chair. It looked incredibly painful, his little and ring fingers both sticking up at odd angles, enormously swollen and the skin livid shades of red and blue and black. 'Clearly these men had a very different agenda. Why did you think they were going to kill you?'

'You know what I do for a living?' Michaelson asked, and she nodded. 'We get briefed on threats of all sorts, financial and physical, and about the only bit of information that I retained from the lecture on kidnapping was that they would always keep their faces covered so that the victim could never identify them after the event. When they dragged me out of my Mercedes on that road in Essex and slung me in the back of their Range Rover, almost the first thing they did was take off their balaclavas. That's when I knew it wasn't a normal kidnapping.

'I thought at first they might be working for one of our competitors, or for a company that we'd acquired, a hostile takeover, that kind of thing, and I tried to buy my way out of it. I offered to pay double whatever fee they had been promised. And they laughed in my face.'

'So they started asking questions and weren't satisfied with the answers you were providing, judging by your left hand. Would that be a fair summary?'

Michaelson nodded, and for a moment it looked as if he was going to break down.

'I didn't think a broken finger would hurt that badly, but the way they snapped these was bloody agonising,' he said. 'Anyway, the questions didn't really make sense. They said they needed information, and I assumed that they wanted something sensitive or commercial, so they could make a serious killing on the stock market. Do a bit of insider trading.'

'Grabbing you for a straight ransom really didn't make sense to us. They had to be after information. So what did they want?'

Michaelson smiled slightly.

'They were looking for dirt. They wanted me to identify any and all of the people that I know in the banking sector and company CEOs, the sort of men and women I deal with on a daily basis, and then tell them exactly what weaknesses they have. Gambling, keeping an expensive mistress, taking drugs, all that kind of thing.'

Evans nodded. That was almost exactly the conclusion the C-TAC team had come to once they learnt of Michaelson's abduction.

'Is this the sort of stuff you actually know about these people?' she asked. 'And I suppose more to the point is, did you tell them? Did you provide the information they wanted?'

'If you work in the City,' Michaelson replied, 'you tend to learn rather more about the people you deal with than you perhaps want to know. You'll hear that a particular banker enjoys a line of cocaine, or the reason why a senior official always leaves work early on a Wednesday afternoon but arrives home later than usual. There's rarely anything concrete. I mean, nobody shows you photographs of some man injecting himself with heroin while he's in bed with a couple of call girls. Nothing like that. But you hear the whispers and the rumours and quite often they do seem to make sense and explain why a particular person sometimes acts or reacts in the way they do.'

Evans opened her mouth to ask the question again, but Michaelson forestalled her.

'I know what you asked,' he said, 'and the short answer is that I tried not to give the answers they wanted.' He held up his left hand again. 'That's when they gave me this – what they called an attention-getter. And it worked, I can tell you. I told them everything I could think of about pretty much anyone I'd ever met. Then they decided that I must be making some of it up – which I was – and so this morning they broke my ring finger as well, to remind me to only tell them the truth.'

Michaelson looked at his hand again and seemed close to tears.

'By that time,' he went on, 'I'd given them everything and I think they knew it. They told me today they were going to question me again, but this time they were changing the rules. Every time I gave an incomplete answer or evaded the question or they weren't satisfied with the information I was providing, they were going to break another bone in my body. I really believe that I had maybe another day left to live. Another couple of sessions and then they'd know that the well was dry. I was expecting that once that happened they'd just march me outside to some field, make me dig a grave and then shoot me.' He shook his head. 'I'm not a religious man. I gave up believing in God about the same time as I realised that the tooth fairy and Father Christmas didn't actually exist. But the thought of my body rotting away in some unmarked hole in a field out here in the sticks, and my wife and children never knowing what had happened to me or why, that was almost more than I could bear.'

Evans had no doubt that Michaelson's analysis of the likely outcome was right on the money. Within a day, perhaps two at the most, the kidnappers would have left and Michaelson's body would have been dumped somewhere.

'I'm afraid,' she said, 'that you're probably absolutely right. But at least you're safe now. The medics will be along in a few minutes to sort out your hand, the police will want a full statement from you and I'll get you a phone so you can call your wife. But there is something we'd like you to do.'

Evans told him what she wanted and he immediately agreed.

'As soon as I can,' he promised.

Waterson had waited while the medics attended to the wounded police officers and the two kidnappers who had been shot. Their injuries were serious but not life-threatening. One of them had been hit in the shoulder by a round from an assault rifle. The other had taken two bullets in the chest, one of which had hit him just below the shoulder, while the other had carved a furrow through the skin over his ribs.

Evans walked over to the superintendent.

'How's Michaelson?' Waterson asked.

'More happy to see a bunch of policemen around him than anyone I've ever met before, and I'm not surprised. They broke two of his fingers and he thought he'd become a loose end that they were going to snip off today or maybe tomorrow, so when your guys smashed their way into this farmhouse you answered all his prayers. I have a feeling that some local police charity might well receive an unexpected donation over the next few weeks. On the other hand, Michaelson's a venture capitalist, so his benevolent feelings may well evaporate once he's safely back in his familiar world.'

'Are you something of a cynic, Miss Evans?' Waterson asked.

'No,' she replied. 'I'm a realist, especially where people who work in the City of London are concerned.'

The senior paramedic walked over to the superintendent.

'That's pretty much it from our point of view,' he said. 'The officer who got shot in the thigh is on his way to Addenbrooke's Hospital in Cambridge in the medevac chopper. He'll be limping for a while, but he should make a full recovery, and your other guys are basically walking wounded. Four of them will need treatment for the shotgun pellet wounds, but that's all. The two kidnappers who were shot will also be taken to Addenbrooke's but by ambulance. In fact, as you specified, in two separate ambulances. But I gather there's another person here with minor injuries that we haven't seen yet.'

'He's in there,' Waterson said, pointing at the door that led to Michaelson's room. 'He's got a couple of broken fingers but otherwise he's okay. And treat him gently, because he's the victim in all this.'

He turned back to Evans.

'You'd like a copy of the report of this afternoon's exciting activities, I assume? Or perhaps just the summary and conclusions, to avoid the whole thing having to be delivered on pallets in the back of an HGV?'

'The summary would be fine,' she said, 'just to complete our records. And you'll notice that there's one question I haven't been asking.'

Waterson nodded.

'I know,' he replied. 'The elephant in the room. We were told there were four people involved in the actual kidnapping and what we have here is one dead body, two wounded kidnappers and a fourth one that my men unaccountably managed to miss when they kicked down the door and filled the place with flying bullets. So who was contestant number five?'

'That was the question I had in mind,' Evans said. 'Any ideas?'

'At this precise moment, no. He ran out of the farmhouse within a few seconds of the first shots being fired, jumped into the car, which was only a few feet away, and simply drove off.'

'I thought you had the place surrounded,' Angela said. 'Why didn't your men stop him?'

'It was surrounded, but we stop cars by boxing them in with other vehicles, by doing a TPAC manoeuvre. What we don't do is open fire on a vehicle to bring it to a stop. I know they do that in America, but over here we prefer to put handcuffs on a suspect once we've dragged him out of the car, not riddle the car with bullets and slide the driver straight into a body bag. My men tried to stop him, even aimed their weapons at him, but he drove straight past them. Perhaps your colleague will have some answers about the man when he comes back in his helicopter.'

Chapter 43

Monday

Near Gamlingay, Cambridgeshire

As Roger Wilson pulled the JetRanger around in a gentle left-hand bank, descending all the time, the scene in the field below looked to Morgan pretty much the same as it had done when they'd taken off about thirty minutes earlier. There were a few less police vehicles parked there, and a few less police officers as well, presumably because most of them were still over at the farmhouse.

Standing beside one of the police cars – in fact leaning on it and shading her eyes as she watched the helicopter descend – was Evans.

Wilson landed the JetRanger about fifty yards from the nearest police vehicle.

'Do you need to shut it down while she gets in?' Morgan asked.

'No. Just get out, walk over to her and then both of you approach the helicopter from the front. Never, ever, go round the back of a running chopper. If you do, the last thing you'll see and feel will be the tail rotor blade reducing your face to minestrone.'

'You do have a way with words, Roger,' Morgan said, removed the headphones and climbed out of the front passenger door.

Instinctively ducking down as he walked under the rotor disc, although he knew the blades were about nine feet above the ground, he met Evans as she headed away from the cluster of police vehicles.

Wilson waited until they were strapped in with their headphones on before he spoke.

'Now are we going back to London?' he asked.

'We're done here, so we might as well,' Evans replied from the rear seat. 'So what happened? You obviously managed to track the car because Superintendent Waterson was able to tell me it was the real thing, which was a bit of a surprise. We'd thought it was probably a ringer. According to Waterson, the Jaguar has a current MOT, valid tax and insurance, though this bit is a little murky. The car's owner is the proprietor of a takeaway restaurant in Bradford, and the insurance policy on the car is for any driver as long as he or she holds a current UK driving licence. The police will be having a word or two with him in the very near future. Anyway, I gather the fifth man made it as far as Sandy.'

'Fifth man?' Morgan echoed. 'I thought he was one of the four kidnappers.'

'We don't know who he was. As well as Michaelson, who's alive and well but hurting because of the degree of persuasion they applied, there were four kidnappers in the farmhouse. One didn't survive the police raid, and the only thing the other three have said so far is "No comment". Michaelson himself only saw the four people who grabbed him, and had no idea there was anyone else in the building.'

'Curious,' Morgan said, and told Angela what they'd seen from the air as they followed the fleeing car. 'So the driver could be anywhere by now, and the only description Roger and I can supply is that we're fairly sure it's a he rather than a she. And that's not desperately helpful, obviously.'

'The police at the farmhouse got a look at him as he ran for the car, and it's definitely a man. A little less than average height, tanned skin and dark hair. That's about it.'

'And what about Michaelson?' Morgan asked. 'Were we right about him being snatched because of what he knows rather than because of who he is?'

'Yes, but they weren't asking him for potentially profitable insider trading titbits. Instead, they wanted him to dish the dirt on everyone he knows in and around the City of London, which is pretty much what we guessed.'

'And I assume he told them what they wanted to know?'

'That's what he said,' she replied, 'and I, for one, don't blame him.'

Chapter 44

Monday
Brent Park, London

'Well, well, well,' Vince muttered as he stared at the computer screen displaying the feed from the lounge camera at Parsons Green. 'It looks as if George Kenton has managed to squeeze in an afternoon appointment.'

'He runs the bank, so I guess he can take a few hours off during the day if he wants to. And that saves having to tell his wife a bunch of lies,' Mike replied, turning from what he was doing to look at the screen.

There had been activity in the flat for much of the day, with Amanda Hart tidying the lounge and working in the kitchen, while the boy they knew as Robert spent most of the time staring almost directly towards the hidden camera, though he was actually watching the large television mounted on the wall close to it. Vince had muted the sound from the camera because they'd heard nothing interesting since Amanda Hart had appeared in the lounge a little after eight o'clock that morning.

They hadn't heard a telephone call and also hadn't noticed when Robert got up from the sofa and disappeared towards the guest bedroom. But the unexpected arrival of George Kenton did explain why the boy was not in the room and, probably, what was about to happen.

Vince immediately turned up the volume so they could hear what was being said.

Kenton and the woman again greeted each other in a cool and professional fashion, and once he'd removed his overcoat she led him down the corridor, returning to the lounge a few moments later.

Vince switched the feed to one of the cameras positioned in the guest bedroom and both men unconsciously leaned a little closer to the screen to see what was happening.

'Good afternoon, Robert,' Kenton said.

'Good afternoon, Master,' Robert replied. He was standing almost to attention on one side of the bed, again wearing the schoolboy outfit, with his hair neatly combed.

'I see that you're ready for me. That's good. And you are going to be a good boy this afternoon, aren't you?'

'I'm always a good boy, Master.'

'He's even given the kid a script to follow,' Mike said, sounding disgusted. 'I bet he's told him exactly what he's got to do.'

Kenton removed his jacket and hung it carefully over the back of the chair, then took off his tie.

'I'm ready for you now,' Kenton said.

Robert picked up a cane that was hanging over the footboard, then handed it to Kenton.

'You promised me six, Master,' the boy said, and Kenton nodded.

'I always try to keep my promises, Robert. Prepare yourself.'

The boy dropped his shorts. Mike and Vince both flinched involuntarily every time the cane made contact with the boy's backside.

On the screen, Kenton delivered the sixth stroke, then put the cane against the wall beside the door and walked back to the boy. He bent down and critically examined the welts that were starting to form across Robert's buttocks.

'Very good,' he said. 'You took them well and I hope you enjoyed them. You've had your pleasure, so now it's time for my reward.'

'Make sure that other camera is getting this,' Mike said, and Vince switched the feed to show the scene from a different vantage point.

'It makes me feel filthy just watching this,' Vince said. 'I fucking hate paedos. And especially gay paedos who're into BDSM or whatever the hell they call it.'

The activity quickly moved onto the bed, the cameras in the room picking up and transmitting clear and unambiguous video footage of exactly what was happening. When it was obvious what was about to happen next, Vince abruptly stood up from the desk.

'I can't stand any more of this,' he said. 'Bastard fucking paedophile and what he's doing to that poor little sod. I swear if I ever see him on the street I'll fucking flatten him. Right, I'm going to have a beer. Just make sure the cameras keep recording. And this is one set of pictures and a DVD, mate, that you can edit by yourself, because I'm not doing it.'

Mike joined him in the adjacent bedroom nearly an hour later, five minutes after George Kenton had paid Amanda Hart and left the apartment.

'Has he gone?' Vince asked, popping the tab on another can of beer.

'Yes,' Mike replied shortly. 'He's planning a return visit tomorrow or the day after.'

'Yeah, but we don't need to watch it all again, do we? The footage we've got today should be enough to bury that bastard.'

'You got that right. I'll splice together him with the woman, selected highlights from the bedroom, and finish with him paying for services rendered. Once I've done that, Kenton will be ours, no question. He either does what we tell him or the Metropolitan Police will get a copy of the DVD and I can pretty much guarantee he'll be inside the slammer at West End Central or somewhere within a couple of hours. He'll never get out of prison alive because the one thing that honest criminals can't tolerate is a paedophile. Somebody will take him in the showers with a shiv and that'll be the end of him. Good riddance.'

'You can't do that,' Vince said, taking another swig of his beer. 'Kenton will go into the programme and make us rich. You can't turn him in. He's too valuable to us.'

Mike opened his own beer, nodded and sat down.

'I know,' he replied, 'but I can dream, can't I?'

Chapter 45

Monday
Chislehurst, Kent

It had actually been easier than James McEwan had expected. Each of the senior bankers that he had invited to his house, ostensibly to give him their professional advice over a problem he had encountered, had been entirely amenable when he had explained that he had some financially critical information to impart to them. He'd provided champagne and canapes for the early arrivals, and when his last guest arrived McEwan walked into the lounge with him. Then he clapped his hands twice to get everyone's attention.

'If you want more champagne or spirits, just help yourselves,' he said pointing at the bar.

He looked around the room, making sure he had everybody's attention. Then he began the explanation that he had worked out that afternoon.

'I want to talk to you,' he said, 'about a company called Professional Security Providers 4, PSP4. I know the name and the initials will be familiar to all of you, because every one of you has signed a contract with the company.'

Exactly as he had expected, McEwan's first words produced a sudden silence. The attention of everyone in the room was wholly focused on him. For a brief instant, he felt a moment's doubt about the wisdom of what he was planning to do, and then decided that he really had no other choice.

'That means all of you, just like me, have a secret that you are not prepared to have revealed to the outside world. Otherwise PSP4 would not have approached you in the first place. What you know as well as I do is that this supposed security company is a front. It's nothing more than a gang of blackmailers. A very efficient gang, certainly, and one that obtains undeniable evidence of wrongdoing before they send anyone to approach the victim.' He paused briefly. 'Does anyone here not know what I'm talking about?'

Nobody answered that question, but one man standing near the bar nodded and then spoke.

'We've probably all met that odious man who calls himself John Harrison,' he said, and several other people in the room nodded. 'What I want to know, McEwan, is why we're all standing here listening to you talk about this. You're a victim too, obviously, so what are you suggesting we do about it?'

'Have you got a plan?' another man asked.

'I have,' McEwan replied, and spent the next few minutes telling the assembled company what he intended to do.

When he finished there was a long and appalled silence, and then the man standing beside the bar spoke again.

'Are you completely fucking barking mad?'

The silence, if anything, deepened at both the language used and the obvious ferocity in the man's voice, and everybody in the room stared at him.

'It's not just John Harrison, or whatever his real name is,' he went on. 'These people are organised criminals, a gang, and you can't frighten them off, because it won't work.'

'I had a more permanent solution in mind,' McEwan said, his voice rising in anger.

'I know, and that's where you've completely lost the plot. If you did manage to kill Harrison, what do you think the other people in the gang would do? We know they've got cameras everywhere because everybody in this room has presumably had a starring role in some activity that we would never willingly admit to, so you can assume that whatever you tried to do would be on video. If you were lucky, they'd just hand it over to the police. If you were unlucky, they'd probably return the favour and you'd end up being murdered. Killing Harrison, or any other members of the gang, won't work.'

'I think it will,' McEwan said stubbornly. 'It'll show them that we have teeth.'

'It'll show them that we – or rather you – haven't got any bloody sense,' the man responded. 'I'd rather pay them ten grand a month than end up standing in the dock at the Old Bailey facing a murder charge. It's cheap at the price.'

McEwan glared round at the people in the room, his anger flaring.

'I hoped some of you would have the balls to help me do something about this,' he almost shouted. 'But as you're all complete bloody cowards, you can all fuck off out of my house. I'll do it myself.'

Without a word, the assembled bankers started to leave the room. The man who'd argued with him was the last to walk out. At the door he paused, reached into his jacket pocket and waved his mobile phone at McEwan.

'It's not just this gang of blackmailers who can record things,' he said. 'I've recorded everything you said. If you persist in this completely fucking mindless scheme, I'll personally send an edited version of what you've said to the Metropolitan Police and tell them who you are and where to find you. That's a promise. And a threat.'

'Get out of my house, you bastard.'

Chapter 46

Tuesday

Vauxhall Cross, London

The rescue of Nicholas Michaelson from the kidnappers didn't mark the end of C-TAC's involvement in the case. Morgan contacted Adam Cross to thank him for what he described as the 'loan of the app' and told Natasha Black at GCHQ she could forget about doing any more work on the data stream.

But none of the C-TAC team believed that was the end of the matter. Grabbing Nicholas Michaelson had been a risky choice for the gang, and Evans's regurgitating of the questions he had been asked and the answers he had supplied – courtesy of the venture capitalist's near-eidetic memory and recall, probably made more acute by the circumstances of his imprisonment – had raised a whole flock of red flags. Michaelson had promised her that he would provide a written follow-up as soon as he got access to his computer.

'So you want to do more with this?' Dame Janet asked from her usual seat at the head of the conference table. 'Why? And why not leave it to the police?'

'Two reasons,' Morgan replied. 'First, the police have done their bit in rescuing Michaelson, effectively solving the crime. Their focus now will be on questioning the surviving kidnappers to make their case for the CPS. But they won't be interested in *why* Michaelson was kidnapped. Angela and I think that's crucial. Second, even if the police were interested in the reason he was snatched, they wouldn't know who to talk to or what questions to ask. In short, we have the knowledge and the access, and they don't, thanks to Andrew here.'

Nuffield inclined his head in acknowledgement.

'There's another factor here that Andrew and I were talking about earlier on,' Dame Janet said. 'I'll let him explain.'

'I talked to the Cambridge Chief Constable a few minutes before you arrived. The room in the farmhouse where Michaelson was interrogated was wired for sound and vision with four cameras, and the cables led into another room in the building. In there, the police found a television that was displaying the feeds. They also found a USB-3 lead that had probably been plugged into an external hard drive. That would allow someone to monitor what was going on in the other room and record everything that was said and done. But the hard drive wasn't there.'

'The implication is that the four-man kidnap gang was working under the direction of a fifth man,' Dame Janet said. 'He was probably telling them what questions to ask and using the equipment to record Michaelson's answers, and he was the man who got away from the farmhouse.'

'He would have taken the hard drive when he ran for the Jaguar,' Morgan said, 'which means the gang will have recordings of the information Michaelson provided.'

'So, armed with Michaelson's list of likely suspects,' Dame Janet said, 'you want to talk to these people and ask what? If their private lives will stand up to detailed scrutiny, or if they spend their weekends taking drugs, gambling away large chunks of their salaries, or having sex with prostitutes or children? I know you're always direct.'

Morgan smiled, but without any humour in his expression.

'I hadn't planned on being quite that direct,' he replied, 'but those are probably the four most likely habits that the kidnappers had been hoping to hear about. Paedophiles are beyond the pale and if I find one of them they're going down, no question, but I was going to try to hint that if they did have some other kind of embarrassing private habit – the sort that could end a career, that kind of habit – it might be worth giving it a rest for a while.'

'Good luck with those conversations,' Dame Janet said drily. 'Okay, you've made your point. Let me know how you get on.'

Chapter 47

Tuesday
Chelsea, London

'George,' Mary Kenton said, standing in the open doorway of her husband's study, 'there's a man downstairs from your office who must see you immediately. Some kind of a problem has arisen over what he described as your position. I've put him in the drawing room. Please try and get rid of him quickly. You know the Sutcliffes are coming over for drinks at eight.'

George Kenton muttered something under his breath, stood up and followed his wife down the stairs. On the next landing, a thought struck him.

'Did he give you his name?' he asked.

'Yes,' she replied. 'It was Hunterston. No. Harrison. That was it. Harrison.'

Kenton felt a frisson of apprehension at his wife's statement. Not only had he never met any member of staff in the bank called Harrison, but never before had anyone from the bank visited his home without being invited. On the rare occasions when his presence genuinely was required in the office, he had invariably been telephoned and then made his own way in. The reality was that the only place he could fix a problem *with* the bank was *at* the bank, so sending a man to his home was completely pointless.

'I'll attend to this,' Kenton said outside the closed door of the drawing room. He waited until his wife had disappeared towards the kitchen then opened the door and stepped inside.

Harrison – if that really was his name – appeared to be a well-dressed businessman of the type that descended upon the City of London in countless thousands every working day. He was standing beside the marble fireplace and looking at the framed family photographs on the mantelpiece above it. As Kenton opened the door, Harrison turned and walked over to him, his hand outstretched and a smile on his face.

Kenton ignored his hand and stood staring at the man, his arms folded across his chest.

'Who are you and what do you want?' he demanded. 'I know you're not from my office.'

Harrison smiled and nodded.

'You're quite right,' he said. 'Please forgive my small subterfuge, but I needed to get in to see you urgently and telling your wife that I was from the office seemed the easiest way.'

'So what do you want?' Kenton repeated. 'And please be quick because we're expecting guests.'

'Very well,' Harrison said. 'I'll get right to the point. I know you live here in Chelsea and that you work in the City, but I also know that you spend some evenings and occasionally afternoons with a friend down in Parsons Green.'

That name hit George Kenton like a blow to the stomach and for a few seconds he said nothing, just looked at the man in front of him. What the stranger had said had the power to make his world implode, and he didn't know what to do or what to say.

'Parsons Green,' he muttered. 'I don't think I know that—'

'Let me stop you right there, George. You're busy and in a hurry and so am I, so let me just show you something.'

Harrison took a sealed envelope from his pocket, tore open the flap and passed over two colour photographs. The first showed Kenton standing and talking to a woman that he instantly recognised.

'You obviously know Amanda Hart, or I believe she sometimes calls herself Amanda Nicholson. She is rather lovely, isn't she? Though I gather your tastes run in a somewhat different direction, as the other photograph shows.'

Kenton barely glanced at the second picture because he already knew what it would depict. It was the young blond boy, and the picture showed both of them naked on the bed in the flat at Parsons Green.

'How much do you want?' Kenton demanded. 'And I'm not paying unless you give me the originals.'

Harrison shook his head.

'This isn't some grubby little blackmail scheme,' he said, and launched into almost exactly the same sales pitch – if that was the right expression to describe what he was doing – that he had delivered to James McEwan. And, in fact, that he had delivered to more than a dozen very senior members of the banking and financial community in London over the previous month or so.

Twenty minutes after he had stepped into the house, Harrison crossed the road to where a Ford saloon was parked, its engine running and a man sitting in the driving seat.

Harrison opened the passenger door and sat down.

'Any problems?' the driver asked.

'None at all,' Harrison replied. 'Our customer base has just increased by one. We're right on schedule.'

Chapter 48

Wednesday

Vauxhall Cross, London

'This is the list that Michaelson came up with,' Angela Evans said, sliding three stapled-together sheets of paper across the table to Ben Morgan, followed by identical pages for Andrew Nuffield, Dave North and Cameron Riley. It was early evening in London and Dame Janet had been called away to some event or meeting – she hadn't elaborated – in Westminster and had left them to it.

In the farmhouse in Cambridgeshire, Evans had given Nicholas Michaelson her card and her private email address and had asked him to provide all the information he could remember about the interrogations he had endured. It hadn't taken him as long to put it together as she had expected. Michaelson had marked the top and bottom of each page with the words 'SENSITIVE/COMMERCIAL IN CONFIDENCE'. And he'd done that because the information was without any shadow of a doubt both of those things.

Each paragraph named a particular senior banking official and stated where he worked, what his job was, and listed his home, office and mobile telephone numbers. That was the limit of the factual information, and what followed was whatever Michaelson had heard or been told by other people about that individual. In most cases, he had couched it in quite vague terms, presumably because he either didn't trust his source or he harboured personal doubts about the veracity of what he'd been told. But in some of the other sections his statements were far more definitive.

One particular entry made Morgan smile. Below the man's name Michaelson had written: 'You know the expression sex and drugs and rock 'n' roll? Well, put it this way: I don't think he does rock 'n' roll but he certainly does the others.' That didn't leave much room for ambiguity.

'So what's the plan, Ben?' Dave North asked. 'Ring up the first of the idiots on Michaelson's list and ask him which flavour of marching powder he prefers: Bolivian, Colombian or Peruvian?'

Morgan smiled at him and shook his head.

'I know the SAS prefers the most direct approach, just as I do, but I have a feeling that would be a little bit *too* direct. I had a slightly more subtle technique in mind.'

'Well, don't keep us in suspense,' Cameron Riley said.

'We're going to need some help from Five to make this work. I was thinking it through, to see the logic behind what's happened. I believe the four kidnappers were just muscle, hired guns brought on board to just grab Michaelson, pump him for information and then dispose of what was left. The fifth guy in the farmhouse, the one who got away, was probably the brains of the operation and he's got the recordings of the interrogations. This operation definitely didn't just involve those five people. I think Number Five – let's just call him that for the sake of convenience – is either the man running the whole thing or possibly somebody near the top of the group. A trusted lieutenant, that kind of thing.

'Now he's got the information out of Michaelson, he's really got to act on it, to blackmail the people that he knows have got weaknesses he can exploit. Number Five and whoever else he's working with will need to approach these men and either demand money with menaces – classic blackmail, in other words – or threaten them with exposure unless they agree to launder money or rig the FOREX markets or fix interest rates, or whatever else it is that these people want them to do so they can make a killing on the markets.'

Cameron Riley raised his hand.

'This is more my world than yours these days, Ben,' he said, 'and the more I think about it, the more I believe this may just be straight blackmail. The volume of funds and financial instruments held or moved through the City is simply enormous, and it would be very difficult for one man, irrespective of his motivation and even his position, to do anything to influence any part of the process.'

Morgan nodded.

'I was thinking about that as well and I agree. Even the most influential City figures would find it difficult to do anything that would move any of the markets in a particular direction. But remember we're not talking about one man. These guys could suborn a dozen or more of the top people working in the City and then, for example, tell them that in a single coordinated move they should all simultaneously begin selling sterling against the euro, or putting all their investments into dollar stocks, or some other financial jiggery-pokery that would make the City lose confidence in sterling. That could start a run on the pound and I would have thought that investors who knew when that was going to happen would make a fortune as sterling crashed through the floor. And remember Libor.'

Riley nodded.

'You make a good point.'

'Libor?' Dave North asked. 'Some City scandal about ten years ago, wasn't it?'

'Yes,' Riley replied. 'Basically, it was worldwide rate fixing. Several banks were fined a lot of money but innocent investors and borrowers who lost out were never compensated. The western world might not survive another major credit crisis like that, and the winner next time might well be China. The Shanghai and Hong Kong exchanges have both got a higher market capitalisation than London, and the Shenzhen exchange is getting close to the City's cap. Their combined monthly trade volume is almost seven times higher than London's. China is a real threat in financial terms.'

There was a short silence as the members of C-TAC considered the feasibility and ramifications of that particular scenario.

'Interestingly,' Evans said, 'when I was talking to Michaelson in the farmhouse, he told me that he was expecting his captors to start asking him for the kind of information that they could use to carry out insider trading. He was surprised when they began questioning him about individual bankers. But what they were actually doing, if Ben is right, was setting themselves up so that they could get insider trading information whenever they wanted it, just by threatening to expose the bankers they've compromised. It's quite clever.'

'Cam?' Ben Morgan prompted.

'You might have something there,' he agreed. 'I hadn't thought about a group of rogue bankers working together under duress rather than motivated by their usual greed. That might work, but we'd need to follow the money to see who's actually behind this.'

'So what do we do now?' Dave North asked.

'That's why we need Five,' Morgan said. 'The people who hired the kidnappers now have the same information that's on these sheets of paper Angela's printed, so they're going to be following these bankers to get photos or videos or other proof that they're doing what they shouldn't be doing. We should do exactly the same. We need to follow these bankers, but not to get some happy snaps of them bonking a couple of call girls. We'll follow them so that we can identify and grab the bad guys who are trying to get incriminating evidence. If we can do that, we should be able to wrap up this entire operation, but we'll need a lot of extra manpower from Five to do it.'

'I like it,' Cameron Riley said. 'And there's something else we can do.'

'What?'

Riley told them, and that really did add an extra, and particularly satisfying, dimension to the operation.

Chapter 49

Wednesday
London

In all, a total of seven people had recorded what James McEwan had said during the meeting at his house. One of these – a man named Stephen Dawkins – had been a 'client' of PSP4 for over a month and was terrified of his own personal secret ever becoming known. He was a predatory paedophile who spent hours every evening dredging the murky and unregulated depths of the Dark Web exchanging images and videos with other men – and allegedly a few women – who shared his depraved appetites. And once or twice a month he donned a rudimentary disguise and ventured out into his usual hunting ground, the streets around King's Cross, looking for a stray boy or a runaway girl – he wasn't fussy about their gender as long as they were young – to service his needs.

When he had heard what McEwan was planning to do, he had actually quivered with fear, to the extent that a couple of the men standing near him had given him suspicious looks. Dawkins had downed what was left of his champagne, and then sidled over to the bar and helped himself to a large brandy as he listened to the rest of McEwan's plan with increasing apprehension.

What he had realised immediately – which McEwan was either too stupid or too arrogant to have grasped – was that if the man who called himself John Harrison ended up murdered, the police would pick apart his life, and the lives of any associates or family members.

And if that happened they would be certain to discover the incriminating photographs Harrison had shown him of one of his encounters with a thirteen-year-old blonde mystery he'd found begging in Taviton Street near Euston Station. He'd never worked out how Harrison's gang had got the photographs, but there was no mistaking him in the pictures, or what he was doing. There were other images he'd been shown that were even more damning, and they'd somehow managed to access his history on the Dark Web, a history that showed his particular proclivities only too clearly. If any of that leaked out, Dawkins knew he was finished. He'd be looking at years in jail, the loss of his job, a messy and probably very public divorce, and all the rest of the shrapnel that would be generated.

And that he couldn't face.

He'd barely slept the night after McEwan's meeting, or the next one, and when he got up on Wednesday morning he knew what he had to do. He had no other choice.

He couldn't call from his office or home in case his location could be triangulated. So around the middle of the morning, he left both his work and private mobile phones on his desk, slipped out of his office and hailed a cab, telling the driver to take him east into Whitechapel. There, he paid off the taxi and walked south to Rope Walk Gardens, a small patch of green surrounded by buildings. He found a seat near the somewhat futuristic outdoor gym with its bright yellow-green machines and took out a pre-paid mobile phone he'd bought a few weeks earlier. He had a slip of paper in his pocket on which he'd written the contact number Harrison had given him, and after a furtive look around, he dialled it.

'Yes?' a gruff voice demanded.

'I have a message for Mr Harrison,' Dawkins said. 'Is he there?'

'He's busy,' the voice responded. 'You can tell me.'

Dawkins took a deep breath.

'Mr Harrison approached a man named James McEwan,' he said. 'I suppose you know about that?'

'Yup. Go on.'

'McEwan is very angry, and he's told me he doesn't intend to pay the subscription. He also plans to try and kill Mr Harrison.'

The man at the other end of the call laughed briefly.

After a brief pause, he asked, 'Are you serious?'

'Completely serious. You need to warn Harrison.'

'Don't worry, I will. We'll take care of him. And who are you?'

'My name doesn't matter. I'm just one of your subscribers.'

Dawkins ended the call, opened up the mobile and pulled out the SIM card. He had a pair of folding scissors in his pocket which he snapped open and cut the SIM card into four sections. As he walked back in the general direction of Whitechapel he dropped one quarter into each of four rubbish bins as he passed them, dead-ending the brief trail he'd left.

Five minutes later he was sitting in another black cab and heading back to his office.

As the vehicle drove through the busy streets of east London he wondered if he'd done the right thing. For a few minutes he forgot about the threat to his personal well-being and focused on one single thing the man he'd been speaking to had said. And on its inherent – and potentially alarming – ambiguity.

When the man had said 'We'll take care of him', Dawkins had assumed, since he'd been warning him that Harrison's life might be in danger, that the man had meant they would take care of Harrison and keep him safe.

But he could equally have meant that they would be keeping Harrison safe by 'taking care' of McEwan. And that was something altogether different.

The prospect disturbed Dawkins so much that when he got back to his office he made another telephone call, this time using one of the landlines and telling the person he talked to exactly who he was.

The message he conveyed in this call was subtly different to his previous conversation, but the core information was exactly the same.

Chapter 50

Wednesday
Brent Park, London

The correct historical meaning of the verb 'to decimate' dates back to the days of the Roman Empire, when decimation – meaning the execution of one soldier out of every ten – was a punishment applied to a Roman legion that was deemed guilty of mutiny, cowardice or some other crime. The modern meaning of the word is more general and simply refers to the removal of a large proportion of a group of things or people. Usually people.

Mr King had no idea of the derivation of the word but he was well acquainted with its effects in the real world. The team he had put together consisted of a dozen men, and in a single afternoon four of them, one third of his total manpower, had been arrested – or worse – by the police at the farmhouse where they had been holding Nicholas Michaelson. He didn't particularly care what happened to those four men, because they were replaceable, but he did care about what they might eventually reveal under questioning by the police.

When he made it back to the building at Brent Park where all the remaining members of his team had been told to assemble, he found he had another problem as well. The call from an unidentified PSP4 subscriber – the man had sensibly used a burner phone to make the call – about James McEwan required immediate action. Taking care of him was an easy decision to make because this eventuality, a target refusing to do what he was told, had been predicted from the start, and one of the men he had recruited, a man with a background in the military, had both the ability and the equipment to solve the problem.

Eventually, Mr King knew, one of the men arrested at the farmhouse would reveal the location of the Brent Park property, so as soon as he had ordered the appropriate action to be taken regarding McEwan, he told the rest of the team to start packing their equipment and weapons to move to a new base, a similar commercial building on a small industrial estate in Aberfeldy Village in east London, a mile or so north of Canary Wharf. Mr King had anticipated that their location might at some point be compromised and had taken a lease on the other premises as a precaution. He was also aware that because he'd had to abandon the Jaguar at Sandy, as well as the Vauxhall saloon at the farmhouse, the police would soon be able to link the other two cars and the white van to the operation. So in the short term, he told his men to use the vehicles only for that evening, then to dump them. They'd source new vehicles the following day.

Because they all remained in contact using mobile phones, the transfer to the new building would have little effect upon their ongoing operation, and the surveillance and recruitment of two new potential targets would continue exactly as planned. Mr King would just have to hire some more muscle, not a difficult task in London.

Less than an hour after Mr King had walked into the building at Brent Park it was deserted, and all traces of the gang's occupation had been removed.

Chapter 51

Wednesday
Mayfair, London

The language spoken in the military world tends to be studded with expressions, acronyms and the kind of mantras that are easy to learn and difficult to forget, typically five-letter shorthand expressions that include four-letter expletives, like SNAFU, SUSFU and FUBAR, all referring to a poor or deteriorating situation. The meaning of 'FU' is fairly obvious, and the other letters refer to, respectively, Situation Normal All FU, Situation Unchanged Still FU, and FU Beyond All Recognition. These may be handy expressions to lob into an operational conversation, but there are other military shorthand expressions that are far more practical and actually work.

One of the most common is sometimes referred to as PAPA 9, the letter 'P' being spoken as 'Papa' in the military phonetic alphabet. This stands for Proper Prior Planning and Perfect Preparation Prevents Piss-Poor Performance, and while there are other, shorter, ways to express the sentiment, it's difficult to argue with the basic principle. Planning and preparation inevitably and invariably have a direct and obvious connection with the outcome of any action or operation.

But sometimes, no matter how carefully and comprehensively something has been planned, some unanticipated factor – either internal or external – can enter the mix and turn any operation into a SNAFU or FUBAR situation. Or, perhaps even less politely, into what is technically referred to as a clusterfuck. And possibly the most potentially damaging factor of them all is also the most innocuous: routine.

The first time any new procedure or operation is put into place, everybody will be alert and watchful, looking everywhere and checking everything, all the time. But when a team is doing exactly the same job at exactly the same time and in exactly the same place for the fifth or the tenth or the twentieth time, inevitably the attention of those involved is likely to slip.

This is particularly true with surveillance operations. A team will be assigned a target and their attention becomes focused on that person, and the importance of not losing contact with them is their overriding concern. The repetitive routine blunts their observational skills.

That evening, when the target turned his 7-series BMW into the short paved driveway beside the elegant townhouse on the northern edge of Mayfair and waited for the electric garage door to open, the essentially invisible mid-range grey Ford saloon that had followed him from his office just off London Wall pulled over about fifty yards away. As they had done on the five previous days when they'd shadowed the man, the driver switched off the engine and he and his companion watched as the car disappeared from view.

'Another day, another dollar,' the driver said as the garage door closed with a faint metallic clunk.

'Tell me about it,' the passenger said, reclining his seat as far as it would go and closing his eyes. 'Wake me up if tonight's the night.'

'With our luck, he'll head for his bed with an improving book and we'll have wasted another evening waiting for something to happen.'

Twenty minutes after he'd switched off the engine, the driver nudged his companion, who sat up immediately.

'Is he on the move?'

'No. I need a coffee and a piss, so get your eyes on. There's a Starbucks or a Costa a couple of streets back. Anything you want?'

'Yeah,' the passenger replied. 'Just bring me a regular coffee, white with one sugar. None of that latte or mocha shit. And a pastry or something.'

'Okay. Keys are in the ignition. If he walks out of his door, call me and I'll head straight back. But if he drives off somewhere or calls a taxi to pick him up, don't wait for me. Follow him and let me know where he goes and I'll get a cab there.'

The driver got out of the car and headed back the way they'd driven. As he did so, the passenger climbed out, stretched and then walked around the vehicle to sit behind the wheel.

And that was what the two-man team from Five had been waiting for.

Some twenty agents had been briefed that afternoon, most being pulled off other tasks, their instructions simple and lacking the kind of background data they were normally given. Twelve of them, working in pairs, had been assigned specific surveillance targets to watch and the actions to take in certain circumstances, and the arrival of the Ford saloon outside the house in Mayfair – one of the half dozen assigned targets – was precisely what they'd been told to look out for. The departure of one of the unidentified watchers was an unexpected bonus that would make their job a little easier. The other agents were just as important, though they were not directly involved in the surveillance, only in making sure that the surveillance worked.

A few minutes after the driver of the Ford had disappeared from view, a street person, a man grey with grime, his unkempt beard looking as if various small creatures possibly used it as a home, emerged from an alleyway between two buildings and headed along the street. He was wearing a tattered black overcoat tied around his waist with a length of rope and carrying an equally battered and torn rucksack over one shoulder. He appeared to have been drinking and weaved from side to side as he walked, muttering almost inaudibly to himself.

There were several cars parked along the street, and as he walked past each he tried the door handle, just in case one had been left unlocked, perhaps with some coins or something worth nicking left inside it.

When he reached the grey Ford he opened the passenger door and reached inside, but he clearly hadn't been expecting to find the vehicle occupied. He stepped backwards in alarm when he saw the man sitting in the driving seat, stumbled and fell sprawling onto the pavement beside the open door.

Immediately, the driver shouted a curse at him, opened his door and strode around the car.

'The fuck are you doing?' he demanded.

The derelict struggled to his feet and backed away, clutching his rucksack.

'Any spare change, mister?' he asked.

'Get the fuck away from here. Touch this car again and I'll kick the shit out of you.'

He slammed the passenger door of the car closed, walked back to the other side and sat down in the driving seat, activating the central locking as he did so.

On the pavement, the tramp took a last look at the Ford and its occupant and then continued his erratic progress along the street, still muttering and pulling at the occasional car door handle as he passed.

'Fucking winos,' the man in the car muttered. He watched the departing figure for a few seconds and then, when he was certain the tramp had left the scene, he turned his attention back to the house he had under surveillance.

—

The Security Service is charged with keeping the people of Britain safe, but usually without directly intervening on the streets. Actually feeling the collars of the bad guys is a task best left to the police, not least because MI5 officers do not have the power of arrest. Or to be specific, they can only carry out a citizen's arrest, exactly the same as any other UK resident, if they see a person carrying out what is referred to as an indictable offence, which typically means a serious crime like burglary or assault.

Its job is to gather intelligence, to identify terrorist plots or other planned atrocities, and to detect and nullify espionage operations mounted against the UK. In order to do this, the service recruits informers and tries to infiltrate its personnel into known or suspected terrorist groups, and it's often necessary for its agents to work undercover, frequently deep undercover, in order to penetrate every level of society.

The wino who had opened the passenger door of the Ford saloon was not quite what he appeared to be. He was a street person insofar as he frequently spent the night in a doorway or under a bridge or in an Underground station or in one of the other more or less sheltered areas favoured by people who had nowhere else to go. And he was to be seen on occasion queuing up at a soup kitchen or another temporary facility that provided hot food. He was also unwashed, as were his clothes.

But inside the rags and the stench and behind the beard the man was very different. Deep cover operations take a lot of planning and are long in execution, and he had been living his present lie for over six months, tasked with nothing more complex than keeping his eyes and ears open as he burrowed deeper and deeper into the shadowy underworld of the homeless. His masters at Millbank had believed terrorists might try recruiting the dropouts of society by promising them drugs or money in exchange for their participation in some planned attack. He had disagreed strongly, pointing out that terrorists like the 7/7 bombers were driven by religious fervour, not the need for another dose of crack cocaine or skunk, but in the end Millbank paid his salary and he'd had no option but to reluctantly abandon the use of his razor, soap and deodorant and take to the streets in the rags he had been given.

In the entire six months that he'd been on task, he didn't believe he'd achieved anything useful at all in terms of intelligence gathering, but just possibly his performance on the street beside the parked Ford, which had ended with him dexterously placing the battery-powered magnetic tracker underneath the car, entirely undetected by the man sitting in the driving seat, might actually be classed as a success. Why his masters wanted to follow the Ford had not been explained to him, the need-to-know principle being applied particularly ruthlessly when it came to keeping undercover agents in the loop. In short, they didn't keep him in the loop, just told him what to do, and when and where to do it.

The only bit of good news, really, he thought as he trudged away down the street, was that he was due to be reassigned within about three weeks, and whatever his new job was it had to be an improvement.

Twenty minutes later and a quarter of a mile behind him, the driver returned to the Ford carrying two coffees and a paper bag containing four muffins. He sat down in the passenger seat and handed his companion his drink and two of the cakes.

'Any movement?' he asked between mouthfuls.

'Bugger all. No sign of him.'

'Okay. We'll give it until about half ten and then call it a day.'

The man in the driving seat nodded agreement. He didn't mention the incident with the homeless person because he'd already effectively forgotten about it. And even if he had mentioned it, the chances of either of them realising that it had been more than just a casual encounter were slim.

Chapter 52

Wednesday
London

The beauty of using a tracker is that the vehicle or vehicles carrying out the surveillance don't have to follow right behind it. All they have to do is stay reasonably close and keep heading in the same general direction as the target vehicle.

The undercover teams sent out by Five to cover the homes of six of the bankers suggested by Nicholas Michaelson as possible blackmail targets had identified only two vehicles whose occupants appeared to be watching the properties. Four of the bankers had attracted no attention whatsoever, which could mean that they had no guilty secrets or, perhaps more likely, bearing in mind the quality of Michaelson's information, they had either already been compromised by the gang, or were on the list but hadn't so far been followed to whatever den of iniquity was their favoured haunt. After all, the gang couldn't have unlimited resources.

Two trackers were attached to the suspect vehicles, one by the wino who wasn't and the other by a young woman pushing a buggy, complete with a child strapped inside it.

The child wasn't an employee of the Security Service, being only about a year old, but his mother was, and it had been her idea to use the buggy to get close enough to the target car to position the tracker without attracting suspicion. Small children throw things out of prams and buggies as a matter of course, and all she'd had to do was to walk up to the target car, then cross the road immediately behind the vehicle. As she passed the rear of the car she bent down and did two things simultaneously. She attached the tracker she was holding to the underside of the rear of the car and picked up one of the toys from inside the buggy, as if recovering it from the road. Then she continued across the road, shaking the toy in her hands as if chastising her child. Only somebody with a clear view of the back of the car and who was paying close attention could have seen what she did. The two suspects inside the vehicle didn't react in any way at all, just maintained their patient scrutiny of the house on the opposite side of the road. The building was owned by a banker who Michaelson believed had an expensive and regular appetite for high-class hookers, the girls usually working in teams of four or more to cater to his needs.

With the trackers positioned and emitting clear signals, the MI5 watchers settled down to wait for as long as it took, which turned out to be most of the evening. Both the trackers started moving just after ten thirty, and each was immediately followed by a surveillance car, two-up, that hung well back, out of sight of the targets.

The two surveillance teams were in contact with each other and with Millbank by radio, and it soon became clear that both target vehicles were heading in broadly the same direction, towards west London.

'Control, this is Sierra One. We're heading north-west through Kensal Green.'

'Copied. Sierra Two, request update.'

'We're a bit further south in White City, and Tango Two is now tracking west.'

Roughly three quarters of an hour after the target vehicles had left the properties, both of them ceased moving. As soon as the surveillance teams were certain the cars had stopped completely, rather than just halted in traffic somewhere, the two MI5 cars headed directly for the static locations.

The results were not exactly what Millbank had expected or hoped.

One car had ended up in Perivale and the other between Wembley and Brent Park, but both vehicles had been parked on the road rather than in a driveway, which would have identified a specific property and tied it to the gang. And, of course, by the time the MI5 teams cruised down the streets where the target cars had come to a stop, the occupants were long gone.

'Control, Sierra Two. Do we leave the trackers in place or remove them?'

The trackers were only about the size of a matchbox but they were expensive pieces of kit. Although the units bore no identification marks, a surveillance equipment expert would probably be able to identify the manufacturer and have a reasonable guess at the agency that had deployed it. The Security Service was always extremely reluctant to have any of its operations exposed to the gaze of the general public and so, depending on the operation in progress, sometimes any electronic tags or devices might be removed if the risk of discovery was felt to be high.

'Leave them both, Sierra One and Two, because this is ongoing. Confirm the registration numbers of both vehicles and get a shot of their VIN numbers as well so we can check if they're ringers or legit. Just make sure you're not compromised. Then we can monitor them through the ANPR and traffic cameras as well as using the trackers.'

'Roger that.'

In the event, the VIN numbers matched the registration plates, which was something of a surprise, and both vehicles had current MOT certificates and were taxed and insured for any driver.

Exactly like the Jaguar abandoned by the unknown gang member at Sandy, both cars were owned by a combined Chinese takeaway and fish and chip shop on the outskirts of Bradford, and subsequent police enquiries with the owner of the business produced the information that he had been paid a cash sum by an acquaintance he was not prepared to name to buy, register, insure and tax several cars, as well as a white van. All the vehicles were fully roadworthy and had the correct documentation and, as the owner, he could allow anyone to drive them as long as they had a full UK licence.

Because what he had done was somewhat unusual but not in any way illegal, that was a hidden and unanticipated shoal on which the investigation temporarily foundered, and neither the police nor the Security Service had any idea of the identities of the people who had been in the two vehicles the MI5 agents had been following.

Specific instructions were issued for both cars to be tracked by the camera system in London and the Metropolitan Police were told to stop them for roadside checks as soon as possible to obtain the names and details of the drivers and any passengers.

But because Mr King had ordered his men to abandon the vehicles, neither the trackers nor the camera surveillance produced any results.

Chapter 53

Thursday
Vauxhall Cross, London

'How sure are you about this?' Angela Evans asked.

'Obviously I don't know the truth of the statement this man Dawkins made,' Cameron Riley replied, 'and I also don't know its source. I suppose it's possible that he misheard or misunderstood something that somebody said.'

'I think we should be taking it seriously,' Ben Morgan said. 'Just in case this is a genuine threat, maybe to encourage other victims to fight back against this blackmail gang Dawkins claims to have heard about.'

'Don't worry, we are.'

'Who is this James McEwan?' Evans asked. 'Was he on the list Michaelson gave us? I don't remember seeing his name.'

'Michaelson didn't mention him,' Riley said, 'and all I know about him is his name and job title, and I've looked at a copy of his CV. Nothing that's relevant to this.'

'Where's Andrew Nuffield when we need him?' Morgan asked rhetorically. 'So we'll be watching McEwan, just in case he tries to do something stupid?'

Riley nodded.

'I've already talked to Millbank and they've put a four-man team on it with immediate effect, as in they're camped outside his office right now, three in a car and one on a motorbike to make sure they don't lose him in traffic. The second and third men in the car are there just in case McEwan goes into a building or gets on a bus or Tube.'

'He's the CEO of a major bank,' Evans pointed out. 'He's hardly likely to risk sullying his Savile Row suits by using public transport.'

'It's just a precaution, and I'd rather see too many people involved in any surveillance operation than too few. Redundancy is always a good thing.'

'Bearing in mind that McEwan is likely to be the instigator of trouble, if what Dawkins claims to have overheard is true, is it worth getting Five or GCHQ to listen to his phone calls?' Morgan asked.

'Probably not,' Riley replied. 'McEwan would be an idiot to try to arrange anything over the telephone. If he genuinely is going to try to have this man Harrison murdered, the one thing we can be reasonably sure about is that he won't do it himself. He'll hire a specialist, a contract killer, and unless he already knows his friendly neighbourhood assassin, about the only way he could set anything up would be to go digging around in the Dark Web, which is a dangerous place for somebody who doesn't know what they're doing. And that's only going to work if he already has access to bitcoin because that's the only means of payment that would be accepted.'

'I don't know this James McEwan, obviously,' Evans said, 'but would anyone as successful as him risk his entire career by contracting to kill a man who's trying to blackmail him? Isn't that a bit of an overreaction?'

'I think that rather depends on what McEwan has been doing,' Morgan replied. 'It'll also depend on how much of a psychopath he is, because most likely he'll think he can get away with it. He probably can't understand how anyone would have the temerity to try to blackmail him in the first place, and he'll believe he was entirely justified in taking whatever steps were necessary to remove the threat. Essentially, he's an intelligent and powerful rat in a corner, and that's a dangerous animal.'

'Andrew didn't answer his mobile,' Evans said, picking up one of the landline phones in the conference room, 'so I'll give Michaelson a ring and see if he knows anything about the man.'

Less than three minutes later she replaced the receiver and looked across the table at Morgan and Riley.

'Michaelson knows of him but doesn't know him. McEwan has a reputation for being a hard businessman and he doesn't suffer fools gladly. In fact, he doesn't suffer fools at all. He just fires them.'

'I think we—' Morgan began, but broke off when his mobile phone rang.

'Morgan,' he said as he answered the call. Then he just listened.

'I have a feeling,' he said, slipping his phone into his jacket pocket and looking at Riley, 'that Stephen Dawkins didn't only call the police to tell them about McEwan. Either that or these blackmailers have a sophisticated intelligence network of their own.'

'What's happened?'

'A site on the Dark Web has just gone live, according to one of my contacts at GCHQ where they keep a watching brief for this kind of thing. It contains about a dozen photographs and three videos of different lengths. The media all show a man stated to be James McEwan – and the site includes his name, job title and contact numbers – snorting what looks like cocaine from a glass-topped table using a rolled-up fifty-pound note. They also show him naked on a bed with a girl who's also naked and young enough to be his daughter. I'm sure you don't need me to spell out what they were doing.'

'So they must have heard about his threat to them and decided to ruin his life anyway,' Riley said. 'But why did they publish it on the Dark Web? There's a good chance nobody will find it down there.'

'They thought of that. They've also scattered a bunch of posts across social media along the lines of "Do you know what your bank manager does in his spare time?" and included the full Dark Web address as a link plus another link to download TOR to access it. That's how GCHQ picked it up, and there's been plenty of traffic already, followed by lots of tweets and retweets as people followed the link and saw the images and videos. The other reason they probably chose the Dark Web was because it's a whole lot more difficult to find the actual location of a site hosted down there and shut it down. That's academic anyway now, because the images and videos have been copied and re-published all over the place on the regular web, so that particular horse has already bolted.'

'Is there anything we can do about it?' Evans asked. 'In fact, should we even be trying to do anything? McEwan brought this on himself by being a bloody pervert and having his picture taken while he was at it.'

'I don't think he knew he was performing on film,' Morgan said, 'but I take your point.'

At that moment Riley's mobile rang. It wasn't a long conversation, and his responses to the caller were largely monosyllabic. He ended the call and looked at Morgan.

'It's amazing how quickly word gets out, especially if it's bad news,' he said. 'I've got tripwires set up through the Bank of England to watch for unusual fluctuations in the market.'

'Let me guess,' Morgan said. 'McEwan's bank's stock has taken a hammering?'

'Got it in one. The City really doesn't like surprises, and a decent-quality video published on the Web showing the CEO of one of the biggest banks in London sodomising a naked girl and snorting coke is almost exactly the kind of surprise it doesn't like. The bank's stock is down nearly eight per cent already. And that's not all.'

He paused for a moment, and Evans filled in the gap.

'Let me have a go,' she said. 'As soon as the market opened this morning there was a flurry of activity amongst the options traders, with investors buying puts on McEwan's bank stock, well before news of these videos and photographs leaked. Something like that?'

'Exactly. An unexpected surge that's already generated impressive profits because the stock's value has fallen so far and so fast. And before either of you ask, almost all the options have been bought by private investors using nominee accounts based outside the UK.'

Morgan looked interested.

'Give me the details and I'll get Cheltenham to backtrack the transactions. We'll probably find that the trail ends in a maze of holding companies with accounts in Vanuatu or the Cayman Islands or some other tricky jurisdiction, but if there is a way through GCHQ will find it.'

Chapter 54

Thursday
City of London

James McEwan sat silently at his desk and stared at the moving images on the screen of his laptop, his mind racing. His own face looked back at him from the computer, his body moving rhythmically on top of the call girl lying face-down on the bed. She was making convincing-sounding moans of pleasure, though the expression on her face suggested the experience was not one of unalloyed enjoyment for her.

The handsets of both his landline phones lay on the desk where he'd placed them when the frequency of calls became virtually continuous. And almost every call had had the same substance, basically abusive disbelief that he could have been so stupid.

McEwan slammed down the lid of his laptop in cold fury, stood up and walked over to the window, staring sightlessly at the familiar buildings and skyline, knowing in his heart – but still not really accepting – that it was probably the last time he'd ever see it, at least from that office. There were some mistakes that could be covered up and eventually forgotten about, and every City institution could produce a long list of such errors and the names of the people who'd made them, but there were others that nobody ever walked away from. The kind of activity he had seen in full colour and HD-quality detail definitely counted as one of the latter.

He moved to the centre of the large double-glazed window that dominated his office and rested his hands on the ledge.

–

McEwan's appearance was just what the man lying prone on the flat roof of a building undergoing renovation a little under three hundred yards from McEwan's office window had been waiting for. In the crowded brick and stone and concrete canyons of the City of London, finding a spot which gave him the view he needed had taken a couple of hours, about half of it using Google's Street View to identify possible locations, and the second hour walking the streets the previous evening to select the best option. It wasn't ideal, but the building did offer a narrow line of sight between two other structures.

He'd been there since about seven thirty that morning, walking onto the building site with the other workers, wearing overalls, carrying a long and battered canvas bag that looked as if it contained something like a pipe bender, and showing a forged work order. Once on the roof, he'd found a secluded corner, moved various boxes and panels to hide himself from casual view and settled down to wait. His weapon was a slightly unusual sniper rifle – an old French FR F1 in 7.62x51mm NATO.

The assassin stared at his target through the optics of his preferred telescopic sight, a Nikko Stirling Diamond long-range tactical unit, which brought James McEwan's face into sharp focus. The rifle was, to use the military term, locked and cocked, with the bullet in the chamber requiring only pressure on the trigger to fire, but for some two seconds the shooter waited, making sure that the man wasn't about to move away and out of sight, because he would only get one chance.

When he was confident that McEwan would remain standing there for another few moments, he lowered the rifle barrel fractionally, adjusting the point of aim to the man's chest. Both the rifle and the shooter were perfectly capable of hitting a target the size of a human head at that range, but the double-glazed window in front of McEwan added an extra layer of complication and aiming at the man's centre mass offered a better chance of a kill. It didn't help that the bullet would hit the window not head-on, but from an oblique angle.

He had already factored in the bullet drop, the difference in elevation between himself and his target, and adjusted the sight for windage.

The shooter squeezed the trigger.

The first bullet took just under half a second to reach the target, but before it had impacted the window the shooter had already worked the bolt of the FR F1 to chamber a second round. As the window shattered, he checked the sight picture and fired again.

The logic was simple. Quite probably the first round would crash through the double-glazed panes of glass and blow a hole through McEwan's chest. But sometimes a bullet could be deflected by something comparatively insubstantial, and it was possible that the first bullet might miss him completely, the angle of the twin panes of glass being sufficient to knock it off course. Hence the second round that would go straight through the hole in the window and definitely take out the target.

The shooter worked the bolt to chamber a third round, his actions instinctive and well-practised, while he stared through the telescopic sight at the target building.

Through the enlarged, state-of-the-art optics, he saw the expression on McEwan's face change from what looked like terminal irritation to startled amazement. He saw the man glance down in total disbelief at the circle of red that had suddenly defaced the front of his white shirt.

The target lurched backwards perhaps half a step, then his body flinched as the second bullet struck and he tumbled out of sight.

The shooter maintained the sight picture for another ten seconds or so, just in case McEwan had only been wounded and managed to stagger to his feet again. At that range, with that weapon and with what he had witnessed through the telescopic sight, the shooter knew it was extremely unlikely. But he was a professional, and professionals always check, so he watched and waited.

McEwan didn't appear, which was exactly what he had expected, and neither did anybody else. He stood up, unloaded the sniper rifle and packed it away in the canvas bag that he'd used to carry it, along with the two fired cartridge cases, reached inside the bag and took out a Browning Hi-Power nine-millimetre automatic pistol and a plastic face mask modelled on Donald Trump. He pulled the mask over his face, picked up his bag with his left hand, holding the pistol in his right, and walked across to the opposite side of the building where a lift had been installed to allow the workmen access to the higher levels.

He knew that the sound of the shots would have been heard and although one shot might have been dismissed as something heavy being dropped, two rifle shots, one after the other, would probably be unmistakeable. Hence the pistol, to dissuade any workmen who wanted to stop him, and the mask to completely disguise his identity. The shooter doubted very much if anyone would have paid him much attention when he walked onto the site, but he was equally sure that people would notice him when he left. And their descriptions would be profoundly unhelpful to the police: Donald Trump, wearing workman's overalls and carrying a pistol.

There were two workmen in the lift when it arrived at the top floor, possibly visiting that part of the building to find out what had made the noises. The shooter waited out of sight to one side of the lift until it reached his level and the men stepped out. He said nothing to them as he came into view, simply gestured with the Browning for them to move out of his way. People waving weapons tend to get what they want and the two workmen stepped to one side and raised their arms above their heads.

The shooter descended to ground level and strode unhurriedly across the building site. Conversation stopped as he came into view, but the sight of the pistol in his right hand ensured that nobody went anywhere near him. Two or three of the workers used their mobile phones to capture his image as he walked past, and one man videoed him leaving. If the assassin noticed any of this, he ignored it. When the police looked at the pictures of him, it would simply reinforce whatever verbal descriptions they obtained but would not help them identify him in any way.

As he stepped onto the pavement a black cab that had been waiting about fifty yards up the road since just after nine that morning drove up and stopped beside him. The shooter climbed into the back seat and the driver accelerated away.

Still wearing his mask, he looked behind the vehicle through the rear window and saw a couple of the workmen using the cameras in their mobiles to photograph the taxi. That, he knew, also wouldn't help the police because the cab was a ringer, displaying the number plate of another black cab that was most likely engaged on entirely legitimate business elsewhere in London.

'Any problems?' the driver asked.

'No,' the shooter replied, pulling off the mask. 'Two shots, both hit him and I saw him fall. That should pretty much ensure we don't have any trouble with anybody else. Mr King should be pleased.'

Chapter 55

Thursday
Vauxhall Cross, London

'So what do we do about James McEwan?' Angela Evans asked.

Cameron Riley's phone rang before he could reply.

'Riley,' he said, picking it up.

Morgan's mobile rang a couple of seconds later.

The two men listened, hardly responding at all, and Angela guessed they might both be receiving similar messages.

Morgan finished his call just before Riley did, and looked at her, his expression grim.

'I guess that answers your question about James McEwan,' he said, 'and what we should do about him. The answer's nothing, because somebody else has just taken care of him for us.'

He explained what he'd just been told.

'They shot him?' Evans asked, the tone of her voice revealing her disbelief. 'In broad daylight? In the City of London?'

Morgan nodded.

'According to the police, the man with the rifle was about three hundred yards away, firing at an oblique angle, and McEwan was hit by two bullets, though one would have been enough. And as far as the sniper was concerned, the daylight helped him see what he was doing. It might have been easier to hit him at his home but I don't think this was just a killing. It was an unequivocal message to the other people who're being blackmailed.

'McEwan made it clear that he wasn't going to lie down and take it and made a threat against the people involved. When they found out about it – and I have a good idea where that information probably came from – they made good on their threat to publish details of his guilty secret. And then they killed him in a very public manner which I'm certain all the other blackmail victims will already have heard about. Knowing all that, I have no doubt that the other victims will do nothing apart from pay, just to avoid ending up like McEwan.'

'We have to do something,' Evans said, 'and now, not in a week or a month. I know investigating McEwan's murder will be a job for the Met, but we still know more about what's going on than they do. We have to stop it going any further. And we have to find these men and take them out of the equation, one way or the other.'

Morgan nodded.

'I'm absolutely with you on this. Those two rifle shots changed my personal rules of engagement. I'm not interested in seeing these people standing trial at the Old Bailey and then watching some liberal lefty judge deciding that they've all had traumatic childhoods and giving them a couple of years in jail and a slap on the wrist. I want to see them end up the way that James McEwan ended up, lying in a pool of their own blood.'

Angela looked at Riley.

'And I suppose you'll be briefing Dave North and getting him to rustle up a few of his playmates from Hereford to come down here to help sort things out?'

'You know me too well, Angela. That's pretty much the first item on my agenda.'

'So what's the second item? And the third?'

'The second thing I'm going to do is make sure that Millbank continues with the surveillance of the bankers Michaelson identified as possible blackmail subjects. But there will be a slight change of plan. I'm not bothered about following these bad guys out to west London or wherever they live. From now on, if the surveillance detects anybody watching these bankers I want them grabbed and given the third degree. The men from Hereford can attend to that. It should be right up their street. We've been pussyfooting around for too long. It's time we took the initiative.'

'I can't argue with any of that,' Angela said.

'That's the kind of backstop, in my opinion,' Morgan said, 'because after this assassination maybe the blackmailers will lie low for a while and wait for the heat to die down. But there's another path we can follow that might provide us with quicker results.'

'You're going to invite Stephen Dawkins to assist the police – or rather assist us – with our enquiries.'

'Exactly. I don't believe for a moment that he overheard McEwan talking about killing one of the blackmailers. I think Dawkins is paying money to these people himself, and I think he's much more deeply involved in this than he's admitting. So, yes, I'd like to have a heart-to-heart with him and see where we go from there.'

Chapter 56

Thursday
182 Bishopsgate, London

An interview room in a City of London police station is a long way from being the most comfortable place in the world, which in some ways is really the point. The last thing any investigating officer wants is for a suspect to feel relaxed and comfortable. Making them feel apprehensive is far more likely to produce pertinent information or even a confession.

Stephen Dawkins looked anything but comfortable, sitting on one side of the table and facing the three men seated opposite him. Just under half an hour earlier, Ben Morgan and Cameron Riley, accompanied by two City of London plain-clothes police officers, had walked into his office and – using the word in its loosest possible sense – invited him to accompany them to Bishopsgate. The warrant cards carried by the officers and Riley's identification meant that it wasn't a request but an order. Dawkins had objected and blustered, and it was only when one of the officers had produced a set of handcuffs that he'd finally agreed to accompany them. The threat of being marched out of his own office in handcuffs was clearly disturbing enough to make him comply.

The City of London officer sitting between Morgan and Riley switched on the recording equipment.

'My name is Detective Sergeant Stuart Howard of the City of London Police. The subject of this interview is Mr Stephen Dawkins. Also present are Ben Morgan and Cameron Riley.'

'Am I being charged with anything?' Dawkins asked, perhaps trying to take the initiative.

'At the moment, sir,' Howard replied, 'you're just helping us with our enquiries and you have the right to have your solicitor present.'

'Do I need a solicitor?' Dawkins asked.

'At this moment,' Riley replied, taking over the questioning, 'I have no idea, but in view of what we already know about you it might be prudent to have one on standby.'

Dawkins' complexion seemed to pale a little at that, but he didn't respond.

'The problem we have with you, Mr Dawkins,' Morgan said, 'is that we think you've been telling us porkies.'

'But I haven't told you anything yet,' Dawkins objected.

'I know. I was talking about the statement you made earlier about James McEwan. You used one of your office telephones to contact the police and gave your name and number. Then you said you had overheard him saying that he was being blackmailed and that he intended to kill the person doing the blackmailing. That's the bit we don't believe.'

Dawkins said nothing.

'We don't believe it for at least two reasons,' Morgan went on. 'First, it seems staggeringly unlikely that anyone seriously contemplating committing murder would chat about it in a location where what he was saying could be overheard by a third party. Second, unless McEwan was talking to a hitman to discuss the details of the assassination, it's difficult to think of any reason why such a conversation would take place at all.'

'I can only tell you what I heard,' Dawkins said stubbornly.

'That, oddly enough, is the bit that we do believe. We think that what you told the police was an accurate account of what McEwan said, but we're also quite certain that the circumstances of that conversation were entirely different to what you're claiming.'

Again Dawkins didn't respond.

'You see,' Morgan said, 'there's one scenario that seems to us to make perfect sense. We think that it wasn't just James McEwan who was being blackmailed. We think that other senior bankers and executive staff working here in the City have been targeted as well. And we also think that McEwan probably discussed his intention to do something about it with other victims. So really that means one of two things. Either you also have some dirty little secret that these people found out about and that you've been paying money to avoid them making public or, possibly, James McEwan was a confidant of yours and he asked your opinion about what he intended to do. Or hoped to do. Or something of that sort. What we can't work out is any other mechanism by which you could have discovered his intentions. He had to have told you directly, face to face, what he was planning. And then, as a public-spirited and upright citizen of this great city, you contacted the police to tell them what you knew about a man who had told you he was going to commit a very serious crime.'

Morgan paused to allow Dawkins to think through the implications of what he'd said and to grasp the metaphorical lifeline that he had just extended.

'So which is it, Mr Dawkins? Are you being blackmailed, or are you just a concerned citizen who wanted to do the right thing?'

Dawkins nodded, apparently coming to a decision.

'Let me be completely honest with you,' he said, which raised an immediate red flag in Morgan's mind, because it normally meant the speaker was about to lie through his or her teeth.

'I've known – or I suppose I should say I knew – James McEwan for many years and he did on occasion use me as a kind of sounding board when he was considering a new business venture, because he knew he could rely on both my honesty and experience. And on my discretion, of course. He called me a few days ago and said he had an important matter to discuss. I assumed, obviously, that it was some kind of financial question and I was shocked when he told me that he had become a victim of blackmailers. I gave him my advice, which was simply to go to the police and not to pay the sums demanded. What he told me next shocked me even more. He said that he dared not involve the police, and at the same time he couldn't risk any of the information the blackmailers had obtained being revealed. And that's when he told me that he planned to murder the only member of the gang that he had come into contact with. He—'

'Did he tell you the name of this person?' Riley asked him.

'Er, yes, he did. The name he gave was John Harrison, though of course bearing in mind his profession that may well have been an alias.'

'Did McEwan tell you how he was going to kill this man Harrison?' Morgan asked.

'No. But I don't think it's much of a secret that there are people who will perform this sort of service for a fee, and I assume he had a contact who could put him in touch with that kind of person. But obviously I don't know any details. We parted on somewhat frosty terms, and the last thing I did before I left was to repeat myself. I told him that he should tell the police and not try to do anything about it himself.'

'Did you tell him that you were going to inform the police?' Riley asked.

Dawkins looked surprised.

'Of course not,' he replied. 'That would have been a gross betrayal of trust.'

'But then you did tell the police,' Morgan pointed out, 'so is that not an even greater betrayal of trust? You told the police in defiance of his express wishes and didn't even have the courage to tell him what you intended to do.'

'I didn't plan on doing that. It was only afterwards when I thought about the situation that I realised I needed to tell someone. To protect McEwan from himself, almost.'

'Did you tell anyone else about his plan?' Morgan asked.

This time Dawkins looked both shocked and indignant.

'Certainly not,' he snapped. 'As I said, I told the police what I knew and that was all. Obviously I have no idea if any member of the police force mentioned it to a third party.'

'And that raises another problem, Mr Dawkins,' Morgan said, 'and I'm sure a man of your intelligence can easily work it out.'

'I don't understand.'

'Think it through. You said McEwan told you face to face what he intended to do, and you passed on that information to the police and to nobody else. If those two statements are true, then why is James McEwan lying on a tray in a fridge in a City mortuary with two bullet holes in his chest? McEwan obviously wouldn't have told the blackmailers what he intended to do, and nor would the police. You said you didn't, so who did? Because we have no doubt whatsoever that the reason McEwan was blown away by a sniper this morning was because someone told the blackmail gang that he was planning to kill John Harrison. That was why they released those images and videos, and then they killed him.'

His voice rose almost to a shout on the last four words, and on the other side of the table Dawkins pushed himself backwards in his chair, as if from the force of Morgan's words.

'So let me give you a reality check, Dawkins.'

Everyone noticed that the 'Mister' had disappeared.

'We don't believe you. We think you're just as much in the grip of this gang as McEwan was. We know you called the police, but we think you probably also called the blackmailers, probably before you called us. We'll be checking the call records of every phone you own, though we know that probably won't work because you'll have used a burner. But we'll also check all your bank accounts and find out exactly how much money you're paying out and who to. And when we find out that you're paying off the blackmailers we'll be charging you with being an accessory before the fact over McEwan's murder. And that's as serious as a heart attack.'

Morgan took a sheet of paper from his pocket and unfolded it.

'Let me read you a definition. "An accessory before the fact is a person who aids, abets or encourages another to commit a crime but who is not present at the scene. An accessory before the fact, like an accomplice, may be held criminally liable to the same extent as the principal." So when we prove you told the blackmailers about James McEwan, you'll find yourself standing in the dock alongside the sniper and facing a charge of murder.'

Stephen Dawkins didn't just look pale and shocked, he looked almost as if he was going to throw up. He opened and closed his mouth a couple of times like a landed fish but said nothing.

Before either Riley or Morgan could resume their questioning, there was a double tap on the door and a uniformed sergeant appeared framed in the doorway.

Stuart Howard looked over at the police officer, his irritation about the interview being interrupted clear on his face.

'I know you didn't want to be disturbed, Stu,' the sergeant said, 'but we've got a walk-in and you're definitely going to want to hear what he has to say.'

Howard glanced at Morgan, who gave a brief nod.

'Interview suspended at 14:23,' Howard said and switched off the recording equipment. 'Would you like a drink, Mr Dawkins?' he asked. 'Coffee or tea?'

'Just water,' Dawkins replied, his voice little more than a croak.

Outside, Howard buttonholed a uniformed constable, told him to get some water and then to wait in the interview room with Dawkins until they came back to start the questioning again.

'So who's the walk-in?' he asked the uniformed sergeant. 'Somebody who works with Dawkins?'

The sergeant shook his head.

'Better than that. Somebody who worked closely with McEwan. His name's Jeremy Somerville and he's in interview room three. He has a list that you need to see to believe.'

Chapter 57

Thursday
182 Bishopsgate, London

'So you knew James McEwan well?' Cameron Riley asked, after they had introduced themselves.

'Rather better than I wanted or needed to,' Jeremy Somerville replied. 'I know you're never supposed to speak ill of the dead, but he was a total bastard to work for. Nothing was ever good enough, you always needed to try harder and he'd happily sack anyone for the slightest infraction if he thought he could get away with it. You know, without falling foul of company or employment law.'

'I was going to say that I was sorry about what happened to him,' Cameron said, 'but in view of what you've just said I don't think I'll bother. The sergeant told us you had a list. What kind of list, and why would it interest the police?'

Somerville explained about the man who'd come in off the street and demanded to see McEwan, and about the research he'd been instructed to do afterwards.

'I had to cut a few corners to do what he wanted,' he said, 'and I suppose you could say that I took the name of the Bank of England in vain, but I couldn't think of any other way of getting the answers that McEwan needed.'

'And all the people on this list were clients of this security company PSP4?' Riley asked, looking at the printout Somerville had given him. 'A security company that I've never heard of. And if it was one working in the City I should know all about it.'

'Did he tell you what he going to do with this information?'

'No. He said nothing, just told me to destroy it.'

'And obviously you didn't do that?' Morgan asked.

'No, I did do that, because I knew that if I didn't there was a good chance McEwan would check my computer to make sure there was nothing there. So I ran a military-standard delete program on that directory, but before I wiped it I made a copy on a thumb drive. McEwan's behaviour was so peculiar that it felt like a good idea. And it just seemed beyond the bounds of coincidence that less than a week after John Harrison walked into the bank, McEwan was shown to be a drug-taking pervert and philanderer, if that's the word I want, and the same day he was exposed for all the world to see he was also murdered. I don't believe these events aren't all connected somehow, and that's why I came here to tell you what I know.'

He pointed at the paper Cameron Riley was still holding.

'I was interviewed at the office by one of the detectives investigating McEwan's killing, and he told me that the City of London police were questioning a man here at Bishopsgate, and he also let slip that it was Stephen Dawkins. Well, of course I knew that his name was on the list, so I printed a copy to give to whoever was in charge here.'

'Can you just talk us through what happened when John Harrison visited McEwan?' Morgan asked. 'And a CCTV or a word picture of Harrison would help.'

Somerville provided a clear and concise account of what he'd overheard when he failed to close the door to McEwan's office, and said he'd check the bank's security cameras for an image of Harrison.

Morgan nodded when he'd finished.

'Thank you for this, Mr Somerville,' he said. 'This is particularly valuable information. Can you please remain here in the station for about another hour, just in case we have any other questions for you. We'll get the desk sergeant to organise some coffee.'

'If it's all the same to you,' Somerville replied, 'and no offence meant, there's a Caffè Nero on the other side of Bishopsgate and I think I'd rather get myself something to eat and drink over there. I also need to call my wife to let her know what's going on, so I'll stay there for an hour and then come back over here in case you've any further questions.'

Morgan, Riley and Detective Sergeant Howard walked back into the interview room. They relieved the uniformed constable, switched on the recorders and sat down facing Dawkins.

'You mentioned this man John Harrison,' Morgan said. 'When did you meet him?'

Dawkins seemed to have recovered his composure slightly, and he immediately shook his head.

'I didn't say I'd met him,' he replied. 'I told you that James McEwan had met him, not me.'

'There you go again, Dawkins, being economical with the truth.' Morgan's voice was laced with steel. 'You see, I think we've now got a handle on the way that this gang of blackmailers operates. They select a likely victim and then follow him around until they find out if he has some kind of secret vice. If he has, they work out how to get unambiguous evidence to prove it, just as they did with McEwan, probably using hidden cameras to photograph their victim in the act. Then they send in this man John Harrison to explain the situation to them, and he probably shows them photographs as proof of what they know. How am I doing so far?' he asked the room at large.

'Pretty well, I think,' Riley replied.

'Good. But what they don't do is demand money. No brown envelopes filled with used twenties and fifties, nothing like that. They're much more subtle in their approach. Instead of making a threat, Harrison offers to provide a useful service, almost protection, to allow them to continue with whatever their particular perversion happens to be, to warn them if there's any indication that the police are taking an interest in what they get up to in their spare time. And all they have to do is sign up with a security company called PSP4. In return for a substantial monthly fee, which would probably be paid by the bank or company that they work for in the belief that it's a legitimate expense, they can carry on taking drugs, doing high-stakes illegal gambling, climbing into bed with underage children or whatever else floats their boat. It's a brilliant system and virtually risk-free as far as the blackmailers are concerned because it appears on the surface to be an entirely legitimate commercial operation. So what's your particular vice, Dawkins?'

The man's face had been growing paler by the second as Ben Morgan spelt out virtually the exact sequence of events that had led to him becoming an extremely unwilling client of PSP4.

'In fact, don't tell me. Let me guess,' Morgan went on. 'You don't look to me like a gambler, somehow, and as far as I can see your septum is still intact so that probably means you don't spend your weekends snorting cocaine or crystal meth. So most likely your weakness is located below the waist.'

'I don't—' Dawkins began, but Morgan immediately interrupted him.

'But you do, Dawkins, you do, and we can prove it because of this.' Morgan held up the paper that Somerville had given him. 'This is a list of CEOs, chairmen, managing directors and other top ranking executives who are paying hefty monthly subscriptions to PSP4. It was compiled by a banking official who worked closely with James McEwan. Your name, oddly enough, is the second on the list. This official also told us about the sales pitch used by John Harrison, and he was able to do that because he stood close enough to McEwan's door to overhear most of their conversation. So we even know what the monthly subscription costs you. McEwan was told it would cost him ten grand to keep his drug-taking and predatory sexual activities away from the public gaze, and my guess is that you're paying the same.'

It looked as if Dawkins was about to nod but he stopped the gesture immediately and just stared at Morgan.

'You can say what you like about this, and deny it all you want, but the reality is that PSP4 is not an authorised security company and the only reason anyone pays money to it is because the alternative is so much worse. The kind of secrets that PSP4 dredges up are so potentially damaging that anyone who refuses to pay is looking at divorce and the end of their career at the very least, and in some cases the certainty, because of the quality of the evidence, of a successful prosecution and a significant prison sentence.'

Morgan thought he could see beads of sweat starting to appear on Dawkins' forehead, despite the fact that the temperature in the interview room was perceptibly cool.

'So here's where we are,' Morgan said. 'We know you've been up to something just because you're a client of PSP4, but right now I'm not interested in that. What I am interested in is what you can tell me about the company, starting with a description of John Harrison – which I hope for your sake matches the one we've already got – and ending with whatever contact arrangements you have with PSP4, like a phone number or an email address. Something we can use to trace them.'

'And if I provide this information,' Dawkins said after quite a long silence, 'what happens to me then?'

'As I said,' Morgan replied, 'I'm only interested in finding PSP4. I don't care what you did to attract their attention or anything else about your life.'

There was another pause, and then Dawkins nodded. Over the next five minutes he explained in considerable detail how he had been approached by Harrison, how much he was paying, and also supplied the contact number that he had been given in case he needed to speak to somebody at PSP4.

'And is that everything?' Morgan asked, looking up from the pad on which he had been making notes.

'Yes,' Dawkins said tightly. 'Can I go now?'

'Of course not, you stupid man,' Morgan said, standing up. 'My interest begins and ends with PSP4, but my friend Cameron Riley here represents the Treasury and Financial Regulators, and I think he's quite enthusiastic about weeding out this cluster of criminals and perverts who appear to be running our banking system. Including you, obviously, so I'm quite sure he'll want a word about your forthcoming unexpected resignation from your position. And of course Detective Sergeant Howard here, who's been remarkably patient while we tried to dig down to the bottom of this, will no doubt want to interview you with a view to prosecuting you as an accessory in the murder of James McEwan.'

'You lied to me, you bastard,' Dawkins spat, half rising from his seat. Howard rose in turn, just in case the confrontation became physical, but then Dawkins sat down again.

'I didn't,' Morgan pointed out. 'I was just being economical with the truth, something with which you seem to be quite familiar. I just said I had no interest in you. I didn't mention my two colleagues.'

And with that, Morgan turned and left the interview room.

Chapter 58

Thursday

Vauxhall Cross, London

'Something rather peculiar has happened,' Angela Evans said.

'Just give me one minute and I'll be all ears,' Morgan replied. He picked up one of the secure phones and had a very brief conversation with Natasha Black out at GCHQ, setting things in motion as best he could with the limited amount of information he had available. Then he made a second almost equally brief call to Dave North, who was doing some kind of Secret Squirrel activity up at Hereford, to warn him.

'Right,' he said 'I'm all yours.'

'You remember the snippet of conversation that sent us up to Cambridgeshire to rescue Nicholas Michaelson? Obviously what we were interested in was the content, what the people involved actually said.'

'As you said, that's obvious. I don't see where you're going with this, Angela.'

'Where I'm going is Cheltenham and the people at the Doughnut. The GCHQ analysts identified that brief conversation and forwarded it to us for action, along with the location where it had been recorded. But they didn't stop there. One of the analysts thought he detected a trace of an accent – a foreign accent – in one of the voices the app picked up, and he decided to check it out. I put in a call to John Waterson and he confirmed that the three surviving kidnappers all speak English as their first language and have regional accents but that was all. The fourth kidnapper didn't survive the encounter, as we know, but he's now been identified and he was born in Ipswich.'

'So that just leaves the one who got away,' Morgan said, 'and if he was the man who told the kidnapper to go and break one of Michaelson's bones, that probably means he was the boss. So who are we dealing with here? The bloody Russian mafia?'

'Oddly enough, no. GCHQ ran a whole series of voice recognition and comparison checks with the take from Echelon and came up with a match, but it was from a lot further east than Moscow. In fact, the voice matched about half a dozen snippets of conversation that had been recorded in Hong Kong and another couple in Macau.'

That surprised Morgan, and he said so.

'Hong Kong? If you'd said Guangdong Province or Shanghai or even Beijing I'd almost have expected it because of the number of cyberattacks that China launches against the UK and America. So could GCHQ put a name to the voice?'

Evans nodded.

'In fact, they put three names to three different voices including our mystery man over here. From references in the conversations GCHQ believes he's called Wang, but whether or not that's his real name or just a name he uses in his business – which is crime, obviously – isn't clear. The Chinese name more or less translates as King. What GCHQ found most interesting was one of the conversations that took place in Hong Kong. The substance of the recording was fairly straightforward, just two men talking with Wang and discussing when he should leave Hong Kong. It was only a few sentences recorded as the three men walked past a bar that was already under surveillance for an entirely different reason. But it was the identities of the two men with Wang that was a surprise. Their names aren't important because they'd mean nothing to you, but both were high-level officials in the mainland Chinese government.'

'Governments consorting with known criminals isn't exactly unheard of,' Morgan pointed out. 'GCHQ can't help any further, I suppose?'

'That's it for the moment, as far as they're concerned. They've put markers on the two Chinese officials and Wang himself, and they'll update us if they learn anything new. But I'm waiting for a call right now that might help.'

'From Hong Kong, presumably?'

Evans nodded.

'Yes,' she replied, 'just because of the time difference. I've asked the questions and as soon as the man who knows the answers gets back to work he'll give me a call. That's what they've told me, anyway.'

Half an hour later, Evans took the call she'd been waiting for. When she rang off, she looked over at Morgan and nodded.

'That man was an inspector in the Hong Kong Police Force,' she said, 'and it looks like Wang is about as bad as you can get. He was being held in jail in Kowloon and facing a charge of what you might call enhanced murder. He not only had someone killed, but he had them tortured over three or four days and then fed what was left to the four-legged residents of a pig farm.'

'And now he's here? That's just what we needed.'

'The Hong Kong police were certain that he was guilty, but before they could charge him he was removed from the jail by two representatives of the mainland Chinese government. They said they were taking him back to China to face charges there, but he never crossed the border. Three days after his release from jail somebody who looked remarkably like Wang but who was carrying a genuine passport in a completely different name flew out of Hong Kong's Chek Lap Kok airport. He had a ticket on a Thai AirAsia flight to Bangkok, and the following day the same man used the same passport to board a non-stop British Airways flight from Bangkok to Heathrow. The Hong Kong police have no idea where he is now, except presumably somewhere in the UK.'

'I think we can probably give them a clue,' Morgan said. 'He's gone to ground somewhere here in London, where he's running a brand-new and very successful business. I think we—'

He broke off as his mobile phone rang.

'That was Natasha,' he said when he'd finished. 'GCHQ's managed to trace the origin of the instructions to buy the put options on McEwan's bank stock. I won't bore you with the technobabble, but the messages reached London after travelling through fifteen different countries and ostensibly originated in Mumbai. But actually they didn't. GCHQ are quite certain that all the instructions came from one specific server in Beijing.'

Evans didn't seem at all surprised.

'It's all starting to come together,' she said.

Chapter 59

Thursday

Vauxhall Cross, London

The C-TAC team were putting together the pieces to form a picture of PSP4. They now knew how the gang operated, the kind of targets they selected, the name of the man running it because of the Echelon intercepts, and the name – real or assumed – of the gang member who acted as a liaison between PSP4 and the blackmail victims. All of which was interesting, but not particularly useful when it came to tracking down the perpetrators.

The police had recovered a Vauxhall saloon car from the farmhouse near Gamlingay and the abandoned Jaguar from Sandy, but neither vehicle had provided significant forensic evidence, and their ownership by the small-time businessman in Bradford was a dead end. The police couldn't force him to identify the person who had provided the funds for him to buy the vehicles because what he had done was not illegal. They knew that, and more importantly so did his solicitor, who had accompanied him to the police station when he was interviewed.

The Metropolitan Police had located and recovered two further saloon cars and a white van with the same ownership from locations in north-west London. Each appeared to have been abandoned, the doors left unlocked and with the keys inside the vehicles. Again, they provided no useful forensic evidence, not least because the forensic scientists had no idea what or who they were looking for. Without a known suspect, they were just wasting their time.

What C-TAC had, and the police did not, was the mobile phone number PSP4 subscribers were invited to call if they had a problem with their chosen activities or with making their monthly payments.

By definition, that number had to be monitored by the gang almost all the time, and because the phone had to be switched on, it also meant that it could be tracked using a technique known as multilateration, essentially timing the radio signals sent between mobile towers and the phone.

As a general rule, tracking a mobile phone in the UK requires both the cooperation of the service provider and a warrant, but through its connections to the Security Service and the Secret Intelligence Service, and its own wide-ranging remit, C-TAC was able to circumvent the legal requirement and simply direct the relevant service provider to supply historic location details.

Which, oddly enough, didn't particularly help.

'Well, I can tell you one thing from looking at this,' Ben Morgan said, staring down at the A3-sized annotated location diagram that had just been provided by one of the desks at Millbank. 'They're definitely based in London, and north of the river.'

'Shit hot, Sherlock,' Cameron Riley replied. 'We probably didn't need this map to work that out.'

The diagram showed an outline map of Greater London overlaid with seven tracks in different colours covering the previous week, each track made up of dots and lines that represented the position of the target mobile phone for one complete day. And the thing that was very obvious was that the phone was almost always in motion and north of the Thames, apart from a couple of excursions down to Richmond and Kingston-upon-Thames. The only oddity was that it was switched off every evening at eleven and switched on again in the morning at seven and was usually somewhere near Brent Park in north-west London when this happened.

That didn't help either, because the Met, acting on information from the Cambridgeshire Constabulary, had already identified a commercial building in that area and had raided it. Inside, predictably enough, they'd found nothing useful, and the place had clearly been abandoned a short time earlier.

'Don't tell me we're back to square one,' Angela Evans said.

'Actually, I don't think we're quite that far forward,' Morgan replied. 'According to this, the phone was switched off a day ago and it's not been back on the network since. King must have guessed that the number was compromised after his men killed McEwan, so PSP4 now has a brand-new emergency contact number. He'll have given that to all his subscribers or whatever he calls them in an email or a text message from his new phone. We can get the number if we ask one of the men on Somerville's list, but I'm not sure knowing it would help us that much. It'll probably generate a very similar diagram and trying to locate that mobile using triangulation would be a nightmare in London.'

The three of them stared somewhat glumly at the paper in front of them.

'I did have one idea,' Cameron said, 'though it does rather go against the grain and it might take a while to implement.'

'Do not,' Evans said firmly, 'keep us in suspense, Cam. Tell us, right now.'

Riley nodded and outlined a possible way forward.

'You can see why I'm a bit hesitant,' he finished, 'because it probably won't give us exactly the result I was hoping for, from my own perspective, I mean. But it could work. In fact, it should work.'

Morgan nodded.

'We'll do it,' he said decisively. 'If you go ahead and make the calls, I'll brief Dave North and make sure that it'll work from his side.'

Chapter 60

Thursday

City of London

What Cameron Riley had suggested was a somewhat circuitous approach to solving the problem they faced, and implementing it turned out to be every bit as difficult as he had expected. He spent almost an hour talking to Nicholas Michaelson in his office – the venture capitalist had returned to work the day after his rescue – gathering the information that he needed and trying to produce what amounted to a league table of people to talk to. Because of his pseudo-position at the Bank of England, Riley knew that they would be compelled to talk to him, but that didn't necessarily mean that they would agree to do what he asked.

His first two appointments that afternoon, based on Jeremy Somerville's list and the information from Michaelson, were inconclusive, to use the kind of terminology commonly employed in business circles. In fact, when he had explained who he was, who he represented and what he wanted, both men flatly refused to even discuss the subject. Reading their body language, Cameron was fairly certain Michaelson was right and that both of them had been shocked when he brought up the subject of their possible extracurricular activities and how what they did in their spare time might impact their future careers.

His third meeting, with another senior banker, began in much the same way but ended rather differently. His name had been supplied by Michaelson but it had not been on Somerville's list.

'I hear what you say, and I agree that it's potentially very disturbing. Can I speak to you frankly, confidentially and off the record? If not, then I'm afraid this conversation will be over.'

'As long as whatever form of recreation you enjoy is not actually illegal,' Riley replied, 'then I can remove my official hat and just talk to you man to man.'

'Good,' Gordon Wiltshire said. 'Between you and me, I enjoy the company of young women who have a particular skill, a skill that my wife does not possess. Perhaps once or twice a week I will visit one of half a dozen ladies who provide this service here in London. They are of legal age, they are independent and not working in a brothel, which would of course be illegal, and we are both consenting adults. I pay them for their time, and what goes on in their bedrooms between us does not break any law of which I am aware. I would, however, not wish my wife to become acquainted with these facts, nor my board of directors or our shareholders.'

'Thank you for your honesty,' Riley said. 'Have you noticed any signs of the activity I mentioned earlier?'

Wiltshire shrugged.

'I drive myself to and from the office and when I go out for an evening. Cars have travelled behind me on the same route for most of these journeys, but in London traffic that's hardly a rarity.'

'Right. You have my numbers and you know what I would like you to do. Speed is of the essence, so the moment you are approached, please call me.'

'I will. And can I assume that that will be the end of the matter from your point of view?'

Riley nodded.

'Doing favours works both ways,' he replied, 'so of course.'

As he left the building near Fleet Street, Riley glanced at his watch. He had two more calls to make that afternoon and he hoped to persuade at least one of the men he was going to see to agree to the same course of action he had outlined to Wiltshire.

C-TAC badly needed to mop up the PSP4 operation and that would require at least three or four of their identified potential targets to work with them.

That wasn't the only string to the C-TAC bow. Every CEO and senior banker that Michaelson had identified as a possible blackmail target was already being watched by agents of the Security Service. But unfortunately, the only two aids they had to identify John

Harrison was a police artist's sketch based on Jeremy Somerville's description and a profile image culled from the bank's internal CCTV system. Harrison had obviously noticed the cameras and had done his best not to look directly towards any of them.

And the man depicted was virtually the opposite of distinctive. He looked like just another one of the tens of thousands of people who worked in the City every day, and in Riley's opinion would be almost impossible to spot in a crowd.

But the sketch and photograph were all they had, so the MI5 agents would just have to do their best.

Chapter 61

Thursday
Vauxhall Cross, London

'Are you sure this is a good idea?' Evans asked. 'And don't you need approval or something?'

'I suppose the two short answers are yes and no,' Morgan replied. 'This is too good an opportunity to miss and C-TAC's remit covers it. Or at least it does the way I'm reading it. China has imposed restrictions to block non-Chinese intelligence services as well as Chinese citizens from having unrestricted access to the Internet. It's known as the Great Firewall. But thanks to GCHQ managing to pick apart the route and the originator of the options' purchase orders for the bank where McEwan worked, we now have a confirmed IP address in Beijing, an address that logically must be used by people connected to this man King and his blackmail gang.'

'Because otherwise they wouldn't have known about the imminent release of the McEwan photographs and videos. Yes, I get that, obviously. But having identified a sleeping tiger, as it were, do you really think that poking it with a stick is such a good idea?'

Morgan grinned at her.

'Nice image,' he said. 'Since at least 2010, China's been the king of cyber warfare. According to one of the latest estimates I've seen, the country employs a hacker army at least 100,000 strong whose only job is to target Western computer systems. Their usual targets are what you'd expect – government, military, commercial, research and industrial websites – and one reason why China is making such strides in the IT field is that they've stolen much of the technology from America and the West. It wouldn't surprise me if the server GCHQ identified was one of those involved in espionage against us, and so getting a look at the contents of its hard disks seems to me to be a really good idea.'

'And if they find out that the originator of this attack on them was GCHQ, how do you think they'll react?'

'I don't think they will, because Cheltenham will cover the tracks so it'll be bounced around the world before it finishes up in Beijing. And the data that the bug will copy from the server will take a similar path on its way to GCHQ. But to answer your question, even if they do work out where the virus originated there'll be nothing they can do because the damage is already done. Don't forget that despite all the unambiguous evidence that China has been hacking us for years, it has never once admitted that it engages in cyber warfare. Instead, it accuses other nations of mounting cyberattacks against China. If there are any protests made about this, nobody'll take any notice.'

'So what will this virus do?' Angela asked. 'What's its payload?'

'It's very small and tightly written, and it'll do two things. First, it will stream copies of every datafile it can identify back to GCHQ. It's a bit of a scattergun approach, but the very first thing it will be sending back will be a copy of the directory structure, so if we get the opportunity we can send a more targeted virus next time. And the second thing it'll do is copy itself onto every other computer in either the local area network, or the wide area network if there is one, and then do exactly the same on every machine that it infects. We don't expect it to last too long out there in the wild – no doubt the Chinese technicians will spot what's happening fairly quickly and take steps to stop it. But I still think it's an opportunity worth taking. And in any case, it's already running.'

Chapter 62

Friday
London

Riley got the call just after two the following afternoon and immediately rang Morgan.

'Ben, it's Cam. It's a go. Can you pick me up on Threadneedle Street ASAP?'

'No problem. We're up in Bishopsgate by the Duck and Waffle. Five minutes, tops.'

Four minutes later a black cab pulled up at the kerb just outside Bank Station on Threadneedle Street, with Dave North in the driving seat.

'Head for Gresham Street,' Riley said, opening the rear door and climbing into the back of the cab. 'I'll direct you from there. Are you moonlighting again, Dave?'

'Nope, though I'm thinking about it. Introduce yourself to the team.'

Riley had seen two figures on the back seat of the cab and had sat down on one of the drop-down seats behind the driver. The man sitting next to Morgan was young and stocky with short hair and forgettable features, but what caught Riley's attention was his open jacket and the butt of a pistol nestling in a shoulder holster under his left arm.

'That's not a SIG, is it?' he asked. 'Wouldn't the armourer at Hereford let you sign out a P226?'

The man shook his head and grinned.

'Nah. They reckon the SIG is too much like a signature weapon for the Regiment so I picked up a Hi-Power instead, because this is all supposed to be like deniable. The Browning's old, but it's solid and reliable, and at the end of the day I don't give a flying fuck what I'm firing as long as it works. My name's Chris, by the way, and I'm bloody sure I've seen you up at Hereford.'

'Wearing one of my other hats, that's quite likely. I'm Cameron Riley. You okay, Ben?'

'I'll be better when this is over,' Morgan said.

'And you're carrying as well,' Riley pointed out, gesturing at a similar shoulder holster and pistol that he could see under Morgan's jacket. 'Is that legal?'

'I'm not entirely sure, but it seemed like a good idea. Dave's tooled up as well, but that's not exactly a surprise bearing in mind who he works for.'

'Take a right up Wood Street and then stop outside the Slug and Lettuce,' Riley said to North, turning to look through the taxi's windscreen.

North braked the cab to a stop outside the pub, and then they waited.

'One of the bankers I interviewed received an unexpected visitor – this bloke Harrison,' Riley explained. 'He told his secretary to make him wait for five minutes before she sent him in and he called me straight away. He'll keep Harrison talking for as long as he can and then he'll ring me when he's on his way down to the street. That should be any time now.'

The taxi had been stopped for under a minute when Riley's phone rang. He answered it and snapped out directions to Dave North who accelerated the cab away from the kerb.

Thirty seconds after that Riley pointed at a slim and well-dressed businessman who stepped out of a doorway on the left-hand side of the road about seventy yards ahead.

'That's the bank,' he said, 'and that has to be Harrison.'

North steered the taxi over to the left and pulled to a stop. Riley opened the door and stepped out as if he was disembarking. As he did so, the figure they believed to be John Harrison opened the passenger-side door of a mid-range Ford saloon and got in. When the car pulled away, Riley climbed back into the taxi and resumed his seat.

'Don't spook him, Dave, just follow him,' he said. 'Then we'll try and find a place to stop him and have a bit of a chat. Where are the others, by the way?'

North pointed backwards with his left thumb.

'Another black cab about fifty yards back,' he said. 'Driver and two passengers. All three of them from Hereford and taking a bit of unscheduled leave to help us out. And they've got a couple of assault rifles as well as pistols, just in case it turns really nasty.'

The Ford headed north out of the City past Liverpool Street Station and picked up the A10 trunk road that ran through Shoreditch and on up towards Stoke Newington and Enfield.

The driver of the target car was not apparently in a hurry and unlike almost everybody else on the road he kept his speed about three or four miles an hour below the posted limit, which both irritated and concerned Dave North.

'I think he's trying to flush out a tail. London taxi drivers aren't exactly famous for sticking to the limit,' he said, 'and if I was him I'd be a bit suspicious of two black cabs keeping pace at this speed.'

But the Ford's driver did nothing unexpected, just kept driving steadily north along the A10 all the way through Stoke Newington and on towards Tottenham.

Traffic was fairly heavy and the distance between the two black cabs increased as other vehicles pulled in front of the second taxi, but North was easily keeping the target car in sight, sixty or so yards in front.

'Now where's he going?' North muttered to himself as the Ford, now four cars ahead, stopped in the right-hand lane at the traffic light-controlled junction with the A503, Monument Way.

Morgan brought up the mapping app on his mobile phone and expanded the scale to show the route ahead.

'He might just be trying to avoid going through the centre of Tottenham,' he suggested. 'That road runs almost parallel to the A10.'

Two minutes later the Ford went straight over the crossroads into Watermead Way and the driver started to accelerate as he approached Tottenham Marshes, where the road was open and the traffic very light. North had no option but to increase his speed, simply to keep up.

And that was obviously what the driver of the Ford had been waiting for.

A couple of hundred yards further on he hit the brakes, spun the steering wheel and then pulled on the handbrake. The car slid broadside across the road with a howl of protest from the rear tyres. Both doors swung open and Harrison and the driver jumped out, running around the other side of the car, each clutching a weapon. North replicated the Ford's actions, slamming the taxi sideways on and stopping about thirty yards from the other vehicle.

'Get out and find cover,' North shouted. 'Cam, keep out of our way.'

Riley had the door open even before the vehicle stopped. Morgan and Chris followed him out of the car a split second later, both drawing pistols.

'Stay down,' Chris ordered Morgan and Riley, pointing his Browning at the Ford. The gang members had ducked behind the vehicle and were aiming their weapons.

Riley nodded and flattened himself on the road surface. He had no weapon and there was nothing he could do to help.

Dave North got out and ran round to the other side of the taxi, reaching inside his jacket for his weapon.

As North ducked down beside Morgan, the driver of the Ford pulled the trigger of the twelve-bore pump-action shotgun he was carrying. Buckshot blasted the side of the taxi. Morgan heard the distinctive click-clack as he worked the action to reload. Then he fired again.

Harrison was carrying what looked like a MAC-10, and then he too opened up, the distinctive blat-blat-blat sound confirming that it was an automatic weapon. But his rounds went very high.

'Oh, shit,' Riley muttered, apparently trying to meld himself into the road surface as bullets and buckshot whizzed over his head and around the taxi.

Chris snapped off a couple of rounds with his Browning, but thirty yards is a long way for accurate pistol shooting, even when the weapon is in expert hands. One bullet hit the side of the Ford but the other one vanished into the trees and undergrowth bordering the road.

Morgan just aimed at the other car and cracked off three rounds. Two of them hit it. Then he heard the sound of a car braking heavily somewhere behind him and turned to look.

Perhaps twenty yards away a dark grey saloon car – it looked like a Vauxhall or Opel – slammed to a stop with a squeal from the tyres.

Morgan assumed the driver had seen what was happening and stopped at the very last moment. But he immediately realised he was wrong when the two men inside the car jumped out, both holding pistols, and began firing at them.

They were outgunned and caught in the middle of a trap and they knew it. Obviously the driver of the Ford had seen that he was being followed and had whistled up reinforcements.

A couple of bullets slammed into the side of the taxi beside Morgan as he aimed his Browning at the new arrivals and squeezed the trigger.

But then Dave North finally managed to pull his weapon out of his jacket and everything changed.

Keeping the bonnet and the front end of the taxi behind him, where the solid lump of the diesel engine would provide him with a measure of protection from the two men firing from the Ford, he crouched down and took aim at the second car.

Two shots cracked out from his weapon, the sound louder and more distinct than the pistol shots. The man standing on the left of the car gave a shrill scream and then tumbled backwards out of sight behind the open door. North switched his aim slightly and fired twice more. The second man had ducked down behind the open passenger door but that didn't do him any good. Both of North's bullets ploughed straight through the middle of the door and the shooting stopped.

'What the bloody hell is that?' Morgan said, glancing at the weapon before he again aimed at the stationary Ford.

'Tell you later.'

North swung round, pointed his weapon at the Ford and waited for one of the men to show himself. Then he fired two rounds.

'We must keep Harrison or one of the others alive,' Morgan said urgently. 'If you kill them all we're buggered and we'll never find King.'

'Now you tell me,' North muttered, as they heard a howl of pain from somewhere near the Ford. 'Chris,' he called out, 'there's only one of them left. You go left and I'll go right. Shoot to wound, not to kill. Ben, go back and check on those two comedians who arrived at the party late. If they're still alive, keep them that way if you can.'

North and Chris made their way carefully towards the bullet-riddled saloon car, preternaturally alert and with their weapons aimed at where the threat – if there still was one – had to be.

But nobody fired at them.

When North rounded the end of the vehicle he altered the aim of his weapon slightly. He saw the man who called himself John Harrison crouched down beside the rear wheel. His head was in his hands and the MAC-10 was lying on the ground beside him, a spent cartridge case jammed in the ejector port of the receiver.

North leaned forward and rested the muzzle of his own weapon against the back of Harrison's head.

'Stay where you are and don't move,' North said. Then he raised his voice. 'Chris. I've got a live one here. He'll do. How are you doing?'

'No problem,' he called back. 'This one's alive too.' Then there was the sound of a single shot. 'Oops, sorry, my mistake. This one's dead.'

'The other two are dead as well,' Morgan said, walking back towards the taxi.

'This is the one you wanted to talk to,' North said, prodding Harrison in the middle of the back and herding him towards the now somewhat less than pristine black cab.

'We're going to need to get this mess cleaned up and bloody quick,' Cameron Riley said, standing up and brushing himself down. He pointed back the way they'd come. 'There's traffic backing up in both directions and no possibility that the local plods aren't already on the way. I'll give Dame Janet a call and tell her what happened so she can provide top cover and hopefully we won't end up spending the night in the cells somewhere.'

'So what is that, Dave?' Morgan said, pointing at the unusual weapon. 'And why did it take you so long to get it out?'

'I'm really sorry about that,' North replied. 'The bloody thing snagged on my jacket and I just couldn't get it free. It's a UCIW – Ultra Compact Individual Weapon – like a pocket-sized assault rifle. It's basically a cut-down version of the American Colt M16. It fires the 5.56x45mm NATO round, which gives it plenty of stopping power, and the magazine holds thirty rounds in all. It's a really good weapon.'

'As long as it doesn't get stuck in your pocket,' Morgan said.

'Yes. True. Right, what do we do with Harrison? And where the fuck was our backup?'

Morgan looked at the dozen or so cars that had stopped about thirty yards from the shootout and pointed.

'Better late than never,' he said as the other black cab, headlights on and hazard flashers working, drove around the stationary vehicles on the wide road and stopped beside them.

'Don't tell me. Traffic?' North asked.

The driver nodded.

'A collision right in front of us. We couldn't get round it.' He climbed out of the vehicle, as did his two passengers, and looked around. 'Some party, eh? You all okay?'

'We are,' Morgan said, 'but we need to move now and get him—' he pointed at Harrison, whose city suit was scuffed and torn '—somewhere we can have a quiet word.'

They all heard the sound of a siren, still a long way off but getting perceptibly closer.

'We can't all bugger off,' North said to him. 'Chris and I are legitimate. We both have military ID cards and we've signed for the weapons, so why don't you and Cameron take Harrison in the other cab and we'll stay here and argue with the plods when they turn up? That'll give you time to sort this.'

'You're sure?'

'Yes. My pension's safe, and Dame Janet will pour oil on the troubled waters.'

'Very poetic,' Morgan said. 'Sounds like a plan. And thanks, both of you. Right, Cam, we're out of here.'

Chapter 63

Friday
London

It had been a bit of a squeeze for five of them in the back of the taxi, but at least they had somewhere to put their feet because they made Harrison lie on the floor until they stopped.

They found a quiet spot near Theydon Bois and the M11/M25 interchange where they could persuade Harrison to divulge what he knew about PSP4. In fact, he didn't take that much persuading, for reasons that quickly became clear. They sat him on one of the drop-down seats in the taxi to face Morgan and Riley.

'We can probably get you as an accessory over McEwan's murder,' Morgan began. 'The shooter would get life and you'd get twenty years, more if we really pushed for it.' He paused for a moment. 'Help us and we might be less inclined to go for the maximum. So now really is the time to talk. You've got one chance at this.'

Harrison looked from one man to the other and appeared to come to a decision.

'Look,' he said to Morgan, 'you probably won't believe me but I'm glad I'm out of it. I'll talk to you because I'm not staring at a couple of detectives and talking under caution. I know I'm in the shit because of what's happened and because I'm a part of it all, but none of this is really my scene.'

Riley laughed.

'You really expect us to believe that? You're in it up to your neck.'

Harrison nodded.

'I know, but I had nothing to do with the killing. You know, when McEwan was shot. I don't do guns.'

'Half an hour ago you were firing a MAC-10 at us,' Riley reminded him, 'so I don't really believe that.'

'That wasn't me. Well, it was but really it was that bloody Reg. He was the driver and he spotted you lot following us in that cab back in the City. Before he stopped he handed me that fucking submachine gun and told me to use it. I deliberately fired well over your heads.'

Morgan knew that was true, though Harrison might just have been a really poor shot.

'What did you have to do with McEwan?' Riley asked.

'Nothing. All I did was recruit him. That was my job. I was the front man.'

'Do you know who shot him?'

'That was a bloke called Vince. He's ex-military. I think Army but I don't know for sure. He's good with guns.'

'Where do we find him?'

'At the new base, probably. It's down near Docklands. I can show you.'

'You will,' Morgan said simply. 'So why are you glad to be out of it? That's what you said a minute ago, and I can't think of any reason why you'd rather be in custody than a free man.'

Harrison looked slightly sheepish.

'OK, I'd rather not be sitting here wearing handcuffs, obviously, but I had no idea of the kind of outfit King was planning when I joined him. Look, I've been a criminal for most of the last twenty years, but always strictly white-collar. Fraud, identity theft, credit card stuff, all that kind of thing. I didn't know what King was like or what he was doing until I got in so deep that I couldn't get out. Or not in one piece, anyway. King hired me because I've got a background in business. In banking, as it happens, and I look the part. I can walk into any bank or office or business in the City and look as if I belong there.'

'You were the front man, you said.'

'Exactly. He wanted me to be the interface between him and what he called his customers. The rest of the people he hired came from the other side of the tracks. They'd all done time for violence, assault, that kind of thing. They were the muscle, the enforcers. My job was just selling the product, I suppose you could say. The meetings weren't pleasant because of what I was telling them but none of the marks ever got physical.'

'How many men does King have?'

'There were twelve of us, but it's been a bad week and I think you know that just as well as I do. We were four down after that fiasco at Gamlingay, and you and your friends just shot another three people and I'm in your custody. So right now Mr King has only got four men with him.'

'What you know about King?' Morgan asked.

'Enough to know that he scares the shit out of me. He's Chinese, or from Hong Kong anyway, and his real name is Wang. He's not a big man, quite small actually. But there's something about him, a kind of aura almost, that just tells you he's more dangerous than you can possibly imagine.'

'We know a bit about what he did in Hong Kong,' Morgan said. 'At least one killing.'

'I'm not surprised,' Harrison said. 'I've seen what he can do. Just after I got involved, a man he'd hired did something badly wrong so King gathered us all in a room, told the man to step forward and explained what he'd done. Then King pulled a pistol on him, tossed him a switchblade and told him he had a choice. He could either take a bullet in the stomach or use the knife to cut off one of the fingers of his left hand. He could choose which finger.'

'Jesus,' Morgan muttered.

Harrison shrugged as much as his handcuffed wrists would allow.

'What did he do?'

'What could he do? A bullet in the stomach would probably have killed him, but if he used the knife at least he could walk away. So that's what he did. He put his hand on the table, opened up the switchblade and cut off the little finger of his left hand. It took him a couple of minutes and he was yelling and screaming the whole time, but he did it. Then he wrapped a handkerchief round his hand, walked out of the room and we never saw him again.'

'The Yakuza in Japan do that,' Riley said. 'If a soldier does something wrong he'll be told to cut off one or more digits and then present the severed bits to his boss. Anyway, we will be taking care of Mr King, one way or the other.'

Harrison seemed to hesitate for a moment, then gave an almost imperceptible nod.

'Look, there's something else you probably need to know,' he said. 'When King recruited me and a couple of the other men at the beginning, he told us that the blackmail scheme was a two-stage process. He called it Phase One and Phase Two. Phase One was doing the surveillance, identifying CEOs and directors who had a guilty secret and then getting evidence about what they were doing, usually photographs or videos. When I went in to show the mark the pictures, that marked the end of Phase One and the start of Phase Two, when he started paying his subscription. That was ten grand a month, so we were really coining it in as soon as the first few started paying. And as far as I knew that was it. A simple twist on the old favourite blackmail.'

Morgan nodded for him to continue.

'But a few times I overheard King talking on the phone to somebody who sounded like he was the one actually giving the orders. During those conversations King kept on referring to Phase Three. And I knew nothing about that.'

'He was speaking English?' Morgan asked.

Harrison shook his head.

'No. That's the point. He was speaking Cantonese and he didn't bother making sure none of us could overhear him. What King didn't know was that after I left university I spent nearly a decade in Hong Kong at HSBC until I was caught with my hands in the till and got kicked out. I picked up the language while I was there. I'm rusty and I didn't get every word King said, but I certainly got the gist of his conversation. And the reason I thought he was speaking to a superior was the way he answered the phone.

'In Cantonese the most common greeting is *haa lo*, which is pretty similar to the English "hello". But if you're speaking to an elder or to a superior you would never say that because it's too casual. Instead you'd say *nei ho*, which literally translates as "you are well?" When King had one of those conversations he always said *nei ho*. King is the local boss of what we were doing but somebody else is definitely pulling his strings. And I was curious enough about this to sneak a look at one of the phone bills. I expected the calls King was taking came from Hong Kong, but they didn't. They all came from the same number in Beijing. I don't know what this means,' Harrison finished, 'but I think King was involved in something a bit more serious than just blackmail.'

Morgan glanced at Riley and nodded. This information was new to him, but if you looked at it in a certain way it definitely made a kind of sense, because of one aspect of this that had been troubling him almost since day one.

'Thank you,' Morgan said. 'It probably won't count for a lot, but I would be prepared to tell the police and your legal team that you did what you could to help us.'

'After your MAC-10 jammed,' Riley interjected.

'Yes. After that.'

Chapter 64

Friday

Aberfeldy Village, London

Ben Morgan had always believed in the essential truth of certain clichés, striking while the iron is hot being one of them. He and Riley were well aware that trying to get police assistance to raid the new premises occupied by PSP4 would take too long. They would need to identify themselves, produce authorisation for what they were trying to do, find some way of proving that the building was occupied by a bunch of violent blackmailers and finally answer numerous questions about why Morgan was wandering around London with a nine-millimetre Browning Hi-Power tucked in a shoulder holster under his arm. And questions like that would be extremely difficult to answer.

Assuming John Harrison was right, and as far as Morgan could see there was no point in him lying, King could only have a maximum of four armed men in the building with him. And as they were travelling towards the address Harrison had provided in a taxi containing three SAS soldiers, one ex-SBS naval officer, and Morgan, who had received small arms training in the past, plus two assault rifles and seven pistols, there didn't seem to be any particularly good reason not to do the job themselves.

And there was also a very good reason why Morgan and Riley needed to finish this. If they stepped back and handed it over to the Metropolitan Police, the operation would achieve its objective in that the Met would storm the building and arrest any gang members in there. But if the raid didn't happen until the next day, there was at least a chance that King and his men would have already moved out, just as they had abandoned their base at Brent Park after the assault at

Gamlingay. King would probably already know – or at least could guess – that the gunfight at Tottenham had gone wrong, because if his men had prevailed they would certainly have contacted him. And Morgan couldn't afford to let the gang get away.

That was the good reason, but the real reason was even more compelling. If the Met carried out the assault, once the gang members had been carted off to hospital, the mortuary or the slammer as appropriate, forensic teams would descend on the industrial unit, take it to pieces and examine everything they found there. And that would be a disaster. Somewhere in that building, Morgan was absolutely sure, was a computer with a big hard drive or maybe an external drive that contained all the material used to blackmail the bankers and other City executives. If the forensic people found it, they would examine it and the Met would have no option but to launch prosecutions against the individuals concerned because they would have unambiguous evidence of criminal activity. And that would be an unmitigated disaster for the City of London. There would have to be prosecutions, but the timing and the sequence would be critical and the Met probably wouldn't agree to that.

It was essential that Morgan and Riley got possession of that disk drive.

—

The SAS always try to reconnoitre any target before they enter it so that they know the layout in detail. That was clearly impossible in the present circumstances, but John Harrison had provided both a detailed word picture and also a rough sketch of what they would find once they got inside the grey painted building on the trading estate, and that was going to have to be good enough.

The unit that King had rented was on a small estate off Leven Road and the vantage point the SAS had picked was at the back of a self-storage unit a couple of hundred yards to the north-west. From there they had a clear view across waste ground to the estate.

'You'd better tell Dame Janet what we're up to,' Cameron Riley said, and Morgan nodded.

'I'll do it right now,' he said, took out his mobile and had a brief conversation.

'She's not over the moon about it,' Morgan reported, 'but mainly because she's worried about us getting hurt rather than the consequences of a gun battle in Greater London. Dave North and Chris, by the way, have already been released by the police. Chris is on his way back to Hereford and Dave will see us at Vauxhall Cross when all this lot's finished.'

'Good,' Riley replied. 'So what's the plan, ladies?'

The three SAS soldiers – one of them a corporal – who were all wearing casual civilian clothing, barely glanced at him before resuming their scrutiny of the building, looking out for any signs of movement. They were all much of a type: compact build, a little under average height and exuding a palpable air of competence and confidence.

'We don't know too much about this place,' the corporal, who had introduced himself as Nick, replied. 'So maybe we should just amble over there and knock on the door.'

'Really?' Morgan sounded incredulous.

'Yeah, but that's a knock Hereford-style,' Bill, one of the two soldiers, replied. 'Because we didn't know exactly what kind of party we'd been invited to, as well as the shooters we've got enough C4 to pretty much flatten that place.'

Greg, the other soldier, grinned. 'Getting the door open'll be no big deal. Just watch.'

'And we've got a few flash-bangs,' Nick added.

Morgan knew just how useful stun grenades could be in an assault. He hadn't expected the SAS team to be quite that well equipped, but on the other hand Dave North had organised them, and he always believed in overkill if he had the option.

'Okay,' Nick said. 'We're gonna have to make this up as we go along, and I really don't like that. So we use a basic plan and we stay flexible. The three of us will be in front, and we'll divide the ordnance so that if one of us gets hit the whole thing doesn't go tits-up. So that's two flash-bangs each and a third of the plastic plus a couple of fuse caps. We've got a M112 demolition block that weighs about half a kilo, so we'll cut that into thirds before we go. Unless that door's a sodding lot stronger than it looks we won't need to use anything like a third of the block. I'll mount the charge on the door and Bill and Greg will carry the Hocklers, the MP5s, so I've got my hands free. You two gents will only be carrying pistols, so keep your eyes open and try not to shoot any of us. And stay well back. I don't want you leaving here in a couple of body bags. Any questions?'

There were none, but Nick went over it a second time to make sure they all knew what was going to happen.

Driving to the target in the taxi was never going to work, and in any case they needed somewhere secure to imprison Harrison. But they did need to get closer, so they all got back in the taxi and found a vacant space on Oban Street, just off Leven Road.

'You'll have to stay here,' Morgan said when they parked the taxi, 'in handcuffs and with the doors locked.'

'No problem,' Harrison replied. 'I'd rather not get shot, thanks. But I'd appreciate it if you opened a couple of the windows so I can get some air.'

There were vehicles of various types on the roads and outside some of the buildings, and people wandering about to and from the vehicles and the business premises.

The three SAS soldiers walked down the road as a group, their weapons hidden from view, then turned into the trading estate, apparently making for the unit next to the target building. Morgan and Riley followed the same route about fifty yards behind them, seemingly deep in conversation. All five of them were covertly watching the windows at the front of the target unit and saw no movement, but there were two cars parked outside it.

'Maybe we're too late and it's empty,' Riley suggested. 'The birds might already have flown.'

'Let's hope not.'

The moment the three SAS soldiers were out of sight of the windows they split up.

A person running will always attract attention and so Nick walked over to the door beside the vehicle entrance, pausing on his way to place his palm flat on the bonnet of each of the parked cars in turn. He turned back to face Morgan and Riley and mouthed 'still warm' at them.

Bill and Greg continued walking to the corner of the target building and then stopped. They opened their jackets to access their Heckler & Koch MP5s on tactical slings, checked them and held the weapons ready.

Nick checked the door was locked, and it took him about fifteen seconds to tear off and mould a piece of plastic explosive around the door lock and insert the fuse cap. Then he struck a match to ignite the fuse and jogged around to the side of the building and safety.

Ten seconds later the C4 explosive detonated with a loud crack and the steel door swung open. Three seconds after that, Bill and Greg were inside and looking for trouble, Nick a couple of feet behind them.

Morgan and Riley took out their pistols and strode closer to the building as they heard the yammer of automatic fire from inside, but they didn't attempt to enter it. The SAS men were professionals and certainly didn't need amateur assistance in clearing a building. And appearing unannounced in a doorway when a firefight was going on was a really good way of getting killed, either by the bad guys or as a blue-on-blue casualty.

They cringed as a couple of stun grenades exploded inside, and instinctively ducked when a line of bullet holes appeared in the steel wall about ten feet above their heads.

And then an entirely different noise grabbed their attention.

Chapter 65

Friday

Aberfeldy Village and Docklands, London

Very early in his criminal career, Mr King had learnt that the most important feature of any base was the way out. It needed to have an entrance that could be defended, or at least securely locked, but what was essential and non-negotiable was another way out. Ideally, several different ways out. At Brent Park the adjacent unit had been empty, and Mr King had had keys made for the connecting doors – it had been designed as a potential double unit – to provide a less than obvious escape route.

The Aberfeldy Village unit was different, but what it had got were two staircases, one just inside the door and the other at the rear of the building, leading down to the back of the warehouse area. Soon after he'd signed the lease, Mr King had hired a local company to fit a second door in the rear wall of the building, a door to which only he had the key.

The crash of the plastic explosive detonating was deafening, making the steel-framed building ring like a drum. But just as at Gamlingay, Mr King didn't hesitate.

He leapt out of his seat, pulled open a tall cupboard and took out a loaded Remington 870 pump-action shotgun and a box of cartridges, and then hurried down the back staircase. The car he'd arrived in was parked at the rear end of the neighbouring unit and the ignition key, like his Walther pistol and a slim external hard drive, was in his pocket.

Mr King started the engine, then stepped down firmly on the accelerator, driving the revolutions almost to the red line. Then he drove forward towards the end of the next unit, stopped and got out of the car, expecting that one of the people who had obviously launched an attack on his operation would come to investigate. And when they did, he and his Remington would be ready for them.

—

There's a world of difference between the sounds of somebody starting a car normally – pulling the door closed, turning the engine on and then fastening their seat belt before moving off – and someone in a real hurry.

The roar of the engine of an unseen car – because neither of the vehicles in sight was occupied – was unmistakeable. The noise was coming from somewhere nearby.

'Where the hell is it?' Morgan asked, guessing the worst.

'It must be beside the next unit,' Riley said, breaking into a sprint and heading for the end of the row of buildings.

He reached the end about a second in front of Morgan and ran out into the open space. Then he instantly swerved to his right and threw himself down behind a car parked against the wall in front of him. As he did so, a shotgun blast tore into the ground just feet behind him.

Morgan stopped abruptly at the end of the unit and cautiously peered round the corner.

Facing him beside the open door of a saloon car ten yards away was a small man with a big gun. He racked the slide to chamber another cartridge and fired. Shot slammed into the wall of the industrial unit right beside Morgan, blasting shards of brick in all directions.

Before Morgan or Riley could take aim at him, King jumped into the car and sped off, driving right between them, heading for the road.

'Are you hurt?' Morgan shouted.

'He missed me, but I've knackered my ankle,' Riley replied. 'Don't wait for me. Get after that bastard.'

'Right.'

Morgan ran to the front of the unit.

He heard a few more shots as he rounded the corner. And then there was silence apart from the shouts of the SAS soldiers as they cleared each room in turn. But he dared not enter until he was sure it was safe to do so.

Nick appeared in the doorway, his left arm hanging loose and his jacket stained deep red, and gestured to him to enter.

'You're hit,' Morgan said. 'Bad?'

'Bastard bullet tore a groove in the muscle, I think. Stings like a bitch but it'll wear off. I'll put a pad on it when we get back to the taxi. There's a first aid kit in the boot. The other two guys are okay. The place is yours.'

'I need the key for one of those cars,' Morgan said, pointing at the vehicles parked in front of the building. 'King got out the back way and he's driven off. The taxi's too far away.'

He went straight to the ground floor office, looking for a key box or anything similar. It was a scene of disarray. Papers and stuff were scattered everywhere, probably blown about by the stun grenades.

'Keys,' Morgan said as Bill walked in. 'Car keys. Have you seen any?'

The SAS soldier shook his head, then looked around and pointed at a filing cabinet in one corner. On top of it was a shallow wooden tray with several sets of keys.

Morgan grabbed two of them, one labelled Vauxhall and the other Ford, and raced out of the building. He aimed both keys at the parked cars and pressed the buttons on the fobs. The Ford obediently flashed its hazard lights. He dropped the other fob on the ground and ran to the car.

'You'll need help,' Nick said. 'Bill, out here, now.'

Behind him, the SAS soldier ran out of the building and over to the car as Morgan dropped into the driving seat and started the engine.

His assault rifle in his hand, Bill wrenched open the passenger door and sat beside him.

'Don't hit anything until I get my seat belt on,' he instructed.

'I'll try not to,' Morgan replied, slamming the car into reverse and spinning the steering wheel. Then he engaged first gear, dropped the clutch and powered away from the unit, front tyres squealing. He clipped on his own seat belt as he drove.

'What's the rush?' Bill asked.

'The boss of the gang got out the back way,' Morgan replied. 'He's the lynchpin, so we have to find him.'

'Okay. What's he driving?'

'A dark grey SEAT on an 18 plate.'

'Got it.' Bill pressed the release on his MP5, removed the magazine and replaced it with a full one. 'Another thirty rounds,' he said. 'Should be enough.'

'I bloody well hope so,' Morgan said, clipping the apex of the corner in front of them as he swung into Lanrick Road. The trading estate was small and that was its only exit. Morgan powered the Ford around the right-hand bend in the road that paralleled the A13.

The SEAT was a couple of hundred yards ahead, where Lanrick Road ended at a junction. A junction where the traffic light was red.

As Morgan accelerated, the saloon car swung to the right and disappeared from view.

'Good trick,' Bill said, looking at a mapping application on his mobile. 'That's a mandatory left turn, not to mention he jumped the light.'

Morgan kept up his speed, then hit the brakes hard, the Ford squirrelling from side to side, just before he reached the junction. The lights were still red, but he moved forward, checking the traffic before he followed the SEAT.

'I hope this isn't a one-way street,' Morgan muttered.

'It isn't,' Bill said.

A black cab was heading straight for them, the driver swerving and blasting his horn as Morgan steered the Ford across the road right in front of him, heading for the left-hand lane.

The road was straight and the SEAT was about a hundred yards in front, King obviously going as quickly as he could. At the end, Abbott Road bent left at the A12 junction.

'He's got two choices,' Bill said. 'Straight on and through the underpass to head north, or hard left onto the A12. That's the Blackwall Tunnel approach road.'

Morgan nodded, changed up a gear and continued accelerating. He had to be close enough to see which way King went.

He was about seventy yards behind the SEAT when King hit his brakes.

'He's probably going left,' Bill suggested. 'Straight on and he wouldn't have needed to brake.'

Morgan made the turn just as King's SEAT disappeared towards the tunnel entrance.

But the car didn't stay on the main road, probably because the traffic heading for the tunnel was an almost stationary queue. Instead, King steered left, up towards the junction with the East India Dock Road.

'He's not lucky with the lights,' Bill commented, seeing the traffic lights at the roundabout turn from amber to red as the SEAT approached.

King slowed down but he didn't stop, dodging to the left to bypass half a dozen cars that had stopped at the lights. He drove into the left-turn lane, hit the brakes again at the end and swung right, cutting through the traffic already on the roundabout to head west.

Morgan had no choice but to follow. Or no choice if he was going to catch the man.

Horns blared all round him as he followed the SEAT.

'We're catching up,' Bill said.

'I'd like to be catching him quicker,' Morgan responded, switching on the Ford's headlights and sounding the horn.

Ahead, the SEAT swung left down what Bill's map told him was Cotton Street, again ignoring the red traffic lights and barely avoiding two cars that had stopped there. About sixty yards ahead of the speeding car two men were starting to cross the road at a pedestrian crossing but scrambled out of the way when they saw the fast-approaching vehicle.

By the time King got to the roundabout at the end of the road, Morgan was only about thirty yards behind him. The SEAT braked, swung left, and then as Morgan closed up even further, King spun the wheel right and accelerated hard, going round the roundabout the wrong way.

'Shit,' Morgan muttered, but kept on going the correct way. 'Keep your eyes on him,' he added.

Chapter 66

Friday
Aberfeldy Village, London

Cameron Riley limped to the front of the industrial unit, outside which a small crowd was beginning to assemble, albeit not close to the building. The sound of assault rifles, pistols, stun grenades and the detonation of plastic explosive charges were not exactly a part of their everyday life.

'Sitrep?' he asked as he approached the open door.

Nick, now holding a blood-sodden towel against his shoulder as a makeshift pad for his wound, looked enquiringly at the limping man.

'It's nothing,' Riley said. 'Just a sprained ankle, I think.'

Nick nodded.

'There were four of them in here, plus the one who got away out the back – three down here at ground level and the other one in the office upstairs. One didn't make it, and the other three are going to need medical help pretty soon.'

'I'll make the call,' Riley said, 'just as soon as I've had a look round. Do you need an ambulance?'

'Nah. This is just a graze. Probably won't even need stitches.'

'Good.'

The dead man was lying just inside the warehouse space, and the SAS team had grouped the three wounded men in there as well.

Morgan had no real interest in them – they were incapacitated, handcuffed using cable ties and under guard by Greg – but the interior of the unit and its contents was a different matter.

The upstairs office was just as much of a mess as the room downstairs, but Riley ignored that. On one side of the office was a desk with a computer on it, the screen displaying File Explorer, which was good news because it meant if there was a password – which was likely – it had already been input so he could view the contents of the hard drive.

Riley sat on the basic wooden chair in front of it, glad to take the weight off his ankle, and started a global search for video files, MPEG-4, DivX and so on. That produced no results, so he searched for image format extensions like JPEG and TIFF, with the same result.

That just didn't make sense. The videos and still photographs that the gang used to blackmail their victims had to be there somewhere. The only other place they could be was on an external hard drive.

He stood up and checked every drawer and cupboard but found nothing. No hard drives or backup devices of any sort, which was odd in itself, because most people had at least one form of backup they could turn to if the computer ever crashed.

Cameron Riley was a computer user, not a computer expert. He knew he had to be missing something, but he didn't know enough about IT to have any idea what.

He needed Ben Morgan to sit down at the machine and work his particular brand of magic on it.

Chapter 67

Friday

Docklands, London

The roundabout went under the A1261, the Aspen Way flyover, and there were probably a dozen cars and vans on the road, all of which Morgan had to avoid. As he jinked left and right, to the accompaniment of a discordant orchestra of car horns, Bill stared across the concrete jungle of support pillars, trying to see which exit King was going to take.

'Not the A1261,' he said, and as Morgan swept past a white Transit van both men saw the SEAT taking the next exit, Trafalgar Way.

'And he's had a prang,' Bill said, pointing at the off-side rear of the car, which now sported a very obvious dent. 'He must have hit someone on the other side of the roundabout.'

Morgan straightened up, his foot flat on the accelerator pedal. About fifty yards in front of him the SEAT swung left at the next small roundabout.

'I think he's lost,' Bill said. 'Or he doesn't know where he's going. Unless he's got an appointment at Canary Wharf.'

The SEAT howled towards the Blackwall Basin, where a dozen or so barges were moored. King apparently saw the roundabout and the guard post in front of him at the last second and braked hard, the car squirming from side to side.

It wasn't just a guard post with a red and white pole that could be lowered across the road. Sunk into the road surface itself on both lanes were steel barriers that would stop any car. And they were both erect, the black and yellow horizontal markings unmistakeable.

The brake lights in the SEAT went out, and then King carried out a competent handbrake turn, spinning the wheel to the right, pulling on the handbrake and then accelerating hard.

Straight towards the Ford.

Bill smashed the butt of his MP5 against the passenger-side window, shattering the glass. As the SEAT approached he leaned out of the window, aiming the submachine gun at the vehicle.

King spotted the threat and jinked away, mounting the pavement on the side of the road and accelerating.

Morgan steered left, slowing all the time. The moment the SEAT had passed, he swung the Ford round to follow it, against the oncoming traffic.

King was dodging his way around other cars. He somehow missed all three of them, Morgan following, and then the road ahead was clear.

'We need to finish this,' Morgan said.

He looked ahead and made a decision.

He put his foot down, closing the distance to the other car as quickly as he could and drew up on the right-hand side of the SEAT.

As he did so, King turned back towards him, a black pistol in his left hand.

Morgan braked and ducked behind the other car and King's shot went wild.

'You want me to ventilate him?' Bill asked, gesturing to his MP5.

'No. I'd prefer him alive. I've got this.'

Morgan swung the Ford out again, and the moment it reached the back of the battered SEAT he steered into it, drawing on his offensive driving training and forcing the rear of the other car over to the left.

He kept the pressure on the SEAT with the left-hand side of the Ford, driving it towards the central barrier made up of heavy metal planters filled with shrubs.

King's car slid sideways, the back of it crashing into one of the planters. It was a neat example of what the Americans call a 'pit manoeuvre'. Morgan had been taught the technique years earlier.

Bill immediately leapt out of the Ford, followed by Morgan, but King was faster.

Even as Morgan reached for his pistol, Mr King, still in the driving seat of the stationary SEAT, aimed his shotgun through the window and squeezed the trigger. At that range, the shot had tremendous energy and the windscreen of the Ford simply imploded, driven back into the car by the blast. He cranked the pump action but before he could fire again Bill opened up with his MP5, a three-round burst slamming into the driver's door of the other car. And at the same moment Morgan snapped off two shots from his Browning that hit the same target.

King appeared pinned in his seat and then, almost in slow motion, the shotgun toppled from his grasp to land muzzle-first on the road. As it did so, King slid backwards out of sight.

'Remember he's got a pistol,' Morgan warned as Bill stepped towards the wrecked SEAT.

'Remind me to tell you about my grandmother and eggs,' Bill said, tucking his MP5 into his shoulder and taking small careful steps, his eyes never leaving the other car.

Morgan approached just as cautiously but well away from the SAS soldier just in case King suddenly started shooting. A basic rule of combat: never get close to your companions because it gives the opposition multiple targets to engage.

'He's gone,' Bill said, looking over the sights of his Heckler & Koch into the car and then checking King for a pulse. 'I count five wounds on his torso, so we'd better share the kill.'

'I don't normally keep score,' Morgan said, 'so he's all yours.'

Bill gave him a somewhat quizzical look at that remark, then shrugged.

Morgan opened the door of the SEAT and looked down at King, the man who'd given him so much trouble over the last few days. He really didn't look like much in death, and probably not much in life either, but as he knew only too well, appearances could be, and usually were, deceptive.

Morgan picked up King's Walther pistol and then checked the man's pockets. He found a spare magazine so he took that, as well as a mobile phone and a solid black object that he recognised immediately.

'What's that?' Bill asked.

'An external hard drive. Hopefully that's what we've been looking for.'

Morgan looked around. Cars were stopping on both carriageways of Trafalgar Way, drivers and passengers staring open-mouthed at the scene in front of them. Death in the afternoon in one of the oldest areas of London, surrounded by water and with the glass and steel and concrete monoliths of Canary Wharf staring down at them.

'Right,' he said, 'let's get away from here before the Met turns up mob-handed. You drive. I'll call my boss and get her to start sorting this out.'

'We just leave him?' Bill asked.

'Unless you've got a better idea, yes. And bring that shotgun. We don't want some local picking it up as a souvenir.'

Chapter 68

Friday

Aberfeldy Village, London

Riley was waiting for Morgan outside the building. He stared at the Ford – dents all over it, no windscreen, and the bonnet and roof peppered with shot – and grinned at him.

'That's really buggered up your no-claims bonus,' he said, 'but I assume you got him?'

'We did,' Bill answered as he got out of the battered car. 'Put it this way, if you want to talk to him you'll need a fucking good medium that speaks Chinese.'

'Ah,' Riley said.

'Ah what?'

'It might have been better if he was still breathing,' Riley said, 'because I can't find the data we need. There's a computer running in the upper office, but as far as I can see there's nothing on it.'

'This might help,' Morgan said, taking the hard drive from his pocket. 'King had it with him.'

Riley looked almost comically relieved.

'Thank God for that. The situation here is that there were four heavies in the building. One's dead and the other three got shot in various places but are still alive and under guard. I've called for an ambulance. In fact, I only called for an ambulance,' Riley added. 'I thought that would give us a bit more time to search. The paramedics will call the police as soon as they get here, of course.'

The two men went up the stairs to the office and Morgan took the seat in front of the computer. He connected the external hard drive and used File Explorer to scan the internal hard drive and the drive he'd just connected.

'I see what you mean. There's nothing on the internal drive, but there are plenty of video files on the other one.'

He selected one at random and played it, but it wasn't what they'd expected to see. Instead of some banker playing away from home and doing something probably illegal, they found themselves watching Nicholas Michaelson sitting in an upright chair, his left little finger clearly broken, telling a man with his back to the camera about a banker named Wellington who he believed had a serious drug habit.

'Oh, shit,' Riley muttered. 'This isn't what we want. This is the drive King took from the farmhouse at Gamlingay.'

Morgan nodded and looked again at File Explorer.

'You're right,' he said. 'I've just checked the file creation dates and they were all recorded after Michaelson was kidnapped. There must be another disk somewhere.'

As they started searching the office again, they heard the first sirens approaching.

'You didn't tell them people had been shot, did you?' Morgan asked.

Riley shook his head.

'No. I just pretended to panic and said three people had been hurt and gave them the address. When they asked how they'd been injured I ended the call and obviously I didn't pick up the phone when they rang me back.'

'Good. So hopefully what we're hearing is an ambulance not a squad car, but we're running out of time. This place will be swarming with police in a few minutes.'

Morgan repeated the search that Riley had done just minutes earlier and found nothing in any of the cupboards or drawers.

'But it must be here somewhere,' Riley said. 'Nothing else makes sense.'

Morgan nodded, and as the two-tone wail of the ambulance siren faded away to nothing, he sat down again at the computer.

'An idea?' Riley asked.

'There is something we can check,' Morgan said. 'We know from the stuff they posted on the Dark Web about McEwan that they recorded him in action – if that's the expression I want – but the video footage was only about ten minutes long and only showed the highlights, as it were. That means they must have edited the original video, and that means they must have video editing software, because there's no other way to do it.'

He brought up the full list of programs on the computer and rapidly scanned it.

'I don't see anything,' he said as he scrolled down the list. 'There's nothing here – oh yes there is.'

'What?'

'Right there. OpenShot. That's a video editor.'

Morgan opened the program, clicked on 'File' and then 'Recent Projects'. A list of names appeared, some of which they recognised from the information supplied by Nicholas Michaelson and Jeremy Somerville.

Morgan opened one of the files to discover the unmistakeable face of Stephen Dawkins looking in the general direction of the camera as he walked down a darkened street holding the hand of a girl who looked about ten.

'Got you, you bastard,' Riley said. 'I knew he was one of the worst. So where's that file?'

'I can tell you where it isn't,' Morgan replied, 'and that's on this computer.'

He stared at the screen for a moment, then went back to File Explorer and checked the list of drives. Then he turned to Riley.

'Stand in the middle of the office, Cam,' he said, 'and say nothing. Just listen.'

'What for?'

'There's a hard drive listed that isn't physically connected to the PC, so it must be a wireless unit and it has to be here somewhere. A lot of hard drives make a very slight ticking sound when they're running. I'm going to open several files at the same time to make the disk work hard. Tell me if you hear anything.'

Riley stood at the centre of the small office and turned in a complete circle, looking at everything. Then he looked up at the ceiling about eight feet above them, and at the fluorescent strip lights mounted on horizontal steel bars that provided the illumination.

'I can hear something up there,' he said. 'Very faint.'

Morgan got up and stood beside him, staring upwards. Then a thought occurred to him and he walked to the door and switched off the lights.

He walked back to the centre of the office, still looking up. Then he grabbed the wooden chair, positioned it below one of the strip lights and climbed onto the seat.

'Here,' he said to Riley, pointing. 'You see this?'

'A couple of white marks. What are they?'

'Plastic cable ties,' Morgan replied, pulling a folding knife out of his pocket and slicing through them. 'And what they were holding in place was this.' He reached up and pulled a power plug out of a socket wired into the room's lighting circuit. He passed the power cable and a heavy oblong box to Riley.

'A wireless external hard drive,' he said. 'That size, it could be six or eight terabytes. That's it. Quite clever, really,' he added, replacing his knife and stepping down from the chair. 'They powered it from the ceiling light and they mounted it vertically on the steel beam so it was invisible from below.'

'Result. Right, let's get out of here.'

Downstairs they found a somewhat nonplussed ambulance team rendering first aid to the three injured men while another medic applied a pressure bandage to Nick's upper arm.

'Have you called the police?' Riley asked one of them.

'Yes. They're on their way.'

'Good. I suppose I should have thought of doing that,' he added without a trace of irony in his voice.

'These three aren't going anywhere,' Morgan said to Nick. 'As soon as they've patched you up, you can go back to the taxi. Wait there and we'll get you out of here. Don't worry about the police. We'll take care of them.'

'Got it. And thanks.'

The first police patrol car arrived seven minutes later. The two-man crew was unimpressed with what both Riley and Morgan told them, but a call from the duty chief inspector, who had himself given Dame Janet a severe listening to a few minutes earlier, seemed to clarify matters and they were allowed to leave.

They walked back to the black cab, Morgan carrying the hard drive.

There was one final surprise when they reached the cab.

Nick met them in front of it, looking worried.

'That Harrison bloke,' he said. 'Did you tell him he could leg it?'

'No, of course not.'

'Well he has. The handcuffs are on the floor in the back of the taxi along with a bent paperclip, and it looks like he managed to shimmy his way out of that window you left half-open for him.'

Morgan looked at the taxi, then at Riley and finally back at Nick. Then he started to laugh.

Chapter 69

Ten days later
The Club at the Ivy, Covent Garden, London

'I suppose this is really more or less what you might have expected,' Cameron Riley said. He was standing at one end of the Loft, the function room that occupied the top floor of The Club at the Ivy, just a short distance along West Street from the much better known Ivy restaurant. It was a discreet and upmarket central location, with easy access from the City. Ben Morgan and Angela Evans were sitting comfortably in a couple of chairs over to his left, watching the proceedings, but it was undeniably Riley's show.

'It's a mixture of good and bad news, broadly speaking.'

He paused for a few seconds and looked over the assembled company, some of whom he knew on a personal level, though that was going to change irrevocably in the very near future. Cameron Riley was somewhat choosy about the people with whom he associated.

'It'll take me less time to deal with the good news than the bad, so I'll cover that first. The reason that you've all been invited, or compelled in some cases, to attend this meeting is because all of you were clients, for want of a better word, of an unregistered security company that called itself PSP4. That company has now ceased to exist, and its surviving employees are being held on remand pending a trial later this year. That, to be brief about it, is the total extent of the good news, except that of course you or the companies for which you work will no longer be required to make the substantial monthly payments you were forced to agree to after John Harrison explained to you his version of the facts of life.'

Riley paused again and took a sip from a glass of water on the table in front of him.

'The question that I'm sure every single one of you wants to ask me is really the start of the bad news. The answer is yes, we have recovered all the photographs, video recordings, audio records and everything else that this gang had managed to obtain of all your various extracurricular activities, and which Harrison – and we still don't know who he was – used to encourage you to sign up with PSP4. I'm sure you'll all be relieved to know that we believe we have recovered their entire database, and that there are no other copies in existence. But the answer to the other question that I'm also sure is preying on your collective minds is no. No, we are not going to either hand over the material to you or destroy it.'

'You have no authority to do that, Riley,' a stocky, red-faced man wearing a classic pinstriped City suit called out from one side of the room. 'If that information was ever made public it could ruin every one of us and you know it. I demand that you hand it over or prove to us that it's been completely destroyed.'

'You can demand whatever you like, Walters.' Riley's tone was cold and clinical. 'But it won't do you any good. I'd rather hand over the hard drive to the bloody *Daily Mail* than give it to any of you lot. You may, or indeed you may not, be interested to learn that I did a very quick survey of the PSP4 material before I organised this little soirée. It was interesting and illuminating, but above all it was repellent.

'In this room, right now, there are four people who are main-lining hard drugs on a weekly basis, two of whom are also acting as dealers, while a third is a compulsive gambler who's racked up debts of the better part of a million pounds this year alone, some of the money coming from funds under his financial control. Five of you are maintaining expensive mistresses that your wives have no clue about. Two of you have a taste for underage girls, another two for underage boys and one for *very* underage boys. Another man in here is happy to abuse underage children of either sex. Two of you enjoy flagellation, one of you preferring to administer it while the other appears to enjoy receiving it, especially if a cane is involved. And finally, three of you in this room spend much of your available spare time in the company of transsexual prostitutes. Several of you combine two or more of these hobbies. None of this, in my opinion, is anything to be proud of.'

It was one of those moments when if a pin had been tumbling towards the floor it would probably have been possible to hear it land.

'When I got dragged into this investigation because of a kidnapping that didn't really make sense I had no idea that I would end up standing in a room full of perverts and deviants and explaining something like this to them. What I also didn't expect was that in the process of taking down this blackmail ring we would end up thwarting a long-term Chinese government-sponsored plan to destroy the reputation of the City of London. We've recovered enough evidence to confirm the full extent of the plan, and all of you were pawns in that scheme.

'What really didn't make sense to us right from the start was why it was only bankers and people involved in financial services in the City who were being targeted. Why hadn't the Chinese also tried to compromise the CEOs of, say, the top fifty companies in the FTSE? I was fairly sure that they could have found just as many perverts in those businesses as they managed to locate within the Square Mile, though looking at you lot now I'm not quite so certain. And it was only a few days ago that we realised what was going on.

'The Chinese plan had three components. First, they identified people working in the City who had something to hide. Then they obtained the evidence they needed to compromise them and began collecting what they called subscriptions from all of you to make sure that your secrets stayed secret. That was the second component: amassing a large amount of money very quickly. We don't know how long they planned to keep that part of the scheme going, but probably at least a couple of years.

'There are fourteen of you in here, which meant that PSP4 would have been collecting one hundred and fifty grand a month if James McEwan hadn't had a brainstorm and got himself shot for his trouble. To save you doing the mathematics, that's just under 2 million pounds every year and we know that they had another twenty or thirty prospects in the City that they were going to try and add to their stable, so it's quite conceivable that they could have ended up making upwards of 5 or 6 million pounds each year.

'The third component was perhaps the most devious. We don't know the timing because the instigator of all this didn't survive, but what we think is that at a pre-determined date the Chinese would have purchased well out-of-the-money options and other financial instruments using the funds they'd amassed – maybe more than 10 million pounds' worth if the blackmail had been running for a couple of years – and gambled on a dramatic fall in the stock market as a whole and specifically in bank stocks. Then they'd have released all the compromising information they'd collected about you onto the Internet at the same time.

'You would all have been publicly disgraced, which in my opinion you bloody well should be, and there would have been a massive fall in the FTSE and the banking sector overall. We saw heavy losses after James McEwan's 'outing', for want of a better word. Bearing in mind the gearing element inherent in options trading, these people could have turned their 10 million into maybe ten or twenty times that. But more importantly, the Chinese government was hoping that the loss of confidence in the London markets and the huge falls would have been enough to permanently shut down the City, to drive London out of the finance business. I have no idea if they would have succeeded. Britain is resilient, and the City might have been able to bounce back, but whether it managed it or not, there would have been colossal losses and any recovery would have taken a very long time indeed. And that was all because the Chinese had found a bunch of people most of whom for some reason don't know how or when to keep their willies in their trousers.'

Riley looked around at the fourteen men staring back at him and shook his head.

'I have zero tolerance for paedophiles and I've already supplied the Met with unambiguous evidence of guilt by those individuals guilty of this crime. Police officers are waiting outside this room right now to take them into custody. The sentences they'll receive will, I hope, be severe.'

A couple of men near the back of the room bolted for the door, which opened to reveal a solid wall of black uniforms.

Riley simply glanced at them as they were stopped and arrested.

'As for the rest of you, when you get back to your offices the first job you are all going to do is to find somebody to replace you, because you are all going to retire over the next year. If you need to find other employment it is not to be connected in any way with banking, financial services or the City of London. I will tell you when you are going to resign. I don't care what reason you give, but the two usual suspects are health problems or family reasons, not that anyone actually believes it when some public figure cites either.

'If you don't resign on or before the date that I give you, the appropriate section of the PSP4 database will be simultaneously released to the media and the Metropolitan Police. And if that happens, I promise you that you'll wish you *had* resigned. Now get the fuck out of my sight.'

Chapter 70

One week later
10 Downing Street, London

It was one of those silences you could cut with a knife, but the man known as John Harrison didn't seem in any way disturbed.

He was sitting on a comfortable sofa across from the Prime Minister's aide, sipping a neat Scotch, his legs crossed and exposing his red socks and expensive hand-made loafers. The expression on the other man's face was one of barely controlled fury.

'I don't appreciate you turning up like this,' he snarled. 'It's embarrassing for me and completely unnecessary. We have an arrangement.'

'We have indeed,' Harrison agreed, 'but I do feel it's a good idea to touch base with old friends now and again.'

'We're not friends and never will be. You know that.'

Harrison looked almost sad.

'Yes, I suppose I do,' he admitted, 'but perhaps our arrangement is the next best thing. At least we have to keep in touch. And rest assured,' he added, 'that your secret is safe with me, and the Prime Minister will never know exactly what you enjoy doing whenever you have a free weekend. As long as your monthly payments continue to arrive in the new account, obviously.'

Author's Note

SIS Headquarters, Vauxhall Cross

Its postal address is 85 Albert Embankment, but it's colloquially known by a variety of less than complimentary nicknames, including the Concrete Wurlitzer, Ceauşescu Towers, the Ziggurat, Babylon-on-Thames and the Vauxhall Trollop, while within the intelligence services it's commonly referred to as Legoland.

The Secret Intelligence Service was formed in October 1909 as exactly half of the Secret Service Bureau (SSB), a grand-sounding title for an organisation that comprised precisely two people: a fifty-year-old Royal Navy Commander named Mansfield Cumming, whose initial 'C' is still used to indicate the head of the Secret Intelligence Service, and Vernon Kell, an Army captain in his thirties.

The SSB grew rapidly during the Second World War, and the two men separated operationally to become, respectively, the first heads of the future Secret Intelligence Service, responsible for foreign intelligence, and the Security Service, tasked with domestic counter-intelligence. By about 1920 the two organisations had adopted their current names and functions. The Security Service was initially named the Directorate of Military Intelligence Section 5, or MI5, and is still popularly referred to by this name today. It's known to the rest of the British intelligence community as 'The Box' or 'Box 500', from the organisation's postal address during the Second World War, or just as 'Five'. Military Intelligence Section 6, MI6, was adopted as a convenient name for the SIS during the Second World War, and is still sometimes used today, though technically incorrect.

The SIS was initially housed at 54 Broadway in London, which bore a brass plaque during the Second World War stating that it was the office of the Minimax Fire Extinguisher Company, and in a faintly James Bond-style twist the building was linked by an underground tunnel to the private residence of the then chief of the SIS, Sir Stewart Menzies, at Queen Anne's Gate.

In 1964 the SIS moved to Century House, a 22-storey building at 100 Westminster Bridge Road, a ludicrously insecure structure that included a petrol station on the ground floor. The function of the building, like the function of the organisation that operated from it, was officially classified information and a closely guarded secret. In reality, London cabbies routinely referred to the building as 'Spook House' and it was even on the itineraries of numerous guided tours of London.

Thirty years later, in 1994, two things happened. First, the SIS moved for the second time, taking up residence at Vauxhall Cross, and for the first time what everybody already knew was officially confirmed when the Intelligence Services Act was passed and put in place the legal and statutory basis for the existence of the SIS.

Bearing in mind that the SIS was then occupying one of the most distinctive buildings anywhere in London, some form of 'coming out' was probably inevitable. Since then, Vauxhall Cross has featured in the James Bond films and other productions, which means that the 'Secret' bit of its name is now somewhat debatable. The organisation even has a website and details suggesting how budding secret agents can apply for jobs there.

Mind you, James Bond-wannabes are likely to be severely disappointed when they discover that they won't be issued with a Walther PPK and a licence to kill, or handed the keys of a heavily modified Aston Martin, but will instead be expected to spend most of their working lives wading through piles of files and papers, just like almost any other office worker. The only difference is that they won't be able to tell their family and friends what they really do for a living because of the blunt instruments that are the Official Secrets Acts of 1889, 1911, 1920, 1939 and 1989.

The Secret Intelligence Service might not be so secret any longer, but the British government knows the value of keeping everything it can, and especially its multitude of mammoth cock-ups, well away from any form of public scrutiny.

The Special Reconnaissance Regiment (SRR) and its gestation

The 9/11 attacks in New York changed the terrorism landscape globally. In Britain, the 2002 Strategic Defence Review identified the need for a specialised and dedicated reconnaissance service, which would need to have a go-anywhere capability and would be principally tasked with counterterrorism operations. On 6 April 2005 the SRR was born. The SRR was the lineal descendant of several unacknowledged or deniable units that began covert intelligence and penetration operations in Northern Ireland during the Troubles. These were the MRF; the Det, Special Reconnaissance Unit or 14 Field Security and Intelligence Company; the Force Research Unit and the Joint Support Group.

Along the way there were scandals, murders, betrayals and numerous changes of names, the British government apparently believing that by renaming something a line can be drawn under a particular chapter and past sins forgiven. In reality, pretty much the only thing that did change was the name. The objectives and intentions remained largely unaltered.

Special Reconnaissance Regiment (SRR)

The SRR was created as a specialised reconnaissance unit that is a part of the British Army, specifically a part of UKSF, the United Kingdom Special Forces. It operates alongside the Special Air Service, Special Boat Service and the Special Forces Support Group (SFSG) under the command of the Director Special Forces.

Its activities are classified, which is unsurprising, but its tasking comprises covert surveillance and reconnaissance of targets in areas specified by the British government and it is primarily involved in activities related to counterterrorism. Since its formation, its members have been active in both domestic theatres, meaning the United Kingdom and Northern Ireland, and abroad. Little definitive information is available about the SRR, for obvious reasons, but its personnel are known to have been active in Iraq during the Iraq War, and in Afghanistan, Libya, Yemen and Somalia.

Triacetone triperoxide (TATP) – the 'Mother of Satan'

TATP, sometimes referred to as acetone peroxide, is fairly simple to make and utilises readily available and individually harmless components. Technically, it's classed as an entropy burst explosive, meaning that when it explodes it releases huge quantities of very fast-moving gas, and it's this gas which does the damage. Its yield is about the same as tri-nitrotoluene (TNT).

TATP is made from products that can be bought from almost any hardware store or chemist. Putative bombers need acetone, which is contained in paint thinner and nail varnish remover; hydrogen peroxide, found in bleach or antiseptic; and high strength sulphuric acid. The last is found in powerful drain unblockers, which may be 85 per cent sulphuric acid.

Details of the manufacturing technique are available on the Dark Web, but in general terms it's necessary to concentrate the hydrogen peroxide by boiling it. Then the acetone and hydrogen peroxide are mixed and the mixture cooled down. When it reaches a certain temperature, the sulphuric acid is added slowly, drop by drop, until a particular proportion has been reached. Then the mixture is cooled in a fridge overnight. If the correct proportions have been used and the right process has been followed, white crystals of acetone peroxide will form as a precipitate. The crystals need to be washed to remove any residual acid and then dried. As well as forming the explosive charge, the crystals can be used as an initiator by compressing them into a length of brass or copper tubing to make a blasting cap.

Perhaps the biggest problem with TATP is its extreme sensitivity. It can be triggered by almost anything – a hard shock, friction or heat of any kind – and it is its inherent instability that has led to so many accidents among terrorists attempting to manufacture weapons using this substance. Maiming and death resulting from carelessness or mishandling of the explosive mixture are more common than is generally known. And the number of casualties and own goals caused by TATP are also the source of its nickname 'Mother of Satan'.

Jean Charles de Menezes

The British police sometimes get things right, but quite often they don't, and the killing of Jean Charles de Menezes was one of the more spectacular examples of them getting it badly wrong.

A location in Stockwell had been placed under surveillance on 22 July and when De Menezes left the premises he was followed by plain-clothes officers from the Met because it was thought he resembled one of the suspects involved in the events of the previous day. The obvious fear was that he might be a suicide bomber and might be wearing an explosive vest under what the police described as a heavy jacket. It was also claimed that De Menezes had been acting suspiciously, and according to one report that he had run down into Stockwell Underground Station and vaulted over the ticket barriers.

In fact, it was later established beyond doubt that he had not been acting suspiciously, that he had walked down into Stockwell Underground Station, used his Oyster card to gain admittance, and was actually sitting in a Tube train when armed police arrived. Witnesses confirmed that no warning was issued by the Met officers, and that they simply shot De Menezes where he sat. The 'heavy jacket' was a figment of someone's imagination: he was actually wearing a lightweight denim jacket. And, of course, he had not been connected in any way with the previous attempted bombings.

De Menezes was shot eight times, seven times in the head and once in the shoulder, and despite the close range of the killing three other shots missed him completely.

The follow-up was moderately shambolic, with at least one police officer altering his evidence, CCTV cameras either mysteriously not working or the video not being available, and conflicting and confusing reports from eyewitnesses. At the subsequent inquest, to the extreme and well justified annoyance of the family of the dead man, the coroner instructed the jury that a verdict of unlawful killing was not available to them despite the indisputable fact that officers from the Metropolitan Police had executed an innocent man in cold blood. The jury were told they had a choice between lawful killing or an open verdict, and it seems reasonably clear that the coroner would have preferred the former. The jury did not oblige and returned an open verdict.

GCHQ *Government Communications Headquarters*

Signals intelligence or SIGINT has been an important source of information and data since the end of the First World War, when the Government Code and Cipher School (GC&CS) was established, a name it retained until June 1946. It was located at Bletchley Park during the Second World War where its principal task was cracking the German Enigma codes. After the war, the renamed GCHQ moved to Eastcote in Middlesex and then in 1951 the operation was transplanted to the outskirts of Cheltenham and two sites at Benhall and Oakley.

The organisation attracted almost no media interest until 1976 when the investigative journalist Duncan Campbell wrote an article for *Time Out* magazine that explained what GCHQ was up to, and public awareness was further increased during the 1983 trial of Geoffrey Prime, a KGB mole working at the organisation. In 2003 GCHQ began operating from a new circular building commonly known as The Doughnut at Cheltenham and since then it has established several monitoring stations to intercept electronic signals and other types of communications. These include Bude, Scarborough and Menwith Hill (operated jointly with the United States) in Britain, Ascension Island and Ayios Nikolaos in Cyprus which was operated by the British Army. Until 1994 GCHQ operated a listening station at Chum Hom Kwok in Hong Kong, but well in advance of the handing over of Hong Kong to the Chinese government in 1997, the operations were transferred to Geraldton in Western Australia.

The two principal components of the organisation are the CSO or Composite Signals Organisation, responsible for intelligence collection, and the NCSC, the National Cyber Security Centre, charged with the security of the UK's communication systems. In terms of its ongoing operations, according to the former intelligence officer Edward Snowden, GCHQ operates two main intelligence collection programmes within the CSO. These are known as MTI, meaning Mastering The Internet, which collects Internet traffic from fibre-optic cables and employs the Tempora computer system; and a parallel programme called GTE or Global Telecoms Exploitation, which monitors telephone communications.

Additionally, and since as early as June 2010, GCHQ has also been able to access the US Internet monitoring programme called PRISM, which provides access to the systems operated by nine of the top Internet companies in the world, including Microsoft and Apple, and the search engines operated by Google and Yahoo, as well as Skype and the social media company Facebook. British and US intelligence organisations have shared data since the Second World War, and GCHQ has always worked closely with the American National Security Agency, NSA.

The Dark Web and TOR

In very broad terms, the Internet has two components: the regular World Wide Web and two darker and more mysterious realms commonly known as the Deep Web and the Dark Web. And if you believe the popular press, those people who venture into the murky depths of the Dark Web can find sites where an assassin can be hired and a contract agreed for a killing, or an automatic weapon purchased or endless quantities of prohibited drugs bought or endless videos of paedophile activity viewed. Some of these statements are even true.

Virtually everybody who has a computer and who uses the Internet ventures into the Deep Web on almost a daily basis, though without knowing that they are doing so. The principal difference between the normal Internet and the Deep Web is that Deep Web sites are not indexed and cannot be found by a regular search engine. So, for example, every time a person checks their bank statement online, that statement is a part of the Deep Web, because if it wasn't then anyone could use Google to locate it and see it.

The Dark Web is different and exploring it should not be undertaken without taking precautions, because dangers do lurk down there. At the very least, explorers should use a VPN, a Virtual Private Network, to hide their physical location and the identity of their computer, and use something like TOR, The Onion Router, which provides some measure of protection and is optimised for use on the Dark Web. The biggest difficulty facing such an explorer is finding anything at all: because the sites are not indexed, a search engine won't help. However, simply Googling something like 'dark web sites' will produce some helpful indexes you can explore. A good place to start is what's known as the hidden Wiki at: http://zqktlwi4fecvo6ri.onion/wiki/index.php/Main_Page, though this address, like many Dark Web addresses, is subject to change.

COBRA

The name COBRA sounds exciting, but the initials stand for Cabinet Office Briefing Room A, which is actually rather dull, and it refers to a committee meeting held in Downing Street. These are usually convened in response to some kind of national emergency as part of the Civil Contingencies Committee and will help determine what action the government should take in response. If any. The composition of the COBRA committee is governed by the event or emergency that required it to be assembled and is chaired either by the Prime Minister or by the minister responsible for that particular area.

The Whippet

The name came from Bonnie and Clyde, the American bank robbers of the 1930s. Either Clyde Barrow or Bonnie Parker – most likely Barrow, because he was known to be the shooter of the pair while Bonnie Parker was an excellent reloader for members of the Barrow Gang – cut down a Remington Model 11 20-gauge automatic shotgun, the intention being that he could 'whip it out' in a bank. His weapon was a lot longer than most home-produced whippets, with only the rear of the stock removed and the barrel cut down to a few inches beyond the end of the magazine. Barrow was constrained by the length of the recoil spring on that model, which extends into the stock, and the under-barrel tubular magazine.

But no such constraints exist if the weapon is a double-barrelled twelve-bore shotgun. The stock can be cut off just behind the grip and the barrels anywhere beyond the end of the chambers. It will be wildly inaccurate and painful to fire because of the recoil, but very easy to conceal and extraordinarily intimidating to face.

Tempora

Tempora is a data mining program that works by buffering Internet communications on the main fibre-optic cables that handle the bulk of worldwide traffic. It monitors the backbone of the Internet and it's untargeted, recording and analysing the telephone calls, emails, social media posts and Internet history of everyone in the UK who uses a computer. It's like a local version of the Echelon monitoring system, but incorporating the US National Security Agency's XKEYSCORE system, which extends the reach of the program worldwide. It went live in autumn 2011 and today more than three hundred analysts at GCHQ are directly involved in sorting the data and metadata that it collects.

The system began trials in 2008, and by 2011 interceptors had been fitted to over two hundred fibre-optic cables, including the transatlantic cables linking America and Europe through the UK, and obviously with the cooperation of the companies that own and operate the cables. It is unclear whether or not this cooperation was voluntary, and according to at least one source warrants were issued to some of these companies requiring them to let GCHQ have access to their cables. The system went live in the autumn of 2011.

GCHQ doesn't just operate out of the Doughnut at Cheltenham and the trial was carried out at GCHQ Bude in Cornwall, more properly known as the GCHQ Composite Signals Organisation Station Morwenstow. This is a satellite ground station and communications intercept centre situated on the north coast of Cornwall on a section of the former RAF Cleave, an airfield used during the Second World War.

The probes installed on the Internet backbone at GCHQ Bude had a capacity of ten gigabytes of data per second, potentially over twenty petabytes of data per day, and once the system was running the data was shared between GCHQ and the NSA. When the system became operational, the capacity of the probes was increased to handle 100 gigabits of data per second. The data are stored offline for three days while the metadata are stored for thirty days to allow analyses to be performed.

There are several different components to Tempora including POKERFACE, a sanitisation program, and the XKEYSCORE global Internet data analysis system developed by the NSA. Various techniques are employed to reduce the volume of data to be analysed, but the principal tool is a system known as MVR or Massive Volume Reduction, which applies certain criteria to filter out traffic. Peer-to-peer downloads, for example, are considered to be high-volume, low-value traffic and are discarded, which cuts down the amount of data by about one third. Then, much like the Echelon system, analysts employ specific searches that include trigger words, known email addresses, phone numbers and names to identify and isolate traffic of interest. Reportedly, the roughly 300 analysts who work on the Tempora traffic at GCHQ employ a list of some 40,000 triggers while about 250 NSA analysts use 30,000 trigger words. Some 850,000 NSA contractors can access the data obtained through the system.

Tempora does not distinguish between identified suspects or targets and innocent citizens, and records telephone calls, emails, social media posts and the personal Internet search histories of everyone on the system, a massive amount of data that is actually far greater in size than that held or accessed by the NSA.

The legal basis for Tempora is somewhat shaky. The Regulation of Investigatory Powers Act or RIPA became law in 2000 and specified that a signed warrant was necessary before any individual's communications could be tapped, such a warrant to be signed by either the Home Secretary or the Foreign Secretary depending upon whether the request came from, respectively, MI5 or the Secret Intelligence Service. But there is a let-out clause. Paragraph 4 of Section 8 of RIPA permits the Foreign Secretary to authorise the interception of data that may be related to either terrorism or organised crime, and it is believed that GCHQ's official authorisation is based upon that clause.

There's also another glitch, or interpretation, depending upon your point of view. Both the US and the UK have legal restrictions on intelligence gathering and surveillance of their own citizens. Because the NSA and GCHQ work so closely together on Tempora and other surveillance projects, it's been suggested that the NSA spies on British citizens, as it is entitled to do, while GCHQ returns the favour and puts American citizens under surveillance. And then they simply exchange the data.

GCHQ has frequently stated that its analysts operate within the law, and specifically obey the terms of the Human Rights Act. This requires that surveillance must be both necessary – the subject has to be suspected of planning or being involved in some form of illegal activity – and proportionate. In another words, they can only look for criminals and terrorists. In reality, because of the extraordinarily broad-brush nature of the Tempora take this is a difficult argument to sustain. On the other hand, it is also been claimed that the surveillance operation has detected planned terrorist attacks in the UK and enabled them to be prevented.

What is certain is that Tempora has provided GCHQ with the most comprehensive Internet surveillance capability of all the so-called 'five eyes', meaning the intelligence agencies of the UK, USA, Canada, Australia and New Zealand.

The Morris Worm

What became known as the Morris Worm was created in 1988 by Ben Tappan Morris, a graduate student at Cornell University. He had identified vulnerabilities in the UNIX operating system – which his father, also named Ben Morris, had co-authored – and claimed he wrote the program just to check the size of the fledgling Internet. He also stated that it was designed to expose security flaws in UNIX. But he only made these claims after he had been identified as the culprit.

And the way he released it in November 1988 showed that his motive was rather different, because instead of using a computer at

Cornell University, he started the worm running from an entirely different machine located at the Massachusetts Institute of Technology in a very obvious attempt to disguise its true origin.

The worm was programmed to analyse each computer it reached to see if it was already infected, and then to copy itself, but Morris's coding was sloppy. When the worm checked a computer, it asked the machine if there was a copy of the worm already running on it, but even if the response was positive, that it was infected, the worm would still copy itself again once in every seven requests. This allowed each computer to be infected multiple times, and each additional copy had the effect of slowing down the computer until it was eventually unusable. The overall effect was the same as a DoS – denial of service – attack, a technique used by modern hackers.

In all about six thousand UNIX computers suffered infections and the total cost of rectifying the damage and cleaning the worm from the machines was estimated to be somewhere between $10 million and $100 million. Morris was charged and convicted under the Computer Fraud and Abuse Act. He received a sentence of three years' probation, a fine of $10,000 and was ordered to perform 400 hours of community service.

SSR

SSR is Secondary Surveillance Radar which uses a small transmitter on an aircraft that can be interrogated by a ground radar station and will display a particular four-digit number on a radar screen right beside the aircraft's primary radar return. It's a way for ATC to identify an aircraft and then keep track of it as it flies through the sky. Air traffic controllers tell pilots what number to use – that's called a squawk – and there are 4096 different codes available in total because each digit is between zero and seven.

London Interbank Offered Rate (Libor) scandal

The Libor is an average interest rate compiled from the rates charged by major banks around the world. The banks report the interest rates they are either paying or would expect to pay if they borrowed from other banks, and the Libor is seen as an indicator of the state of the entire financial system. Banks that feel confident about prospects report low interest rates, while higher rates are quoted by banks that feel uncertain.

The scandal came to light in April 2008 following an article in *The Wall Street Journal* that suggested some banks had quoted artificially low interest rates during the 2008 credit crunch. Despite immediate denials of this by the British Bankers' Association and other authorities, the can of worms was opened. It was later proven that some banks had been submitting false rates to increase their trading profit or enhance their creditworthiness.

Because Libor underpins over 350 trillion dollars' worth of derivatives, the effects were both massive and felt worldwide. Libor is used as a reference rate for student loans, mortgages and financial products as well as derivatives.

The fixing wasn't even a new problem. In July 2002 a former trader stated in the *Financial Times* that Libor manipulation had been common since at least 1991. The scale of the problem was summed up by Andrew Lo, a professor of finance at the Massachusetts Institute of Technology, when he said: 'This dwarfs by orders of magnitude any financial scam in the history of markets.'

In Britain, the Serious Fraud Office opened a criminal investigation into interest rate manipulation by Barclays and other banks, while in an affidavit filed in Singapore Tan Chi Min, a trader for the Royal Bank of Scotland (RBS), stated that his bank was able to alter global interest rates through Libor. He also stated that Libor fixing was being run by what was essentially a cartel based in London, with traders around the world colluding to fix rates to enhance or protect their financial positions.

In 2012 Barclays was fined $200 million by the Commodity Futures Trading Commission (CFTC), $160 million by the United States Department of Justice (DoJ) and £59.5 million by the UK Financial Services Authority (FSA). In December 2012 UBS was fined $1.2 billion by the US DoJ and the CFTC, £160 million by the FSA and 59 million Swiss francs by the Swiss Financial Market Supervisory Authority. In September 2013 ICAP Europe was fined

$65 million by the CFTC and £14 million by the FSA. In October 2013 Rabobank was fined €774 million by American, British and Dutch regulators.

In December 2013 UBS avoided a fine of about €2.5 billion by telling regulators about bilateral cartels fixing Libor rates for the Japanese yen between 2007 and 2010, rate fixing in which the bank had participated. Citigroup did the same for one of its infringements, avoiding a fine of about €55 million, but had to pay €70 million for other infringements. RBS was fined €260 million, Deutsche Bank €259 million and J.P. Morgan €80 million.

In July 2014 British and American regulators fined Lloyds Bank a total of $370 million for Libor fixing and other matters. And in April 2015 Deutsche Bank agreed to pay a total of $2.5 billion in fines and penalties over its involvement, the biggest such fine ever imposed.

In January 2014 Libor started being administered by Intercontinental Exchange.

The Security Service (MI5) – breaking the law

In March 2018 an article in the *Guardian* newspaper revealed that the British government had admitted for the first time that MI5 agents are authorised to commit criminal acts in the United Kingdom. At least by implication it was assumed that these acts directly related to intelligence gathering, and that those agents were protected by the agency from prosecution.

That might have come as something of a shock to most people, but they would have been even more startled in October that year when the same newspaper reported that at a tribunal it was revealed that MI5's informants were provided with legal protection to participate or commit crimes right across the spectrum, including sexual assault, torture and even murder, a policy that came into force during the early 1990s.

Unlike the police, and according to its own website, the Security Service is a publicly accountable civilian intelligence organisation and not a law-enforcement agency. In fact, bearing in mind the above, it could be argued that MI5 is the exact opposite of a law-enforcement agency: it is actually a law-breaking agency.

FR F1 sniper rifle

Produced by the French company MAS – Manufacture d'Armes de Saint Étienne – between 1966 and 1980, the FR F1 gained a reputation for reliability because of its bolt action and also for extreme accuracy out to its normal practical range of 800 metres, almost half a mile. Like many French weapons, it was initially chambered for an unusual French round, the 7.5x54mm MAS cartridge, but versions were also produced chambered for a standard NATO round to provide a degree of commonality with other European forces. It came equipped with a Model 35 *bis* telescopic sight, a bipod about halfway along its length, and a distinctive combined muzzle brake and stabiliser on the end of the free-floating barrel that looked a little like a small suppressor.

Sniper rifles do not generally use suppression systems for two very good reasons. First, using a suppressor can slightly slow the speed of the bullet and because by definition most rounds fired by snipers are aimed at targets a long distance away, the faster the bullet can get to the target the better. The second reason is related to the first. Suppressors only really work if the bullets are travelling below the speed of sound, and the rounds fired by sniper rifles are almost invariably supersonic. This means that the bullet reaches the target well before the sound of the shot would be heard by anyone standing nearby. The muzzle velocity of the FR F1 is about 2,600 feet per second, meaning that at its maximum range of 800 metres, the bullet would cover the distance in about one second, while the sound of the shot would reach the target in about two and a half seconds.

Many people believe that bolt-action weapons are virtually obsolete because they have such a slow rate of fire and that a semi-automatic mechanism that allows a shooter to fire rounds as fast as they can pull the trigger are much superior. And, like many beliefs involving weapons, this one is wrong.

The vast majority of sniper rifles are bolt-action because the single most important characteristic of such a weapon is accuracy, the absolute requirement to make sure that every shot is as accurate as possible because the shooter may only get a single chance to pull the trigger, and bolt-action weapons are both accurate and reliable.

They can also be fired much more rapidly than most people think. The bolt-action weapon that's generally accepted to have achieved the highest rate of accurate fire ever was the British Short Magazine Lee-Enfield rifle, or SMLE. In 1908, Sergeant Major Jesse Wallingford, firing at a range of 300 yards, scored 36 hits on a 48-inch target in 60 seconds. Firing fast is one thing, firing fast and hitting the target, especially a comparatively small target at quite a long range, is another matter altogether, making this an impressive feat of both speed and marksmanship, particularly when it's remembered that the SMLE had only a ten-round magazine, meaning that Wallingford had to reload three times during that minute.

It's also worth saying that Wallingford was exceptionally gifted in this field. He was a competitor in the 1908 Olympic Games in both rifle and pistol events and won the title 'Gold Jewel', awarded to the best shot in the British Army at Bisley on no fewer than five occasions.

Acknowledgements

As every author recognises, writing a novel is a collaborative effort, and this book involved more than just the two people with their names on the cover.

Our thanks go out to the usual suspects, including literary agent Luigi Bonomi, our media agent Jane Compton and the talented staff at Canelo Digital Publishing, particularly Michael Bhaskar and Kit Nevile, as well at to the more unusual suspects who played a part in bringing this project to its completion. These include Richard Berry, Angela Edwards, Andrew Hill, Dr Robert (Bob) Nowill, Professor Cameron (Buck) Rogers, Dame Janet Trotter DBE CVO and Nicola Whiting.

About the Authors

Peter Smith, who writes under the name James Barrington was an officer in the Royal Navy's Fleet Air Arm for 21 years, a career which included service on the aircraft carrier HMS *Illustrious* during the Falklands War. Later, he worked at Headquarters Military Air Traffic Operations in London which required continual access to, and work on, a variety of projects classified 'Top Secret', including United Kingdom preparations for war and transition to war (the 'War Book'), and he became very familiar with techniques for intelligence gathering, dissemination and related subjects. After leaving the service, he started a new career as a professional author. Using several pseudonyms, he's been published by Macmillan, Penguin (UK and USA), Simon & Schuster and Transworld, and is now published by Canelo. *Cyberstrike: London* is the first of a series of novels that will explore that most destructive and insidious of modern threats: cybercrime.

Richard Benham is best known globally as a pioneer in the world of Cyber Security, Artificial Intelligence and Cyber Warfare. As well as being an academic he has worked for many years for governments, law enforcement agencies and businesses on security matters. He continues to serve as a British Army Officer and sits as a council member on the Winston Churchill Memorial Trust.